ALEXANDER BOTTOM
SERIES
BOOK ONE

Alexander Bottom

&
The Dreamweaver's Daughter

LEE RICHIE

Right Track Publishing

Hill Top, Australia

RIGHT TRACK

PUBLISHING

Lee Richie/Right Track Publishing
49 Cumberteen Street
Hill Top, NSW 2575

www.leerichie.com

Cover art© 2017 by Richard Austin Lee

Alexander Bottom & The Dreamweaver's Daughter/Lee Richie. -- 1st ed.

ISBN 978-0-6482564-0-3 Hardcover
ISBN 978-0-6482564-1-0 Paperback
ISBN 978-0-6482564-2-7 E-Book

For Christine

Without whom I would be washed out to sea

&

In loving memory of
Mum, Dad and Ken

Alexander Bottom
&
The Dreamweaver's Daughter

Perdidit Somnia

In the fleeting moments between dreams and waking, a boy searches for his mother. He doesn't find her; he never does before reality creeps in, and he opens his eyes to the world he knows without her. He thinks he saw her this time, but he can't be sure. He tries to hold on to the fading memory, but it melts like ice in the heat of a fire, turns to haze, and as always, disappears forever. He tells himself it doesn't matter; it was just another dream.

CHAPTER 1

The Dreamweaver's Daughter

ottom. The word is like 'fart'; you can't say it aloud without bringing the curl of a smile and a snicker to even the most miserable lips. It wasn't as though he had asked for the name, not like he went to the front of the line, hands cupped in the shape of a begging bowl and said, 'Please, sir, may I have Bottom?' No, Alexander was born a Bottom and would die a Bottom, just like his father and his father before him. He had no intention of changing his name or hiding behind a *nom de plume* as writers often did. Had he been an actor, he might have given himself a catchy stage name, such as Alexander Hurricane or Alex Le Mars. An American uncle on his father's side of the family had simply substituted the letter 's' for one of the 't's. His line of the family will now and forever be known as the Bostoms of Corm Valley.

Even though it was like having a 'Kick Me' sign permanently pinned to his back, Alexander was rather fond of the name. The unusual surname had in many ways contributed to his positive character and confidence. Perhaps if he had been born Alexander Fart it would be different, then he might well have considered a change for the better.

'Hey, Butthead,' said Malik.

Malik Ashkar stood a little under six feet seven inches tall and towered over every other student in his high-school grade and those in every year above, including teachers. To say Malik was big for his age was like saying King Kong was big for a monkey. The same age, Alexander was almost a foot shorter and probably only a third of Malik's weight.

Malik's oversize proportions intimidated people. But it was his constant ridiculing of others that got under the most skins. He picked on anyone, but especially those a little bit different, which was strange seeing as Malik himself was a lot different on account of his extraordinary size. Alex had only recently come to know Malik; the boy had joined the school mid-term after supposedly being expelled from another school. While most kids had grown tired of thinking up new ways to ridicule Alex and his unusual surname, Malik had found it impossible to encounter Alex without laughing at him and throwing out insulting twists on his family name. Butthead was Malik's go-to line when wittier insults failed to come readily to mind.

This day, for once, Alex did not find himself the prime focus of Malik's attention, and the bizarre sight now greeting Alex as he turned the corner could only be described as, well, bizarre!

'Did you ever see anything like it?' said Malik. 'It's like a doll only it moves and talks. I've seen French fries with more fat on them.'

And ate every one of them, thought Alex.

The 'it' Malik was referring to, was in fact a girl, a petite girl. Alongside Malik, the extreme difference in size seemed utterly ridiculous; together they could have been an exhibit in a sideshow circus. Although exceptionally small, she was not a young child. She had short blonde hair covering her forehead with a bob cut. Her facial features were chiselled and hard, and sky-blue eyes twinkled with a hint of mischief. She wore a pair of tiny blue shoes, slim fitting calf-length pants the colour of grass, and an even tighter fitting orange sleeveless top that only served to accentuate her petite stature. Sitting cross-legged on a low wall just inside the Morton Bay High School gates, she looked for all the world like a...

'Pixie! She looks like a Pixie,' Malik said, delighted to have someone new to ridicule.

Alex couldn't help thinking the new girl did indeed look pixie-like, in fact, alongside the hulking frame of Malik, she looked positively like a tiny elf.

'My name is—' Alex began.

'Alexander, yes, I know. My name is Nim,' the girl said.

'Most people call me Alex, except Malik of course, who thinks he's being funny.'

Malik wasn't listening; his attention had gone to a teacher emerging through the double doors at the entrance to the gym. The teacher, Edward Evans, had a unique crab-like figure. Long, lanky legs and spindly arms, all of which appeared far too long for his frame, extended from an undernourished body like withered branches on a dying tree. He had a large hook nose, once broken in the middle so it now followed the contour of a dog's back leg. His pallid face looked painted with whitewash, and he struggled to breathe during classes, making noises like a steam engine puffing up a hill. He slinked his way through school rather than walked, sending students scurrying to avoid contact with his coal-black eyes. Fellow teachers called him Ed while students knew him as Phys Ed, or just Phys, a nickname that when spoken carried with it just a hint of fear to those within earshot.

Mr Evans was, of course, the master in charge of physical education. He took his job very seriously. If he had been in command of a legion of soldiers, it was doubtful he could have applied himself with more aggressive passion. Demanding did not even begin to describe Phys Ed. Old fashioned in his ideas about teaching, he would gladly have his pupils thrashed with a cane at regular intervals, just to teach them respect. Ed was not an old man but he was a dinosaur amongst his colleagues; Alex thought he belonged in a Charles Dickens novel.

'Oh no, I forgot to report to Phys for early detention,' Malik said, cringing at his blunder.

Malik crept away under cover of the toilet block before Phys Ed saw him. Alex watched him go with a shake of his head and a 'serves you right' kind of smile.

'Don't mind Malik,' he said, turning back to Nim. 'He's not as obnoxious as he first...' But when he looked she was nowhere in sight. A small dust devil picked up a discarded snack packet and a handful of leaves, spinning them in its vortex and dropping them where Nim once sat. There's something very odd about that girl, thought Alex.

Just how odd, Alex was about to find out.

Leanne Chambers checked her phone for text messages, but there were none. She opened Facebook just in case she had missed something. Nothing had changed since she last looked, exactly three minutes and twenty-five seconds ago. She just wanted to be sure no one had mentioned her in a post. Not that they ever did. Perhaps she should change her profile picture, which for reasons known only to her, featured a close-up of the back of her head.

Exceedingly intelligent, Leanne cruised through classwork that bored her to tears while others struggled to cope. She hid at the back of the class, yet she couldn't resist shouting out answers before any other student could respond to the teacher's questions. Full of contradictions, Leanne liked the fact she was different to most kids, and yet she often craved to be normal. She groaned when picked for the track team, but she made sure she won every race she entered. And she didn't want to be flashy like some of the popular girls, but she tinted her hair in three primary colours. Students were asked in class to describe themselves in one word, Leanne had answered without hesitation; 'complicated', and that's just the way she liked it, or not, she couldn't make up her mind.

The back row of class 4C contained three double desks and one single. The single desk in the rear corner of the room had been named 'Purgatory' for as long as anyone could remember. Purgatory being, as Miss Derbyshire explained, a place to suffer for one's bad deeds. At the start of this year, all desks in this back row had occupants except Purgatory, which was reserved for the form mistress's troublemakers. Modified so the desk and chair stood several inches lower than all the others, students believed this was deliberate, so the unlucky occupants would feel small and humiliated. No one knew who had been responsible for the modification. Leanne had never sat in Purgatory but spent her days in class looking down on the tiny desk and chair from the adjacent row, and sometimes wishing she were bad enough to suffer the fate at least once just to show she could run with the cool kids.

Alex sat next to Leanne, not out of choice, but because he had been asked to swap with Joslynn Prassat soon after the start of term when it became evident she could not hear from the back of the room. At first, Leanne had been horrified at having to share her personal space for the entire year with a boy of whom she knew very little. But Alexander turned out to be okay, and he treated her with the kind of respect she rarely saw from other boys his age. Always pleasant towards her, never patronising or fawning over her, he didn't seem to feel the need to show off like most boys. And he was confident, which she thought surprising given the burden of his surname.

The next double desk was vacated only a week earlier by the Ashley twins, who had apparently moved to America with their parents. Malik Ashkar and Jani Nasri completed the current back row.

'Good morning, ladies, gentlemen, and Malik,' Phys Ed said as he entered the room carrying an enormous pile of papers. Malik's face turned paler than his spotless white shirt. 'I'm very pleased to tell you,' Phys Ed continued, 'that due to Miss Derbyshire's unexpected absence, I will be your guide and leading light for the remainder of the week.'

The class gave out a collective groan. Malik Ashkar placed his head on his desk and pretended to cry.

'First order of business, Malik,' said Phys Ed.

'Yes, sir,' Malik answered. He knew what would come next.

'I hear Purgatory calling!'

Malik bowed his head and took the walk of shame, accepting he was now paying the price for getting distracted on his way to the gym. He blamed that little new kid.

'And Malik, don't think this gets you out of detention. You'll do double time after classes.'

Malik groaned and squeezed himself into the Purgatory chair where his knees came up to his chest, much to the amusement of the entire class. He glared, and the giggles stopped.

'Right,' said Mr Evans. 'Let's see who we have here.' The teacher looked around the room, starting at the front and working his way to the rear. As he came to the back row, he smiled. 'Ah, Mr Bottom.' Phys Ed took great pleasure from Alexander's company in class. While other more responsible teachers would set a good example, Phys Ed saw it as his God-given duty to entertain the other students at Alexander's expense. And though there were only so many ways to make fun of someone's name, Phys Ed was not above repeating his jokes and puns on a regular basis. 'Take a Seat-Bottom.' Giggles.

'I am seated, sir,' Alex said.

'So you are, Bottom, and no butts about it,' said the teacher. 'And still Bottom of the class I notice.' More giggles. 'Well then, now that we have that out the way, let's kick on, Bottom, shall we?'

Alex rolled his eyes.

'And who do we have here?' asked Phys Ed.

'Nim, sir.'

Alex turned to his right, surprised by the sight of the new girl seated at the twins' empty desk.

Leanne whispered in Alex's ear. 'Where did she come from?' Alex shrugged.

Nim barely appeared above the desktop.

'New girl?' said the teacher. 'Well, Nim, what are you doing slouched down in your seat?'

Alex chuckled. 'She's not slouched, sir, she's sitting up straight. Nim is just small.'

'Small?' Phys Ed marched to the back row and was shocked to confirm that the girl was indeed small. 'Good Lord, child, I...' The teacher appeared to be lost for words for a moment. 'Yes, well, sit up as far as you can. Do you want some books to sit on?'

'No, sir, I'm fine just as I am.'

'Right.' Phys Ed returned to the front of the class and proceeded to wipe the blackboard clean, sending clouds of chalk dust into the air and choking poor Joslynn Prassat in the process. 'As Miss Derbyshire is not here and she normally teaches your Thursday morning Social Studies class, I'm pleased to inform you there will be no Social Studies today.'

The class gave a loud cheer.

Phys Ed sneered. 'I'm glad to hear your enthusiasm, 4C, because you will be even more pleased to hear that in its place we will be discussing the origins of our wonderful universe.'

Grumbles all round and at this news, more than half the class dropped their heads and started to scroll through their smartphones.

'AND, if I see one single phone in the hands of its owner, I will confiscate everyone's for the remainder of the week. Do I make myself clear?'

Everyone shuffled as phones were rushed from sight and into pockets and bags. Phys Ed turned his attention back to the board and started to draw a very rough graphic depicting a timeline of the universe.

'We start around 13.7 billion years ago with the Big Bang,' he said.

'Ha!'

Phys Ed turned and scowled. 'I won't tolerate interruptions.' No one responded. Returning his attention to the blackboard, the teacher continued. 'As I was saying, if we look at the universe as a timeline starting almost fourteen billion years ago, we can see the different phases of its development, and as the universe is constantly expanding—'

'Ha!'

Everyone turned to the back of the class. The new girl stood on her chair.

'You have something to say, little lady? Or would you like to take a seat in Purgatory?'

'I said, HA!'

'I understand you are new, but unless you want to take Malik's place—'

'Yes!' Malik said, delighted at the suggestion.

'Shut up, Malik,' said Phys Ed. 'Alright, little lady, I'll humour you. What exactly is it you find so amusing?'

All attention now focused entirely on Nim. 'My father says people who teach theory as though it is a fact should not teach at all. If you don't know it's a fact, how can you teach it as though it is? You'll be telling me you believe in evolution next, and that that is a fact.'

The class sat in stunned silence, waiting for Phys to explode in a fury. He didn't. Phys Ed seemed as stunned as everyone else.

Nim continued. 'Your facts about your universe are fundamentally flawed. For a start, you talk about time as though it has a beginning and an end when everyone knows there is only now. Everything has, is, and will happen now.'

Phys Ed appeared dazed by the girl's rudeness. Alex's mouth gaped wide, and Leanne looked on in awe of Nim. In what seemed the blink of an eye, Nim skipped across the rows and stood on Alex's desk.

'How...' stuttered Malik.

'And where are the poles, good and evil?' Nim continued. 'Other dimensions, infinite worlds?'

'Infinite worlds?' Phys Ed looked perplexed. Never had he been challenged by a pupil, let alone a new girl on her first morning. 'Perhaps you would like to come down here and explain how science has been getting it wrong?' Phys Ed looked around the class as though he needed their support. He looked like he might burst into hysterical laughter at any moment. 'What do you think, class, shall we hear what the little lady has to say about the dimension of the universe?'

'Not dimension of the universe,' Nim said, suddenly standing on a chair at the blackboard.

Phys Ed seemed bewildered, as though the events were going too quick for him and he was trying to catch up.

'I'm talking about other dimensions, other universes, other worlds,' she said. 'You haven't even mentioned the eighth and ninth dimensions, let alone the tenth.'

Alex started to shake. His hands dithered as though he were cold, and he had turned so pale Leanne thought he was about to be sick.

'What's wrong, are you ill?' she said.

Alex answered in a whisper. 'I dreamed all this.'

'Dreamed what?' Leanne put her hand on Alex's arm to try and calm him. 'What are you talking about?'

'I dreamed it,' Alex said. 'Me, you, Malik in Purgatory, Phys Ed taking Miss Derbyshire's class...it was all in a dream I had once.'

'You're imagining it. Déjà vu maybe.'

'Déjà what?'

'Déjà vu. It means you have an unexplained feeling you have already experienced the present situation at some time in the past, even though you are sure you haven't.'

'No, I mean, yes, I know what it means, but I did dream it. I don't remember the details, but we were all together in this classroom, and... and that wasn't the end of the dream, something bad happened and...' Alex stopped mid-sentence. 'I have a horrible feeling about this.'

Phys Ed also started to flush. Small beads of sweat formed on his forehead, and the veins in his neck bulged and throbbed like angry snakes. He focused on the girl and ground his teeth, snarling at her like a rabid dog. She drew on the blackboard and pointed to the graphic with a ruler as though she were teaching the lesson, and Phys Ed could do nothing to stop her.

Nim pointed to the board and said, 'Imagine this is the Megaverse. The Megaverse is infinite, and like time, it has no beginning and no end. Within the Megaverse, there are multiple dimensions. Who can name some?'

Leanne was quickest to raise a hand. 'Length, height, depth.'

'That's right, Leanne. Any more?'

Someone at the front started to speak, but Leanne was already on it. 'Time!'

'Oh, you're good, Leanne. But those are only the tip of the iceberg. There are many dimensions, and within them, there is an infinite number of identical worlds. There is also an infinite number of worlds that are not identical, as in the seventh dimension. Stay with me, class, you're doing fine so far.'

Phys Ed seethed.

'Shall I go on, teacher?' asked Nim.

'Oh, please do,' Phys Ed said, turning his grimace into a snort of disbelief.

'The Megaverse is full of energy,' Nim continued. 'And like all energy, there are negative and positive poles. At one pole we have Agathos, which is made up of positive energy and represents all that is good. At the opposing pole, we have Angra, a pole of negative energy, representing everything bad. These forces are held in balance, and the poles separated by neutral energy within the Megaverse create a state of equilibrium.' Nim directed her attention towards Phys Ed. 'It's just basic physics.'

'Basic physics?' Phys Ed said, unable to regain control.

'Basic,' Nim repeated. 'The Megaverse depends on order and balance for its continued survival. Any disruption to this balance could be catastrophic. Evil energy—'

'I'm sorry, evil energy?' Phys Ed interrupted, turning to the class and chuckling, expecting to see the class laughing also.

Instead, he saw everyone's attention hanging on Nim's every word.

'That's right, evil energy is becoming a problem we can no longer ignore.'

'So this is your theory, no Big Bang, no expanding universe?' Phys Ed mocked.

'Oh, it's no theory, and as for the Big Bang,' Nim said, 'it just hasn't happened yet.'

Phys frowned, he had noticed something familiar about the girl. 'Have we met before?' he said.

'Absolutely we have, and it wasn't a pleasant encounter. But you can be certain, Ed, we will meet again very soon and the tables will turn.'

The class gasped as one. *She called him Ed!*

Phys Ed turned to the class. 'Did she just call me Ed?' His jaw dropped, and his eyes grew wide in exaggerated outrage. His knees began to buckle as though he had lost control of his legs and the room started to spin. When he turned to the blackboard, Nim had gone.

The class erupted into chaos. Students talked over other students excitedly, recounting what they had seen and each shouting over the other to be heard. Laughter rippled through the room while Phys Ed stumbled back to his desk to sit, seemingly stunned into a confused world of his own while anarchy spread through his classroom unchecked.

Alex jumped to his feet and turned to Leanne with wide eyes. 'We have to go after her,' he said.

'Why? I don't understand,' said Leanne.

Alex ran to the door. Leanne glanced at Phys Ed, who seemed oblivious to the world around him. She grabbed her school bag and followed.

'I'm coming too,' Malik said as they rushed from the class-room, leaving the bedlam behind.

What's in a name?

Alex, Leanne, and Malik ran to the yard as Nim disappeared behind the library block.

'Do you think she's a new student, or someone pretending to be, a joke perhaps?' Alex said, hurrying to catch up. 'She's tiny, but when you think about it, she looks much older than us. She has a mature face. I think she could even be in her thirties. I don't think she's a student at all.'

'Did you see Phys Ed's face?' said Malik. 'Priceless!'

'I felt sorry for him,' Leanne said. 'But I've never seen anyone so brave and yet so small as Nim. It was almost like she was the teacher and Phys was the student. I think you're right, Alex, it must have been a practical joke.'

Malik grinned. 'Do you think Phys will ever want to step in for Miss Derbyshire again?'

'I doubt it,' said Alex as he came to a standstill at the edge of the sports field. 'She's gone,' he said, scanning the area for any sign of her.

'Who's gone?' Nim said out of the blue, causing all three to jump as she appeared without warning behind them.

'I wish you would stop doing that,' Alex said as he recovered from the shock.

'What?'

'Sneaking up on people from nowhere and...and disappearing without warning. It's very annoying and very rude.'

'Sorry,' she said with a cheeky smile. 'What did you think of class?'

Leanne spoke first. 'I thought you were awesome, but I thought maybe you were a little hard on Phys. He looked ready to have a heart attack.'

'Oh, he's tougher than you think. Much tougher in fact.'

Alex seized on the comment. 'Ah, so you do know him. And I'll bet it was a practical joke wasn't it? It was all set up by you and some of his friends. I'll bet they are all waiting for him now at the pub, having a good laugh about it.'

'It wasn't a joke, Alex,' said Nim. 'Sit with me and I'll explain.'

All four sat on a wooden bench overlooking the sports field and watched as four young track athletes competed in a sprint. One of them finished far ahead of the others, and Alex commented on how fast he was.

'That boy will win a gold medal at the Olympics one day,' said Nim.

'Probably,' Alex agreed.

'No, not probably, he *will* win gold.' Nim spoke as if she knew for sure.

'Hey, Bottom, why don't you go to the Olympics?' Malik paused for the punchline and laughed. 'You could do the shot-butt.'

Alex had to admit it was one of Malik's better ones.

'Why do you have to be such a jerk, Malik?' Leanne said. 'You're the only one who finds your comments funny. In fact, when you say stuff like that and people laugh, they're laughing at you for being so pathetic.' Leanne turned away in disgust.

'It's okay, Leanne,' Alex said. 'It doesn't bother me. I've heard them for so long now, comments like that go right over my head. And besides, Malik doesn't realise he's an idiot.'

'Hey! That hurts,' Malik said. 'Where does a name like Bottom come from anyway?'

'My dad says we come from a proud line of Bottoms.'

Malik covered his mouth with his hand to stop himself making a funny remark.

'Ignore him, Alex. Go on, you were saying?' said Leanne.

'Family names often come from what people did in the past for a living or where they lived. Like Miss Derbyshire for instance. Her family probably lived in Derbyshire many years ago. Max Wheeler's ancestors might have made wagon wheels for a living.'

'So your family were just bums, right?'

'Malik!' Leanne reacted.

'According to my father,' Alex continued, unfazed by Malik's wit, 'our family name dates back hundreds of years to a time when we farmed the low country. Some families farmed the hills, and I guess they became the Hill family or the Tops.'

'Like ZZ Top,' said Malik enthusiastically.

'That's a band, not a person, Malik,' said Alex.

'I know that.'

'Anyway,' Alex went on, 'as farmers who worked in the valley fields, our ancestors became known as the bottom farmers, and later, just Bottoms.'

'Why didn't they just call themselves Vale? It would have made life easier for you,' Leanne said.

Alex went on. 'Actually, I prefer my grandad's theory. He says we descended from seafarers. Once known as the Boatmen, the name was shortened and corrupted by local dialects and eventually became Boatom, and later still, just Bottom. Grandad says we may even have been pirates like Captain Black Beard.'

Malik sneered. 'Captain Black Bottom! Somehow it doesn't have the same ring, does it?'

'Well, I wouldn't change it even if I could,' said Alex.

'Perhaps you wouldn't change your name, Alex,' said Nim, 'but if you could change something, anything, not just you, all of you, if you had the chance to change the world, what would you change? What would you do?'

Leanne answered first. 'You mean after kicking Malik's butt?'

Malik was quick to respond. 'Hey, don't say butt, Bottom will be offended.'

'Ha, ha,' Leanne said, trying hard not to be amused. But everyone couldn't help giggling, including Alex. 'Okay,' Leanne continued, 'I would find a way to make everyone accept people's differences and respect their choices in life. Like with Mary Riley for example, why does everyone, especially you, Malik, pick on her because she chooses to dress like—'

'Like a weirdo?' Malik said.

'See, Malik, that's what I'm talking about,' said Leanne.

'She's a Goth. What isn't weird about her?' said Malik.

Mary Riley was indeed a Goth. Jet-black hair framed her snow-white face and masses of black eyeshadow made her face appear skull-like. Black clothing, black lipstick, and heavy silver piercings in her ears, nose, lips, and tongue completed her mysterious look. Leanne couldn't help admiring Mary. She was a loner who sulked her way through life in gloom and resentment, showing her dislike for anything and everything and refusing to smile as if her life depended on not doing so. She mumbled and snarled at every attempt to include her on a social level. Leanne thought she was the perfect example of being true to oneself and not conforming to what other people think of as normal.

'She may be a Goth,' Leanne continued, 'but having the courage to be different makes her strong in my eyes, not weird. If I could change the way people think about being different, that would be a good thing. The world might be a better place.'

'Sounds dumb to me,' Malik said. 'I would just make sure everyone was rich, so you could do what you want or go where you want, and no one would care if you were different.'

'You're so lame, Malik,' Leanne snapped.

'What about you, Alex, what would you change?' Nim asked.

Alex seemed distant. His thoughts had carried him off to some faraway place or time long ago. When he finally answered, he had a sad expression and looked to be on the point of tears.

'What's the point of dreaming?' Alex asked. 'The fact is, you can't change the world and you can't change what people do or think.' Alex stood and began to walk away; something had upset him.

'You're wrong, Alex.' Nim skipped off the bench and stood to block his way. 'Your mother would never want you to stop dreaming.'

Alex looked stunned by the mention of his mother. His surprise turned to irritation. 'How would you know what my mother would want? My mother—' Alex stopped himself saying it.

'Your mother never wanted to leave you all those years ago, Alex,' said Nim. 'One day you will know the truth.'

'How did...Why are we even talking about my mother?'

'Because you were thinking about her. You were wondering why she disappeared when you were just three years old, where she is now, and how things might be different if she were still here. Sit down, Alex,' Nim said.

Alex returned to the bench.

Nim continued. 'Time will give you answers, Alex, but first I need you all to understand why I'm here.'

'I thought you said there was no such thing as time?' Malik said.

'It's complicated,' Nim said.

'So why are you here?' asked Alex.

'As I said in class, there has been a serious shift in the balance of the Megaverse,' said Nim. 'Terrifying forces are growing in Angra. I urgently need your help.'

Malik laughed. 'Forces of evil, right! Angra and the bogeymen are coming to destroy us all, along with the Megasphere.'

'It's Megaverse, not Megasphere,' Nim said. 'And yes, Malik, the bogeyman is very real and comes in many disguises, you would do well to remember that.'

'The bogeyman, eh? NUTS! Bottom line is...Sorry, Bottom... the bottom line is you are one crazy little girl,' said Malik. 'I'm going home to grab some lunch before going back to school.'

'Who is going to feed you when you get home, Malik? Your parents are overseas,' Nim said.

'How did you know? They only went yesterday and the trip was unexpected.'

'I know you had a great argument before their sudden departure,' Nim said. 'I also know your parents would have preferred you went with them, or at least have them go with your blessing. Instead, they left with heavy hearts.'

'This is freaking me out,' Malik said. 'How do you know these things?'

'Yeah, this is starting to get more than a little weird,' said Alex. 'Who are you and where have you come from?'

Nim smiled. 'Here, there, and everywhere in between,' she answered.

'Riddles, great!' said Malik.

'I'm sorry, Malik, I don't mean to be vague. And don't be alarmed when I tell you I am not human like you. I am a Figment,' said Nim.

'Oh man, this gets worse,' said Malik. 'Nim is not a human lunatic after all, she's just a figment of our imagination!'

'Give her time to explain, Malik, please,' Leanne said, trying hard to give Nim the benefit of the doubt.

'It's okay, Leanne, this is hard to explain never mind understand, and if I were Malik, I would think I'm crazy too. I am not a figment of your imagination, Malik, I am a Figment. Figments exist in the Dreamscape.'

'The Dreamscape?' said Alex.

'The Dreamscape is the space between dimensions where souls and spirits transcend worlds. There are many Figments within the Dreamscape, and it is our job to maintain order in the transit of spirits. Some Figments are Guardians, some are Navigators, and some are Dreamweavers like my father. It might be hard for you to accept, but what I said in class was the truth. Everything you think you know about your universe is wrong.'

'Okay, I've heard enough,' Malik said.

'I understand you want proof, Malik.' Nim thought for a minute and said, 'We need mirrors, two of them. But we need to hurry.'

After a moment of silence, Malik jumped to his feet. 'Okay, I'll bite. My house is close and I have mirrors, big mirrors. But as soon as we're done, I'm getting online to find you a doctor and a straightjacket.'

'What about school?' said Alex.

'Believe me when I tell you,' said Nim, 'you will not be missed.'

CHAPTER 3

Smoke and mirrors

Malik led the way to the Ashkar family home; a modern double story house set in a prosperous neighbourhood of showcase homes and immaculate landscapes. Retrieving a key from under the doormat, he unlocked the front door and let everyone inside before disarming the house alarm system.

'You set the alarm and then leave a key under the doormat? Brilliant,' said Alex.

'I only half trust people,' Malik said, smirking.

Alex admired the spotlessly neat interior but felt uneasy, like he had entered a church or a fine art gallery where he should touch nothing and speak only in whispers. He half expected little signs that read: no photographs, please stick to the path and do not enter the designated areas.

Beautiful Persian rugs covered shiny hardwood floors, and classic mahogany furniture, dustless and polished, gave the home an opulent feel. Luxurious gold satin armchairs and sofas had white lace slipcovers protecting arms and backrests, an indication of the owner's pride in every detail within the home. Alex thought it curious that someone like Malik, who appeared so rough, tough, and aggressive in many ways, could live in such a pristine environment.

Smiling faces of parents, aunts, uncles, nephews, and nieces stared out from gilt picture frames on beautifully waxed table tops. Many more family photographs adorned the walls, almost shrine-like. This was a family with values. Perhaps there was another side to Malik, one he kept hidden behind his endlessly annoying self.

'Upstairs,' Malik said. 'The mirrors are in my bedroom.'

Malik led the way two steps at a time. Alex and Nim followed while Leanne came after, making it clear Malik's bedroom was not at the top of her list of places to visit. She paused on the stairs to view a photograph of a younger Malik, sitting on a beach with his parents. They looked happy, but something about the boy's smile just didn't fit with the Malik she had come to know in school.

Typical for most boys his age, Malik's room contained a mix of past and present treasures. Early childhood toys lined up on shelves alongside model motor cars and remote control drones. Toy soldiers, no longer used, remained as mementoes of happy play-days past. Psychedelic colours flashed across a large computer monitor as a screensaver bounced abstract images endlessly back and forth, and a games machine stood on standby, its joystick controllers ready and waiting for the next cyber battle. Two more computers stood idle with the power switched off at the wall, and a dozen Rubik's Cubes formed a pyramid on a desk. A bookshelf filled with an assortment of storybooks, computer manuals, and technical books about writing software appeared to be arranged in alphabetical order. Pictures of wrestlers flexing steroid-filled muscles adorned the walls next to a poster of Beyoncé and several other female personalities Leanne could not readily name.

'Beyoncé? Really, Malik?' Leanne had never imagined Malik as a music enthusiast, let alone a Beyoncé fan; yet another surprise.

'It's my brother's,' said Malik.

'Right. And the rabbit is his too, I suppose.' Leanne pointed to a large stuffed toy sitting in the corner of the room, looking goofy. 'Anyway, you don't have a brother.'

Malik ignored the comment.

A bank of built-in wardrobes ran down an entire wall from floor to ceiling while four mirrored doors set on sliding tracks enclosed the contents, making the room appear much bigger than it was.

'You asked for mirrors,' said Malik.

'Well you did say they were big,' said Nim. 'But we need them to stand opposite so they reflect each other.'

Malik complied, with Alex's help, by lifting the mirrors from their tracks and setting them in the appropriate position while Nim directed and Leanne looked on. To everyone's surprise, removing the doors revealed an immaculate wardrobe full of perfectly displayed clothes. Folded shirts and sweaters were neatly stacked up on shelves while regimented lines of jackets and trousers hung neatly from rails. Socks and underwear filled out sliding trays alongside racks of highly polished shoes.

'Holy cow, Malik, this is your wardrobe?' said Alex, amazed at the perfect organisation.

'I like things tidy. What can I say?' replied Malik.

'Tidy!'

'And there you have it,' Nim said, bringing their attention back to her demonstration. 'The sixth dimension.'

Reflected images ran one after the other into the distance, getting smaller and smaller until they disappeared from view.

'This is it...this is your demonstration?' Malik deliberately banged his head against the wall. 'I don't know who is more crazy, her, or us for listening to her. I don't want anyone to know we came here today and did this, or they'll think I'm the biggest fool for going along with it.'

'What, bigger than you already are?' asked Leanne.

Nim pleaded for patience. 'Tell me what you see when you look in a mirror, Malik?'

'I see me,' Malik answered impatiently. 'In this case, I see me a hundred times over looking seriously fed up with the games you keep playing.'

'Do you really?' said Nim. 'What if I were to tell you what you see are other worlds entirely? Identical in almost every way, but other worlds nevertheless, just as real and full of life as your own. These mirror reflections are just a glimpse into the sixth dimension.'

Alex sighed. 'Other dimensions and parallel worlds, and that's not me looking back I suppose?' Alex was beginning to get as impatient as Malik. 'I'm sorry, Nim, but they are just reflections in the mirror. One mirror reflects the other, the other reflects that and so on into infinity. This is not the Megaverse, and I'm starting to agree with Malik that you are a little crazy.'

'Infinity, Alex, the images disappear into infinity,' said Nim. 'Don't you remember what I told you? There are an infinite number of worlds, and the Megaverse itself is infinite. You learned mirrors are mere reflections and so that is what you believe, but you need to open your mind to what lies beyond.'

'Our eyes don't lie, Nim. Seeing is believing,' said Alex.

'Malik, I see a pack of playing cards on your desk. Take the pack and hold it up to face us,' Nim said.

Malik complied.

'Now, Alex, Leanne, what do you see?'

'A pack of cards,' Alex said stubbornly.

'No you don't,' said Nim. 'Tell me what you see and nothing else.'

Alex thought for a moment. 'I see the back of a card.'

'Correct. One card. Now turn the pack sideways and what do you see?'

'A pack of cards.'

'Exactly! Fifty-two cards and two jokers if I'm not mistaken. Just because you didn't see the pack from the first angle didn't mean it wasn't there.' Nim knew they were still unconvinced. 'Okay, one last example. Imagine you are one of a million microbes living on a grain of sand in a vast desert. If you are a very clever and advanced breed of microbes, you may have observed there are other grains of sand nearby, capable of supporting life like your own. Sound familiar?'

'Like looking for life on other planets,' Alex said.

'Exactly,' said Nim. 'But as a microbe confined to your grain of sand, how could you possibly imagine the scale of the desert and how many identical grains of sand there were, each supporting its own population of microbes? And how could even your smartest microbe scientists predict that beyond the desert there would be vast oceans with all manner of life and mountains that reach for the sky? How could they imagine some life forms were thousands of millions times bigger than the average microbe in the form of great mammals that roam the earth? Could they understand that while their lives are measured in hours, there are trees on Earth that have lived for thousands of years? Are you starting to get the picture? There is no way for those microbes living on a little grain of sand to know what lies beyond, just as you cannot be expected to know the scale and all the secrets of this vast and wonderful Megaverse.'

Silence followed while they digested Nim's logic. Eventually, Leanne spoke. 'It's all wonderful in theory, Nim, but you were the one who said we need facts. These are just reflections in a mirror unless you can prove otherwise.'

'It's difficult to accept, I know, but it's really simple. Reflections like these are windows to the cosmos, and each plane, or reflection as you like to call them, is a real-time view of a different world entirely. Worlds within this particular dimension are virtually identical with only minor differences, such as a hair out of place or a freckle you don't have. Most times you will look in the mirror and never notice even the tiniest difference. But if your eyes were capable of following the reflections further, you would move away from your world and the changes would become more evident. Eventually, perhaps a billion worlds away on a different dimensional plane, similarities cease and life becomes unrecognisable. Slip into the seventh, eighth, and ninth dimensions, and, well, you don't want to know! Scientists spend lifetimes searching through telescopes for answers, when all the time the truth about life and the Megaverse is staring them in the face.'

'So we could just walk through the mirror into another world, is that what you're saying?'

Nim looked frustrated. 'Don't be silly, Malik. If you did, you would crack your head on the glass. It's a window, not a door.'

'Oh, of course, how stupid of me,' said Malik. 'And there I was thinking I could just trot on through to the other side like Alice in Wonderland. I'm sorry for my confusion, Nim, I really am. Perhaps we need to climb down a rabbit hole instead.'

Malik's sarcasm brought an exasperated groan from Nim, who seemed at a loss to explain. She had noticed the Alice in Wonderland novels on Malik's bookshelf.

'You are right, of course,' said Nim. 'When Lewis Carroll wrote his books about Alice, he simplified the whole experience and had Alice walk through the looking glass or disappear down a rabbit hole before appearing in another world. But his Alice in Wonderland and Through the Looking Glass stories were actually an expression of Lewis Carroll's real-life experiences. He was the first of his kind to travel across dimensions and return to tell the story. He remembered his experiences enough to write about them.'

'Wait a minute,' Alex interrupted. 'Are you trying to tell us Alice in Wonderland is a true story?'

'Why of course it is, silly. Maybe it contains some fiction, Lewis Carroll did enjoy a great deal of poetic license, but essentially his stories are based on his own experience after crossing over to a world in the seventh dimension. A rather bizarre world by your standards. There is even a clue in the pen-name he chose and that of his main character. His name was Charles Dodgson, but when he crossed over to another world, he became Lewis Carrol and embarked on his adventure with Alice, Lewis Carrol's sister. When he eventually wrote his stories, he chose Alice for his character and Lewis Carrol for his pen-name. It was his in-joke.'

The trio looked sceptical.

'Okay,' said Nim, 'I can see you still don't believe me, but you are all missing something compelling to prove I am who I claim to be and that I am telling the truth. If you will look again and tell me what you see in the mirrors, please.'

'Reflections! Hundreds and hundreds of reflections,' said Leanne.

'And what are they reflections of?' asked Nim.

'Us!' said Alex.

'Are you sure, Alex? What don't you see reflected?'

They studied the reflections as though they were taking part in a guessing game until it dawned on them one after the other.

'Oh, good grief,' Malik gasped. 'There's no reflection of Nim!'

What they also failed to see, including Nim, were the two black-clad figures slipping into Malik's house through the unlocked front door.

CHAPTER 4

Not a minute to lose

Kale and Slade entered the house, stealthily moving their taut, sleek bodies from room to room, ready to strike if and when the right moment came. They communicated in silence, using only hand gestures, body language, and eye contact so each knew what the other was about to do next and so each could respond accordingly. Kale took a framed photograph of Malik and his parents from a polished table top, studied the image, dropped it on the soft rug, and smashed the glass under the weight of his foot.

'Okay,' said Alex, unaware of the intruders making their way through the house, 'let's say for one moment this is not a magic trick and you are truly a Figment of the Dreamscape.' Malik opened his mouth to object, but Alex silenced him with a wave of his hand and continued. 'You still haven't told us why you're here, Nim.'

'Because, my dear friends,' Nim said, 'I have come to ask for your help.' Instantly, she appeared cross-legged on the floor next to the giant rabbit.

'And that's another thing,' said Malik. 'How do you do that? How do you move without anyone seeing?'

A mischievous smile curled on Nim's lips. 'Oh, that little thing,' she said, as though it were nothing at all. 'Actually, I have trouble moving freely in your world...this is my slow mode. There is no gravity or atmosphere in the Dreamscape you see, and movement comes just by thinking it. I've never had to take physical form before, and it takes a fair bit of practice. But what was I about to say? Oh yes. Remember Agathos and Angra?'

'Good and bad,' answered Leanne. 'Opposite poles of energy.'

'That's right, Leanne. You can only imagine such extremes within these poles, where on one side everything evil and bad comes together in a fiery cauldron of torment and mayhem. Worlds within this dimension are terrifying beyond belief. On the other hand, Agathos is filled only with peace and love, where worlds abound in the warm glow of paradise. Harmonic forces separate the poles, resulting in the balanced neutrality of the Megaverse core, where neither Angra nor Agathos dominates.'

'Kind of like heaven and hell, with Earth in the middle,' Leanne observed.

'Exactly,' said Nim, now appearing back on the bed. 'For all eternity this great balance has existed. Good deeds within the Megaverse make up for the bad ones and vice-versa. But the nearer one gets to the poles of Angra and Agathos, the more influence each has on life there. There are some worlds as black and dark as the darkest pit in Angra itself. And there are worlds so full of love and peace you would be forgiven for thinking you were already in Agathos.' Nim's expression turned dark and serious. 'Sadly, these days, there are more bad deeds than good, and the neutral forces are becoming weak. Every new war, every new conflict and selfish act makes Angra more powerful, causing dimensions to deform and break apart, pulling Agatha ever closer to a cataclysmic event.'

Leanne asked, 'What will happen if the forces of Angra and Agathos come together and dimensions collide?'

'Then, dear Leanne—'

'The Big Bang,' Alex finished for her. 'That's what you meant in class when you said the Big Bang hasn't happened yet.'

'And if it does happen?' asked Leanne.

'Chaos and destruction,' replied Nim. 'It's a fate for the Megaverse too terrible to imagine.' Nim sprang to her feet. 'But there is still hope, we are not beaten yet. We must swing the balance back in favour of Agathos. And that's where you come in, my dear young friends.'

Kale and Slade crossed the landing, pausing to listen at Malik's bedroom door. Kale signalled and they moved on, entering the adjoining bedroom without a sound. Slade closed the door and put his ear to the dividing wall while Kale stood by and waited.

'What can we do?' said Alex. 'Surely if the Megaverse is as vast as you say, we are as insignificant as those microbes you described. We cannot influence the outcome of events, evil or otherwise.'

Nim looked kindly at Alex; her expression was warm and understanding. 'If only you knew how wrong you are and understood how much influence you have. There are countless ways you inhabit this Megaverse, Alex. You take many forms as part of its physical existence and its invisible consciousness. At this very moment, you are a child, a man, and a babe. You are a wizard, a soldier, a scholar, and a doctor all at the same time. Each of you exists in other worlds in all your manifestations and incarnations. History repeats itself. Roman legions are once again creating an empire. Dinosaurs roam worlds. The first man is stepping onto a moon somewhere, and you are part of it all. Then there are future worlds. Worlds where technology rules, where robots are as common as stars in the sky, and space travel is as easy as stepping on a bus. To think of yourself as singular and confined to this one life is to misunderstand your entire existence.'

Malik had remained unusually quiet until now. 'I still think this is a joke and I don't understand half of what you're saying, but let's say it isn't a joke. You said mirrors were only windows not doors, so seeing as how you have somehow slipped into our *dimension*, where is the door?'

Nim instantly appeared propped against the pillow beside Malik, making him jump off the bed in alarm. Leanne immediately doubled up in laughter at the sight of Malik's panicked retreat.

'That's what I like about you, Malik,' said Nim. 'You like to get right to the point.'

'What I like is to eat, but until we get to why you're here, that doesn't seem likely, does it?' said Malik.

'It's a good question, Malik, and the answer is in your dreams,' said Nim.

'Here we go again, more riddles,' said Malik.

'Not riddles, the answer is literally in your dreams. Let me explain. When a living entity such as yourself dies, they transit through the Dreamscape and stay there until a new life begins. All very simple and a process known to you as reincarnation. When you sleep, you also drift into the Dreamscape, and your non-physical being, or soul for want of a better word, moves briefly into the Dreamscape. During these short excursions, you encounter glimpses of other lives and other incarnations.

Dreams are remnant memories of your experiences in different lives, woven delicately into your consciousness.

'The Dreamscape can get very confusing,' Nim continued, 'when one incarnation encounters another. Sometimes, two sleeping entities meet within the Dreamscape and go through a kind of spiritual fusion. It is the job of a Dreamweaver to sort out the two realities, so when you wake, you can go on with life with a sense of normality. Very occasionally, two entities change lives completely. This process is called a crossover and can cause all sorts of problems. But normally, if the Dreamweaver does a good job, your experience in the Dreamscape fades very quickly into what you believe are simply half-remembered dreams.'

'And your father is a Dreamweaver?' said Alex.

'That's right, Alex. Weaving is simple enough until an entity ventures too far and gets lost in distant dimensions, or encounters another version of itself and the two cannot be easily separated. You have all had nightmares at some time, and they are a result of encounters with worlds very far removed from your own where many horrors reside. It takes a Master Dreamweaver like my father to settle you back into safe reality.'

'Is this a form of time travel?' Malik asked, already sounding like he half-believed Nim's story.

'Not time travel as you imagine it, Malik. Don't forget, time is not linear as it has no beginning and no end. Every event and every moment in your life is happening now, as are all your other lives. On some distant world you are just being born, on another you're dying of old age, and on another you are just becoming a father for the first time. It all happens now because yesterday and tomorrow do not exist.'

'My head hurts,' said Malik.

Leanne joked. 'Mine too...just from imagining you as a father, Malik.'

'What do you want us to do, Nim?' asked Alex. But he had a horrible feeling he already knew.

Like an ink-black spider, Slade stood flat against the wall with his arms spread wide and his gloved hands clinging to the surface as though it were a spider's web. He pressed his ear to the wall to hear Nim speak.

'A terrible war is coming, and a great crime will be committed on a world, not unlike your own, called Trinity in the seventh dimension,' Nim said sadly. 'Trinity is a world halfway to the Angra pole, many billions of worlds from here.'

'Just a hop then,' said Malik.

'Not really,' Nim replied, unaware of Malik's attempted humour. 'While Trinity is far removed from your world, the effects of this immoral war will have dire consequences throughout the Megaverse. Flowing over into the sixth dimension, these acts of war will be mirrored across billions of worlds, spreading like a virus and contaminating all in its path. The magnitude of this crime against life and its repercussions will throw an already imbalanced Megaverse into complete disarray. Worlds will fall like dominoes, bringing all life to an end, and Angra will have triumphed.'

Stunned into silence, Alex, Leanne, and Malik reacted with the same look of horror upon hearing this grim news. Having only just learned of their new Megaverse, the existence of new dimensions, and a billion new worlds, they now had to also contend with its possible destruction.

'Shouldn't you be talking to leaders, prime ministers, and presidents, the United Nations even? If what you say is true, this affects everyone. Why waste your time with us?' said Malik.

Nim was sympathetic to Malik's comments. 'In a perfect world, you would be right, Malik. You should be able to count on leaders for solutions, but sadly they are part of the problem. Unfortunately, history does not reflect kindly on so-called adults and leaders, or their solutions. I told you before, history repeats itself. The same wars are fought over and over, but the same lessons are never learned. We chose you because we believe you can stop this war before it begins and prevent an unforgivable crime. You have innocence uniquely suitable for this role.'

Leanne laughed. 'Malik, innocent?'

'Trust me, Leanne,' Nim said seriously, 'in another incarnation on Trinity, you are directly involved in the events leading to war. Each of you has a part to play in the outcome.'

'Another incarnation,' Malik said.

Leanne was quick to respond before Nim could elaborate. 'Incarnation means another life. Some people, like the Buddhists for instance, believe we are reincarnated when we die. To be reincarnated simply means to be born again. Buddhists even believe we can be reborn as animals or insects. So, next time you're pulling the legs off a fly, remember it might be your great-great-grandma, Malik.'

Malik shook his head. 'I don't pull the legs off flies. I eat them alive on toast.'

'Yuck! You are revolting, Malik,' said Leanne.

Malik felt delighted with Leanne's disgust. 'I know what incarnation means, Leanne. It's like you have to prove how clever you are. How do you know stuff about Buddhists anyway? Did you swallow the Wikipedia or something?'

'I'm not showing off, and I don't know stuff,' Leanne said defensively. 'I must have just heard it somewhere.'

'Hey, I just had a thought!' said Malik. 'If Bottom knew as much about stuff as you, Leanne, he would be a smartarse, or maybe even a wisecrack.'

Leanne screamed. 'Malik! That's completely gross.'

Alex shook his head but couldn't help laughing. Malik was quick-witted and turning out to be quite funny in a cruel sort of way. Though he tried very hard not to, Alex was beginning to like him.

'There is no shame in knowledge, Leanne,' said Nim. 'And you are right about reincarnation. It forms the very basis of the Megaverse.'

Alex interrupted. 'Tell us what you have in mind, Nim?'

Nim looked hesitant. 'I...I want you to cross over to Trinity.'

Everyone appeared stunned for a moment. Malik laughed.

'Cross over? You're not serious?' Leanne said.

'I am,' said Nim. 'You have to go to Trinity and take the place of your other selves until the crisis is averted. Conditions are right for a crossover, but we must hurry because we only have a small window. I will assist you to fall soundly asleep, after which, a Figment Navigator will guide you to Trinity. Once there, my father will weave your consciousness with your Trinity incarnations and you will use your influence on the key players to prevent a catastrophe.'

Alex looked sceptical. 'How will we do that?'

'The way you proceed will only become clear to you once on Trinity. You will become one with your other self and have access to everything they know. At that point, you will understand the situation. The crossover is not a permanent switch you understand. Once your quest is complete, you will return here to your world.'

'And if we don't go?' asked Alex.

Nim smiled sadly. 'Without the four of you, there seems little hope.'

Leanne looked miserable. 'You said without the four of us there is little hope, but there are only three of us, Nim.'

Nim appeared on the floor, the bed, then next to the rabbit, all within the blink of an eye. 'Oh, didn't I mention it? Jani Nasri is coming too.'

Kale pulled the ceremonial dagger from its sheath. The finely honed blade could split a single human hair by simply dropping it onto the sharp edge. Kale's fingers wrapped around the jewelled handle, caressing the diamonds and rubies embedded within. But Slade placed a hand on Kale's arm, indicating he should stay his hand and wait a little longer as there would be an addition to Nim's little group. They would hold off until everyone was together. Kale replaced the dagger in its sheath and joined Slade to listen at the wall.

'Jani Nasri?' Malik asked, confused and seemingly irritated by her sudden inclusion. 'The Jani Nasri who sits next to me in class?'

'The very same,' Nim said.

'Well that's me out,' said Malik.

'Why, what have you got against Jani?' asked Leanne.

'Everything,' said Malik. 'I don't like her kind.'

'Her kind?' Leanne felt the hairs stand on the back of her neck.

'Her lot,' said Malik, clarifying his comment. 'They probably came on a boat.'

'Came on a boat! Are you for real? That's a terrible racist remark.'

'Why is it racist? Anyway, I can be racist if I want. If I don't like people,' Malik continued, 'I should be allowed to say so. Why is that wrong?'

Leanne could not believe her ears. 'Because it just is! You can't say you don't like people just because they're different to you. And what makes you think she came on a boat?'

'Their lot always does.'

Leanne was horrified. 'How would it be if I said I don't like you because you come from where you do, because you look different to me, or just because I don't like the colour of your skin?'

Malik looked defiant. 'I wouldn't care because I'd say I don't like you either. Your choice, my choice.'

'What about our parents, Nim?' asked Alex, changing the subject and hoping to put an end to the bickering. 'What if the school calls to say we're not in class?'

'I can assure you they will not,' said Nim. 'No one will miss you until you return.'

Several minutes of silence followed as Malik and Leanne cooled their tempers. Alex wondered how they were going to complete their task if they couldn't get along before they'd even started. He still had doubts about Nim's extraordinary story, half-expecting Phys Ed to walk through the door with cameras in tow, declare they were all fooled and that the resulting embarrassment would promptly be posted on YouTube so the world could laugh at their gullibility. Still, he felt compelled to go along with Nim.

'How long will we be gone anyway?' asked Alex.

'You will be back before you know it, Alex,' said Nim. 'Remember, time—'

'Is not linear,' Alex completed. 'Yes, I know.'

'Make a phone call and tell your parents you may be a little late home from school. Nothing more is necessary as I will do the rest,' said Nim.

Leanne was still stewing over Malik's remarks. After seeing his home environment, she had begun to wonder if her opinion of him might have been just a little unfair, and there might be another side to his character. After all, she reasoned, how could anybody be such a mean-spirited person when they came from such a good home? But now he was proving to be the nasty individual she always thought him to be.

'What's wrong, Nim,' Leanne asked, having noticed a change in Nim's appearance.

Nim looked worried. She closed her eyes and held her hands outstretched before her. Her fingers moved as though they were feeling the air, and she started to flit from one place to the next in quick succession, mumbling as she did so. She moved so fast the others could not keep up with where she would appear next. She stopped with her hands on the bedroom wall and gave out a squeal as though she had been stung by its touch. Alex, Leanne, and Malik looked on, alarmed by Nim's erratic behaviour.

'Nim?' said Alex. 'Are you okay?'

Nim's eyes snapped open. 'You must leave now,' she said. 'We cannot wait for Jani, she will have to follow later.' Nim sprang to the bedroom door and turned the key in the lock. 'Please lie on the floor,' she said, guiding them quickly to their positions in the centre of the room. 'We must hurry.'

'What's going on, Nim?' asked Alex. 'Why the sudden urgency?'

'Everything is aligned and the time is fast approaching when you must leave,' Nim said. 'But, just as I have come to find you, so have others. I told you of Figments who inhabit the Dreamscape, Navigators, Dreamweavers, Guides, all good spirits. But just as Angra and Agathos are present throughout the Megaverse, they both exist even within the Dreamscape. There are Figments whose intention it is to swing the balance in favour of Angra. They are the Quacksalvers, Charlatans, and Assassins. I feel their presence, and they are here to stop you.'

'You're frightening me,' said Leanne.

'Trust me, Leanne,' said Nim as she arranged the three young adventurers on Malik's bedroom floor on their backs, each with their head to the centre like a three-pointed star.

'Unfortunately, I cannot join you on your journey, but I will meet up with you later.' A worried expression passed between the three youths. 'If it were possible, I would be at your side from the very beginning,' Nim added, realising their concern, 'but the laws of Megaverse physics mean you must cross over on your own. Once you awake on Trinity, your destination is the city of Mariana where hopefully your quest will become clear.'

'Hopefully?' squealed Alex.

'There are no guarantees, Alex. Crossing over is not an exact science. But all being well, you will each find yourself in the identity of your Trinity incarnation. I have faith in all of you that you will know what to do and your path will be clear.' Nim inclined her head, smiled and tried to reassure them. 'Though this is an important mission, you must be prepared for some very odd encounters, some of which you may find quite amusing. What may seem impossible on one world can be quite normal on another. While Trinity has many similarities to your own Earth, there are going to be things to surprise you. It will be a great adventure, but you must remain focused and not get distracted from your quest. And remember, I will join you as soon as permitted.' Nim looked at the door. She could not hide the concern on her face or the urgency evident in her eyes. 'The time has arrived,' she said.

A loud bang hammered the bedroom door.

'Who's that?' asked Leanne, but she was already starting to feel groggy as Nim stroked her head and spoke in a strange tongue like she was reciting a chant or praying. With growing urgency, Nim did the same for each of the boys.

'Are there any final questions?' asked Nim, ignoring the continuous pounding on the door.

'Yes, when do we eat?' asked Malik.

'I'll take that as a no, Malik.' No one else responded. 'Once you enter the realm of sleep, I will disappear from here and we will only meet again on Trinity.'

'I'm scared,' Leanne mumbled.

'Don't be,' Nim reassured her. 'The Navigator will take you safely on your way, and my father will do the rest. So now we must begin. Please hold each other's hand.'

Leanne took hold of Alex's hand and squeezed for good luck, while on the other side, Malik's huge fingers enclosed hers so tightly she had to force herself not to pull away. They stared at the ceiling in readiness for what would come next as Batman images looked down on them from the overhead light shade. Before Alex could comment, and as if by magic, they instantly fell into a deep sleep. At the exact same moment, Nim vanished.

Eyes flickered, faces twitched, and dreams stirred in each of them. Moments later, Alex opened his eyes to a blinding array of dazzling lights, and as he did so, he thought he saw two men. They were dressed in black from head to toe and rushing across Malik's bedroom to stop him, but they were too late. The journey had already begun.

CHAPTER 5

Awakenings

Shivering against the chilled morning air, Leanne struggled to wake from a deep yet restless sleep. With half-opened eyes, she peered through a murky haze that swirled around her head and made her think she was still dreaming. Her breath billowed and caused lingering clouds of vapour to hang in the air, and her fingers failed to move in the frigid conditions while her toes had no feeling at all. Her neck ached through lying in the same position for too long, and her left arm had gone numb underneath the weight of her body. A makeshift shelter of palm leaves formed a blanket to cover her, scarcely enough to protect her from the harsh winter chill. Was she asleep or awake? She couldn't tell.

Sunlight burned through the hanging mist, and she shuffled into a shaft of light to feel its warmth. She felt disoriented.

Squinting, she surveyed her surroundings but the light hurt her eyes. She realised she was lying in a ditch at the side of a narrow road. Through the fog, she could make out the shapes of people passing; some were riding ponies, and some drove animals pulling carts. The clatter of cartwheels and the clomp of hooves on cobblestones echoed through the air as the simple forms of transportation passed her by.

Leanne reached automatically for her smartphone, which she always kept in the same place at the side of her bed. The phone was not there, and neither was the bedside table. Waking more thoroughly, she became aware she was not in her bedroom, and she was not emerging from a dream. Startled by this sudden realisation, she sat bolt upright and remembered the events in Malik's bedroom. Frantic, she called for her companions.

'Alex! Malik!'

Leanne saw the unmistakable bulk of Malik lying beside her, his head buried deep beneath the fronds of his makeshift shelter. He grumbled at the coming of daylight and the sound of his name. Beyond Malik, enveloped in mist, others emerged from their overnight beds in the same dry ditch, but none she recognised. She called again. 'Alex!' Nobody answered. 'Malik, I can't see any sign of Alex. I think we've been separated and I don't know where we are. We seem to have been sleeping at the side of a road, and there are people everywhere.'

Sunshine soon burnt away what remained of the night, the fog cleared, and Leanne climbed out of the ditch onto the road. She saw people making their way on foot or horseback, dressed in odd-looking clothes. There was not a car in sight.

Malik poked his head from beneath his cover, dazed and half-asleep, he stretched his arms and yawned.

A horse rider passed at a gallop and as he went by, he shouted. 'Hey! No Greens without a leash.'

Leanne thought it was a strange comment from the rider, whose remark was directed at her. She heard Malik behind her.

Malik said, 'What did he mean, no greens without a leash?'

'I don't know. He looked like a soldier dressed for a historical re-enactment.' Leanne turned to Malik and her face turned pale. 'Oh, Malik.'

'What?'

'Look at your hands.'

Malik raised his hands, and his sleepy expression turned to one of horror. 'My hands,' he said, 'they're green.' Dumbstruck by the sight of his own hands, all he could say was, 'Green! They are green!'

'Malik, I don't want you to panic.'

'Don't panic? They're just green hands, right?'

'It gets worse, Malik.'

'How...how can it possibly get worse? I've got green hands for crying out loud.'

Malik held out his hands as living proof so that Leanne could grasp the magnitude of the problem. But she was looking at him weirdly.

'What?'

'Promise you won't get angry.'

'What!'

'Your face, Malik, it's kind of the same green colour as your hands.'

Alex opened his eyes. He had the strangest feeling of movement. The rolling motion made his head swim and his stomach nauseous. He pulled the sheets up around his neck and closed his eyes tight to settle himself, but the shifting sense of his surroundings made the feeling worse. Turning on his back, he opened his eyes once more and took in the immediate environment. Wooden beams crossed the ceiling and terminated at panelled wood walls. Light entered the room through a row of three windows with small panes of thick glass, so thick it was impossible to see outside. An old-fashioned oil lamp swung lazily back and forth on an overhead beam as its flame flickered on a low burn. Alex suddenly realised the motion he was feeling was not in his head; he was on board a ship.

Alex came to his senses, and the situation became clear. He appeared to be alone on a boat, an ancient ship. Anxiously looking around the cabin, he saw it housed a bunk, a large desk strewn with maps and charts, a bookcase, a cupboard, and a dressing table. Alex surveyed the room, inspecting its contents with interest. Charts lay open on the desk, indicating a recently plotted route through oceans and seas to lands he did not recognise. Geography was one of his best subjects, but the names of these places were entirely unknown to him. Also on the desk was an hourglass standing ready to be turned, and a collection of brass navigation instruments lying next to a set of compasses. He picked up a feathered quill from an ink bottle, scrutinised it, and returned it to the container. His clothes looked odd and were made of wool that scratched at his skin. A loud knock on the cabin door startled him.

'Who's there?'

'Little Jim, sir,' came the reply.

Alex opened the door just enough to observe a young boy of maybe nine or ten years old standing before him. He opened the door wider.

'You asked me to wake you at dawn, Captain Boatman, sir. The sun has just crept over the horizon.'

Malik had calmed down and no longer spoke with the high-pitched squeal of a mouse sucking helium from a party balloon. Leanne reassured him that even though his green appearance might be a little traumatic at first, the condition was probably temporary. It was a side effect, she told him, and he would soon return to his loveable, colourless self. Until then, she added, they must not lose focus over silly things such as this.

'Silly things!' Malik was unimpressed at Leanne's lack of sympathy.

'Come on, Malik, we need to figure out where we are and where in hell's bells Alex has disappeared to.'

They sat at the roadside, taking stock of their situation and recalling the events in Malik's bedroom that had led to their miraculous transportation to Trinity. Convinced now Nim had told the truth, and with only half the team in place, they decided they had no alternative but to start making their way to Mariana and hope Alex would do the same. Jani might also soon follow according to Nim's plan. Malik was unhappy with his new identity and his green appearance, muttering under his breath as Leanne spelt out their current situation. She knew he would sulk all the way to the city and prepared for a long and challenging journey.

'I have to go,' said Malik as they prepared to set off.

'Go where?'

'Go! I have to go.'

'Oh, sorry. Well hurry up, we need to get moving.'

Malik promptly disappeared behind a nearby tree to answer his call of nature, but a short time later, Leanne heard an ear-piercing scream erupt from his chosen toilet spot.

'Malik, what is it?'

'It's green!' came the horrified reply.

Once on the road, Malik and Leanne decided to ask for help before wandering off in the wrong direction. Their hope was someone would know the city of Mariana and direct them on to the correct path. Leanne made several approaches, but each time her questions were ignored and she found herself shooed away. The narrow road was bustling with small groups of people who appeared to be travelling around dressed in period costumes from the Middle Ages.

It's like we just stepped onto a historical movie set, Leanne thought. 'We could easily be in Europe during the fifth or sixth centuries. But I don't think this is Europe, and I don't think they are dressed up for a film shoot. Look at our clothes, Malik. I think this is what people wear every day.'

Clothed in what could only be described as dishevelled potato sacks with hoods, Leanne and Malik would have blended perfectly with other simple travellers had it not been for Malik's green skin and extraordinary size.

'I feel dumb,' Malik said.

Leanne had a reply but decided to keep the wisecrack to herself. The vast majority of travellers headed up the road to the east, so Leanne and Malik followed the flow of traffic. At Leanne's suggestion, they pulled their hoods down to partially cover their faces. Leanne felt the urgent need to remain hidden as much as possible, though she did not understand why this seemed so important. Malik, given his rather green exterior, needed no coaxing to take a more secretive approach.

'If I run into someone I know, I'll just die,' he moaned.

'We're halfway across the Megaverse, Malik, who are we going to run into?'

As they walked, he continually complained about his colour change, as though his whining would somehow magically rectify his appearance.

How come it was me who got the paintbrush? Why is it you get to be yourself? How come Nim never said anything about being green? On and on went the pointless questions and dissatisfied grumbles. Leanne wanted to scream.

'Malik, give it a rest please.'

'Alright for you to say give it a rest, you don't look like the jolly green giant.'

The crowd grew thicker as they neared a bottleneck in the road. Standing at the portal of a covered bridge spanning a vast river gorge, a group of soldiers dressed in leather and chainmail tunics stopped random travellers before allowing them further passage to the bridge. One of the soldiers spotted Malik's approach from a distance. His unusual size and frame became the focus of attention as the pair neared the checkpoint.

'You,' the soldier said, ordering them to stop. Malik stayed back while Leanne met the soldier with head bowed low. 'Papers,' the soldier demanded.

Leanne went for an inside pouch in her sackcloth smock and produced a set of identity papers. The grim soldier read them, looking from the papers to Leanne and back again, as though he were checking the traveller against the details of her documents. Leanne kept her head low, allowing the hood to flop over her face to shade and partly conceal her features while Malik watched on nervously.

'It says here you're travelling from Caprine to Mariana. What's your business in Mariana?'

Leanne realised the soldier was speaking a strange language, yet she understood every word. Not only could she understand the language, but she could also speak it. 'We are on a pilgrimage to the Great Pyramid, sir. To kneel and pray before the Lux Temple and to touch the Hand of Gods.'

'Caprinese people have a long history of treachery, why should I let you pass?'

'Sir, it has been many millennia since the Caprinese and Mariana came into conflict. Peace has been stable between our two provinces since the great extinction. We share the same Gods.'

'That may be, but things have changed. Mark my words, there is a war brewing. How do I know you're not spies?'

'We are just simple pilgrims, sir.'

The soldier eased Leanne aside and came face to face with Malik. At least he would've been face to face had the soldier been two feet taller. 'Take off your hood,' the aggressive soldier ordered. Malik complied without a word of protest. 'This Green has no collar, no leash.' He aimed the observation at Leanne.

'He's a free man,' Leanne said. 'I have his papers right here.' She produced a second set of papers from her pouch and pushed them into the soldier's hands. Malik stood in silence. 'This man has been a loyal servant of our family since he was a small child,' Leanne continued. 'My father freed him as a reward for his long and faithful service. His papers have been signed by the high court of Caprine to verify this.'

The soldier snarled as he spoke. 'You are not in Caprine now, Green lover. This Green cannot travel without a leash. End of story.'

'But I don't have a leash, and he is free to walk unshackled. His papers say so.'

The soldier turned to his comrades and laughed. 'Then he is free to turn around and walk back to Caprine. His kind are not welcome here, free or not, and neither are you. Go with him, Caprinese woman, walk your dog and don't come back. You'll never cross this bridge while I have anything to say about it.'

Malik went to speak, but Leanne silenced him with a look that told him how dangerous it could get if he said the wrong thing. She turned away and Malik followed.

'And get him on a leash,' the soldier shouted after them. 'Free or not, in these parts, you will soon be arrested.'

They walked a while in silence, and Leanne imagined how the soldier's cruel words must have sounded to Malik. Simmering, he raced ahead, making it hard for Leanne to keep up with his long, relentless stride.

'Malik, wait up.'

Malik quickened his pace.

'Malik, stop!'

'I'm going home,' he said without looking back.

'And how do you expect to do that, catch a bus?'

'I've had enough already, and where's Nim?'

'Malik!'

Malik stopped. 'Did you hear that soldier? Did you hear what he said about me?'

Leanne caught up, irritated by the unnecessary exertion. 'I did, Malik, and it was cruel, and it was wrong. But until we understand the situation and figure out where we fit in, we have to be careful how we react to these setbacks.'

'How did you know all that stuff anyway, all that about Caprine and Mariana and the Great Pyramid?'

Leanne sighed. 'I don't know, I just did. How did you know to keep your mouth shut? I mean, that was not the Malik I know. I thought you were going to bust him in the chops at any moment.'

Malik's features softened as the hint of a smile curled his mouth. 'I almost did. It was hard to say nothing, but did you see his sword? And the others had swords and spears too, sharp ones. I somehow knew how a Green should react and what would happen if I opened my big mouth. Where the hell are we, Leanne?'

They stood to the side of the road to let a large group of pilgrims pass on their way to Mariana.

'At least we know which direction we should be going,' Malik said. 'If all these people are making a pilgrimage to Mariana, all we have to do is follow them.'

'If we can get past the guard on the bridge,' Leanne said.

'That's another thing, you knew about the papers in your pouch and why we would need them. Where did they come from, and how did you know they were there?'

'I just knew. It's as if I am this Caprinese woman. She's somewhere deep inside me, telling me things. I know the things she knows. It's very unnerving. Then again, in my head, I'm still the Leanne I always was.'

'Not quite,' said Malik. 'I've been so wrapped up in my appearance I haven't had the chance to tell you. You may be the same Leanne, but you're older, much older. Probably in your late twenties, maybe even older.'

'I had a feeling I had changed. Our papers say we are both twenty-three. And thanks for pointing it out to me, Malik, you're so kind.' Leanne paused and a mischievous smile crossed her face. 'Oh, by the way, nice tail, Malik.'

'WHAT!'

'Only joking.'

They laughed together for a few moments, easing the tension. Malik turned to the west, looking back to another time and another place.

'Do you think it's true what you said about your father? I mean this Caprinese woman's father. You think they kept me as a slave and later freed me?'

'Yes, it's true,' she said sadly. 'We may have moved halfway across the Megaverse, Malik, but some things never change.'

Overboard

Aboard the Mariana ship, M.S. Klaw, Captain Alexander Boatman made his way to the main deck to find his newly adopted crew assembled before him. He scanned the faces in the hope he would find his missing companions. Despite the large crew of male and female sailors, Alex could pick out neither Malik nor Leanne in their midst. He was about to address the crew when a shout came from a lookout on the mainmast above.

'Ship on the port bow, Captain. Looks like a Man o' War.'

Alex called for a telescope and confirmed the lookout's observations. The ship was in the middle of a wide turn. 'She's spotted us, lads and lasses. All hands to battle stations.' He gave this order in a calm and confident tone; somehow he knew what to do. *This is crazy...I'm a ship's captain and my name's*

Boatman, how mad is that? And what was it I just said? Lads and Lasses? Oh no, I sound like my grandad.

'First Officer Stark,' Alex said, 'prepare to take evasive actions if you will.'

'Aye, aye, Captain.' The first officer, a stout woman of ample proportions and rosy complexion, sprang into action and bellowed orders to all stations. Alex looked on with a satisfied smile as she pressed the well-drilled crew into operation. Sails flapped and ropes snapped through turnbuckles and capstans. Lurching in immediate response to the new settings, the Klaw heeled over to thirty degrees and surged to starboard, sending a plume of salt spray high into the air.

The M.S. Klaw had once been a battleship of the Mariana Navy. Sixty feet long, she had three masts and an excellent set of Black Spider silk sails. She was fast, and she needed to be because her guns had been removed, all but two twenty-four pounders only capable of firing small cannonballs the size of a grapefruit; useless in a fight with a warship. Now an explorer come trader, her survival and that of the crew depended on her ability to outrun the enemy. In this case, however, the Klaw was no match for the newly built Man o' War now bearing down on her. Alex knew his only hope was to use his knowledge of the sea to out-manoeuvre her.

Unlike the Klaw, the Man o' War had a full complement of guns at her disposal. Lining three decks on either side, they included two huge sixty pounders that could sink a ship with one direct hit to the waterline. This overabundance of cannon, Alex thought, could be used to his advantage. For although the Man o' War was a newer, faster ship, she had the weight of almost one hundred cannons to slow her down, while the Klaw had only two. If Alex could push his ship to the limits, with a little luck he could still outrun the other vessel.

'Tack hard to port now, Ms Stark!'

The order relayed throughout the ship brought a sudden shift in direction, sending the ship's bow crashing deep into the surf and sending an explosion of white sea foam shooting skyward. Alex braced himself against the mast as a wall of water pounded the vessel, leaving crew members tumbling helplessly before spilling into the ocean on the opposite side of the deck. No sooner had the ship stabilised than the order to tack to windward came and the ship lurched again, smashing against the waves.

'She's still gaining on us, Captain, we have to lose more weight.' First Officer Stark approached Alex, and the urgent expression on her face told him he had to make a decision. 'Captain,' she said, holding on to her hat against the wind and sea spray, 'we need to throw the cargo overboard.'

'The cargo?'

'Yes, sir, we have a full hold, and the difference in weight might just be enough to see us to freedom.'

Alex felt his stomach churn, not because of the sea, not out of fear, but because he suddenly knew what Stark meant by cargo. 'Take the helm, Ms Stark. Second Mate Gates, come with me.'

With difficulty, Alex and the second mate made their way through the decks of the rolling ship, pausing every few feet to maintain their balance until they arrived at the hold, located in the hull, well below the waterline. The second mate unlocked the door and stood aside. The sight sickened Alex.

'Shall we start throwing them overboard, Captain?'

Alex took a moment to regain his composure. He closed his eyes and tried to understand the scene before him. When he opened them, he knew this was a slave ship. He looked over his cargo of Green men and women, row after row of whom looked up to where he stood with terror on their faces, apparent for all to see. Alex would never forget the misery or pain in their eyes. Chained together in cramped and squalid conditions, they moaned as one when the ship lurched and thundered against a wave. These were his prisoners, his slaves, his cargo. Alex had been responsible for their capture, and the realisation gutted him.

Greens had been slaves for hundreds of years on Trinity; it was only in recent times that the practice had become less acceptable and in many places, outlawed. Caprine and its provinces had given Greens freedom and equal rights. Mariana had looked ready to follow their example. But distrust had developed between the Caprinese and the Mariana nations; a war was imminent, and Green reforms withdrew from Mar-

iana's parliament in the process. Worse still, increased suspicion of the Greens as a threat in their own right had led
to Alexander Boatman being sent to the islands to round up
members of the so-called rebellion. An overreaction, according to more moderate members of the high counsel who called
for evidence of such a threat, an opinion shared by Alexander.
Nevertheless, the captain had obeyed the queen's orders, and
for this, Alex was angry at his Trinity incarnation.

'No, Mr Gates,' Alex said eventually. 'We will not be throwing them overboard.'

Returning to the top deck, Alex tried to shake the scene
from his mind. He told himself he had not chosen this role.
Captain Alexander Boatman was not a person of his own cre-
ation, but it did little to ease his guilt.

'But, Captain—'

'I won't hear any more about it, Ms Stark.' The news there
would be no dumping of cargo did not please the first officer,
who seemed to think it was an easy decision to make. 'We'll
outfox her if we can't outrun her,' Alex said. 'We need more
sail, Ms Stark. Unfurl the gennaker and come sharply about.'

'Aye, aye, Captain.' Stark gave the orders, the ship's wheel
spun hard, and the ship once again plunged deep into the
waves in response to the sudden change.

'And back again, Ms Stark.' Alex had little time to think
about his transformation from high-school student to ship's
captain. His actions as a commander came automatically,

as though he had found the knowledge to take control deep within him, as if leading his men in a battle with the seas had always been his calling and the most natural thing he could imagine.

The Klaw leapt high on the swell, its keel breaking out of the water before crashing once more with a mighty splash, throwing everyone to the deck and sending them scrambling to take hold to save themselves against the wash. Above the mighty roar of wind and waves, Alex heard a cry. He spun in time to see Little Jim, the cabin boy, washed over the side and into the unforgiving turbulence of the ship's wake.

Alex acted without thought for his own safety. Taking a knife from his belt, he cut through a bowline, wrapped the thin rope around his waist, and before anyone could stop him, he leapt from the ship into the pounding sea. Submerged beneath the waves, Alex disappeared into the depths. He held his breath and felt the icy water shocking his body, urging him to panic and breathe. Struggling in the murky darkness while being pulled this way and that by the deep ocean currents, he thought his lungs would burst at the effort. He resisted the urge to take a breath, determined to stay focused in his frantic search for the boy. Was he upside down or downside up? He couldn't tell. Disoriented and out of air, he kicked for what he hoped was the surface and broke the waves in a last desperate lunge. He took a gulp of air between waves as the churning water crashed around him, and he disappeared below the foaming sea once more. Fight, Alex, he told himself. Fight for your life and Jim's.

He did not give up until out of breath again, breaking the surface only to see Little Jim slip from view. Mistiming his gulp for air, he took a mouthful of water. With no time to lose, Alex kicked for where Jim went down, but the bowline was now at its limit. He felt the line pull around his waist as the Klaw took the slack, and Alex made a split decision. He untied the rope and dove one last time. With his final desperate effort, he caught Jim's shirt and kicked for daylight. Once more he took a frantic gulp of air, strengthening his grip on the boy and hoping the Klaw was still within reach. He saw the ship turn against the wind, and for a few moments the sails fluttered lifelessly, causing the ship to stall. With all his strength he swam towards her, the limp body of Jim grasped under his arm. The treacherous sea fought against his effort and all seemed lost. But as if by a miracle, he felt the bowline in his outstretched hand and with what little remained of his strength, he took hold. The crew hauled them both to safety, but the drama was far from over.

'He's dead, Captain. Little Jim has drowned.'

Exhausted, Alex picked himself up from the deck and pushed the crew aside. They watched in bewilderment as Alex placed his hand on Little Jim's forehead, the other under his chin, and tilted his head. Alex pinched Jim's nose, covered his mouth with his own, and gave two short breaths. He followed this action by clamping his hands together on Jim's chest, pumping the boy's ribcage in quick succession. He repeated the cycle, desperate for a response while the crew looked on in amazement. Jim coughed and spluttered, opened his eyes and whispered, 'Th-thank you...Captain, I-I nearly d-died.'

The crew cheered, and Alex looked around at the astonished expressions and laughed. He said, 'Don't thank me, Little Jim, thank St John's Ambulance Brigade for coming to Morton Bay High School and teaching us CPR.' No one understood the comment, which made Alex laugh even harder.

'Captain,' said the first officer. 'The Man o' War has come around our port bow; she's preparing to fire her guns.'

Alex hurried to the top deck and found the enemy ship preparing for battle. A devil-like figurehead carved into the Man o' War's prow gave the warship a fearsome appearance. But it was the name painted in gold letters along its gunnel that frightened Alex the most. 'Angra,' he said to himself. 'The ship is named Angra.'

The Klaw lay still, dead in the water. She would be a sitting duck once the Angra came to starboard and her big guns came into range.

'Sir, shall we run up the white flag and surrender?'

Alex considered Stark's request. 'I somehow doubt they intend to take us prisoner, Ms Stark.'

'Captain Boatman,' came the call from the lookout. 'We're drifting towards the Convergence.'

The Convergence, Alex somehow knew, was an area of the ocean all sailors feared. Sailors are superstitious folk, and many myths had been created over the years to explain this strange and mysterious place of terror were many hundreds of ships had mysteriously been lost, never to be heard of again. A little bit like the Bermuda Triangle, Alex thought. Alexander Boatman's grandfather, who was an accomplished naval captain, had explained the Convergence to his grandson as an occurrence of nature. At this exact location, four of the world's oceans came together in a fierce tempest of currents and tides, one crashing into the other with terrifying force and making it impossible for any ship to survive the tumult. Alex imagined New York traffic converging at speed on its main intersection without traffic lights. The result would be catastrophic.

'Sir, if we drift any further, we will be pulled into the currents and there will be no escape.'

As the first officer spoke, a crack of thunder broke across the space between the ships. The Klaw's crew froze in anticipation before the whoosh of a massive cannonball split the mainsail and disappeared harmlessly into the ocean.

'They're finding their range, Captain. What shall we do?'

'Still drifting, Captain,' came the cry from above.

Alex saw only one way out. 'Turn her fifteen degrees with the wind, Ms Stark. Give her some slack in the sails.'

Stark's reaction told of her fear. 'But, sir, we'll sail right into the Convergence.'

'Do as I say, Ms Stark.'

Stark complied with the orders. She knew her captain well enough to trust him, though this was a manoeuvre she feared went too far. Once in the Convergence, they would face perils unknown and almost certain death.

The Klaw responded quickly, leaving the Angra little time to adjust. The Angra fired several harmless shots before swinging around and shooting a full volley of cannonballs broadside. This time, many shots found their mark, sending shards of timber splintering through the air like deadly arrows. A sixty-pound ball sliced through the forward mast like a knife through butter, bringing the top of the mast crashing to the deck and sending sailors diving for cover. Dazed by the close call, First Officer Stark had just lost her hat as a smaller cannonball had taken it from her head. An inch lower and the Klaw would have been without her second in command.

Several cannonballs found their target, shattering parts of the ship to sawdust. But the damage from the volley proved minimal. Currents swept the Klaw out of range of the Angra's weapons, and the Angra's captain didn't dare follow, instead resigned to watch as her quarry disappeared from view. What the Klaw and her crew faced now, however, was more terrifying than the fate any one ship could deliver them, even one as mighty as the Angra. Inside the Convergence, Captain Alexander Boatman, his crew, and his cargo sailed into the unknown at the mercy of the Gods.

CHAPTER 7

The bone man

Exhausted, Malik and Leanne stopped at the side of the road. They had spent the day travelling side tracks and trails in the hope they could find an alternative crossing of the deep river gorge. Most of these dirt roads had come to nothing, fading out and disappearing into dust. Two promising tracks had come to an abrupt end on the rim of the river gorge, leading the unwary to a deadly plunge of one thousand feet down the sheer cliffs to the water and rocks below. Their latest attempt, however, had taken them in a full circle and ended back on the cobbled road to Mariana with the covered bridge and the soldiers' guard post only a hundred yards away. Night had already begun to fall. Disheartened and spent, the pair slumped to the ground in despair. Winter days were short, and the sun had long since disappeared below the horizon. Malik imagined another night in a ditch.

'I can't walk another step,' said Malik. 'And I'm cold.'

'Me too, frozen. We passed an inn just a few miles back on the side track. I've got tokens in my pouch so we could pay for some rooms.' Leanne carefully removed a sandal from her foot and inspected the blisters. 'I don't even know if I have the strength to walk back that far,' she said, replacing the footwear. 'But it's getting colder, and I don't want to spend the night here under a bunch of leaves.'

'Right.' Malik made the first move, and with a lot of effort he got to his feet and began walking back. Leanne followed with a limp.

When they reached the inn after a slow, painful walk, darkness had descended fully and completed the transition to night. Orange flames glowed from a series of outdoor oil lamps, inviting weary travellers to stay and promising a warm welcome within. The sign above the door had a picture of a man riding a horse and read: The Pilgrim's Rest Inn. Malik imagined a hearty meal of beef and vegetables beside the fire and a soft, warm bed for his tired body.

When they stepped through the door, they were not disappointed. A massive log fire burned in the hearth, oil lamps and candles flickered around the room, and travellers sat around in groups drinking ale and eating hot, delicious looking food. Voices competed with each other in the cheerful atmosphere, and Malik decided there was no place he would rather be at this very moment in time. The room fell silent, and all heads turned to Leanne and Malik as they completed their entrance and closed the door behind them.

A short, balding man they presumed to be the innkeeper, stood behind the bar and stopped in the middle of pouring a mug of ale for a customer. Beside him, a smiling girl had just delivered two steaming plates of sausages to a hungry patron. Several moments passed in silence as all eyes focused on the newcomers. Eventually, the innkeeper spoke. 'Can't you read the sign?'

The sign to which the man referred had been nailed to a wooden beam facing the door upon entry. STRICTLY NO GREENS! Leanne's heart sank. She turned to see Malik's shattered expression and thought for a moment he was about to cry. She pleaded with the innkeeper before Malik could say something they would both regret.

'Please, sir. Just one night?'

'You can stay, girl. There's one single left vacant at the back, but the Green has to sleep in the stables.'

Malik took a step forward, and a group of men instantly jumped to their feet to block his way. The average height of the men brought their faces level with Malik's chest. But there were many men in the inn, and the odds of Malik receiving a good beating for his troubles were great indeed, even if he was bigger than all of them. Leanne held Malik back and asked the innkeeper what he would charge for them both to sleep in the stables. She paid the necessary tokens, and the pair retreated to the somewhat rickety outbuildings adjoining the inn.

'You could have stayed in a room,' Malik said as they lit an oil lamp and settled down in the straw.

'Oh right, me in a warm bed and you sleep with the animals,' Leanne replied. 'I'd never hear the last of it until we got back to Earth. Anyway, we can save some tokens by staying here. I don't have a lot. I wonder if they have Wi-Fi,' she joked. They both chuckled, and Leanne added, 'My gosh, I do miss my phone.'

The stables were warm at least, though they both had longing visions of the roaring fire inside the inn. Since leaving the bar, they could hear the return of loud voices and laughter and could only listen with envy at the sound of happy customers within. The stable stalls contained a variety of horses, but they were all smaller than the ones on Earth and had strange heads with a bump in the middle and nostrils the size of saucers. They grazed on hay from nets hung on the side of each stall. Several blue chickens, perched on the beams overhead, clucked with enthusiasm as though discussing the new arrivals.

'Blue chickens. What next, red eggs?' said Malik.

'Would go down a treat at Easter,' Leanne added.

The stable door opened and the friendly faced girl from the bar came in carrying a tray. On the tray were two bowls of hot stew, two mugs, and a jug of ale. She said, 'Don't mind my dad. He has to keep up appearances, and they would arrest him if he put the Green up inside. It's not his way, you understand, it's just the law says he can't.'

'The Green has a name,' Leanne said, unimpressed by the apology.

The girl looked embarrassed as she turned to leave but stopped before reaching the door. 'My name is Sally,' she said without turning back.

'I'm Leanne, and my friend is Malik. Thank you for the meal, Sally.'

'You're welcome,' she said and returned to the inn.

Satisfied and warmed by the delicious stew, which they ate in silence, the pair settled back down to rest. Malik looked from the jug of ale to Leanne and back again. Leanne said, 'No, Malik!'

'It just seems such a waste,' Malik said as he inhaled a delicious lungful of the brew.

'Have you ever drank ale?'

'No. I had some of my dad's wine once. I didn't like it.'

'I don't think this is the time to start drinking alcohol, Malik.'

'I am twenty-three,' he laughed.

'Yeah, the body of a twenty-three year old and the mind of a stupid young teen.'

'Want some?'

Leanne hesitated. 'Okay, I'll taste it. Just a drop.'

As Malik poured the ale into the mugs, a pungent stink wafted into the building. 'Geez, what is that awful smell?'

Leanne caught the odour too and covered her nose with her hand. 'Malik!'

'I swear,' said Malik, 'it wasn't me.'

The door opened and a very hairy bull stepped into the stable, followed by a pumpkin shaped man, taller than most men they had seen so far but broad and round. He had a long, tatty beard and wore a tall, pointed hat, much like a wizard would wear. He looked somewhat menacing with the long whip he carried, which he flicked against the bull's hide to drive the animal into a free stall. The bull turned to look at Leanne, snorted, shook its head, and sent a stream of snot and sticky mucus through the air towards her. She ducked, and the snot hit an unsuspecting Malik full in the face. Malik wiped the disgusting gunk from his eyes as Leanne moved away from the ugly animal before she copped the same treatment. Satisfied that Malik and Leanne posed no threat, the bull started feeding at the trough. The bull's owner seemed oblivious to Malik's unfortunate condition, and without a word of apology, he settled down in the straw nearby.

Groaning as though he was in pain, the man removed his boots to reveal a pair of dirty, smelly feet, causing Leanne to shuffle away and hold her nose in disgust. She could not help speaking up.

'Sorry if I sound rude,' she said. 'But what the heck is that stink? Maybe you should check into a room in the inn and have a bath.'

The stranger did not appear in the least bit offended and scoffed at Leanne's suggestion. 'They won't let the likes of me in there, girly. Everyone wants their bones collecting, but none of them wants to come anywhere near the bone collector.'

'Bone collector?' Malik said.

Leanne answered before the stranger could respond. 'He collects bones from slaughterhouses and butcher shops, and dead animals from wherever he can find them. He sells them, and they are boiled down to make glue and waterproofing. By the time he's finished his trip, the bones are well rotted and rancid. That's why they stink.'

'Very interesting,' Malik said. 'Who needs school to teach us useless facts when we have Leanneapedia at our disposal?'

'Girly is right, lad, I have nearly a full load. One more day will do it. Then I'll return home to my dear wife who will bathe me and shower me with perfumes, leaving me clean and pure until the next stinking load. That's the life of a bone man, my dears.'

Leanne peeked through the barn doors and saw the bone collector's cart outside, piled high with rotting bones and animal carcasses. The horrendous stink was almost too much to bear, and she quickly shut the doors against the stench. She returned to Malik's side as he continued to grumble and curse at the sticky mess still covering his face and clothes.

'Malik,' Leanne whispered. 'I think I know how we can get past the guards on the bridge.' She told him of her plan, careful not to let the bone collector overhear.

'NO WAY!' Malik blurted.

'Shush,' Leanne said in a panic. 'He'll hear you.'

Malik lowered his voice to an urgent whisper. 'There is no way on earth I am going to hide in a stinking load of...who knows what. I have had enough of this Green rubbish and I won't stand for more. Listen to me, Leanne, it's too much to ask. There is no way on earth I'm doing it, no way.'

'No way on earth? Okay, but you're not on Earth are you? We all have to make sacrifices, Malik.'

'Oh, and what sacrifices are you making?' Malik cursed under his breath. 'Stealing. What you propose is stealing. If we take this poor man's cart, we'll be branded thieves. Have you considered that?'

'I am prepared to do whatever it takes, Malik. How about you? Think about it, you are six feet seven inches tall and like it or not, you are green. How else do you propose to get across the bridge without anyone noticing?'

'Yeah, green, green, Leanne, I get it! I'm sick of it.'

'Oh, Malik, so you have a green pee pee...so what, get over it.'

'Leanne!' Malik turned his head away and sulked in disgust.

'Just saying,' she said, unable to keep the smile from her lips.

Reluctantly, Malik agreed to Leanne's plan, with the proviso this was the last time he would be humiliated for the cause. They planned to make small talk with the bone collector, who introduced himself as Fergal, and get him drunk. They set about gaining his trust by asking about his family and other personal details. Despite his fearsome look, Fergal proved eager to talk and seemed more than happy to share their company. Conversation was a rare occurrence for a man most people avoided, and he took the opportunity without much persuasion.

Malik took a mug and pretended to drink ale. Leanne gave Fergal her drinking cup so he could share in the jug of beer, which he did with great relish. Once Fergal started talking, there was no stopping him. He had a tale to tell on every subject. As the jug emptied, Leanne acted as a waitress and ran to the bar for a second. By the time the third ale arrived, Fergal was well and truly drunk, and the plan was in motion. In the middle of a story and halfway through the last jug of ale, Fergal mumbled something neither could understand, slumped on his back, and closed his eyes to sleep.

Before daylight, Leanne and Malik rose, untied the bull from its stall and made their way out of the stables, being careful not to wake Fergal who appeared to be in the deepest of sleep. Snoring like a chainsaw, Fergal rolled onto his side and farted. Malik giggled and led the bull into the breaking dawn where he hitched it between the stays of Fergal's wagon while Leanne stood by as a lookout. The grey morning had a sharp chill, causing clouds of condensing air to billow from their mouths. The bull snorted, and Malik ducked in fear of another drenching of snot. The night had laid down a heavy haw-frost, thickening the branches of trees with icicles. Leanne stamped her feet to keep warm.

Malik was about to climb onto the wagon when the stable doors crashed open, and to their dismay, Fergal staggered dizzily into the yard. Looking gaunt and sick, he took two paces forward, grunted, raised the whip and fell flat on his face, unconscious in the dirt. A sigh of relief passed between them and without hesitation, Leanne picked up the whip and climbed up to the driving seat. Malik took a deep breath and slid into the space he had cleared beneath the stinking bones. Leanne pulled the oilskin cover over the load and flicked the whip, sending the bull into a slow saunter on the road to Mariana.

CHAPTER 8

The Convergence

Snowflakes the size of rose petals tumbled slowly from the sky; a dense veil of grey and white, endless in number. So thick was the snowfall that Alex saw nothing beyond the forward mast of the Klaw. The wind had died, leaving the sails limp and nothing more than great sheets of soaking gossamer, useless without a breeze to fill them. The crew huddled against the cold as heavy flakes settled all around them. Fearful of what lay ahead, they cowered together for comfort as the Klaw travelled steadily and silently on the ocean current, despite the lack of wind. Alex wiped the ice crystals from his face, but each slight movement allowed snow to find its way beneath his jacket, and he could feel the freezing slush begin to pack itself against the bare skin of his neck. He shivered.

Alex had no time to stop and think since waking aboard the Klaw after his transit from Earth to Trinity. Though he had no expectations of this new world, he could never have imagined the life and death situation in which he now found himself. Without his companions to share in the escapade, he couldn't help feeling alone and scared by thoughts of what lay ahead. He wondered if the others had even made the journey to Trinity. After all, his last image on Earth had been of two strange Ninja-like men rushing at him with knives drawn, apparently trying to do him harm. Perhaps none of the others had made it through. What if the men in black had caught Malik and Leanne, and he alone would have to complete the task? Whatever the task was, he still had no idea what he was supposed to do now he was here. The thought of Leanne and Malik being killed by those men did not bear thinking about. And where was Nim? She had promised to be here to guide them, had she not?

A call came from overhead and the lookout told of a change in the ocean colour. The Great Southern Ocean in which they travelled had been joined on the starboard bow by the rose-coloured Great Eastern Ocean, so ominous looking black water lay on one side of the boat and rose-coloured on the other. And still, as if pulled by a gravitational force, the Klaw forged onwards into the unknown.

Nim's father had clearly succeeded in weaving Alex's consciousness into Captain Boatman, but he had been unprepared for the body of a man. Despite some knowledge of the captain's thoughts, his mind still belonged to Alexander Bottom. He knew instinctively what to do and what to say to the crew when needed, but beyond the next step, he knew nothing. The revelation of slaves in his cargo had come as a huge shock. The ship rolled, throwing everyone off balance, and the relentless snow kept falling.

'It's getting choppy, Captain,' said Stark.

Alex came out of his daydream and focused on the way ahead. Occasionally the snow would ease and allow him a fleeting glimpse forward, where whitecaps gathered and clashed as the two oceans collided against the bow. Unhindered, the Klaw carved a path through growing waves, causing great plumes of spray to burst into the air.

'Have your crew stand to, Ms Stark.' Alex's order placed his crew at the ready, and they could do nothing more than anxiously watch as conditions deteriorated.

The Klaw continued to move forward at a quickening pace, driven only by ocean currents as the sails had yet to take on wind. They flapped and slapped against the rigging with each lurch of the ship, causing falling snow to swirl and curl around them in blinding gusts. Alex took the helm and gripped the ship's wheel with his bare fingers, although he was hardly able to hold it in the freezing conditions. Pain throbbed in his knuckles, and he dreamt of a warm fire to thaw his aching bones.

Pitched into a massive wave, the Klaw groaned, and First Officer Stark made her way across the deck with her head bowed and her body straining against the breaking waves crashing over the gunnels.

'It's getting very rough, Captain. I fear we should have taken our chances with the Man o' War,' Stark said, grimacing against the sting of driving ice. Her cheeks were red and swollen like two ripe apples, and chunks of freezing snow had gathered in her hair.

Alex could not help thinking she was right. What madness had he brought them to with his decision to take his chances in the formidable Convergence?

'Devils await us, Captain,' Stark said, looking out to the ocean in terror.

'Not devils, Ms Stark. Rough water and terrifying seas, yes, but no devils. It's just us against the worst nature can throw at us.'

Before Stark could respond, a mighty flash of lightning emblazoned the sky, followed by a deafening crash of thunder so loud and threatening it shook the crew to their knees. The oceans boiled and a sudden gust of wind curled the snow into a sheet of stinging crystals. The sails suddenly filled like big balloons and the bow lifted into the air like a whale breaching. Crashing back down into the cauldron, the Klaw buried its bow beneath the waves before surging ahead in response to the increasing gale.

Alex braced himself against the force of the wheel as it violently fought him for control. 'Heaven help us,' he said as the view ahead cleared momentarily, offering him a glimpse of what lay before them.

Rising like mountains, the Great Western and Great Northern Oceans joined the Convergence and climbed for the dark sky like immense giants, towering over the Klaw and her crew. Onwards the ship forged through the waves, carried by the southern and eastern currents while being tossed back and forth like a child's toy in a turbulent spa. Emerald green in colour, the Great Western Ocean hurled the surf skyward where it broke into sparkling green jewels against the black backdrop of sky. Lightning flashed, and the emeralds turned to a glittering gold.

The Great Northern Ocean, as if to match this magnificent show of colour and force, crashed against the Western in a tsunami of purple and blue. The resulting spectacle brought to mind fireworks on New Year's Eve, though a hundred times more spectacular. But this show caused fear, not delight.

The wind howled like a wolf to the moon and the thunder became a continuous roar. Snow and ice lashed the ship, sending slivers of crystal through the air like knives. Terrified by the growing storm, the crew looked to their captain for guidance and strength. Alex called for the second mate and Little Jim.

'Take Jim and go below, Mr Gates. Unchain the prisoners.'

Mr Gates looked horrified. 'But, Captain, if we unchain them, they...'

Alex looked directly into the second mate's eyes so there would be no misunderstanding over his order. 'If our fate is to die here today in this cruel sea, Mr Gates, we will face it as free men. And if those poor souls are to meet the same fate, they should do likewise. Unchain them, Mr Gates.'

The second mate and Little Jim headed for the hold without further objection, and Alex turned his attention to the roaring oceans into which they sailed while Ms Stark clung to the rigging in readiness for the captain's orders.

'Your instructions, Captain?' she shouted above the roaring hurricane.

A wave from the west exploded over the bow and Alex was suddenly in trouble. Unable to move or speak, he had lost all thoughts of the captain he needed to be, and all that remained on the deck of the rolling ship was the frightened mind of a schoolboy named Alexander Bottom. He told himself to clear his head, stay calm, and search his mind for the lost captain. But there was nothing. No experience, no calculated decision making, no sailor's instincts. Nothing. All that stood between the Klaw and disaster was Alexander Bottom.

'Captain, your orders,' the first officer repeated above the storm.

'I...I don't know what to do,' Alex mumbled as the ship surged into a trough, sending the crew scrambling.

'Sorry, Captain Boatman, I can't hear you above the noise.'

Without the captain's skill and leadership, all was lost. Alex tried to concentrate but to no avail. He had no solution to offer and no orders to save the Klaw and her crew, so he urged himself to tell Stark the truth, hand over command to her, and beg for forgiveness. Stark had a better chance of saving them; at least she had experience. As he was resigning himself to the fact all hope was lost, Alex felt a sharp tug on his sleeve, looked down, and saw Nim at his side.

'Nim! Thank the heavens you're here. I've lost the captain's thoughts,' he said. 'There's nothing, and I have no idea what to do!'

'I'm sorry, Captain, I still can't hear you,' said the first officer.

Nim was invisible to Stark, who remained oblivious to Nim's presence as she hopped onto a rope ladder leading to the mast. A blast of snow took Nim's breath, and she swung freely in the wind before bracing herself with a hand on a line. The gale had now reached hurricane force, and Alex thought she would be carried away on the gusts. Forks of lightning split the sky and thunder crashed all around them with a vengeance. Nim called Alex closer, and although she spoke in a calm, unhurried manner, Alex heard her voice quite clearly above the din.

'You must find him, Alex. Your fear has clouded your mind, and so you must dig deep for the answers. Look around you.

Each of these souls are depending on you. They look to you for their strength. Find the captain.'

'I want to save them, Nim. But I can't, I don't have what it takes.' Another crash of thunder boomed through the air as the sails flapped out of control. Alex cringed at the noise.

'Find the man within you, Alex. He's always been there, you just have to open your mind, see the world through his eyes and think with his thoughts.'

'Captain!' Stark cried. 'Hell is upon us!'

The Great Southern Ocean climbed with a ferocious howl, carrying the ship high above the depths in its great watery hand. As if not to be outdone, the Great Northern Ocean whipped the sea into a whirlpool, threatening to drag the Klaw down again as The Western Ocean opened a chasm-like mouth, bellowed its displeasure, and tumbled into the Eastern Ocean. The Klaw buckled and groaned, the central mast cracked and timber fractured in the hull, but the ship battled onwards.

Alex closed his eyes and summoned his strength and will to survive. Two mainstays snapped, causing what was left of the forward mast to come crashing down to the deck, narrowly missing the crew. A large capstan broke loose and disappeared overboard, leaving the mainsail lines flapping dangerously in the wind. At last, Alex found his inner strength and sprang into action. It was as though Alexander Boatman had just returned to find his ship in mortal danger.

'Haul in the mainsail lines, Ms Stark.'

'But, Captain, we can never hold her against the force of the storm.'

'But we'll try, Ms Stark. Every available crew member on the lines. We'll sail through this.'

Answering the captain's call, all available crew took the strain with twenty men and women to each line to hold the mainsail tight. Alex turned the ship's wheel and headed for the centre of the tempest. Great Oceans fought amongst themselves to claim the little ship and her crew. Through the thrashing storm, Alex saw the ghosts of ships, long since lost to the powers now locked against them. Grim faces of captains who had gone before him called out from their watery graves; give it up, there is no escape! But Alex held his course, summoned his strength, and prayed.

'We can't hold on, Captain,' Stark screamed above the uproar.

The ship veered as the mainsail tore loose from the weak hands of the crew. Despite the sailors' desperate struggles to recover control, the lines snapped and whipped like furious eels, pulling the sailors from one side of the ship to the other. All strength now depleted, the crew could do nothing more. First Officer Stark felt the rope slipping through her bleeding fingers, and she screamed all was futile. With all other options spent, she called for the Gods to save her.

Like an answer to her prayer, an extra hand appeared on the rope, then another and another. Green hands. The unchained prisoners had taken the strain and were hauling the lines tight. The sails billowed and pulled the ship through the seas like a dolphin riding the waves. Alex steered the ship into chaos, but on and on they went, cheering in triumph as the ship carved its way forward and battled wave after wave in defiant response.

'We'll survive!' Alex screamed. 'Or we'll die trying, me hearties.' Alex laughed hysterically. *Me hearties, really, Alex? Who do you think you are, Jack Sparrow?* He laughed some more, now safe in the knowledge they would make it through.

As though the oceans had heard his thoughts, or as if by a God-given miracle, they conceded; the curtain of darkness lifted, the oceans parted, sunshine split the clouds, and blinding radiance filled the sky. The survivors had to shield their eyes against the beauty of a new dawn. The Klaw had withstood the Great Ocean Convergence and emerged in glory.

Behind the ship, the oceans appeared to sigh in admiration and respect for the Klaw and her crew. Everyone cheered as hands slapped backs, welcome hugs were offered all around, and even the Greens were embraced and thanked joyously for their part in the miracle.

'Hip, hip, hooray for the captain,' a voice shouted from the foredeck as all aboard cheered in reply.

'And a cheer for the Greens,' said another, followed by another loud cheer. Elated, Alex scanned the deck for Nim, but she was nowhere in sight.

CHAPTER 9

Hide and seek

Puddles of frozen water crunched and cracked under the wheels of the bone wagon as it moved at a crawl up the road to Mariana. A great many pilgrims had already set out along the way, and all gave a wide berth to the vile and smelly transport. Leanne had a good view of the road ahead from her seat high above the ground, and she gently flicked the whip to keep the bull going forward, though he seemed to know the routine without much need for encouragement.

'How much further?' Malik asked from his hiding place.

'A mile or two,' Leanne answered. 'I can see the bridge in the distance.'

'Have you any idea how bad it is under here? It smells like a sewer. I swear to you, Leanne, this is the last time—'

'Shush! Soldiers ahead.'

Leanne smiled to herself in satisfaction. There were no soldiers, but she had silenced Malik before he could continue his complaining. She did sympathise with him over his unfortunate predicament, but hearing him go on and on about it was driving her crazy.

The wagon trundled on in silence, and ten minutes later they were drawing close to the bridge. Leanne could make out the guard post now and could see four soldiers on duty; none of which was the senior officer who had stopped them the previous day. Breathing a sigh of relief, she pulled the hood down low over her head and urged the bull forward. Unlike the random checks of the previous day, the soldiers appeared to be stopping every traveller, which was creating a bottleneck at the crossing. Even at this early hour, a long queue waited to show their papers and the line moved slowly, causing Leanne's anxiety to grow.

As the wagon approached, one of the soldiers said, 'What in hoo-ha is that awful stink?'

All heads turned to Leanne.

'You in the wagon, you can't bring that stink through here. What have you got in there anyway?'

Leanne spoke without meeting the soldier's gaze. 'Bones, sir. I'm just a lowly bone collector trying to make a living.'

'And where are you headed?'

'The pilgrim camp, sir. Queen's orders.'

'Queen's orders?'

'Yes, sir. Apparently, discarded bones and dead animals is causing a stink down by the city walls, and she wants it cleaned up, real quick like.'

The guard hesitated. Not wanting to contradict the queen's orders, he waved the wagon through. 'Go on, get that blooming stench out of here.'

Leanne flicked the whip, and the crowd of waiting pilgrims more than willingly parted as the wagon rolled forward.

'Wait!'

Leanne turned her head in the direction of the order and saw the senior soldier who had detained them the day before emerging from his guard post. The officer walked halfway towards the wagon, stopped, and held a cloth handkerchief to his nose. He turned to one of the guards and asked, 'Have you searched it?' The soldier replied he had not. 'Then do so now,' the officer ordered.

Leanne's heart raced. She considered cracking the whip and driving the animal forward to escape, but she couldn't imagine the beast reaching anything more than a fast walk. Meanwhile, under cover of the oilskin, Malik heard the commotion and squeezed further into the space below the bones. As he did so, he came face to face with the rotting carcass of a dead cow. Its milky-white eyes seemed to stare at him, and its tongue was hanging limply from its mouth covered in flies. Malik almost screamed in horror. It was all he could do to remain hidden.

The unlucky soldier covered his face with his hand and pulled the oilskin back from the load. 'It's just bones, sir,' he said without really looking.

'Check it properly,' came the command.

The guard half looked through the bones and dead animals. He was repulsed by the sight and smell and promptly vomited on the road.

'Properly,' said the officer, undeterred.

While his colleagues looked on and giggled, the guard composed himself, wiped his mouth on his sleeve, took his spear and thrust it into the wagon. The razor-sharp point missed Malik's leg by a whisker, and he thought best to pull himself up closer to the rear of the cart. The dead cow slid along with him and eventually trapped him, spilling dozens of finger-thick maggots and worms over Malik's head and shoulders. He wanted to jump out and surrender to get away from the disgusting creatures, but he couldn't move without causing even more foul things to drop onto his face. The guard thrust his spear several more times into the wagon, but the dead cow protected Malik, and the lance probed harmlessly.

'All clear, sir,' the soldier said, relieved his ordeal was now over. The officer hesitated. Leanne looked away.

'Move on,' said the officer eventually. Followed by a quick, 'No, wait.'

He called two soldiers over and whispered instructions. They trotted off quickly to the guard post while Leanne waited in terror, unaware of their motive. A moment later they returned carrying a heavy bucket between them. As they brought it towards the wagon, the officer spoke.

'We haven't seen the poo man for over a week, and the toilet bin is overflowing. I'm sure you won't mind carting it away with the rest of your stinking load.'

Before she could object, the two soldiers tipped the big can of poo into the wagon, splattering its putrid contents over the entire load.

Leanne thought she could hear Malik crying as she pulled away and crossed the bridge to Mariana.

Within Mariana's grand palace, Queen Cleoron paced back and forth, muttering angrily as she waited for the royal doctor to emerge from her daughter's bedroom with word of her condition. Anxious for good news, she went and stood on the balcony overlooking the city and its harbour, where her warships held in readiness for her command to deploy. The queen watched as stores and weapons were loaded on board and vowed to destroy all those responsible for her daughter's condition. *If she dies, I will show no mercy. Caprine will feel my fury.*

Malik shivered beneath the overhang of a large rock as Leanne washed spots of excrement from his smock in the fast running stream.

'Apart from the big bit on the sleeve, it's mostly just spotted, Malik. I can't wash it completely or you'll freeze to death. It won't dry in this cold weather.'

She finished as best she could and passed the top back to Malik, who turned his back modestly before putting it back on. Simmering with anger, Malik remained stubbornly silent.

'We were lucky,' Leanne said, trying to sound bright and positive. 'No one thought to ask why we were carrying a full load of bones to the pilgrim camp when we were supposed to be taking bones away from it. But it was the only story I could think of to tell them under pressure.' Malik flared his nostrils but did not answer. 'Anyway,' Leanne continued, 'we made it past the checkpoint, and it should be only a few miles further to the city walls. From there, hopefully, our next move will become apparent.'

Leanne had more bad news for Malik but didn't know quite how to tell him. Eventually, she plucked up the courage to approach him. After she had taken the leather harness from the bull and left him to graze freely near the flowing stream, she carried it to Malik and joined him on the rock.

Before she could speak, he said solemnly, 'I know.'

'Malik, I am so sorry.'

'Just get on with it and let's get going.'

Without another word, Leanne fashioned a collar and lead from the leather and pulled it into a knot to form the necessary restraint. Malik sat resigned to his humiliation as Leanne placed the collar over his neck and completed the setup with a loop for her hand. She gave Malik a sad, sympathetic smile and the two of them set off along the road, leaving the wagon behind and the bull happily grazing by the water's edge.

Sunshine had thawed the morning frost by the time they came over the high breast of a hill overlooking the magnificent city of Mariana. Located beside a shimmering blue sea with its sheltered harbour, the walled city dazzled in the sun's early rays.

'I've never seen anything so wonderful,' Leanne said, taking in the sight.

Unlike the simple wooden structures they had so far encountered, the buildings of Mariana were grand on a spectacular scale. Constructed with multi-coloured marble, they sparkled like wet pebbles on a beach. Domed topped roofs dominated the styles, and tall minaret-like towers climbed high into the sky at regular intervals across the horizon. A tremendous wall surrounded the entire city, and from their vantage point on top of the hill, Leanne and Malik observed the snowflake pattern of streets radiating from the city centre. But for all the beautiful buildings laid out before them, their eyes were irresistibly drawn to the one taking centre stage. Reaching skyward to the clouds, the breath-taking Great Pyramid of Mariana appeared strikingly out of place. Clad in gold mirrored glass, the massive structure seemed to float above the ground like a spaceship just lifting skywards. To the right of the pyramid, the towering Lighthouse of the Gods looked out to sea. Seen for hundreds of miles in every direction, these were indeed wonders of this new world.

But Malik's attention was not focused on the city's beauty, for he studied the city walls with renewed dismay. Apart from being high, they were topped by lines of soldiers. Where the walls came down to the sea, they ended on steep cliffs that fell away to the rocks and surf below. One central gate and two side gates seemed to be the only way into the fortified city, but heavily guarded by soldiers, the gates looked impassable. Beyond the wall and cliffs, he saw the masts of hundreds of ships at anchor and a busy port abuzz with activity. Turning his attention to an encampment of tents and shelters outside the main gate, he saw they formed a vast city in their own right. Smoke drifted up from hundreds of cooking fires, causing the low-lying area to be covered in blue haze. A separate fortified compound stood close by, and Malik noted more soldiers housed within the battlements.

'I have an awful feeling about this,' said Malik.

The walk down the hill to the pilgrim encampment was a deceptively long one. When at last they reached the heart of the camp, they were tired and hungry. As a temporary accommodation for travellers, the pilgrim camp was a bustling hive of activity and appeared to provide every type of facility necessary for life. They saw bathing houses and laundries, butchers and grocers, each with a salesperson spruiking for business from passers-by.

'Let's find an internet café,' Leanne joked, fending off a pushy vendor.

'Right, and a burger house selling soft-serve ice-cream in dipped chocolate waffle cones for dessert,' Malik said, causing him to salivate at the thought.

Oilskin hides formed domed tent shelters where people slept and spent their days waiting for permission to enter the city. Along the main thoroughfare, dozens of cooking stations had been set up to cater for the hungry crowds. Fires burned orange under large pots of food, and Malik felt the pains of hunger strike his empty belly. He saw seafood of every variety, including fish, crabs, lobsters, and eels. He saw meat roasting on spits above the flames, and despite his recent episode in the bone wagon, the glorious smell of barbequed flesh meant he could no longer wait to eat.

Leanne went to her pouch and produced enough tokens to purchase a meal of roast beef on fresh bread with vegetables for each of them. The woman behind the stall took payment and filled two plates. She looked at Malik's size and smiled before adding an extra dollop of potatoes on the side for free. They sat at crude tables nearby and enjoyed the feed under the warm winter sun. But on the horizon, storm clouds gathered.

'Better enjoy it while you can, Malik, there's rain on the way.'

'Don't care as long as I have food,' said Malik.

'I think it's beef. It tastes like beef, but I wasn't about to ask,' Leanne said between mouthfuls.

'It's perfect no matter what it is,' he said.

Malik stopped eating and watched two men on horseback lead five green men and women through the crowd on leashes. Hands bound, the captives walked with their heads bowed and looked thoroughly miserable. Malik appeared spellbound by the sight of other Green people.

'They are the first Greens we've seen,' Leanne said. 'I wonder where they're taking them?'

Up until now, Malik had viewed his green skin as an irritating side effect of his crossover, an effect that had caused him nothing but trouble ever since he emerged from the ditch. He had pushed the more profound implications of his status as a Green from his mind; they had enough to worry about already. But as he watched the Greens led away, his stomach rolled and he knew he was on the wrong side of a great injustice.

'What's going on here, Leanne? Who the hell am I?'

They were questions he did not expect Leanne to answer. Grimly, they watched the Greens disappear into the crowd, then ate their meals in silence.

Malik couldn't help feeling angry, though he was unsure at whom. He also felt conned, like he was the butt of a joke. Maybe Nim had tricked him into coming along for the entertainment and the others were in on it. Why else would Nim choose him out of everyone in the class, and why was it he turned out to be the only Green?

I bet she thinks it's all very amusing, Malik thought as he watched Leanne with a growing sense of suspicion. He wondered if she'd known he would be a Green right from the start. He didn't know what it was about her, but he found her confusing. Some things he liked about her, others were just maddening. There were times she played dumb, but she was no dummy. She was tougher than other girls he knew and was confident in every way, though at times she seemed almost apologetic for being that way. He was sure she thought he was an idiot, and who could blame her? He let people think he was daft. She got under his skin, but he could not put his finger on why.

Malik had always played the fool. Joking about and making sly comments had been his way of putting up barriers around himself. He had no friends; he didn't want them. He made people avoid contact by driving them away with his behaviour. He knew his great size frightened some people, and yet he encouraged their fear of him so he would not have to get close to anyone. Perhaps that was what they all had in common; they were all loners, each in their own way. Alexander, Leanne, even Jani Nasri; none of them had friends at school. Then again, perhaps they preferred to keep their social lives away from school. Maybe they did have friends and people they met when school was out, and perhaps he was the only one without a social life.

'Come on,' Malik said, sweeping the paranoid thoughts from his mind and racing off before Leanne had finished eating. 'We need to get this blooming thing done,' he shouted over his shoulder.

Leanne had to run to catch up, grabbing at Malik's leash as it trailed on the ground as though she were chasing a runaway puppy. They headed for the gate and joined the long line of pilgrims. Shuffling their way towards the entrance, they eventually came to a standstill several yards short of the gate. People grumbled and groaned as faces turned angry and disappointed. Several pilgrims even walked away in disgust.

'What's happening?' said Leanne.

The average height of people on Trinity stood at about five feet for a full-grown male and even less for a female. At five feet seven inches, Leanne was already taller than most. But at six feet seven inches, Malik towered over everyone like a man on stilts. His extreme height gave him an advantage in as much as it allowed him a clear view over the crowd and all the way to the city gate.

'They've closed the gates,' Malik said. 'Looks like they're not letting anyone else in the city.'

A man beside them said, 'The city has been cordoned off, no one in or out. That soldier said they are expecting war to be declared at any moment.'

'War with whom?' asked Leanne.

The pilgrim looked at Leanne as though she were mad. 'Where have you been these past weeks? War with Caprine of course. Oh, and you better get your Green off the streets, I heard there's a new order to have them all rounded up and impounded.'

Leanne and Malik made a hasty retreat from the line and out of sight of the soldiers gathered at the gate.

'What now?' Malik asked. 'We can't crash our way through.'

'I'm thinking,' said Leanne.

Malik's height may have given him the edge when it came to the best view in town, but as far as keeping a low profile went, he faced an impossible task. He spotted two soldiers on the far side of the crowd who had turned their attention to him.

'Time to leave, Leanne. Soldiers are heading our way from the left.'

Without hesitation, the pair fled, and the soldiers seeing this gave chase. Had Malik been an average size man, they could easily get lost in the mob, but wherever they ran, he served as a beacon for them to follow. Dashing between tents, they found a spot where Malik could lay low and wait for the soldiers to pass. But just as they thought they had succeeded in avoiding capture, a man spotted them and sounded the alarm. More soldiers joined the chase.

In and out the lines of tents they hurried, all the time hearing shouts to stop. In panic, they dived inside an empty shelter and pulled the flap shut. Soldiers gathered nearby and searched tents one by one. Malik and Leanne could hear them barking orders when the tent flap suddenly flew open and an old woman looked inside. They thought she would shout the alarm, but instead, she put her finger to her lips in a sign of silence. With a whisper, she had them lie down on the floor and covered them with thick animal fur blankets. She sat on the floor at the entrance to the tent and waited. When soldiers arrived, she started coughing and sneezing, making out as though she were ill.

'Who is in this tent?' said a soldier.

The old woman answered in a weak and painful tone. 'Just me and my sick husband, sir. I fear we have the pestilence,' she added, coughing for effect. 'Come inside, perhaps you can help him. Let me wake him so you can take a look at his horrible rash and tell me what you think.'

The soldier covered his nose and voiced his disgust before walking on to the next tent without checking further. When the voices of the search party had disappeared into the distance, the woman pulled the blanket back and told them they were safe, for a while at least. Leanne thanked the old woman for her help and asked if they could rest awhile.

'You're welcome to stay,' she answered with a toothless grin. 'Not everyone agrees with the queen's decree. As far as I'm concerned, Greens is just like any other. It's a crying shame what's being done to them...to you,' she added, looking directly at Malik to assure him of her good wishes. 'If I had my way, all you lot would be free to walk the streets whenever you wanted.'

'Oh, I'm not really a—'

Leanne gave Malik a sly kick, and he stopped speaking mid-sentence.

Hours passed before they felt safe enough to leave the old woman's hospitality. They thanked her again and slunk away in the direction of the wall. Rounding the last row of tents, they had just stepped into the open when a rope lasso dropped over Malik and cinched up around his arms. Two horse riders came into view, the first pulling the rope tight around Malik and smiling in triumph.

'Got you, Green bugger!'

He tried to struggle, but Malik could not escape the restraining line. Leanne sprang forward, grabbed the rope and pulled in an attempt to free Malik from the horseman, but her efforts were futile as the second rider knocked her to the ground.

'You like him so much,' said the second rider. 'You can share a cage with him.'

CHAPTER 10

Parisos

Anchored in shallow water just off shore, the Klaw quietly bobbed on the calm water of the bay. The sound of pounding hammers and grating saws echoed across the sheltered cove as crew members worked alongside Greens to repair her damage as best they could until they returned to port. On the sandy beach, two large cooking fires burned while the ship's cook prepared a meal of freshly caught fish. Alex sat with Stark on a driftwood log, alongside the Green they now knew as Callum, and discussed his plans. He drew in the sand with a long, pointed stick.

'Here we are in the Great Western Ocean on the island of Parisos. It's a half-day sail to Ikadies, which is here.' Alex circled the spot and planted the stick in the middle.

'This island has been a forbidden place ever since the great extinction. We could hang for being here if the queen finds out,' Stark said.

'Well, let's just hope she doesn't,' Alex countered.

Alex came to the island for more than running repairs to his ship. Nim had appeared in his dreams the previous night and directed him to proceed to Parisos, where he must search for a sacred relic among the ruins of a lost city. Retrieval of the relic was a vital part of his mission and one he must undertake with the utmost caution. Nim warned him of dark forces out to stop him with every trick they could conjure; he must trust no one. Frustrated that their conversation had been a one-sided affair, Alex had been unable to ask questions of Nim. Upon waking, he wasn't even sure if Nim had come to him, or if his dream was just a dream. Nevertheless, here he was on Parisos, following her instructions.

Nim had also told him things had not gone to plan during the crossover. Her father had been unable to pinpoint Leanne and Malik's exact location. Though they appeared to be close to Mariana, it was impossible to say where exactly until they slept and he could pick up their thoughts through their dreams. Jani Nasri had been unable to follow. This was not good news and according to Nim it would make their mission just that little bit harder.

'Work on the ship is almost complete, Captain. The Klaw took a beating but stood up better than we could have hoped.

And it's thanks to your father's Black Spider silk sails we are here to tell the tale. No other sail ever made could have pulled us through that storm.'

Alex agreed with Stark. He wanted to ask her if she knew his father; he wanted to ask her what John Boatman was like but didn't because he would sound mad for asking about things he should already know. He decided to wait for a better opportunity to quiz the first officer.

'You're right, Ms Stark, he's the finest sailmaker there is. They are the only Black Spider sails in existence.' That much he knew, and facts like these just popped into his head and spilt from his mouth without warning. And yet he couldn't bring a picture of the captain's father to mind no matter how hard he tried.

Alex gave Stark new instructions. 'Once repairs are complete, Ms Stark, you will take the ship and sail to Ikadies, returning the Greens to their homeland where they belong. I will need six of our best men to stay with me, so ask for volunteers and have them ready to climb the mountain.'

Callum stood tall and said, 'I will remain with you, Captain. It will be my honour.'

'You understand we can't take you home later? If you stay with us now, you will have to return to Mariana with us. If you don't go now with the others, you'll lose your opportunity.'

'I'm with you, Captain. I'll take my chances,' said Callum.

'We have only three more moons before the war counsel meets, Ms Stark. You must drop the Greens and return to pick us up no later than tomorrow night. Please hurry.'

'You can count on me, Captain.'

Alex turned to Callum. 'Last chance for freedom, Callum.'

Callum looked thoughtful, as though he had something important to say. 'Ikadies, Mariana, all of Trinity, this planet has been home to our once great civilisation for many thousands of years. Once upon a time, our people lived freely in every corner of this world. Now they are slaves with no freedom unless freedom is bestowed on them by overlords, such as those you serve, Captain. I don't want to sound ungrateful, and I thank you for releasing my people, but you and I know we are far from free, no matter where we are on Trinity. Circumstances have brought you and your crew to recognise us as equals, but there are those who want us chained, even exterminated. Olo and I will return with you to Mariana where my people are in desperate need of help. We have to find a friend there who we have recently lost contact with.'

You're not the only one, thought Alex.

Callum continued. 'I don't pretend to know your plans for when you return to Mariana, but I do know you are struggling with a great conflict. For the moment I place my trust in you, Captain. Nevertheless, the time will soon come when you will have to take a stand. Who knows, the Gods may look down and find us on the same side when that day comes.'

'Who knows,' Alex said.

After eating, those leaving for Ikadies boarded the Klaw and prepared to set sail. Green men and women worked alongside the crew, making light work of the departure procedures and further binding the two groups together. First Officer Stark climbed into a longboat and waved her goodbyes. 'We'll be back before the second moon, Captain.'

'Godspeed, Stark. If we are not here waiting for you, you must leave for Mariana without us.'

Alex, Callum, and the expedition party watched as the sails were hoisted high on the mainmast and the anchor raised. Responding to the manoeuvre, the Klaw's sails filled with air, she leaned to port and departed the cove. Alex couldn't help thinking he would be lucky to see her again.

Five crew members and a second Green named Olo formed the expedition party of eight. Contemplating their next move, Alex remembered Nim's final warning. *Don't trust anyone, Alex; not all is as it may seem.* Alex wondered what she meant by 'Not all is as it may seem.' He had a loyal crew but decided he would be wary of all and say little about their objective.

A source of great frustration for Alex was he had no endgame in sight and no real idea of what he was looking for on the island. That he should find a holy relic was so vague a task it seemed almost impossible. Nim said he should follow his instincts and would know what to do when the time came, but this line from Nim was wearing thin, and her reluctance to explain was beginning to annoy him. He had a strange sense of someone at his shoulder, a presence he assumed was Captain Boatman, who would take control of his words and actions at any given moment. The thoughts in his head were those of Alexander Bottom, but the words he spoke were often those of the captain. Was he a mix of the two identities, or was it just Captain Boatman reaching out to him from the Dreamscape?

The Green men from Ikadies seemed genuine enough, but Alex knew little of such people and decided to keep Callum and Olo in his sights. He didn't want to end up a victim of trickery by placing his trust in men who had up until recently been his prisoners. Second Mate Norman Gates led the way, the others falling in behind him in single file. Nim planned for them to follow the mountain track to a village where they would find a hermit named Frog. Every time Alex thought about the instructions, he couldn't help visualising a little green Muppet.

They set off at a brisk pace, ascending rapidly along the winding path. The sun was high in the sky when they rounded a bend to find the hillside dotted with dozens of stone mushrooms, many of which lay half buried in volcanic soil. Each mushroom was, in fact, an abandoned house carved from solid blocks of granite. The round dwellings were small by Earth standards. Roofs had very large overhangs, giving them their distinctive mushroom appearance, and Alex noted each had a fireplace and a small kitchen inside. The builders had carved beds into the walls, and every dwelling had two windows and a door. Covered in pumice and ash, personal belongings lay scattered around, discarded where the owners had left them. It was as though the occupants of these homes had just gone for a walk or left in a hurry one day and never returned.

Moving on up the mountain, the number of mushroom houses increased until they arrived at a village of considerable size. Identical dwellings lined dirt roads in a labyrinth of backstreets, and above the deserted village, the volcanic mountain towered like a brooding giant. Alex saw the snow line and wondered how far they would need to climb before they reached the ancient city and the temple ruins. A plume of smoke rose from the summit, warning Alex and his companions the giant was only sleeping and should be viewed with the proper respect.

Turning to look back to the distance, Alex saw the Klaw, a tiny dot on the glistening ocean near the horizon. They were making good progress, and Alex hoped they would meet with favourable weather and no pirates on their way.

It was Callum who noticed them first. Ants the size of mice, scurrying from dwelling to dwelling, pausing to scan the air with antennas that waved like long-stemmed flowers in the breeze. Alex had the feeling they were watching the party with more than just a casual interest.

Advancing into the heart of the crumbling town, Callum asked, 'What happened here? Why is this place a ghost town?'

Norman Gates, an educated man, answered. 'The Island of Parisos was once home to the Caprinese people. It was their capital. This place was a thriving paradise of unique plants and animals. The peace-loving Caprinese lived an idyllic life here until Tiran, the mountain you see before you, woke from his sleep. There were many eruptions over several years, and towns were buried and rebuilt again, only to be buried once more by the lava and ash caused by the great explosions. Trying to stay alive became the national pastime. At the same time, unbeknown to the Caprinese, events were taking place across the ocean that would change the world forever, and in so doing, provide the Caprinese with a new home for their weary people.

'Across the Great Northern Ocean,' Gates continued, 'in the land of Leemonadies, the Leemon people worshipped their own unique Gods. They built great temples high in the mountains where they could get close to the heavens to pray. At that time, the whole of Trinity was a diverse and wonderful place full of unique cultures and races. Peace had dominated the planet for as long as anyone could remember. Greens like you lived free in many lands, Callum, but Leemons were different because their religious leaders were dissatisfied with their place in the world. The high priests of Leemon were part of a growing culture bent on power and control. They had grand ideas of conquest, and they believed *their* Gods were the true Gods and anyone who worshipped false Gods should be punished or even eliminated. Their plan was for a holy war. At the same time, a young Leemon man, named Carchi, took up a fondness for scientific study.

'Carchi believed he could find the cure for common diseases such as colds and flu, and more serious ailments such as plague, pox, and pestilence by crossing one bad germ with another and using what he called antibodies to work a kind of magic.'

Alex smiled to himself. If these people only knew where that science would end up, they would be amazed, he thought.

'His theory was,' Gates continued, 'each race of people had evolved uniquely and could fight different types of disease using this new magic. These diseases had evolved independently among races. He believed if he could get the virus to evolve from one specific race to another and induce resistance in people, he could find a cure for all disease. He went back to the origins of the races to find the vital clues.'

'It didn't work out as he planned, did it, Mr Gates?' Alex asked as the story suddenly played out in his head, and Captain Boatman's knowledge of the tale came to the fore.

'No it didn't, Captain. Oh, he was successful alright. He even recorded his research in a scientific journal, entitled Origins and Leemons.'

Alex burst into laughter, and everyone stopped to watch with bewildered expressions. 'Origins and Leemons,' said

Alex, which was met with blank stares all round. 'Oranges and Lem...Sorry, go on, Gates,' he said, regaining control.

Gates didn't get the joke. He continued, 'As I said, he did identify different strains of the virus and proved they attacked only certain races. But before he could start working on the cures, the High Priests heard about his research, confiscated his work, and threw Carchi in prison for his troubles. The Priests took Carchi's work, and using their own holy medicine men and wizards, they somehow perfected his deadly strains. They tested some by releasing them against outlying, remote populations. A wildfire could not have spread more quickly. Within months, two-thirds of the planet's unique races had been wiped out.'

Horrific images of dead and dying populations flooded Alex's mind, and Alexander Boatman's knowledge of historical events became his dominant thoughts. Alex took up the story and spoke with this new-found authority, telling Callum what happened next.

'Carchi was mortified, or so the story goes,' Alex said. 'His research had been used to destroy rather than save lives. With the help of friends on the outside, he plotted his escape from prison and once free, went underground to work on the problem from a hidden location. But, by the time he emerged, only four races remained. Out of hundreds of diverse races, the Mariana, the Caprinese, the Ikadiens, and the Leemons were the only survivors. It was a global catastrophe.

'Carchi called for a meeting between the leaders of the four surviving races, including the High Priests of Leemon who had been responsible for the extinctions. He warned them he had created new viruses, capable of spreading through the populations and wiping out what remained of the planet. Each strain of virus had been sealed in a stone pot. Leaders of the four races would receive an unmarked pot, knowing the virus within might be any one of the four that had the potential to wipe out one of the races. No nation could open their pot for fear of killing off themselves and their entire population. And if one race should use the virus as a weapon, the other nations would follow suit and retaliate, releasing their version of the virus in revenge. Carchi called his solution M.A.D, Mutually Assured Destruction.' Where have I heard that before? Alex thought over his own voice.

Callum listened in awe as Norman Gates took over and finished the story. 'Carchi's plan worked for a short time, and the world was at peace once more. But the High Priests of Leemon were not ones to give up their ideas of world domination. After reading Carchi's original research papers, they tested a virus on the Ikadiens. When no Green died, the Priests convinced themselves Carchi had tricked them. Confident there had been a deceit, they opened their stone pot, believing it to be empty, but within a matter of only days every Leemon had been wiped from the face of the planet. The priests had opened the pot containing their own destruction, having based their theory on their tests against the Greens. But unbeknown to the High Priests, the Green Ikadiens were immune from all the diseases.'

Callum said, 'This story is tragic. Everyone could have lived together in peace for all time, but now only three races remain.'

'That's right,' said Gates. 'Not many years later, Tiran erupted violently in the greatest explosion ever seen, and the Caprinese fled for their lives and left Parisos forever. As the fertile lands of Leemonadies were no longer inhabited by the Leemons, the Caprinese settled there, and it has been their home ever since. The capital of Caprine was once known as Leemon, the home of Leemon High Priests and their subjects for centuries past. And that is why this island, once home to the Caprinese, is uninhabited and abandoned.'

Alex and his party walked in silence, each contemplating the impact of the historic tale.

Eventually, one of the crew broke the silence. 'There's more of them, Captain. Ants as big as rats and they're watching us. I think they may attack.'

'They're just ants, sailor. Keep your eyes on the track,' Gates said, though he looked warily behind just in case any followed him.

'Don't look now, Mr Gates, but I think the man's right. These creatures have been following our progress,' Alex said. 'They're gathering in numbers.'

At first, it appeared to be a black torrent of water running down the mountain towards them. Everyone stopped to look.

'What in the name of the Gods is it, Captain?' asked a crewman.

Alex hesitated, squinting to see more clearly. 'It's not water,' he said. 'It's...'

No one gave the order to run; they didn't need to. What appeared to be liquid was very much solid matter, in the form of rat-sized insects numbering in their thousands and heading their way at speed. Panic rippled through the ranks as they stumbled and tripped to escape. More ants joined the attack, increasing in numbers until it seemed there were millions coming from every direction. Flowing from every dwelling, through windows and doors and from every hole and shelter, streams of insects converged in a continuous river of clicking, snapping life.

Norman Gates squealed after being bitten on the ankle. 'Faster!' he said as blood poured from his wound.

They reached the edge of town in a desperate sprint with a flood of pursuing ants massing on their heels. Alive, the surrounding hills swarmed with insects donned in black armour and razor-sharp pincers snapping at the air as they poured towards their prey. Still more emerged from holes in the ground, creating a continuous organism to consume all before it.

A crewman slipped. Alex watched, unable to help as the man disappeared in the rolling tide of deadly insects. Nothing could be done to save him. Alex stumbled and fell to the ground as the army approached, and he resigned himself to the sailor's apparent fate. But the insects stopped. It was as if they had reached an invisible barrier and could go no further. Antennas waved, tasting the air for stragglers. Alex checked his crew, and apart from the one unfortunate sailor, the group had somehow survived. The party slowed to a walk and eventually came to a standstill, dropping to the ground one by one in exhaustion, relieved for the chance to recover.

'Why did they stop?' asked Callum.

'No idea,' said Alex. 'But I thought I was a goner.'

'We lost Seaman Coles, sir. He was a good man,' Gates said, nursing his bleeding leg.

They sat in silence as they watched the insects return to their homes and remembered their fellow crewman, silently thanking the Gods for their own lucky escape.

'They will not come any further,' said a voice from nearby.

The party turned as one to find a man in grey woollen robes standing on the track before them. He carried a long walking pole with a ram's horn handle, and he wore sandals upon dirty, big feet that Alex thought must be size fifteen at least. He was sure even Malik had smaller feet. Tattered, grey, and matching the colour of his robes, his long beard and ragged hair stood from his head like the tentacles of an octopus.

'The name is Frog,' he said.

CHAPTER 11

Archimedes' Key

Heavy winter rain fell over Mariana, turning the prison compound into a frigid, muddy swamp. Leanne and Malik crouched under a waterproof skin, watching rain water spill from their cover to form rivulets, spreading like liquid fingers across the ground to the perimeter fence where it collected in pools. The fence, fifteen feet high and topped by hundreds of sharp spikes, encircled a holding compound where thirty to forty Green men and women had been imprisoned and were awaiting their fate. Oilskin tarps had been strung over posts to form shelters, and a small wooden hut housed a toilet that served as the only permanent facility. Two oak barrels collected rainwater runoff from the toilet roof to provide drinking water, the thought of which disgusted Leanne. A heavy wooden beam latch, only accessible from the outside, secured the compound door. Two guards stood watching the new arrivals with interest, pointing to Malik as though he were a zoological exhibit.

'These Greens get fatter. Look at that one...he probably arrived on a boat from the islands,' one guard said to the other. 'Hey, fat boy, we don't want your kind here. By the Gods, I have never seen anything so big and ugly,' he taunted.

Malik yelled back in response. 'Oh yeah? Well, you should take another look at your mother.'

The guard turned angry and made as though to enter the compound to punish Malik, but his comrade held him back.

'Come on, let's get out of this rain. He'll wait. He'll get what he deserves when they take him to the Hellefyr.' The guards laughed, covered their heads against the downpour, and disappeared in search of shelter.

'You shouldn't antagonise them, Malik,' Leanne said.

They sat in silence for several minutes until Malik spoke. 'Hey, Leanne, what do you call a big Brussel sprout with legs?'

'I don't know, Malik, what do you call a big Brussel sprout with legs?'

'Malik of course!'

'Well, at least you haven't lost your sense of humour,' Leanne said.

'I never had one to lose in the first place,' he said.

Leanne thought about it for a few moments and said, 'You did, you just used it to hurt people.'

More minutes passed and the rain increased, which eventually flooded the area as the rivulets became streams running through the compound. So intense was the fall that the city walls were no longer visible, and daylight had turned to an oppressive dark grey beneath the storm clouds.

'Thank you,' Malik said.

'For what?'

'For not saying it.'

'Not saying what?'

Malik thought for a while and said, 'For not saying I deserve everything that's happened to me. You could have told me this is Karma for what I said about Jani. But you didn't, so thanks.'

They sat a while longer in silence until Leanne said, 'You can be cruel to people. What do you have against Jani Nasri anyway?'

Malik thought about it. 'I don't have anything against her. That dumb stuff just comes out of my mouth without me thinking. It's a habit or something. I hurt people's feelings before I even know what I'm saying, and then I feel obliged to stick with what I've said. Too proud to apologise.'

'But you come from a good family. I saw your loving home, the photographs. I'm sure you didn't learn to be cruel from your parents.'

'Foster parents,' Malik said. 'They are my foster parents. My birth parents died during conflicts in our homeland, along with my three brothers and my sister. Our house got bombed, and I was the sole survivor.'

'I'm sorry, I didn't know.'

'How could you know? Anyway, it was a long time ago. I don't remember any of them because I was only two years old at the time. My foster parents were our neighbours. They pulled me from the rubble, unaware they'd lost their own children in the blast until later. They escaped the troubles soon after as refugees, took me with them and made their way to safety. They're the kindest people you could ever meet. So no, I didn't learn to be cruel from my parents, or my foster parents, I managed to achieve that all on my own.'

'I can't imagine how terrible that must have been for you. I'm so sorry, Malik.'

'Don't be, it was long ago and I have no memory of it.' Time passed in uncomfortable silence as the torrent increased. Eventually, Malik asked, 'What about you, how did you come to be so smart?'

Leanne laughed. 'Smart? I don't think so.'

'Why do you deny it? You're the smartest kid I know.'

'Kid! I'll have you know I'm a twenty-three-year-old woman, thank you very much.'

'Don't avoid the question,' said Malik.

Leanne thought about it. 'I guess I've always found learning easy. I could read fluently before I was three. I played a piano concerto when I was five and spoke four languages by the age of six. My parents are really into all that child prodigy stuff, but as a result, I never had time for children's games and just being a kid. They want me to be a concert pianist, my dad does at least. I decided I don't want to be, and Dad went bonkers when I told him. It caused all kinds of problems at home. I started rebelling, doing stuff I knew they would hate and that didn't involve music.'

'Such as?'

'I enrolled myself in gymnastics classes during school lunch breaks, and my parents didn't even realise for three terms. I became good at it, but when they found out they put a stop to it because they were afraid I would hurt my fingers. I had spent so much time playing the piano that I didn't know how to get on with other people my age. I tried to be cool at school and act like I didn't care about anything, but other kids somehow knew I didn't fit in, that I was faking it.

'My dad was furious when I stopped playing. I've hardly touched the piano seriously for so long now, I don't know if I could even play like I used to. Last summer I made a deal with them. If they let me go away to a summer camp of my choosing, I would knuckle down, finish my year at school and go on to music college. They agreed. I got a place in an extreme sports program. I went rock climbing, sailing, wakeboarding, and mountain biking, learned kickboxing, you name it, if it involved risk we did it. It was as far from music as I could get. They were horrified of course, but they had my word on college and music so they let me stay the whole summer, hoping I would keep my word and start playing again.'

'Did you say you tried to be cool? You are the most uncool kid in school,' Malik said, grinning. 'And I'm not trying to be cruel.'

'Yeah, well, this uncool kid is going to get us out of here. I've just given myself an idea.'

'How?'

'We need to move fast before the rain eases and the guards return. How much do you weigh, Malik?'

'A lot,' he said.

'Help me roll that water barrel over by the fence and rip a wide plank of wood off the side of the toilet hut.'

The other Greens watched with curiosity as Leanne gave instructions and Malik lay the plank across the barrel like a seesaw.

'Remember I told you about gymnastics? At the time I wanted to join a circus. I once saw these amazing circus acrobats performing backflips and somersaults. I wanted to be the one flying through the air and have the crowd clapping wildly with excitement.'

'You can't be serious! That fence is probably twenty feet high, and if you haven't already noticed, it's topped by razor-sharp spikes. Plus, you may have the mind of a teenager, but you have...' Malik paused and passed his eyes over Leanne's body as though he had only just noticed her mature figure and curvy new look. 'You're...um...old,' he stuttered. '*Older* I mean. Older.'

Leanne didn't notice Malik's embarrassment as she was too busy studying the fence. 'Fifteen feet,' she said. 'Anyway, have you got a better idea?'

Malik gauged the fence again and shook his head. 'It's impossible, Leanne. One mistake and you will end up on the spikes. There has to be another way.'

Leanne had made up her mind and actually looked excited by the challenge. They rolled the second barrel across and stood it upturned in place near the seesaw. Leanne stood at the very end of the plank with her back to the fence and Malik nervously climbed onto the second barrel.

'What if I'm not heavy enough?' he asked, desperate for Leanne to give up the idea.

'You know the slogan, Malik. Just do it!'

Malik closed his eyes and appeared to pray. Without another word, save a few internal curses, he leapt from the barrel and onto the plank. There followed a crash and a thud as the wooden board pivoted over the barrel and splashed into the wet ground, sending mud in every direction. Leanne's ascent came swiftly as the force of Malik's sudden arrival propelled her skywards. Three backflips sent her tumbling over the spikes, clearing them by less than a hair. She landed on the far side on two feet, bent her legs to lessen the shock, stood straight, and raised her arms above her head in triumph as though she had just dismounted the high-bar after completing a gymnastic routine to perfection.

'Perfect score,' she shouted. 'Every single judge gives a ten.'

Amazed and elated, Malik began to clap but realised where they were and what they were doing. 'Eh, I think we should hurry.'

Leanne went to the compound entrance and tried to lift the heavy wooden latch. It had taken both guards to lower it in place.

'Oh my gosh, it's heavy.' She tried again but only managed to lift it a quarter inch before it crashed back into place. 'Malik, I can't lift it, it's too heavy.'

Malik's heart thumped. 'Think, Leanne, you're the smart one, remember?'

'Smart, not strong,' she said in a panic.

'Listen to me. Think it through, Leanne. It's just another problem you can solve. Google it for crying out loud!'

'Ha, ha, very funny.' Leanne took Malik's advice. She calmed herself and analysed the problem. After a few moments, she said, 'Who was it said 'give me a lever long enough, and I'll move the world'?'

'Not a time for quizzes, Leanne.'

'Archimedes,' she said. She had Malik pull up a support pole from the tarp shelter and hurl it over the fence. Leanne then took the tapered end of the pole and drove it between the wooden beam latch and the latch holder. Using only one hand to demonstrate the leverage effect, she pushed down on the end of the pole and lifted the latch free and clear. The door opened, and Leanne sang, 'Da da!'

Given their freedom, the prisoners scattered while Malik and Leanne ran for the edge of the pilgrim camp nearest the city wall. Under cover of driving rain, they were able to reach the very last tent.

'What now?' asked Malik.

The tent flap opened and a curious face appeared from inside. 'Come in out of the rain,' the man said.

Inside the tent, they found a family of seven. A man and his wife, their three children, and the father's ageing parents. The children were tucked up under warm animal skins, one of which slept soundly but wheezed out of bubbling lungs.

'He's sick, poor little blighter,' the mother said. 'There's others going down in the camp too. We fear it's the pestilence.'

Leanne exchanged looks with Malik, and though she never spoke of her concern, she worried they might catch the disease and wanted to cover her mouth in response.

'We'll be gone soon, when the rain eases,' Leanne said.

The grandmother eyed Malik thoughtfully. After a while, she spoke. 'We had a Green with us two days ago, a free man. Not big like you, but strong and good. They came for him,' she said sadly.

Leanne asked, 'Why do they treat the Green people this way?'

'Fear,' said the old woman. 'They fear the Greens will join the Caprinese and fight alongside them.' The old woman re-capped the story of Carchi's virus. 'After the Leemons died away, the peace-loving Greens destroyed their own version of the virus and encouraged Caprine and Mariana to do likewise, but they were too suspicious of one another and the threat of Carchi has hung over us ever since.' She went on to say how af-ter the extinctions, the planet had suffered a great shortage of labour. Greens were defenseless, they were taken into slavery. It had been so ever since.

Malik sat in silence and listened.

'This all happened centuries ago,' said the woman. 'With the Greens in chains, Mariana also had one less potential ene-my to worry about. The Caprinese were not much better. They took advantage of the situation by taking their share of cap-tives and making them slaves.'

Leanne knew this story, but she let the woman go on. She did not want to reveal she was herself Caprinese.

'That all changed a few years ago,' said the woman. 'Cap-rine has been steadily freeing slaves. Last I heard, the prac-tice had been outlawed. These days, slaving only exists here in Mariana and a few of its provinces. Now with all the unrest, the queen has a fear of Greens rising up against her and tak-ing revenge. That's why she's rounding everyone up.'

They sat in silence as rain pounded the tent like a never-ending drum. 'We need to get inside the city,' Leanne said after a while.

The father shook his head. 'No one gets in or out. The city is closed to everyone.'

'There must be a way,' Malik said.

The grandfather joined the conversation. 'When I was a young man, I worked on the city drainage system. There is an outfall on the wall below the third tower. You can enter the underground passages and make your way into the city from there.'

'We must find our way to the palace,' Leanne said.

The old man raised his eyebrows, surprised by the comment, but did not ask why. 'It is possible,' he said, laying out his knowledge of the tunnel complex and how they could reach the palace if the tunnels remained open.

They waited without further discussion as the hours passed. The sleeping boy tossed and turned, beads of sweat covered his head, his face looked pale, and his eyes were so dark they appeared bruised. He cried out, causing Malik to reach for the boy's arm to comfort him. 'Poor little fella,' he said.

Alarmed by this contact, Leanne met Malik's eyes as a worried look crossed her face. *Do you know what you just did?*

Malik responded to the unspoken question by simply shrugging. He rubbed the little boy's arm again and wished him well.

As well as worrying her, Malik's compassionate gesture moved Leanne, making her wonder once again who the real Malik was behind the scornful mask he wore.

The rain eased a little. On the hills above the city, torrenting waterfalls could be seen filling gorges on the way down to the rivers below, and Malik and Leanne prepared to leave.

The old man gave his final instructions. 'Once in the labyrinth of tunnels, you must keep track of your twists and turns. It would be easy for a person to get lost in such a maze.'

The husband gave Malik an oil lantern to light the way and wished them good luck.

'We'll need luck,' Malik said.

The sleeping boy woke and smiled, his fever broken.

'Well, there's a sign,' said the mother. 'You have brought us good fortune, and you go now with our blessings for yours.'

Malik winked at the child, who waved back weakly and grinned a toothy smile.

Outside, the rain persisted, albeit marginally lighter than in previous hours. Soldiers had disappeared from the battlements, keeping dry no doubt rather than keeping watch. Malik and Leanne agreed they were ready for what lay ahead. They crossed the barren no-man's land, reached the wall in a run, and headed for the third tower.

No one saw their dash through the downpour, and they reached the outfall without incident, finding it exactly where the old man had said it would be. A steel grate covered the entrance, and a steady stream of water flowed out from the tunnel. Without difficulty, Malik pulled the rusting barrier free. They stepped inside and lit the lantern.

'Now,' said Leanne. 'One hundred paces north, then east for two hundred.'

'I hope you can remember,' Malik said. 'Because I'm already starting to forget.'

CHAPTER 12

The King of Caprine

Climbing at a steady pace, Frog led the party along the winding mountain path. He used his walking staff as an aid, digging it deep into the soft volcanic earth before pulling himself forward two huge steps at a time. Alex found it extraordinary that the old man breathed so easily, unaffected by the steep climb or the altitude. Everyone else gasped for oxygen in the thinning atmosphere as they tried to keep up with the old man's punishing pace. An unusual looking man, Frog's eyes were dark as coal yet sparkled like diamonds. Wrinkled, prune-like skin gave him the appearance of age, but he travelled the path like a teenager on steroids.

'How long have you been alone on this island?' asked Alex, panting.

'Since I don't know when,' answered Frog.

'It must be a lonely life,' Alex said.

Frog stopped and said, 'If you mean being solitary, then yes, I am alone. But lonely? Not while I have the wind to converse with and the rain to come calling.'

Frog turned back to the path and continued to climb, causing the others to step up the pace to catch him. As they gained altitude, the air grew thinner and colder, and men who thought they were fit for the climb now had doubts about their ability. Alex gasped for oxygen, and one man slumped to the side of the track, unable to go further.

They reached the snowline quickly, in spite of the effort needed. Temperatures plummeted, and walking became increasingly laborious in the deep snow. Above, with its head occasionally disappearing in the cloud, the ever-present spectre of Tiran stood over them, puffing out clouds of rotten egg smelling gas at regular intervals that made the ascent even more unpleasant for the struggling climbers.

Gates wheezed. 'How much further?'

Frog grinned at the faces looking at him for an update and hoping for a rest. 'Not much further,' he said.

At first, Alex thought he had a dizzy spell. He swayed back and forth several times before realising the others had felt it too. Beneath their feet the mountain rumbled and shook, causing a small landslide to appear on the slope below. They watched the loosened ground tumble down the mountain as rocks bounced through the air on their way to the foothills.

The shake ended, and the worried crew looked once more to Frog for reassurance.

'Oh, there's nothing to be concerned about, friends, it's just Tiran letting us know he's watching.' Frog laughed aloud and continued to lead, giving them no time to recover.

'What's he been taking?' Alex asked, watching the old man leap from rock to rock.

'I don't know, but I want some,' said Gates.

Silence fell on the climbers, all energy now diverted to the effort, giving Alex time to consider what might lie ahead. Nim had mentioned an ancient relic, but this was all the information he had. What form this relic might take and where he might find it was anyone's guess. He wondered if Leanne and Malik were faring any better.

'Look, eagles!' a crewman shouted.

Everyone stopped to look skyward as two large birds circled high above.

Frog held a hand to shield his eyes from the sun. 'No, not eagles,' he said. 'They are vamps. I'll wager they are taking a look at tonight's dinner menu.'

As if on cue, the great wings flapped and the pair swooped low over the group, causing all except Frog to dive to the ground in fright. Once up close, Alex saw the vamps had bat-like, featherless wings with ten-foot spans casting shadows across the sun. Broad, gargoyle heads snarled and snapped at the group, and canine teeth dripped big gobs of saliva from the air like rain. Reptile legs terminated in sharp talons with which to grasp their prey. A crewman screamed in terror as they made another torturous pass before disappearing high into the clouds.

Frog chuckled, amused by everyone's panic. 'Have no fear, friends, vamps only hunt at night.'

They returned to the slog and soon reached the upper edge of the snowline, which ran around the mountain like a priest's white collar. Above this mark, the volcano's inner heat prevented snow from settling. Thick black ash replaced soft snow on the ground, offering little relief and only further draining their flagging energy reserves with every tired step. At last, they came to a plateau. Frog halted and raised his staff to bring everyone to a standstill in front of a crumbling city wall.

'Welcome to the Temple City of Kerano, home of the Caprinese immortals. These blackened walls once protected a great and thriving civilisation. Tomorrow we will enter the gates.'

Alex gauged the sun and said, 'We still have daylight. We should go further while we can.'

'Night falls quickly, and Kerano is no place to be when it's dark. There are many dangers within the walls. We will make camp here and rise with the sun to explore.'

The mountain rumbled as if to confirm Frog's warning, and Alex gave orders to bed down for the night.

Frog was right; night fell within minutes. In the orange glow of a campfire, the exhausted group recovered from the climb with a hot feed of broth before laying out their bedrolls and turning in for the night. Alex volunteered to take the first watch along with Olo. Frog said he would stay to keep them company; he did not need sleep. Alex wondered again how this old man could be so spritely.

In the flickering firelight, Frog had an unsettling appearance. Alex thought he looked eerily different in the glow; it was as though he was looking at another person, a ghostly spectre of something not quite of this world.

'How old are you, Frog?' Alex asked.

Frog's eyes sparkled. 'Older than the fire and younger than the smoke,' he said with a sinister grin.

'I don't know what that means,' Alex said. 'You talk in riddles.'

'It means, my young friend, age is a concept only fashioned by time. And as time itself is just a worldly notion, it could be I am no age at all.' Frog stood. 'I must be more tired than I thought, Captain. I think I will retire after all.'

Frog disappeared into the shadows, and Alex watched him go as he considered the cryptic answer. Perhaps Frog had more in common with Nim than anyone else.

Hours later, Olo and Alex, relieved of their watch, settled down to sleep by the fire that had dwindled to a smouldering mound of glowing coals. The watch had set lanterns at intervals around the perimeter, and Alex gazed at the flickering lights and thought of home. Tiran rumbled, sending an orange plume into the sky. Stars gathered in their millions and a red moon floated above the horizon. Alex lay on his back and wondered how many other Alexs were out there looking down on him, and how many times this adventure would be played out across the Megaverse. He exhaled a tired sigh as his eyelids began to droop and close.

It was as if a hand had just passed over his face and he lost sight of the moon. Was he dreaming already? Yes, he was probably falling asleep, and not a moment too soon, he thought. But it happened again, and this time he knew he was not dreaming. A black silhouette covered the moon for less than a second, causing each of Alex's senses to jump to high-alert. He waited in silence while holding his breath, wondering if what he had seen could have been a passing cloud.

'Arrgh! Arrrrrrgh!'

Blood-curdling screams woke the camp as one. Panicked, they sprang to their feet and gathered near the fire. Screams continued from the darkness, but it was unclear who was crying out. Alex held a lantern aloft as he cautiously stepped forward to investigate. Callum joined him with a second lamp.

Confronted by a terrible sight, they froze in their tracks and baulked at the horror. The lamplight caught a vamp in its glow, its fearsome eyes warning them not to proceed further.

The beast snarled, baring its teeth in a vicious display of power as its wings covered and protected its gruesome kill like cloaks. Nearby, a second vamp stood ready to spring with its formidable predator eyes fixed on Alex and Callum. The first vamp gave out a guttural growl, loud enough to shake both men to their knees. With a flap of its great wings, the animal took to flight, carrying an unfortunate crewman in its talons as though he were nothing more than a child's ragdoll. Callum and Alex leapt forward to save him, but they were too late, the beast had taken its prey. The second vamp bellowed and spat before following its mate into darkness with a mighty flap of its wings.

Over in seconds, the drama seemed surreal. Stunned survivors gathered and watched the sky for the horrific animals to return. Alex saw Frog in the lamplight, watching the terrorised travellers with no hint of alarm to spoil his serene expression.

'Go back to sleep,' Frog said in a chilling voice. 'These demons only take one each night.'

Morning came, though few had slept more than a wink after the night's terrifying drama. No one spoke of the horror; they ate breakfast quietly, struck camp without conversation, and made their way into the Temple City before the morning mist had cleared.

Half buried and half destroyed, the blackened buildings here were much more prominent than those they had seen on the hillsides below. Frog described them as the homes and offices of the rich and powerful.

'Those who once resided here were the Masters and Overseers,' said Frog. 'They lived a privileged life of wealth and good fortune.'

'Until their good fortune ran out,' Gates added.

Frog smiled. 'You are right, of course. Living so high on the mountain, these lords and ladies believed they were close to the Gods and would benefit from their protection. But I don't believe they counted on meeting the Gods in person and at such close quarters. There was no escape for these advantaged few; they were swallowed by the mountain while many of the poor people living below fled to safety.'

Tiran roared, sending a cloud of black smoke skyward. The ground shook violently, and fear appeared on every face.

Frog laughed. 'It's just Tiran farting,' he said as the mountain settled once more.

Progress through the rubble of the ruined city was slow. They walked single file, Alex leading the way and Olo taking up the rear. Solidified ash crunched underfoot. Occasionally, someone would break through the meringue-like crust and flounder in the black dust before being dragged to safety by another. Colourless and dark, there was not a single thing that had escaped the effects of the larva and ash. Steam rose from numerous vents and belched gases of stinking sulphur. They crossed bridges of pumice and felt them creak and crack, sometimes dropping large chunks into chasms far below where pools of red-hot larva bubbled and popped.

'This world is dead,' said Callum. 'But the mountain lives,' he added.

After a slow march through the outer sanctum, they approached an inner wall and a gateway to the High Temple. They passed beneath the arch and came to a halt, astonished at the spectacle before them. Two thousand soldiers stood in regimented lines, spears in one hand, shields on the other. These ordered ranks of warriors, drilled to perfection, formed a shield wall to protect the high altar.

'Impressive, aren't they?' Frog commented, looking over the assembled ranks as though they were his to command. 'You men are privileged. Not many have witnessed the mass formation of the Imperial Guard.'

They stood in silence for several long moments until Frog spoke again. 'Shall we?' he asked, leading the way between the columns. Alex and the others followed, eyeing the fighting men with cautious fascination.

A king stood overlooking the assembled ranks. Frog stepped forward, bowed, turned to the others, and said with a crooked smile, 'May I introduce to you, His Immortal Majesty, the King of Caprine.'

Thirty miles out to sea, First Officer Stark scanned the slopes of the volcano through her telescope looking for signs of life. A blast of smoke billowed skyward from the cone, causing Stark to shudder. Seconds later she heard the rumble.

'Can you see them, Ms Stark?' Little Jim asked anxiously.

'No, too far away, Jim. But I'm sure the captain is safe if that's why you're worried. We've made rapid headway and will be on the shore in good time.' Stark watched another belch from the volcano and hoped she was right.

CHAPTER 13

The Charlatan

T he King of Caprine, like his two thousand elite soldiers, stood lifeless before them. Petrified to stone, the blackened remains of the once great ruler captured his final moments in a dramatic pose. Hands held high to the mountain, frozen in time, his offering was now a featureless lump of stone in his brittle hands. The offering was never enough to satisfy Tiran and save the king's life. The fate of His Majesty and that of the Imperial Guard had been sealed in an instant as Tiran's blast had encased them where they stood, preserving them forever like statues of granite. Alex wondered if their faith had ever wavered, or if they had believed in their immortality to the end and placed their lives in the hands of the Gods.

'As you can see for yourself, Captain Boatman, there is nothing to discover here. The mountain consumed everything I'm afraid. Your quest is futile.'

Alex could not help agreeing with the old hermit as he surveyed the scene before him. Every living thing, every brick and stone, every timber structure, plant and tree, every window and wall; they had all become fossilised, at one with Tiran. Nothing remained but the gruesome black casts of what had once been living beings, eternally preserved along with the charred remains of the city they'd once called home.

'You're right,' said Alex. 'We've wasted our time.' Heavy with disappointment, his voice tapered off as he accepted defeat. The city was nothing but a blackened wasteland.

After an hour of aimless searching through the charred remains of the temple, Alex gave the order to depart and the party made ready for the descent of the mountain, each glad they could leave the desolation behind and return to the safety of their ship. Callum appeared fascinated more than most by the preserved army of soldiers, lingering to imagine their final moments on the mountain. He placed a hand on one stone warrior, running his fingers over the rough surface and wondering who this person might have been in life. *What was your name?*

Alex joined him, and together they looked over the ranks of lost souls.

'It reminds me of the Terracotta Army discovered in China,' Alex said.

Callum tilted his head and frowned. 'China?'

Alex smiled, careful to maintain the secret of his life on Earth. 'It's a land far from here,' he said. 'I've never been there myself, but I would like to go one day. There are many wonders to see, ancient and modern. Great palaces and long walls stretching for thousands of miles across mountains, and cities of steel and glass where people live in their millions.'

Callum considered this for a moment and said, 'I would like to go too one day.'

'Who knows what the future will bring,' Alex said. 'Many things are possible when you follow your dreams.'

Callum's eyes met Alex's for a moment, almost as though they were both in each other's heads, and each knew the truth about the wonders of the Megaverse and their part in its future. The feeling passed and Callum turned back to the stone warrior.

'This was once a living, breathing man. I imagine *he* had dreams beyond this mountain,' he said. Beneath his palm, he could almost feel the soldier's heartbeat. He paused. *This cannot be.* Callum put his ear to the stone chest; he could hear a sound, he could feel a quiver.

'Captain, I can feel his life force. How can this be?'

Alex placed his hand on the soldier's chest beside Callum's. He felt it too, the pulsing tremor beneath his fingers. But this was no heart beating. The soldier was shaking, and cracks appeared across his chest as the ground began to rumble and move beneath their feet. Everyone stopped what they were doing and looked to one another for answers. The soldier continued to crumble under Callum's hand, and an almighty crash split the air, causing all heads to turn in the direction of Tiran's smouldering cone. Moments later, as if hell itself had broken loose from the earth, the mountain erupted in a catastrophic blast.

'Run for your lives!' came the cry.

No one argued. The party hurried across the unstable ground while the earth shook like jelly around them. Cracks appeared across the ground, and molten lava oozed from below like toothpaste squeezed from a tube. Stone soldiers shook to pieces and turned to dust, while others opened like cracked eggs to reveal red-hot liquid centres that spilled magma rivers to join the torrents now rumbling seaward. The crew stumbled and fumbled their way to escape, running on legs that refused to stand firm on the treacherous slope. Alex and Callum joined the race as the volcano erupted again, the second blast sending smoking lumps of burning rock the size of houses hurtling into the air with a series of terrifying squeals. Alex slipped as the earth beneath him ripped apart, but he managed to roll to safety just in time to miss a boulder as it hurtled by. Stone soldiers cracked and crumbled all around him, dis-integrating before his eyes. Amid the mayhem, Alex saw the glint of metal and realised it was the tip of a spear tumbling to the ground. More glimpses of steel. Could it be the metal had survived until now, encased in stone? Alex watched as more soldiers collapsed, and stared in amazement when the steel of a breastplate appeared from within one of the stony shells, shining as though it were new. Another soldier shattered, leaving behind his shield and sword intact; again they appeared as if newly forged.

Alex had an idea.

'Go on ahead,' he told Callum. 'I'll meet you at the shore-line.'

Alex turned and made his way through the remains of the temple as more pillars fell and more walls tumbled, leaving in their wake great holes filled with the glow of liquid rock. Alex saw the king, still fixed in his pose with his arms out-stretched to the mountain as debris crashed down around him. Alex reached the stone king with a desperate leap across an opening chasm, but the once mighty ruler was fast breaking apart. His head broke loose and tumbled from his shoulders while his arms fragmented and helplessly dropped to the ground. Alex reached out and started to dig in the rubble for the hands and their offering, now merely a featureless lump of rock among many. After a few agonising moments of frantic searching, Alex picked it from the ruins and saw the prize within. *The relic.*

Alex had no time to savour his moment of triumph. He tucked the relic in his shirt and turned to run, only to be stopped short by the scene before him.

'I do believe that belongs to me,' said Frog amid the chaos.

Callum was on his knees with Frog holding a dagger to his throat.

'Now why am I not surprised,' Alex said.

The ground shook violently once again, causing them to sway and almost fall, but Frog held the blade steady. 'Toss it over here,' he said.

'You're not the real Frog, are you?' Alex said.

'No, that old hermit died many years ago. Eaten by ants, I believe. I replaced him in the Dreamscape. Now, enough small talk. If you value the life of your friend, you will hand over the relic.'

'What do I care about a Green? He's just a slave!' Alex bluffed.

'Nice try,' Frog replied. 'I think you care a lot, for whatever unfathomable reason. But I'm a reasonable man. I'll take your little prize there, and in return, I will let you both leave so you can run for your lives.' No reply. 'Well...deal?'

Alex hesitated.

'Don't take too long deciding,' said Frog. 'Tiran may have other ideas about your escape from this island.'

As if on cue, Tiran thundered, sending another angry blast of rock and ash into the atmosphere.

'You say you replaced Frog in the Dreamscape. I do believe that makes you a Charlatan,' Alex said. 'Nim warned me of Charlatans. She said they were Figments like her, only Charlatans are from the dark side of the Dreamscape, aren't they?' Alex hoped he was right. 'She also told me something fascinating about Figments.'

'Oh, and what was that?' said Frog.

'Figments can't physically interfere with events. You're an illusion. In fact, I bet if I held up a mirror, you would not even be here.'

'Pity you don't have a mirror,' said Frog.

'You can't kill Callum any more than you can kill me.'

Frog's expression turned sour. 'Try me,' said the Charlatan.

Alex gambled. 'Walk away, Callum. This Figment can't harm you.'

Cautiously, Callum stood and stepped away. 'Now go, Callum,' Alex said. Callum didn't waste a second and ran away as fast as his legs could carry him.

'Very good,' the Charlatan congratulated Alex. 'There are many stupid rules for Figments and as you have rightly observed, I am a Figment and cannot act against you physically. But perhaps Nim also mentioned one exception to the rule. Indeed, you may have already made the acquaintance of the Assassins, Kale and Slade.'

One on either side of the Charlatan, the two black-clad Assassins appeared as if from nowhere. They closed in on Alex with their daggers drawn as Tiran thundered above them in yet another blast. Splitting the air and shaking the mountain, the eruption caused everyone to stumble. Alex took the opportunity, leapt from the high altar, skipped over the opening crevasse, and miraculously landed on his feet on a flat piece of rock. He was about to thank the Gods for their holy assistance when he realised Kale and Slade were doing the same, coming to rest in a perfect position to block his path to freedom. The ground fell apart around them, but Kale and Slade deftly circled away with gratified smiles on their faces. Alex closed his eyes in acceptance of his fate, but much to his surprise, he heard Nim's voice.

'You are the one, Alex. Only you can deliver the relic safely. Have faith in yourself and your ability to out-think your opponents. You have done it before.'

Alex opened his eyes, expecting to find Nim at his side. *Where are you, Nim? I could use some help right now!*

Kale continued to close in from the front while Slade circled behind. Despite the lava spurting in scalding fountains from every fractured rock, Alex managed to steady himself. *Okay, Nim, I think I know what you mean. I've done this a thousand times before on my video games.*

'It's no different to Donkey Kong,' he said aloud, watching as the safety of the stepping stones disappeared into the fire. He had to move or burn.

Alex jumped. *Confidence, Alex; the secret is confidence.* Kale and Slade shadowed his every move, but Alex was too quick. Leaping from one crumbling platform to another, he glanced back as fires destroyed the path in his wake. Explosions boomed and crashed at every turn, and fireballs and lightning peppered the sky as the mountain voiced its anger by launching every possible obstacle in his path. Alex took control but had no time to pause; he moved like a champion gamer, leaving the Assassins to stumble and falter in the chaos left behind. Enjoying the challenge now, Alex half expected Super Mario to jump up before him at any moment and applaud his agility.

Alex reached the temple wall to see Callum racing down the mountain only thirty feet ahead. Behind him, the scene had deteriorated to utter destruction, and he saw Slade disappear with a high-pitched scream down a fiery crack with Kale tumbling after him. The mountain crashed again, sending clouds of choking gas into the air. Alex ran, stumbled, picked himself up and stumbled to the ground again, then rolled and returned back to his feet all in one motion. He caught Callum, urging him to go faster as they raced to escape the fury. Rocks crashed around them, some burning bright red, and bounced down the mountain in an unstoppable shower of deadly sparks.

'Ants!' Callum cried.

Ants massed in their thousands on the path ahead of them, and with a quick glance over his shoulder, Alex saw molten rock surging down the mountain behind him. Alex screamed, 'Faster!'

They picked up the pace, all the while dodging hot rocks and boulders as if they were hurdlers locked in fierce competition. At times it seemed as though their feet never touched the ground; if they had wings, they would have been airborne. A burning chunk of molten rock as big as a truck crashed beside them, but they quickly sidestepped and kept on running without a pause. With an army of ants now swarming around their feet, Alex soon realised the insects had no interest in him or the crew; they were fleeing for their own lives as the mountain belched its fury. Many had been caught in the lava flow, incinerated by the thousands. Alex could hear them popping and snapping like popcorn.

Exhausted and barely able to walk let alone run, Alex and Callum saw the beach at last, but the once golden sand had turned to a living black mass as a million ants scrambled in confusion and panic, some diving into the sea in a desperate bid for safety. Beyond the swarming insects, Alex saw what was left of his expedition party, already in boats on their way to the Klaw. The ship had arrived and was now anchored a short way from shore. Rafts of ants followed, swimming in the surf like a writhing slick of oil.

Arriving at the water, Alex and Callum saw nothing but the black-armoured backs of insects clamouring across the ocean. Alex led the way by jumping onto the shining insect backs and using them as stepping stones. So thick were the layers of insects, they could support a man's weight like a living jetty, taking them out to sea and beyond the waves to the Klaw. Callum and Alex reached the lead insects, dived over their heads into the surf, and swam the remaining yards to the ship where the crew hoisted them to safety.

'Set the sails! Pull the anchor, Ms Stark. There's no time to lose!'

Already in motion, the crew were quick putting the ship into action. Ants tried to climb aboard in a last bid for freedom but were fended off with swords and clubs, soon left behind as the wind caught the sails.

Alex looked back to the mountain that had almost claimed his life, and his stomach turned at the sight. A massive bulge had formed on the slopes facing the sea.

'I've seen this on National Geographic,' Alex said. Callum stood beside him, puzzled by the comment. 'No time to explain, Callum.' Alex screamed his orders. 'Hard to starboard, Ms Stark, and follow a course close to the shore, as close as we dare, please.'

'But, Captain, we should head straight out to sea.'

'We don't have time. As I ordered, Stark, hard to starboard.'

The first officer complied, heaving the wheel hard. The sails flapped and the lines were adjusted, bringing the ship into a tight turn and running her parallel to the shoreline. Alex watched the mountain and prayed as the ship tacked and zigzagged into the wind.

'Pray we can put enough distance between us and the blast, Ms Stark,' Alex said.

'What blast?'

Without further warning, the bulge in the mountain exploded with an earth-shattering eruption, sending a thundering cloud of white-hot gases surging at breakneck speed down the slopes towards the beach, consuming everything in its path. From the ship, they watched a million ants evaporate before their eyes. Trees, ancient houses, the blast destroyed everything in an instant. Beyond the beach, the speeding flow continued out to sea for several miles, slowing eventually at its limit in a billowing toxic cloud of destruction. The crew covered their faces against the smoke as dirty grey ash fell like snow all around them. The ship rocked violently, but they were just out of the blast zone and soon made for open water and clean ocean air.

Stark looked stunned. 'The flow would have swallowed us had we headed straight out to sea,' she said. 'How did you know that would happen, Captain?'

Alex winked. 'TV documentary,' he said smiling. 'That was a pyroclastic flow if I'm not mistaken.'

Stark shook her head. She had given up trying to understand the captain's strange comments.

The Labyrinth

Weird and shadowy shapes, bearing no relation to Malik and Leanne's human forms, loomed eerily on the passage walls under the flickering lamplight. Malik led the way and held the lantern high, ducking under low support beams as the passage narrowed into a brick-lined tunnel.

'I don't like small spaces,' Malik said, bumping his head as if to make the point. 'This is insane.'

'Shouldn't have such a big head,' said Leanne.

'Thanks a lot. I'll have you know it's full of brains.'

'Pity they're scrambled.'

'I think this roof is getting lower by the way. It certainly wasn't built for someone my size.'

'Nothing is built for someone your size, Malik.'

'Stop with the insults, please. Talk about me being a smartarse.' Malik hit his head again, only this time harder, causing a trickle of blood to run from his scalp. 'Geez!' he screamed. 'That's it! I've had it, we should go back. We'll never find our way through here, and this tight space is giving me the creeps.'

Small spaces had an unnerving effect on Malik at the best of times. But these dark and damp passages brought the term claustrophobic to a whole new level.

'We can't go back, Malik. You know what's at stake.' Leanne counted under her breath. 'That's two hundred and thirty paces. We should turn left here.'

'Do we know what's at stake?' asked Malik. 'What if Nim is not what she seems? How do we know she's telling the truth?' Malik ducked too late and caught a spider web full in the face. He cursed, spitting silk threads from his mouth while hoping there were no spiders in the tangled web. 'She told us we would know what to do when we got here,' he continued. 'Which we don't. We're still working blind.'

'Have a little faith, Malik. It's not been easy, but we are making progress.'

'Progress? You call this progress?'

'Malik, I'm trying my best to remember the way here, give me a break. I'll figure it out, don't worry.'

'At least you get to figure it out. You get ideas. What am I doing? I have no practical use. You get all the premonitions, you know what to say, what to do next. I'm just a big green blob, attracting unwanted attention wherever I go. I haven't a clue why I'm here or why they chose to make me a Green. You would be better off without me.'

Tell me about it, Leanne thought. 'Are you going to whine like this all the way?'

'I am not whining, I'm just saying there's no point in me being here.'

'Wait!' Leanne said.

The passage took a step down, and Malik felt water suddenly up to his knees. 'Arrgh! That's all I need...as if I'm not wet enough already,' he said.

'Which way now?' Leanne said to herself more than to Malik.

They tried to remember the old man's instructions, but each remembered differently.

Malik offered his opinion. 'We turn right here, then pass five tunnel entrances on the left before turning left again.'

'Are you sure? I thought it was four,' said Leanne.

'It's five,' Malik said confidently.

They walked in a crouch until they reached the fifth tunnel entrance where Malik turned.

'Were we supposed to turn at the fifth tunnel or pass it and turn at the next?'

'Don't confuse me, I know what I'm doing,' he insisted.

They travelled for several minutes, passing tunnel after tunnel before coming to a standstill.

'Dead end,' Malik said.

'Malik, I told you we had to go one more entrance before turning.'

'You didn't,' he argued. 'You asked me if it was the fifth or sixth where we turn, you didn't say the fifth was wrong. You let me take the wrong turn.'

They retraced their path, but every tunnel looked the same.

'This is a labyrinth,' Leanne said. 'How many tunnels did we pass after turning?' Malik didn't answer. 'Are you sulking, Malik? Did you count the tunnels?' Malik didn't answer. 'I think we've come too far now. We should have turned right one tunnel back.' Malik still didn't answer. 'There's no point in sulking, Malik. I mean, if you can't remember, just say so.'

Malik stopped, turned, and gave Leanne the lantern. 'I can't remember. Happy? So here, let's see you do better.'

Leanne took over the lead, but within a matter of moments, she paused and turned, unsure which way to go next. Malik stood facing her, wearing a smug expression on his face.

Leanne looked him in the eye and sighed. 'There's good and bad news, Malik. The good news is you don't look green in the lamplight, the bad news is we're lost.'

Malik felt the water now well past his knees. 'This water is getting deeper,' he said.

'It will be because of all the rainfall. Did you see all those swollen waterfalls foaming down the mountainside above the city?' Leanne said. 'That's what this drainage system is for, to take away stormwater.'

'We're in a flood drain?' Malik said, instantly terrified.

She wished she hadn't told him. 'Don't worry, we'll be out of here well before the drains fill.'

'Fill!'

'Water travels downhill,' Leanne said. 'The main tunnel probably runs all the way to the harbour and out to sea. So if we follow the flow, it will take us through the city where we are sure to find drains to climb out of.'

Malik looked sceptical. 'What if we don't?'

'Got any better ideas?' Leanne said.

Malik simply stared at Leanne with wide eyes and a blank expression.

'Thought not,' she said after a pause. 'Let's go,' she added before Malik could dwell any further on their fate.

Following the water flow seemed like a logical idea, but Leanne also knew if all the drains flowed in the same direction, they would eventually merge and things might get a little bit tricky. She kept the worry to herself and changed the subject to keep Malik's mind off the rising water level.

'Hey, Malik, what were you thinking coming into contact with that little boy in the tent back there? If he had the pestilence, you could have caught it yourself.'

'I don't know what pestilence is.'

'It's a plague or something I guess. One of those diseases that spreads like crazy, killing thousands of people. Like bird flu.'

'You are just one constant fountain of knowledge, Leanne, a regular prophet of doom. Well, it wasn't pestilence or bird flu,' he said in his defence. 'He probably had a bad cold, poor kid. You saw it for yourself, he was on the mend even before we left.'

'Yeah, but you didn't know that when you touched him. You have to be more careful. There are things here we know nothing about. Who knows what disease he might have had.'

'Enough with the lectures.'

'Just saying, is all.'

'Just keep your fat butt moving.'

'Hey! That's horrible, Malik, you can't say stuff like that to a girl. Haven't you learned anything?'

'You're not a girl, you're a woman.'

'That's even worse.'

'You called me fat head a while back.'

'That's different.'

'Why is it different? You implied I have a fat head, so how is that any different to me implying you have a fat butt?'

'It just is. Anyway, I didn't say you had a fat head. I was saying you were stupid.'

'Oh, so now I'm stupid, and that's not insulting, right?'

'I didn't mean you *are* stupid, I was saying you were *being* stupid.'

'How's that any different?'

'Give it a rest, Malik.'

They made their way in silence for a while, making blind turn after blind turn. At times it seemed impossible to tell in which direction the water flowed, as sometimes it flowed in more than one direction at the same time.

'Have I?' asked Leanne.

'Have you what?'

'Have I got a fat butt?'

'I don't know.'

'Well, you said I did.'

'Okay, yes, you have a fat butt,' Malik said, exasperated.

'Malik!'

'No then, you don't. It looks fine to me.'

'Oh, so you've been looking.'

'Leanne!'

'What about boobs, have you been looking at my boobs?'

'Arrgh! Leanne, shut up. I'm not listening.'

Leanne giggled. 'Well, they did appear out of the blue. It's kind of freaky actually.'

'Not listening! Da da da, la la la.'

'What, you don't like boobs, or you don't like talking about them?'

'Leanne, for the last time, shut up about boobs! It's giving me the willies.'

There followed a long pause before Leanne said, giggling, 'What, green willies?'

'LEANNE!'

The passage narrowed further, and as a result, the rising water flowed even faster. It had reached Leanne's waist now, making progress difficult and causing her to worry about getting out before the tunnel filled completely.

Malik struggled to walk upright in the low tunnel, resorting instead to half walking, half floating on the fast flowing current. He didn't want to say anything to Leanne but found himself constantly fighting panic in the increasingly claustrophobic space. She would probably call him a wimp and tell him to get a grip if she knew.

Leanne kept turning to check on Malik's progress, and from the concerned look on his face, she sensed he was in trouble. She was about to stop and ask how he was doing when a sudden surge of water burst from a side channel, knocking Leanne off her feet and causing her to drop the lantern.

'Malik, the lantern!'

Leanne watched helplessly as the current carried the lamp beyond her grasp. The flame dimmed and flickered before being completely extinguished as the lantern sank below the surface of the water, leaving the tunnel in pitch-black darkness.

A last-ditch stretch threw Leanne off balance, and she stumbled and fell below the surface. Gripped with sudden fear, she struggled to regain control, but the slippery surface beneath her feet gave little purchase. She tried to stand but took a mouthful of water before she could recover. She slipped again and took another desperate gulp. Whether it was the sudden cold plunge or the fact it happened in pitch-black conditions, the result was the same; Leanne found herself fighting for life. She tumbled and slipped again, flailing for a hand or foothold as she battled to reach the surface.

Usually the one to take the unexpected in her stride, this kind of fear was new to Leanne. She surfaced, gasped, and slipped once more on the slimy tunnel floor. Carried by the current so every time she managed to gain her feet, the force of the water pulled her off balance, she couldn't help panic with every failed attempt to stand.

Mercifully, though it seemed like an eternity, Malik grasped her arm and pulled her clear, holding her steady until she could regain her senses. She gasped and coughed until at last she could stand on her own two feet without Malik's support.

'Thank you, Malik,' she said, trembling. 'I'm so sorry...I lost the lantern. I'm so sorry, Malik,' she said breathlessly.

'It's okay, you couldn't help it.'

'No, it's not okay, Malik. Without it, we can't possibly find our way out.'

'I can see,' he said.

'What do you mean you can see?'

'I mean I can see clearly. I can see everything as though I'm wearing night vision goggles. It must be a Green thing,' he said. 'When the light went out, the vision came on like someone flicked a switch. Take hold of my hand,' he said.

Leanne took hold in the dark and they moved slowly forward, following the flow once more and the prospect of an exit. Leanne's stumble had taken Malik's mind off his fear. Now with renewed confidence, he was the one charged with guiding them to safety.

Above, in a tower upon the city wall, Manchuie, who was in charge of city water, looked high into the mountains. The deluge had swollen every watercourse, turning streams into torrents and thundering waterfalls. He studied the sky and decided there could be no end in sight. The reservoirs were full to overflowing, and there was a danger of the main dam bursting under the weight of too much water. He signalled the order to open the spillway and release the excess volume into the stormwater drainage system where it would be carried out to sea.

CHAPTER 15

Seeing is believing

Leanne grasped Malik's hand tight, growing in confidence with every step as she realised she could trust Malik's ability to see in the dark. She now knew what it must feel like to be blind, the importance of trust and what it must be like to totally rely on someone else.

'So you think it's a Green thing,' Leanne said.

'What?'

'Seeing in the dark. You said it's a Green thing.'

'Must be I suppose.'

'Hey, Malik, you asked what the point of you being here was. Maybe this is the reason. Without you and your night-time vision, I wouldn't have had a chance. Game over. You saved my life, and maybe being a Green was the only way to do it.'

'Maybe,' he said, somehow doubting he had been brought halfway across the Megaverse simply to see in the dark. Wasn't that what they had carrots for? 'The water is getting deeper,' he said.

Leanne could hear the fear returning to Malik's voice.

'Malik,' she said.

'What?'

'Talk to me.'

'About what?'

'Anything. About you, tell me more about you.'

'Like what?'

Leanne sighed. 'What do you want to do when you leave school?'

'I don't know, maybe I'll never leave school, held back every term. I'm stupid, remember?'

'I've seen your grades, Malik, you are anything but stupid. You must have some idea what you want to do?'

Malik thought about it. 'Something with computers I guess. I'm pretty good with computers. My parents run a small chain of fruit and veg stores, and I created the software for their management system. Inventory and all that stuff.'

'Wow! That takes brains. See, you're not so stupid, are you?'

'What do you want?'

'What do you mean?'

'I mean, what do you want? You're being nice to me. But it sounds patronising.'

Leanne snickered to herself, gripping Malik's hand tighter as she stumbled slightly. What she wanted was to keep his mind off the narrowing tunnel and rising water.

'I don't want anything, Malik, I'm just interested.' Silence followed between them, the only sound coming from the running water. 'So you're going to write software,' she continued after a while.

'Games. My main interest would be writing games. I've written three already, though they weren't great. Dad took them into one of the big software companies. They said I could have a future if I applied myself. They said to come back after I finish school.'

'That's great, Malik.'

'If we ever get out of here and—' Malik stopped mid-sentence. 'Listen,' he whispered.

'I can't hear anything.'

'That noise, you don't hear it?'

Leanne strained to listen. 'I don't h...Oh, wait. Like a growing rumble?'

'Yeah, like a growing...'

'It sounds like a train, like we're standing in a subway station and a train is approaching.'

They could imagine it. The distant hum when you first sense your train is coming, and then a louder rumble follows; the air in the station starts to stir as the train pushes air through the tunnel before it, and you know any second it will emerge into sight. Except, this was not a train station, and there were no trains.

'What can it be?' Malik asked.

Hairs stood on Leanne's neck, and she felt a chill of dread running over her skin, turning it to goose flesh; she knew what was about to happen.

'Oh my gosh, Malik, we're in big trouble.'

'What,' he said, 'in bigger trouble than we already are?'

The rumble became thunderous.

'Much bigger,' she shouted. 'Take a deep breath, Malik, NOW!'

Though there were no such things as trains in the medieval world of Trinity, the wall of water that hit Malik and Leanne sure felt like one. Bam! It slammed into them, an explosive blast of water travelling at speed, carrying them off their feet and along with the raging current. Instantly, their world had transformed into a terrifying battle for life.

Thanks to Leanne's quick thinking, both she and Malik had taken a deep breath of air moments before the surge struck. But the volume of water released from the dam raged through the tunnel and gave them little chance to replenish their burning lungs.

They tumbled through the torrent. Tossed and turned in the confusing rush, they were helpless, disorientated, lost. Malik's night vision gave him no advantage in the foaming tsunami. Leanne maintained her grip on Malik's hand, desperately clinging to her lifeline. Propelled like fast-moving submarines, it was all they could do not to open their mouths and scream for help.

A tight turn and the tunnel narrowed again, causing Malik to bind against the tunnel walls, slowing his passage along with the flow and increasing the pressure now building behind them. They had left the mainline and found themselves being swept through the confines of a smaller tributary. A further narrowing of the tunnel brought with it a whole new danger; Malik was becoming a plug in the pipeline.

This can't be happening. I'm going to get stuck and drown in this dismal tunnel, Malik thought.

Too big for the smaller tunnel, the enormous pressure of water wedged Malik like a cork, and his bulky body now blocked off most of the water. With his head clear, it allowed him to breathe and get an unobstructed view down the line, but being behind him, Leanne had no such luck. He could feel her rising panic as she punched and clawed desperately at his back. Wedged in the tunnel, he was the equivalent to a human bung in a high-pressure hose. Fountain sprays of water burst through the narrow gaps between him and the tunnel wall like leaky plumbing. The tunnel walls were slimy, and Malik slipped forward under the pressure. He slid three feet and stopped, then another foot and stopped again, all the while being slowly squeezed ever tighter against the tunnel walls with one arm stretched before him like a swimmer, the other trailing behind so he could keep his hold on Leanne's hand. She shook him off, and he sensed her hopeless struggle for oxygen. Immersed entirely, Leanne was in the final stages of her fight to survive.

Malik noticed an open shaft in the tunnel roof three feet ahead, tantalisingly close, yet painfully out of reach. The shaft had a steel ladder, the rungs of which came just beyond his grasp. Must be an inspection shaft, Malik thought. If only he could grab the last step. But he had come to a virtual stand-still now, wedged even tighter. Precious seconds ticked by, and Leanne was slowly losing her fight. Malik wriggled and squirmed, inching forward before stopping just short of the shaft opening.

I can't go any further. We're going to die here and rot until some-one sends a plumber to clean the drains. Boy, are they going to get a surprise. 'Help!' he screamed.

The futile call for help went unanswered. Six inches more would be enough for him to reach the ladder and pull himself into the shaft. Malik exhaled, pushing the air from his lungs in the hope he would shrink. His body slipped against the walls, but only another inch.

Malik stretched with all his might and reached for the lad-der, gripped the bottom rung and pulled, edging his upper body into the shaft. In his left hand, he still grasped Leanne's arm; she felt limp. He pulled on the ladder and felt the pressure easing him into the shaft; the plan was working. *Must hurry.*

Without warning, and with the force of an exploding hydrant, the pressure released and sent Malik and Leanne shooting upwards through the shaft like launching rockets. They emerged inside a cavernous chamber like two corks popped from the same champagne bottle and landed on the stone floor with a splat, coughing, spluttering, and gasping for air. In the tunnel below, stormwater rumbled and roared, unobstructed and now on its way to the sea. They lay in silence for nearly a minute.

'I...I don't think...I don't think I will ever look at a spa bath in the same way ever again,' Leanne said, coughing up water and recovering her breath.

'That would make a great water ride at the theme park,' Malik said, panting.

'Keep it,' she laughed. 'I'll settle for the slippery dip anytime.'

The chamber they now found themselves in had high walls and vaulted ceilings of bricks and stone. Torches burned on the wall, lighting the immediate area and giving them a sense of the vast cavern. The chamber smelt damp and musty, like something rotten had filled the air with a stench unfamiliar to either of them. They picked themselves off the floor.

'Someone has been here and left torches burning,' Malik said.

'If they find us, we could get into trouble,' Leanne said.

Malik replied. 'I don't think we could get into any more trouble.'

Malik took a torch from its holder on the wall and began to explore their new surroundings with Leanne following closely behind. Malik tried the handle of a wooden door and found it to be locked from the outside. Massive steel hinges and rustic locks indicated an impenetrable barrier unless one had a key. Leanne tapped on the door, but the wood appeared so thick and heavy it hardly made a sound.

'What is this place?' Malik asked.

Leanne took a second torch from the wall and made her way deeper into the chamber. Arched columns supported a high domed roof, and their footsteps echoed off the surfaces. Wooden racks stood in alcoves along the outer walls that held objects not quite identifiable, so she moved closer for a better look.

Leanne reacted with a start. 'Oh my gosh!' she exclaimed. 'They're bones.'

On closer inspection, the racks revealed lines and lines of skulls and bones stacked a hundred deep. Years of dust and grime covered the surface of these ancient remains, a gruesome collection of dismembered corpses.

'I think it's a catacomb, a burial chamber,' she said. 'It's ghoulish.'

They made their way between the banks of racking, all of which carried the same old remains. Skulls with unseeing eyes seemed to follow their progress, and a snake slithered out of one, startling Malik before disappearing into another.

They came to a new vault, which was grander and more elaborate than the previous one. Instead of hundreds of skeletons, the racks carried bones arranged in individual sets and labelled in ancient script.

'What does it say?' asked Malik.

'I'm not sure, but I think these are kings and queens.'

'Look.' Malik waved his torch and pointed to a newly prepared vault. Workmen's tools lay scattered on the floor. 'Whoever left these torches burning must have been working here. It looks as though they're expecting an addition to the collection.'

Leanne's torch flickered and died. 'Malik, pass me another torch, please.' Malik didn't answer. He had wandered off, deeper into the dark and cavernous chamber. The faint glow from his torch flickered in the distance. 'Malik?' Still Malik didn't answer. Leanne made her way to join him, but without a torch now, she moved with caution in the dark. Something brushed the back of her neck. 'Malik?' She felt it again. 'Quit it, Malik, I know it's you.' Still no answer. The distant light from Malik's torch had faded almost to nothing. 'Come on, Malik, stop fooling around.' Leanne's heart began to race. If Malik was trying to scare her, he was doing a pretty good job of it. 'Malik!'

The vault brightened as Malik rounded the corner with two torches in hand. He passed one to Leanne. 'What's the matter?'

Leanne felt silly for being afraid. 'Nothing, I just felt something on my neck is all.'

'Spider webs,' Malik suggested. 'Anyway, come and look. I found another shaft, and it may lead us out of here.'

Malik led Leanne to a spot on the vault floor and held his light over a new shaft. A dry passage ran eight feet below.

'How do we know where it goes?' asked Leanne.

'We don't. But I don't see any other options unless we wait for whoever was here to come back and find us. Which, judging by the age of these bones, could be long after we become part of the collection.'

'I don't know, Malik, I've had my fill of tunnels and passages. Maybe we should wait. Oh dear, what is that stink?'

'Wasn't me,' Malik replied.

'Do you smell it?'

'Yeah, smells like rotten meat. So what do you think, shall we go for it and try the shaft?'

'Let's recheck the perimeter of the chamber first. If there's no other way, we'll take the shaft.'

Leanne went left, Malik right, and they checked the outside walls for an exit. On returning to the main chamber, they agreed the shaft was their only option.

'There's that stink again,' Leanne said, holding her nose.

'No, that was me that time,' Malik said laughing.

Leanne punched Malik in the arm. 'Of all the people to get stuck with. You're so gross, Malik.' She was about to say more when she heard a noise from the far end of the chamber. 'Shush. There's someone down here.'

'I heard it too,' said Malik.

They stood in silence, listening to the shuffling sounds of feet across the stone floor. Hearts began to race again, a feeling that was becoming all too common. Due to the enormous size of the chamber, torchlight could only brighten the immediate area. Leanne peered through the shadows as the strange sounds became louder.

Leanne whispered, 'That smell is getting stronger and don't tell me it's you, Malik.'

'Definitely not me,' he said. Malik doused his torch; he could see better without it. 'There's movement behind the racks and a luminous glow.'

As he spoke, the culprit, a rat-like creature as big as a medium size dog, emerged from behind a wall of bones. Glowing a phosphorous blue, the animal looked unreal, almost like a computer-generated hologram. Hairless and with skin covering its eyes, the blind creature sniffed the air and dripped sticky saliva trails behind it like strings of glue. A second animal appeared from the right-hand rack, followed by a third and a fourth. Malik backed up next to Leanne and relit his torch for protection.

'What in the Megaverse are these foul, stinking things?' he said.

'They are cadaverines,' Leanne answered with new-found authority. 'Creatures of the underworld that dispose of rotting flesh. They are scavengers by nature, but vicious pack hunters when food is scarce. Once bitten by a cadaverine, the victim is infected by toxic bacteria from their saliva, and death is assured once the bacteria enter the bloodstream.'

'Oh, thank you for your reassuring overview, Leanne, upbeat as always. How do you know this?'

'It just came to me like everything else here. These animals once lived in remote parts of the Caprinese provinces, where it's said they lived off the remains of Leemons for centuries before disappearing suddenly. Most think of them as mythical creatures, stories to tell around a campfire.'

'I've got news for you, Leanne, they don't look very mythical to me.'

'Nor me. Use your torch to keep them at bay. I think it's time for us to exit via the shaft.'

Cautiously, they made their way back to the shaft while circling each other with the flame of their torches low down to the ground, making sure they covered the blind side. The cadaverines followed, sniffing at the air, baring their teeth and dripping big gobs of saliva onto the ground. Malik stepped in one and felt the sticky pull on the soles of his shoes.

'Ugh, that stuff is everywhere,' he said.

Seven or eight animals joined the pack, stalking the duo as they made their way towards the open shaft. One animal lunged, and Malik stabbed it in the face with his burning torch, sending it scurrying away with a squeal. The others moved in closer, keeping just enough distance between them and the flames. Leanne and Malik kept their torches moving, stabbing at their rodent faces at the slightest sign of attack. More creatures circled, perhaps fifteen or twenty, all focused on the prospect of fresh meat. They took turns in lunging and snapping, and all the while, Leanne and Malik held them away with fire.

The shaft had an eight-foot drop to the passage below. Malik figured he could hold the animals off while Leanne took the plunge. He would follow once she was clear. The plan had one big problem, however; what was to stop the cadaverines from following?

'Leanne, we need your brilliant powers of reason again. How do we stop them following us down the shaft?'

'How do we know there's not more of them down there?' Leanne answered.

'We don't, but we don't have a choice. Come on, Leanne, how do we stop them following?'

Malik swung his torch and caught a charging animal, sending a shower of sparks into the air. The cadaverine shrieked in pain and retreated.

'I've got nothing,' Leanne answered.

'Think, Leanne!'

'I am thinking. You think!'

'Okay, okay.'

Malik noted that instead of wood, the old timber racks had sack-cloth hammocks for shelves stacked with bones. Tinder-dry with age, these frames of timber, cloth, and old bones would burn quickly. Upturned over the shaft entrance and left burning, they might create a barrier to keep the predators at bay.

Malik explained his plan. 'We set the racks alight, you jump down the shaft and I'll follow, pulling the burning racks on top of me as I leap.'

'What if you set yourself on fire?'

'Then you're on your own,' Malik said.

Leanne didn't have a better plan. As she prepared to jump, Malik held his torch to the nearest rack and watched the flames take hold, turning the racking and its contents into an instant raging inferno. But before Leanne could take the plunge, the cadaverines attacked in numbers, coming at them from all sides at once. Leanne and Malik thrashed out with torches as the animals ignored the flames and sensed the kill. The racking burned fiercely, catching hold on one bank after the next, roaring up to the vaulted ceiling and lighting the entire chamber in a raging orange glow. Leanne screamed as Malik smashed his torch into a bloodthirsty animal, sending it tumbling while another jumped in to take its place.

'NOW!'

Leanne jumped, landing on her feet in the passage below. Malik tossed his torch down after her, grasped the blazing racks and pulled. Burning bones tumbled as he plummeted through the shaft in a shower of flaming debris. The shelves crashed down behind him, covering the opening and consuming the rodents in flames. Cadaverines could be heard squealing as they burned in the inferno.

Malik landed heavily, followed by an avalanche of burning bones and wood. He cried out in pain, twisting his ankle on landing.

'We need to move quickly before the fire dies and they have time to regroup,' Malik said, hobbling to his feet.

Malik snatched up the burning torch, held it high and turned to Leanne. Sat with her back propped against the passage wall, she wasn't making any effort to move and had the strangest look on her face.

'What?' he said.

Leanne's eyes filled with tears and she started to tremble. 'I've been bitten,' she said.

CHAPTER 16

Majestic Mariana

E ven though he were seeing Mariana for the very first time, Alex found the sight of the magnificent city somehow reassuring and familiar. The monsoonal winter rain had finally cleared, leaving Mariana to shimmer under perfect blue skies. Domed roofs glistened in a multitude of colours, the palace's gold dome standing out amongst the others as it marked the kingdom's centre of power. Sparkling like a yellow diamond, the Great Pyramid rose majestically to the sky, reflecting the morning sun and making it impossible to stare at the scene for more than a moment without going blind. Alex had first glimpsed the pyramid hundreds of miles from port. Along with the flat topped lighthouse, he had watched these landmarks drawing nearer over a period of hours. Now he stood in awe of their full grandeur and unique construction.

Drums thundered from minaret towers to announce the Klaw's arrival in port. Alex watched as the ship's sails were furled, ropes and lines stowed, and the Klaw glided to anchor alongside the dock to the coordinated shouts of a scurrying crew. Mariana harbour was a hive of activity. Waiting dockworkers stood ready to unload cargo, make repairs, and resupply the ship with provisions for its next voyage. Alex stood on the foredeck and wondered if the voyage just finished might have been his first and his last. For all his adventures so far, the details of his quest remained a mystery. But somewhere in his mind, he knew Mariana was where the story would unfold and the future would be made clear.

'Ship secured, Captain.'

'Thank you, Ms Stark. Where are Callum and Olo?'

'Below decks, sir. But they've acted very strangely since we came into Mariana waters.'

'Can you blame them? I think it would be wise for them to remain hidden until we sail again. Put them in my quarters and inform the crew to tell no one of their whereabouts. Ms Stark, there's danger in freeing slaves, and I take full responsibility. If you believe you must turn me in to protect yourself and the crew, I would understand. I only ask that Callum and Olo are allowed time to escape.'

Stark smiled. 'There's not a man or woman in this crew that wouldn't stand by you, Captain. We've taken those Greens into our hearts, so have no fear, we're with you all the way. We'll be ready to sail again just as soon as you say the word.'

Alex thanked the first officer and turned his attention to the harbour. A vast forest of masts swayed gently on the swell, making the scene deceptively peaceful. Never had he seen so many warships gathered in one place. Even modern naval fleets would struggle to compare with the might of the Mariana navy. On closer inspection, each vessel buzzed with excited activity as crews prepared for duty and war. Startled by its presence in port, Alex cast his eyes over a three-mast Man O' War berthed at the far end of the quay. Its black masts and sails a familiar sight to the Klaw and her crew.

'Since when does Mariana open its ports to pirates and brigands, Ms Stark?'

'I noticed it too, Captain. There's no name on her bow anymore, but it's the Angra as sure as night follows day.'

'Keep a close eye on her. I'm going ashore. Have the ship ready to cast off at a moment's notice. We'll go without repairs if we have to.'

Making his way through busy streets, Alex frequently stopped to take in the sights and sounds of the bustling market stalls lining the route. Animals crowed, quacked, brayed, and mooed, and voices did battle to be heard over the other.

Vendors plied their wares, competing to attract buyers by shouting offers of discounts and tempting visitors with free samples of food. Customers ranged from the wealthy to the poor. Servants accompanied well-to-do citizens who loaded them up with all manner of purchases. Their masters dressed in colourful, flamboyant robes with elaborate jewellery of gold and silver gave little thought to how much their servants could reasonably carry. They bargained and haggled with merchants over exotic items of food, many of which Alex had never seen before. Live animals were traded. Snakes being high in demand; snake sellers were by far the busiest stalls in the market. The writhing, wriggling mass of reptiles caused a stir when some escaped in a bid to slither to freedom while laughing children chased with excitement and the desperate stall holder followed. Other live animals included birds of great variety and colour, monkey creatures with fish-like heads, snapping turtles with gold coloured shells, and stick insects, two feet in length and with eyes the size of apples.

'Av a taste, sir,' said a vendor, offering an exotic fruit to Alex.

'Try mine,' said another, who looked exactly like Julien Taylor from school soccer. Alex declined with a friendly smile after he saw no recognition on the man's face. He wasn't the first to appear familiar.

'Good to see you back, Captain,' said a trim young woman at a clothes stall. 'I've got them red pantaloons you wanted.'

Alex flushed. 'I'll get them next time,' he said, moving on. *Red pantaloons, I'm sure they'd go down well at Morton Bay High. I'd be the coolest kid in school. Not!*

Once past the market quarter, the roads became quieter and Alex found himself driven to his destination by instinct alone. Pausing at a blacksmith's workshop, Alex stepped inside. A large man stood beside a burning forge, pumping an enormous bellows the size of a small family car. Sweat rolled from his forehead as he laboured to bring the coals up to temperature. He stopped as Alex approached.

'Captain, you're back,' he said, wiping his face with his forearm and smudging black soot on his cheeks in the process.

'You're Landor,' Alex said.

The blacksmith quizzically furrowed his eyebrows. 'Last time I checked. The name hasn't changed since we were lads together, Alexander. Months at sea rattled your brain av they? Can't remember your best mate?'

Alex saw the friendship unfold in his newly formed memories as he grinned and hugged Landor.

'How could I forget a big lug like you,' he said as if he'd been joking. 'It's good to see you, my friend.'

'Tell me about your voyage,' Landor said.

'Later. How is the sword coming along?'

Landor beamed and held up a hand, telling Alex to wait where he was as he disappeared into the back of the workshop. He returned a short time later, proudly carrying Alexander's new sword. 'Forged in the finest steel,' he said, presenting the weapon to its owner.

Alex's eyes sparkled with delight. 'It's perfect, Landor.' Alex slid his old sword from the scabbard and replaced it with Landor's newly minted version. 'I'll treasure it,' he said, hugging his friend once again.

After promising to catch up later, Alex left Landor's workshop and made his way down side streets and passageways until he stood before his destination, a small blue building with a yellow front door. Having made his way here as if on autopilot, he now realised this was the place of Alexander Boatman's birth and the home and workplace of his parents. Above the door, a painted sign depicted a ship in full sail and the words: Boatman & Son, Sailmaker.

Alex paused. His experiences since leaving Earth had unfolded like the pages of a book, and he didn't know what to expect until the next page had turned. With each new page, however, he realised the characters and stories were so familiar to him; it was almost as though he had read the book before. Behind the low front door, Alexander Boatman's parents had lived and worked while raising their son from birth to manhood. So far, he had no picture of them in his mind and could not see their faces or remember his childhood. But he knew that would change the minute he walked through the door. *What will she be like?*

'It's not what you imagine, Alex. I don't want you to be disappointed.'

Startled by the voice, Alex turned to find Nim standing nearby. 'Nim,' he said, surprised and relieved at her appearance. 'Disappointed?'

'My dear Alex, your desire to meet your mother is understandable. That day will come, but not today. Behind the door, you will find Captain Boatman's mother, not yours.'

'I just thought maybe...'

'I'm sorry.' Nim saw Alex's disappointment. 'Every living person is born a billion times over. Each time, their life begins anew, sometimes in the same world, sometimes in a new world or a different dimension. When re-born, you will almost certainly be born to new parents and bear no resemblance to your previous self. For you to have the same physical appearance as Alexander Boatman is quite coincidental. Your Trinity parents, John and Ida Boatman, bear no resemblance to your Earth family, and Ida Boatman is not your missing mother.'

'I understand. I didn't know what to expect and thought maybe they would look like... Anyway, it doesn't matter.'

Nim smiled sympathetically. 'Did you retrieve the relic?'

'Yes, I have it here,' he said, pointing to a shoulder bag.

'You've done well, Alex. But there is still much to accomplish. It's vital the relic is protected, for it must not fall into the wrong hands.'

'I understand,' he replied.

'Alexander's parents can help you achieve your goals. You can trust his father with your life.'

'What if they realise I'm not the real Alexander? I don't know what they will expect of me. Being so close to their son, won't they see I'm an imposter?'

'The moment you walk through the door, they will be as familiar to you as you to them. Just follow your instincts, and the rest will take care of itself.'

'All this secrecy is driving me nuts, Nim. Why can't you just tell me exactly what I have to do? Tell me what will happen next so I can be prepared.'

'Because I don't know, Alex. I heard you thinking this adventure is like reading a book. How true. Unfortunately, we are all reading the same book, and I have no better idea of what lies on the next page than you.'

Reluctantly, Alex accepted he would have to find out the hard way. 'Any word of the others?'

'We picked up a faint trace, but it was not clear. It might have been Leanne somewhere under the city, but the power of the Great Pyramid is blocking any communication. We will keep trying. I must go now. Stay true to the quest and have faith, Alex.'

Nim did her disappearing trick before Alex could ask any more questions. He worried about Leanne and Malik and hoped they were now safe within the city walls.

Inside the sailmaker's cottage, Alex greeted his new mother and father in the way most people do after a long journey. They hugged and kissed and made a fuss of his arrival as they would usually do on his return home. As Nim had promised, they were familiar to Alex in every way, just like he had known them all his life. Ida Boatman was a short, stout woman with homely features and a ruddy red complexion. She wore a cotton bonnet on a head of silver-grey hair, a navy blue dress, and a white apron bearing signs of cooking and other household chores. She busied around her son like every doting mother does, making him sit while she prepared his food and drink, excited to have him home from the sea once more. She constantly babbled about things that had happened while he had been away, pausing only to breathe between stories. Alex ate his meal and listened dutifully before excusing himself and seeking out his father in the workshop next door.

Adjoining the kitchen, a sailmaker's workshop housed everything needed to make and repair ships' sails. John Boatman had taken over the trade from his father and his father before him. His great-great-grandfather had been a famous boat builder. John had hoped Alexander would follow in the family trade of sail making but soon realised his son had other ambitions. As a teenager, Alexander had begun an apprenticeship with his father and learned to make patterns and sew sails. But their close contact with ship owners and naval captains, and hearing their stories of adventure, had eventually turned

Alex's head to the sea. John had accepted his son's choice of career, knowing whatever he set his hands to, he would excel in the Boatman tradition.

John could not be more proud of his son who had received his first command at just thirty-one years of age. With swash-buckling style, Alexander had gained the attention of the queen. His daring adventures at sea and the treasures he secured for her realm were a constant delight for the monarch. Now a great favourite of the queen, she liked to sit and listen to his stories of far-off lands, and much to the irritation of several high-ranking members of government, often sought his private opinion on matters of state.

Alexander, in turn, was proud of his father and had the utmost respect and admiration for the dedicated family man. As well as a sailmaker, John Boatman was an inventor. He saw new ideas in everything he touched and had visions of a world full of technology and learning. Alex watched John working, his thick fingers manipulating the fabric of a new sail with the skill of a master craftsman and knew his mind would be concocting some new invention as he worked.

'How did the Black Spider sails perform?' John asked, looking through thick glasses that he had invented to help him see.

'They were everything you said they would be and more, Father. Without them, I think we would all have been drowned at sea.'

John Boatman paused, caught between his pleasure at the successful trial of his new sail design, and the stomach-turning knowledge of his son's dangerous occupation. 'I'm glad they brought you home safely,' he said, going back to work on the stitch. 'I have already begun designs using Red Spider silk, even lighter and stronger, a hundred times finer.'

Alex wandered around the workshop, picking up items and studying them as though seeing them for the first time, yet recognising his father's handiwork in every new piece he admired. In his mind's eye, he saw visions of his life as Alexander Boatman. Childhood memories flooded his mind, at play around his father's feet, watching as John toiled into the night to make a living, following John's instructions while whittling wooden ships; these memories were as real to him now as his own.

John routinely created working drawings in an attempt to develop new ideas. Recently drawn on parchment paper, Alex turned over several pages of these sketches and smiled when he saw his father's latest inventions. The illustrations reminded him of those he had seen on the internet, drawn by Leonardo da Vinci. Wing-like structures had all the details necessary to build prototype flying machines. Alex knew they lacked the science needed to take them to the next step and for them to succeed, but he found himself intrigued by the possibilities in John's ideas.

Alex's interest in flight stemmed from his experience in paragliding. Back on Earth, his father had taken him up on a tandem flight when he was just ten years old, and he had been hooked ever since. He took his first solo flight as soon as he was heavy enough at fourteen years of age. It was the only real sport he enjoyed and one he could share with his dad. With his father's guidance, Alex had become quite an expert flier.

'You've been working on your ideas for flight again, Father,' he said.

John put down his work and came across to look over Alex's shoulder. 'What do you think?'

'I think you are on the right track. But let me show you something,' said Alex.

Alex took up a quill and dipped it in ink. He sketched a profile of an aeroplane wing for John with some written details before explaining his drawing.

'With this wing design, you decrease the air pressure on the upper curve and increase it on the underside, speeding up the passage of air at the trailing edge giving you the lift you need for the wing to fly.'

John stood with his eyebrows raised and his jaw dropped open in amazement. 'Why of course,' he said as the realisation hit home. 'All we need is forward thrust. I see it all now. Alexander, that's brilliant!'

'It's the basic principle of how aeroplanes work,' said Alex.

'Aeroplanes?'

Alex hesitated, realising what he had said without thinking. Eventually, he answered with a vague explanation and said, 'Oh, it's just a name I thought up for your flying machines.'

John thought about it for a moment. 'Yes,' he said, delighted with the suggestion. 'Airplanus! I will call my invention an airplanus.'

Together they studied the drawings, making alterations and calculations based on Alex's knowledge of physics and his experience as a paraglider. They discussed various forms of flight. As a sailmaker, John's enthusiastic approach came from his vast knowledge of sails. He explained his vision for a hot air balloon and a parachute. Alex suggested the necessary changes to the design and before he could stop himself, he had helped John with the finishing touches needed to make his designs a reality.

'We can call this design a paraglider,' Alex said. 'Made from Black Spider silk, it would be the strongest and lightest design ever made. Strong enough to carry two people or more.'

John laughed. 'Yes, my son, it would be the strongest ever made, because there has never been a paraglider ever made.'

'Of course,' Alex agreed with a chuckle. 'Yours will be the first. Build one, and we can test it together from the mountaintop.'

John nodded, excitement evident in his grinning face as he studied his plans. Alex noticed a light in the older man's eyes, telling of his passion and visions for the future. It would not be long, he thought, until John had built his flying contraptions and in doing so, possibly change his world forever in the process. Feeling good about his contribution, Alex returned his focus to the mission and the coming war.

'The fleet is preparing for war, Father. I have never seen such readiness to fight.'

'Yes, it is true,' John said sadly. 'I spoke with Admiral Trask only yesterday when we discussed my designs for his new sails. He tells me a great armada of Caprinese warships have been sighted off the Bally coast. All foreigners have been expelled from Mariana or imprisoned, and the Greens...' John shook his head in despair. 'There is talk of extermination. Every Green has been rounded up and placed in detention camps throughout the city. The queen is taking all her counsel from Drabek the Black Lord, and he holds great power over her decisions. Princess Li is gravely ill, and Drabek has placed the blame squarely on the Caprinese. He is a dark soul, Alexander, a very dangerous man.'

Ida Boatman interrupted. 'There's a lad at the door,' she said, wiping her hands on her apron. 'Says he needs to see you urgently, Alexander.'

Little Jim stood anxiously at the doorstep. When Alex appeared, he wasted no time in getting to the point of his urgent errand.

'It's the Queen's Special Guard, Captain. They're on the ship demanding to search her. Ms Stark is trying to hold them off, but they are armed and ready to use force if needed. The officer said they were acting on Lord Drabek's orders.'

CHAPTER 17

End of the line

S tand up,' Malik said, trying hard to remain calm. 'If we move quickly, we can get you to a doctor before the poison spreads.'

Leanne slumped against the wall, a picture of despair. 'You don't understand, Malik...it's over for me. There is no cure for a cadaverine bite. I've got no chance of surviving.' Tears ran in rivulets down her distraught face, making her cheeks glisten in the torchlight.

A flaming skull dropped through the shaft, followed by a burning cadaverine. The creature writhed and rolled in agony, squealing like a pig until it died in a smouldering, stinking heap before them. Leanne stared at the charred carcass, a mixture of bitterness and regret in her defeated expression. The fire raged in the catacomb above, spreading through the vaults and causing more racks to take hold. Cadaverines caught in the blaze met their fiery end with terrifying screams, and it sounded as though hell itself were burning above them.

'We have to go,' Malik said, as another burning creature fell through the shaft.

The passage was a dry and dusty access tunnel, not part of the drainage system. Though still too low for Malik to walk without bending, it was wide and did not have the same claustrophobic conditions. They had brought two flaming torches from the vault, the light of which carried a long way down the passage. Malik saw no signs of danger.

'Walking will only send the poison quicker through my bloodstream, Malik. You have to go on without me.'

'I'm not leaving you,' Malik said firmly. But he knew Leanne was right about the poison. He also knew that without treatment she would die anyway. *Not much of a choice.* 'I'm not leaving you,' he repeated.

'What are you going to do, die here with me? Get out, Malik, the cadaverine has killed me. I'm as good as dead.'

'You don't know that. You don't actually know anything about these animals, you're just going by some stupid old wife's tale. It's the old *Leanne knows everything* routine again. How can you be sure these animals are deadly? Where did you get your facts? It's not like you can look them up on the internet. For all we know, this bite on your leg could be nothing more than a nip from a big blind mouse.'

'A nip from a mouse? I've never seen mice the size of dogs before, Malik.'

'And another thing. I've got news for you. Leanne doesn't know everything. You said yourself they were believed to be mythical creatures. There are no facts about myths, that's the whole point!' Leanne said nothing. 'Facts! Unless we have facts and until we know otherwise, we get moving and get you some help. I'll bet they have natural antibiotics or old fashioned cures for things like this. There'll be some miracle herb or something to cure every ailment known to man.'

'I know you're trying to help, but—'

'I'm not taking no for an answer,' said Malik.

He held out a hand for Leanne to take hold. She paused a long moment before taking it and allowing Malik to help her to her feet. The bite had penetrated her skin just above the calf. In the torchlight, it looked dark and wet. She felt pain in the form of a dull throb, which seemed to be already spreading up her leg. Leanne turned to Malik.

'What about you? Your leg is hurt, did you get bitten too?'

'No, I just twisted my ankle. Let's get going,' Malik said, trying his best to look strong and confident, even though he felt terrified for Leanne.

To anyone watching, they would have a made a sorry sight. Hobbling side by side, the pair appeared to have matching disabilities. But with only a few yards covered, it soon became clear Leanne's fears might be justified. Sweating profusely, she had turned a ghostly white, and her infected leg trailed in the dirt as she painfully dragged herself forward.

'Here,' Malik said. 'Drop your torch, put your arm around my shoulder and let me take the weight.'

Leanne gave an ironic laugh. 'You can hardly take your own weight, Malik. There's no point in us both struggling. I told you before, I'm done for.'

'Put your arm around me and stop whining. You're starting to sound like me,' he said.

Leanne accepted Malik's support, leaning on his arm and willing herself forward. Progress was slow but steady, putting space between themselves and the cadaverine crypt.

Malik checked Leanne's condition regularly and observed a rapid deterioration. Her eyes rolled and she appeared to be struggling for breath. He needed to keep her talking so she would not pass out.

'Hey Leanne, you're always on that phone of yours. It's a good thing you didn't have it in the flooded tunnel. It would have been ruined.' Leanne did not reply. 'What would happen,' he continued, 'if you dropped your phone and your laptop into the water at the same time?'

'I don't know,' Leanne mumbled, barely able to stay conscious.

'They would sync, of course.'

Leanne managed a half smile. 'That's the...That's the worst joke I...ever heard.'

No longer able to walk, Leanne dropped to the ground and Malik slumped beside her.

'Look at me, Leanne. Don't go to sleep.' Leanne opened her eyes. 'Talk to me...tell me about this music you do. The piano, wasn't it?'

Leanne made an effort. 'Yeah, piano. Malik, you don't want to hear this.'

'But I do. How else am I going to make fun of you when we get back to school and I tell everyone you play classical music?'

'Don't you dare.' Leanne huffed and puffed, giving in to Malik's request. 'I started playing when I was two. My parents hired a tutor.' Leanne closed her eyes as Malik helped her to her feet.

'Go on...they got you a tutor?'

'They had this idea I could become a great performer and composer, and I'd be famous. It's an obsession really. Malik, I'm tired.'

'But you were good, right?'

Leanne sighed. 'It was easy at first. I enjoyed it, couldn't wait to play. But it was never enough for my dad.'

They shuffled forward.

'What did he expect?' Malik asked, trying to keep the conversation going.

'More than I could give.' Leanne paused. The effort of speaking was exhausting her. She took a deep breath and continued. 'Practice became a nightmare in the end. He had me practice five, sometimes six hours per day. Before school, after school, every weekend.' Leanne stopped, slumped to the floor once more, and closed her eyes again.

Malik fought against panic. Leanne was sinking fast, and it seemed there was nothing he could do to stop it. If he didn't get help soon...He didn't want to think about the consequences.

'I'm going to pick you up, Leanne, so don't freak out.'

With no response from Leanne, Malik placed an arm under her shoulders, the other under her knees, picked her from the ground, and started walking.

'Okay, Leanne, we're on our way again. So you were saying?'

Leanne's eyelids opened just a crack, and her lips curled into a smile. 'Never thought I'd see the day when you had me in your arms, Malik.'

'Yeah, well don't get too cosy,' he said, trying not to smile.

The effort of carrying Leanne was causing Malik great pain. Under normal conditions, he could carry her weight without difficulty, but being doubled over in a stoop to avoid the passage roof, and with the extra strain on his twisted ankle, Malik was struggling badly.

'Why were your parents so obsessed with wanting you to play?'

'Malik, I'm so frightened.'

'Nonsense, you're the most fearless girl I know. Keep talking. What about your mother, did she want it as much as your dad?'

'My mother...My moth...' Leanne appeared to pass out before she could say more.

Malik checked Leanne's breathing, which was shallow and laboured, and she was hot and clammy to the touch. He knew time was now critical and without help soon, Leanne would die as she had predicted. *Don't you leave me, Leanne.*

Malik carried Leanne onwards, despite being near to collapse himself and the fact the low passage seemed endless. He negotiated a series of steps and was horrified to find the passage stretched on until it disappeared in the distance. *I'll never make it. Where the heck is this taking us?*

'Hey, Leanne, can you hear me. Wake up! We're almost there.' *I wish.*

Leanne mumbled. 'Mal...I...So ti...'

'Okay, I know you can hear me, so I'll do the talking, shall I?'

Leanne did not answer. Malik prayed and trudged bravely onwards.

'You know, you're not the only one with parent problems.' *Keep her awake.* 'When you asked me before about mine, I lied. Well, I didn't lie exactly, I just missed stuff out.' Leanne did not respond. 'Shall I tell you the story?' A grunt. 'Okay, I hear you. Well, what I said about the bomb was true, what I didn't say was it was my father's bomb.' Malik pictured the place of his birth. 'We lived in a small town near the border. Our town had been a disputed territory for centuries, and it changed hands regularly. They told me my father was a passionate man, particularly when it came to his country, his rights and freedoms. He believed fighting and bloodshed was a fair price to pay for his beliefs. He joined a resistance group to fight for repatriation of lands lost long ago. He learned how to fight and build bombs.

'The bomb that destroyed our home was a bomb he had made and had hidden away in the children's bedroom of our house. Smart move eh?' Malik felt the anger at his father grow in him as he told the story. 'It was an accident waiting to happen, and it did. My father was away at the time, and no one knows how his bomb exploded. Perhaps my brother found it and was playing with it, not knowing the dangers. Everything was destroyed in a split second, and my mother, brothers, and sister were killed instantly.

'My foster father is my real dad's brother. It's true they lived next door, and they lost their own children in the blast. Everything I told you about my foster parents was right. They raised me as their own, and I call them Mum and Dad. My birth father disappeared after the explosion, went on the run, and his family disowned him for what he had done.

'I knew none of this until Mum and Dad told me when I turned ten years old. They thought I had a right to know the truth. Maybe it would've better if they hadn't. I started seeing people in a different light...cynical, you'd call it. I guess I've been carrying a big chip on my shoulder ever since. The row I had with my parents was because...' Malik paused to check on Leanne. She was still breathing, barely. 'News came my father had died, murdered by someone in his own organisation. My dad told me the news. He said he had given it a lot of thought and had decided it was time to forgive. He wanted to go back and lay my father to rest. Mum and Dad wanted me to go with them, saying it was time for me too.

'I told my parents I had no intention of forgiving him, and I didn't want to hear any more about him. To me, he'd been dead for a long time. That's where they are now, burying my father and forgiving the unforgivable. When I told you I didn't like Jani, it was because she comes from the same country that gave my father sanctuary. It's where he made his home after killing his family. He married one of them.' Malik looked down at Leanne. 'Are you listening because I'm spilling my guts here? This is like my confession.' Leanne grunted.

Malik struggled up another flight of stairs, taking him above ground level. Another long passage, only this time, daylight filtered in through narrow slits in the passage walls, and through the openings, a vast paved square milling with people came into view. Malik laid Leanne down and called through a gap.

'Help!' No response. 'Help!' Still, no one heard his cries. They were too far away to register his desperate calls. Exhausted and disheartened, he sat next to Leanne and propped her up to be more comfortable against his shoulder.

'I can see the palace square, Leanne. Can you smell the fresh air?'

Leanne was now unresponsive. Malik put his hand on her leg; it felt hot beneath his touch. Black in colour, the wound was swollen and weeping. All colour had now drained from Leanne's face, leaving it a deathly grey, and her eyes looked sunken and dark like the skulls in the catacomb. Her tangled hair dripped with sweat, and she burned with a fever so hot he thought she would melt away before him. Malik held her in his arms and rocked her.

'Please don't die,' he said as tears filled his eyes. 'PLEASE HELP US!' Malik's scream echoed through the empty passage, full of anguish and anger. 'Help us...' he repeated, his voice petering out to a whisper and a sob. This was Malik the boy, frightened and fragile, helpless. He kissed Leanne gently on the forehead, holding her tight and trembling as his tears rolled down and dropped onto her pale face. She was dying, and there seemed nothing he could do to save her.

'I'm sorry I was always so mean to you,' he whispered. 'I'll never be again, I promise. Please don't give up,' he wept.

Malik sat silently, unmoving, staring at Leanne's lifeless body, her last breaths barely passing her lips. Minutes passed.

What are you doing, Malik, feeling sorry for yourself? Get up! Instead of doing something to save her, you're wallowing in self-pity. What do you think she would say to you now if she could? She'd say you were pathetic, that's what she would say. If the tables were turned, Leanne would find a way no matter what it took. Get up and do something!

Malik brushed the tears from his face. 'I'm not giving up, Leanne, and I'm not letting you give up either.'

With one last great effort, he lifted her in his arms and staggered onwards as reserves of energy surged through his body. He covered a lot of ground quickly. He could hear voices now, people in the square getting closer. 'Help!' he cried. 'Help us!'

Malik grimaced, hurrying forward as he sensed an exit. 'Help us!' he screamed again. Ahead he saw a shaft of daylight and at last, a large opening at the end of the passage.

'We've made it, Leanne. Hang in there. Don't give up.'

Malik staggered up one last short flight of steps and emerged through the exit into the open palace square. Blinded by intense sunlight, it took him a moment to adjust his vision. When he did, he came face to face with the sharp end of a spear.

'Hello, fat boy!' said a soldier of the Queen's Special Guard.

CHAPTER 18

Drabek's orders

On arrival at the ship, Alex found a dozen soldiers of the Queen's Guard held at bay by the Klaw's angry sailors. The crew, armed only with belay pins and knives, would be no match for the elite guard who stood ready with cutlasses drawn. Alex gave the order to stand down and placed himself between the guard's senior officer and his crew. He recognised the soldier at once and knew him as a disciplined man who would carry out his orders to the letter. If he encountered resistance from the Klaw and her crew, Alex had no doubt he would command his soldiers to use force.

'What is the meaning of this, Lieutenant Ryan?'

Though the Lieutenant was a determined man who had the backing of Lord Drabek's orders, he also knew the courtesies to offer when faced with a senior officer such as Alexander

Boatman. 'Begging your pardon, Captain, but we have orders to search the ship.'

'Whose outrageous order?'

'Lord Drabek gave the order, Captain. I apologise for any inconvenience, but if you will allow my men to carry out—'

'Drabek?' Alex interrupted. 'Since when does Lord Drabek command the Queen's Special Guard? And under what authority does he see fit to search the queen's vessel?'

Ryan replied confidently. 'Under the queen's own authority, Captain. While you have been away on your voyage, Lord Drabek has been given complete command of the queen's armies, including the special guard and her ships of the fleet. He has total authority as commander in chief.' Ryan fixed his gaze on Alex so the captain would understand there would be no backing down. 'Please, Captain, allow my men to carry out their orders so we may avoid any unpleasantness.'

Alex stepped aside. His crew followed his lead, allowing the soldiers to disperse about the ship. Alex took Stark beyond earshot of the Lieutenant and asked, 'What of Callum and Olo?'

'They had little warning, Captain. Where could they go when the soldiers had the decks? I believe they are still in your cabin.'

Though the Klaw was a sizable ship, she had very few places to hide during a full search of the vessel. Alex took a deep breath and hoped the Greens had hidden successfully.

Drabek's sudden rise to power was a disturbing development. Alexander Boatman had never personally met the little-known lord, who up until now, had remained an obscure lower order member of the assembly of the parliament. How he had come to gain such power and trust in such a short space of time was a mystery. Alex intended to find out more from the queen.

Stark watched as soldiers worked their way to the lower decks. 'What will we do if they discover the Greens?' she asked Alex. 'We can't allow them to be taken without a fight.'

Alex agreed. 'Have your crew ready, Ms Stark. If they find our friends, these soldiers can't leave the ship alive. It will be all our heads if they are allowed to take the news of the Greens back to Drabek. If the time comes, we must haul anchor and make a run for it.'

Alex could not believe the words coming from his very own lips. Talk of killing these soldiers flew in the face of everything his father taught him. A chill of dread ran through his flesh, and he hoped he would never have to make such a decision.

'Pray for a miracle, Ms Stark, pray for a miracle.'

Lieutenant Ryan returned to Alex's side and waited with the captain while his men did a methodical search. Eventually, after a nervous wait, a soldier appeared from below decks and reported to Ryan.

'Nothing, sir. We have searched everywhere except the captain's quarters, which are locked and guarded.'

Ryan looked at Alex and said with a smile, 'Captain, if you would be so kind.'

Ms Stark sprang forward before Alex could respond. 'No one enters the captain's quarters. It would be an outrageous slur on the captain's honour.'

Alex intervened. 'Thank you, Ms Stark, but we have nothing to hide from the lieutenant. Come, I will escort you personally if you wish to search my private quarters.' Alex was bluffing in the hope the officer would dismiss the idea.

Ryan paused, thinking about the invitation and perhaps wondering if he should consider the search complete and allow the captain to preserve his dignity in front of his crew. He studied Alex as though looking for signs of deception. Eventually, he said, 'Thank you, Captain, please lead the way.'

The short walk to the captain's quarters proved to be an anxious one. Soldiers stood eye to eye with crew members in a tense standoff while Alex and Ryan made their way aft. Stark had previously warned the crew they must be ready to fight; she only needed the order from the captain before giving the signal. Alex turned the key in the lock, opened the door, and with his heart racing and his hand on his dagger, he stood aside for Ryan to enter.

'You maintain a simple cabin, Captain,' said Ryan, browsing the room slowly. Noting the charts on the table with interest, he paused to look them over. 'Your voyage took you far from port. I wonder that you returned with such little cargo to show for your effort.'

'That's the nature of the sea, Lieutenant. On voyages such as ours, there is a great deal of luck.' Alex eyed the space beneath his bunk, one of the few hiding places within the room. Ryan stood beside it as he talked.

'Still, after six months at sea, one would expect to find your hold at least partially filled.' Ryan sat on the bunk with a bump causing Alex to flinch.

'It's as I said, Lieutenant, it's a matter of luck. Sometimes the Gods look down on us favourably, sometimes they don't. Now, if you've finished with my ship, I'll bid you good day.'

Ryan rose from the bunk, walked to the door and turned. 'One more thing, Captain.'

Alex held his breath. 'Lord Drabek would like to see you before you report to the queen. He will expect you before this afternoon is over.'

Alex watched the soldiers depart before returning to his cabin with Stark. They looked under the bunk and to their great surprise found only dust. Callum and Olo had vanished from the ship.

Later in the afternoon, Alex attended the palace for his meeting with Lord Drabek. The spectacular palace complex, designed around a central square, included government buildings bordering three sides, and a formal garden surrounding the lake and the Great Pyramid on the fourth. Beyond the pyramid, the towering Lighthouse to the Gods stood as a focal point, and beyond came a public square and the dreaded Hellefyr, a place of great sacrifice. Royal architects had planned the city on the ancient lines of power, running all the way through the Great Pyramid, the Royal Palace, and the centre of the lighthouse, finishing at the Hellefyr. Every roof and wall of these buildings had colourful mosaics of marble, and pathways were also made up of multi-coloured stone tiles, making the city one of the brightest and most colourful spectacles Alex had ever seen. Above all else, the golden pyramid stood proudly and protectively, like a mother watching over her children.

Lord Krug, a senior senator in the Queen's Counsel, greeted Alex upon his arrival. The soft-spoken senator had been a confidant of Alexander when the captain first came to court. He had coached the young seaman on correct etiquette and behaviour before first meeting the queen. Over time, they had struck up a friendship, and Alex knew Krug could be trusted.

Lord Krug had always been a charming and cultured man. He wore richly decorated clothes of silk and gold but managed to look classy and understated in his robes. Alex walked with him towards the gardens where, apparently, Lord Drabek awaited his presence.

'Much has happened since you went away, Alexander,' Krug began. 'A strange pestilence has been spreading through the city and its outskirts, and the princess has been struck down by the disease. Drabek claims to have evidence the Caprinese are responsible. He says they have released small quantities of the Carchi virus and are planning a full-scale attack on Mariana and our people. There has been much internal fighting over the issue in the Senate, resulting in Drabek emerging with great power, though no one quite understands how. Distraught over her daughter's condition, the queen has allowed him to influence her to the point where she has given him complete control of her forces. He also commands his own, newly formed secret police who have come together from the nastiest elements of the army. They have been tasked with rooting out all those who oppose him, trumping up false charges against them whenever they feel the necessity. Arrests have been frequent, and now no one is prepared to speak up against Drabek. For your own good, you must stay out of his way, Alexander.'

'But how did he gain this position of trust in such a short time?'

'Magic, witchcraft, or just plain brainwashing, who knows. But the fact remains he is in complete control. The queen has lost all interest in anything but her daughter's condition, and she wants revenge against Caprine.'

'I can't believe the Caprinese would be stupid enough to contemplate releasing the virus. They must know it would seal their own fate and would surely expect retaliation. Mariana would disperse our own version of the virus in response, would we not?'

'That logic has preserved the peace for so long. Mutually Assured Destruction was a concept meant to save us all from the horrors of war, now it appears it will drive us towards it,' said Krug.

'On our travels, we heard rumours the King of Caprine is gravely ill,' Alex said. 'He is old and has no living heir to the throne. Talk is of a new democracy and power residing with the Caprinese Parliament. They are preparing to elect a new leader, a president, as soon as the king passes.'

'Yes, we have also heard such rumours, and I'll admit that does not sound like a nation bent on destruction.' Lord Krug paused. 'Alexander, you know I feel responsible for you. I see myself as your mentor and friend. So there is another matter on which I must warn you. Drabek does not like the idea of any other influence on the queen but his own. He is aware of the queen's fondness for you and your special relationship, and he is determined to undermine it I'm afraid. News has reached him that a cargo of Greens on-route to the capital has been released against the terms of the Royal Decree. I do not pretend to know what occurred on your voyage, Alexander, but be very careful when you speak to Drabek.'

Krug departed before they reached the gardens, leaving Alex to make his way amongst the beautiful flower beds to where Lord Drabek awaited. The gardens surrounding the pyramid were unique in that they bloomed regardless of season. In the very depths of winter, such as now, they maintained the warmth and vigour of long summer days. He found Drabek standing near an ornate fountain, and with his back turned to Alex, he appeared to be studying a rose. Taller than most other men on Trinity, Drabek wore a tall hat, which gave him a lofty appearance, like a long-legged stick insect wearing a top hat. Always dressed in black trousers and tunic, he had snubbed the colourful robes of other lords and senators, labelling them vulgar and loud. Alex thought black a most suitable colour for a man with such a dark reputation.

Alex approached. 'Lord Drabek, I believe you wished to see me.'

Drabek turned. 'Captain, thank you for coming.'

Alex wobbled with shock and his head swam, almost to the point where he had to sit down. 'Phys Ed!'

'I'm sorry, Captain, what did you say?'

Alex took a moment to recover his composure. Seeing the familiar face of his physical education teacher had thrown him completely. He stuttered, 'I-I said...it's *red*. The rose. The rose is red...very red.'

Drabek glanced at the flower. 'Ah, yes, yes it is. Blood red, my favourite colour.'

Drabek invited Alex to join him. 'Come, I want to show you something.'

Alex's mind raced as he tried to make sense of the situation. How did Phys Ed's appearance fit into all of this, and did Drabek know Alex's true identity, that he was Alexander Bottom? Drabek gave no sign of recognition, but Alex could not help feeling nervous as Drabek led the way. He engaged in conversation to hide his jitters.

'Congratulations on your new position, Lord Drabek. Your rise to the top must have been unexpected.'

Drabek snorted, a noise sounding somewhere between a pig and a horse. 'Not really,' he said. 'I have always believed the assembly lacked leadership, and my rightful place was at the queen's side. For too long the queen has been surrounded by cronies with self-interest. I will make it my business to drain this swamp of a capital and give Mariana a new respect for authority. Those who took me for a fool and snubbed me in the past have already fallen on their swords. But let us not dwell on that. Let's talk about you, Captain. It has come to my attention your cargo has mysteriously disappeared. My sources told me you left the Northern Archipelago with a full hold of slaves. And yet here you are in Mariana four months later with nothing but rats aboard your ship.'

Alex could not help thinking Drabek was referring to his own crew when he talked of rats. 'Your information is correct, Lord Drabek. Unfortunately, pestilence soon took hold of the Greens, and we were forced to throw them overboard or face infecting the crew and bringing the disease back to Mariana.'

Drabek considered the answer before speaking. 'I am well aware of the queen's affection for you, Captain Boatman, but let me make it clear. Freeing slaves has always been an offence. These are times of coming war, and Greens are known to be allied with the Caprinese so aiding their escape would now be treason. I don't need to remind you of the punishment for such a crime.'

'No need at all, Lord Drabek.'

Arriving at the palace jail, Drabek led Alex into the drab facility. Alex was scared, fearful of Drabek's intentions.

Am I about to be thrown in prison?

'These cells were almost empty when you left on your voyage. Now we can't find enough room for prisoners.'

Alex struggled to conceal his emotions. Confronted with packed cells of Greens held behind bars of steel, he felt sick to his stomach and could do little to hide his disgust. Cell after overcrowded cell contained men, women, and children in miserable conditions, yet Drabek flaunted his prisoners with evident pride.

'Word has reached me the Greens have a new leader. They are planning an assault on the capital to free all slaves and to overthrow the queen and my government. They have thrown their lot in with the Caprinese. Caprinese agents have begun spreading the Carchi virus and will stop at nothing to succeed. What you see in these cells is just the beginning, we must eliminate the Greens quickly and turn our armies against Caprine.'

Drabek had brought Alex to the jail to intimidate him, perhaps to get a reaction so Alex would incriminate himself. Alex wondered if the queen was aware of Drabek's barbaric treatment of prisoners and what she might say if she did. Alex felt the need to put his fears aside and challenge Drabek's view of the situation.

'With respect, Lord Drabek, I am far from convinced the Greens are plotting against us. In my experience, Greens are a peace loving race. I don't think I have ever heard of a violent Green, whether he be a slave or a free man.'

'There is a first time for everything, Captain. We cannot trust our own people let alone the Greens and the Caprinese. I will not stand idly by while they poison us with their viral germs and infiltrate our city. The Caprinese would dance on our graves, and these Greens would join them, given a chance.' Drabek stopped and stood to gloat through the bars into a crowded cell. 'Look at them, Captain. Look at them and tell me they are not savages.'

Alex wanted to tell Drabek he was the only savage in the room. 'This supposed plot by the Caprinese to spread the Carchi virus doesn't make sense. If they intended such an action, why not just do it? Why release a little here and a little there? It would only warn us of their intention and give us time to retaliate. Frankly, I find the prospect of an attack on the queen to be highly unlikely. I think we should think carefully before reacting with war.'

Drabek stopped and turned his attention to Alex. 'Your opinion is duly noted, Captain. But there is clear evidence of a plot, and we will not wait for its completion. When the princess dies of the virus, and I'm afraid she *will* die, there will be no hiding the fact Caprinese scum are responsible. You would do well to remember whose side you are on, Alexander Boatman.'

CHAPTER 19

Parlay

S trange images, savage animals fighting, soldiers marching in mass formation, and lightning crashing with frightening power all melted away as she regained consciousness and allowed her nightmares to fade into oblivion. Leanne opened her eyes slowly, struggling to make sense of her surroundings. She closed them again because they ached at the effort of focusing in the intense light. *The light is so bright.* Perhaps she had died and this was heaven. The thought frightened her. She did not want to look. The seconds ticked away and she became aware of a nearby presence, waiting for her to wake. She did not want to in case she was dead.

'How are you feeling?'

The soft male voice startled her, making her heart skip up a beat. The speaker sounded friendly and genuinely concerned, so Leanne opened her eyes cautiously, forcing herself to adjust to the brilliance. A man, the source of the voice, stood at the foot of the large bed in which she now found herself lying. Silhouetted against a large window, his face appeared as a featureless blur. Leanne tried to move, but the aches and pains she felt throughout her body caused her to sink back into the soft bedding.

She squinted for a better view of the hazy looking man and asked, 'Where am I?'

Seeing that Leanne found the intensity of sunlight difficult to deal with, the stranger turned to the window and pulled the wooden shutters closed, throwing the room into a more subdued level of light.

'Is that better?' he asked, returning to the foot of the bed.

'Yes, thank you,' Leanne said. 'Where am I?' she asked again.

'You are in the royal palace, in the guest chambers. My name is Fallon, and I am the royal doctor. Your Green told us a cadaverine bit you.'

Leanne's stomach turned as the memories of her ordeal flashed into her mind.

'Examination of your wound and your obviously dire symptoms appeared to confirm his story,' Fallon continued. 'We first gave you up for dead. But your condition started to turn for the better. It's quite extraordinary really. No one has ever recovered from such a bite in all of history, and yet here you are alive and well.'

'Where is he? My companion, where is he?'

'That I cannot answer,' said Fallon.

A rustle of clothing and the shuffling of feet indicated someone had entered the room, and they were now standing in the shadows, out of sight behind a dressing screen in the corner near the door.

'You may leave us, Doctor Fallon,' said a woman from her hiding place.

With more than a little effort, Leanne managed to prop herself up on her elbows. She saw only the woman's shadow as it danced on the wall. The doctor bowed and backed out of the room, closing the door behind him. Remaining hidden from view, the mystery woman waited until they were alone before speaking again.

'You say the Green was your companion. A free man so his papers claim.'

Leanne reached for the pouch inside her smock and realised she had been undressed and placed in a white gown. Her papers had gone along with her clothes.

'Mal...' Leanne paused. 'Slavus Loss is a free man. He accompanied me here of his own free will.'

'And you,' the woman continued. 'You are...' She paused as though she were checking her information. 'Leonora Loss, a pilgrim from Caprine.' It was a statement, not a question.

'Odd that a Caprinese woman would choose to make the long and dangerous pilgrimage to Mariana when war is about to break out at any moment. Unless you are a spy of course, the forerunner of an invasion.'

Leanne answered with caution as the fog in her brain cleared. 'I am no spy.'

'And yet you are not the Leonora Loss described in your papers. Have you forgotten you emerged from the sewers accompanied by an illegal Green soon after fires destroyed a sacred vault in our holy crypt? If not a spy, a saboteur perhaps?'

Leanne struggled to clear her mind and find the right thoughts with which to defend herself. She could not think of anything to say in her confusion. The woman's questions were meant to provoke a reaction.

'I must speak to the queen,' Leanne said, desperate to buy herself time to think.

'Tell me your real name and your purpose here in Mariana, spy.'

'I told you I am not a spy, and I must speak at once to the queen.'

'You carry false papers and go by a false name. If not a spy, then what?'

'I must speak to the queen,' Leanne repeated, ignoring the question.

A long pause followed until eventually, the woman spoke again. 'You wear the White Bird of Genkatan, the sacred symbol of Parlay.'

Leanne felt her chest and found a medallion hanging from a chain around her neck. The necklace depicted a white bird, the symbol of Parlay, and she had been wearing it since arriving on Trinity. Her mission was now clear. Defiantly, she repeated her demand for an audience with the queen. The woman emerged from behind her screen.

'Jani?'

Older by far, Leanne estimated the woman's age at forty-five. Nevertheless, the resemblance to Jani Nasri was so remarkable that Leanne was sure they were the same person. *Perhaps Jani made the crossover after all.* But something about the woman's demeanour caused Leanne to hold her tongue until she learned more.

'I am fluent in the dialects of Caprine, but I don't know the word *Jani,*' the woman said, opening the window shutters just enough for a better view of Leanne. 'I am Queen Cleoron, Queen of Mariana and the lands of the ten provinces. But of course, you know already.'

Which shock was the greater, Leanne didn't know, seeing Jani Nasri's likeness or the sudden realisation she had been talking to the queen all along. Leanne regained her composure and found the strength to slip out of bed. She knelt on the floor with her head bowed in submission.

'Forgive me, Your Majesty, I had no idea. I am Ambassador Elandra Mezza, envoy of the King of Caprine and Senator of the Caprinese Assembly.'

The queen gave no hint of recognition. If she was Jani Nasri, she was not letting on. She allowed a long pause to hang in the air between them before giving Leanne leave to rise.

'You are still weak. You may return to your bed,' she said, taking a seat by the window.

Dizzy from the sudden exertion, dazed and a little confused, Leanne welcomed the chance to return to her bed. A stiff gust of breeze picked up strength and entered the room through the window, causing the sheer curtains to billow like sails. Leanne smelt the ocean. She breathed deeply, collecting her thoughts along with those of the ambassador, whose place she had taken.

'Speak,' the queen said abruptly, startling Leanne with her sharp tone. 'If you are Ambassador Mezza, what is the reason for your deception? You carry the protection of Parlay, and yet you enter my city in secret, out of the sewers no less. If not for your injuries, would you have made your way to my room and slit my throat in the night? Are you an assassin, Ambassador?'

'No! Your Majesty, I come in peace.'

'I warn you, Elandra Mezza,' the queen continued, 'using the White Bird of Genkatan to perform treachery will be rewarded with little mercy. Unless you can explain your presence here, I will have no choice but to hand you over to Lord Drabek.'

'Your Majesty, there is no treachery, at least not on my behalf. We travelled in secret and under cover of false identities because there are forces desperate to stop our peace mission. There are those who would have our nations enter a war neither can win, and they will stop at nothing to see my assignment fail.'

The queen laughed ironically. 'Peace! You talk of peace while the Caprinese are killing my people with vile diseases. How can you talk about such things and look me in the eye? My daughter lies dying, and it is her blood on the hands of Caprine.'

Leanne struggled to respond. 'But...'

'Tell me, Elandra Mezza, how is it you can talk of peace and at the same time assemble a powerful war fleet, the one which now stands off our coast to the north and waits to attack?' Queen Cleoron rose with an angry flourish and clenched her fist into a ball. 'You insult me with your lies, Ambassador. I promise you this, the Caprinese will not live to enjoy their victory. Your people may have made the first strike with your germ warfare, but we will finish the war by annihilating every last one of you.'

Leanne felt stunned by the queen's reaction, and was now sure this angry woman was not Jani Nasri. If the plan had been for Jani to replace the queen, it had apparently failed.

The question on Leanne's mind now was how to deal with a queen hell-bent on vengeance.

'Your Majesty, it is no secret King Loris is not long for this life. He is weak and unaware of the world around him. I represent the Assembly of Caprine and have been chosen to plead for restraint while we prepare for the king's departure from this life. There are no plans for war, only defence against a growing hostility towards our nation.'

The queen did not respond. She looked furious.

'This pestilence sweeping your country,' Leanne continued, 'may have similar characteristics to the Carchi virus, but it cannot have come from our pot, as has been claimed. The pot has never been opened and never will be. It remains sealed. The disease running through your population must be the result of a natural ailment.' The queen looked sceptical. 'Your Majesty, we have fine doctors in Caprine, and we would like to offer any help we can give in this matter.'

'If you were telling the truth, it would be a simple enough matter to prove your innocence by producing the sealed Carchi Pot.'

Leanne's heart sank. She suddenly knew the truth about the virus, and it was not good news. 'We cannot produce proof,' she said sadly. 'We do not have the Carchi Pot. The disease has been lost for many centuries.'

Queen Cleoron appeared stunned at the revelation. She stood and paced back and forth as she considered the information. Leanne could almost see the wheels turn in her head. Eventually, the queen said, 'I don't believe you.'

'Why would I lie when the truth exposes us? I'm telling you this because I believe it's the only way to convince you of our innocence. Legend has it, during the evacuation of our people from Parisos, a ship carrying the Carchi Pot became engulfed by a terrible storm and sank in the Great Southern Ocean, lost forever in the deepest sea. With the threat of the other virus hanging over our heads, Caprine's rulers decided to conceal the loss. Locked away in a secure vault, what was believed to be the Carchi Pot was, in fact, an ordinary ironstone cask of red wine. Only a few trusted leaders of the High Counsel knew the deceit, and the secret has been handed down to a select few throughout the ages. Your Majesty, the only virus still in existence is in your own hands.'

The queen listened, her expression a mixture of bewilderment and scepticism. Eventually, she said, 'I cannot believe such a secret could go unchallenged in the centuries that have passed.'

'But it is the truth. I wish only to be allowed to plead our case for peace before Your Majesty and the Mariana Senate.'

'The High Counsel of Mariana will determine the truth of your words one way or another. If you are lying, we will have your head, or worse. In the meantime,' the queen said, making her way to the door, 'we will honour your protection under Parlay. Until the counsel meets, you are my guest and will be treated with respect, Ambassador. You will join me for dinner in the great hall tonight if you are feeling strong enough.'

'What about Malik?'

'Malik?'

'As my travelling companion, he is entitled to the same protection under Parlay.'

'Ah yes, the large Green with whom you crawled out of the sewer. He is unharmed and will remain so until we determine your fate. But I am afraid the day will never come when a Green sits down to dinner with the Queen of Mariana, Parlay or not.' The queen opened the door to leave but hesitated. 'Your survival of the cadaverine bite has left some senators wondering if you are a witch.' She said this with an amused smirk, not quite a smile. 'They call for a witch trial and would have me throw you into the Hellefyr. If you survived, you would be proved a witch, and we would chop off your head. If you burned in the Hellefyr, you would be proved innocent. Doesn't seem fair does it, my dear? But one way or another, the truth always wins.'

Silence followed the queen's departure. Her threats had left Leanne with an overwhelming sense of doom. A wave of emotions washed over her, and she started to shake. Frightened once again, she felt lost and alone like a child without her mother. But that's precisely what she was, trapped within this woman's body, she was still a child. She felt inadequate and ill-equipped for the challenges she faced. Her vision blurred as tears filled her eyes, spilling out and tumbling down her cheeks in a steady, salty flow. She wanted her mum and dad, the safety of home, and the comfort of her own bed.

Up until now, she had stayed strong by thinking on her feet, staying true to her mission, and taking on the role of this woman named Elandra Mezza. But recent events and the queen's threats had shaken her, and now on her own, she was falling apart. In reality, she was just a young girl named Leanne Chambers, and for the moment, in her despair, this was all she could be. She wrapped her arms around her body and tried to comfort herself in her own embrace. She started to sob, quietly at first, then long, loud convulsive sobs followed that shook her body to the core. She had reached breaking point. All her anxiety of the last few days, all her fear and frustration had combined to bring her to this, the edge. The sobs soon became a wail, giving vent to all her terror, pain, and desolation. How could she ever find the strength to get through this? *I'm still a child.*

Leanne cried until the tears had dried and there were no more left to weep. She resolved to be strong once again. *I have to get through this. I will get through this.*

CHAPTER 20

Claustrophobic

Malik stood before the open cell door with his heart galloping. This was his worst nightmare. Thirty or more prisoners crammed into the small space, all observing him in silence. Packed like frightened sardines, they watched and waited for Malik's next move.

'I can't go in there,' Malik said, desperately trying to reason with his captors. They looked anything but sympathetic. 'I'm claustrophobic,' he pleaded.

Short of patience, the lead guard pushed Malik forward. 'I don't care what your name is, get in there before I knock you in.'

The guard, a grim-faced man, urged Malik in with the point of his sword. Encouraged by one final shove from behind, Malik stumbled into confinement and heard the cell door slam behind him. The loud clang of steel only increased his anxiety. He closed his eyes, took a deep breath and told himself to stay calm. *It's not as though you're traumatically claustrophobic, you've already endured the confined space of the labyrinth.* But being locked in an overcrowded cell with barely enough room to raise his arms was enough to make anyone experience a panic attack, even the strongest of characters. Malik had to fight his fear.

Curiosity over the enormous man had caused others in the cell to back away and form a circle of space around him, relieving his confinement enough to make him relax just a little. No one spoke until Malik broke the deadlock.

'Just like peas in a pod, eh,' he said, attempting to break the ice with a joke. No one laughed, and he imagined even peas in a pod never felt so cramped.

'Why are you so big?' a little voice asked.

The innocent question came from low to the floor where a young girl, no older than three or four, shyly peered from behind her mother's legs. She twirled a ringlet in her hair with her fingers. Malik squatted so he could face the tiny infant.

'Too many chocolate bars and cans of cola when I was growing up,' he answered with a smile.

'What's a cansacola?'

Malik laughed, causing a release of tension and a noticeable change of atmosphere to ripple through the cell as smiles lit faces and the mood lightened. The child's mother took her by the hand.

'Her name is Loti. She never stops asking questions I'm afraid. She has never seen anyone so big...no one has.'

'I do attract attention, don't I?' Malik introduced himself to clear any confusion. 'My name is Malik by the way, not Claustrophobic.'

'What is claustrophobic?'

'It means I'm scared of small spaces. What's your name?'

'I am Shari,' the woman said, reaching up and hooking a hand around Malik's neck to draw him closer. To Malik's great surprise, Shari rubbed her nose against his in a traditional Green greeting. Malik pulled away quickly, embarrassed by the encounter.

'I...I am sorry, have I offended you?'

'Not at all,' Malik said, waving away her concern. Now he felt embarrassed for being embarrassed. He had heard of such greetings in cultures on Earth, the most well-known being the Inuit of North America. He felt angry at his ignorance, but Nim should have prepared him for his role as a Green. Unlike Leanne, who seemed to know her part instinctively, he had gained little knowledge of his Green culture and stumbled from one embarrassment to the next. He didn't even know his proper name. Leanne's papers listed him as Slavus Loss. This literally meant he was enslaved to the Loss family, and he was their property for most of his life. Like most other Greens, he had long since lost his identity. He was just a nobody.

'Where are you from?' he said as they sat together in a tiny corner of the floor. Loti, having decided she liked Malik, sat on his lap.

'I was born right here in Mariana, as was Loti. We belonged to Lord Tagus of the High Counsel.'

Malik could not help staring at Shari's skin. Smooth like silk, it had a luminous sheen and gave her a beautiful glow. This was the first time he had been close to another of the same race.

'My ancestors have been in his family's service for many generations,' Shari continued. 'They were kind slave owners who treated us well until Lord Tagus was arrested by Drabek's secret police. He never came home again. Eventually, his family was thrown into the streets, and their slaves were taken into custody. My husband is somewhere in the camps outside the wall. We don't know if we will ever see him again. Our numbers have been dwindling for many years, Malik. I heard my lord say only three or four thousand Greens are still alive, most of whom are here in Mariana. They have rounded up many more from the islands, and it is clear they plan to eliminate our race completely.'

Malik's anger grew as he listened to Shari's story. It was a story repeated by Greens across the city. 'It won't happen, I promise. Don't give up hope, Shari, you must never give up hope.' *Something needs to be done about this Drabek.*

'Yes, there is hope. We believe in such a dream. We have heard of a Green, a king who comes to save us. Legend says he will come from the dark world beyond Ikadies. It is said he will be wise and strong, a leader who will stop at nothing to free our people from their chains. When the people here saw you and your great size and strength, they thought—'

'They thought I was their king,' Malik finished for her.

'Yes,' she said sadly.

'You, Claustrophobic!' The guards had returned, and their leader had singled out Malik. 'Get up and come with me.'

Initially shocked by Phys Ed's appearance as the fearsome Lord Drabek, Malik quickly realised he was not what he seemed. Bizarre didn't even come close to describing his adventure so far, and Phys Ed's incarnation as Drabek came at the end of a long list of crazy circumstances. With a tall top hat perched precariously on his head, Phys looked even more laughable than when he'd hopelessly tried to control Miss Derbyshire's class, an incident that now seemed so long ago. Malik's fear of being brought before Drabek eased when he saw the pathetic teacher in Drabek's place. But Malik was smart enough to know the man before him was a different and dangerous man, capable of great cruelty, and his appearance as Phys Ed was just an illusion. Watching Drabek now, he couldn't help feeling the fate of all Greens lay in his evil hands.

Two guards and an ugly looking man dressed in what could only be described as cobwebs entered the room. Spider silk had long since been used to make the finest and most beautiful fabrics from which clothes were fashioned, but this man's garment looked like it had just been spun directly by the spider. Drabek introduced the man as Cork, who appeared to cower in the dark lord's presence.

'Cork is a Mindbender,' Drabek said coldly. 'Cork, this is Claustrophobic, or so he claims to be. We shall soon find out.' Malik did not attempt to correct Drabek. The whole claustrophobic bit was becoming his inside joke. 'The queen has issued orders he is not to be harmed under the rules of Parlay,' Drabek went on. 'Sadly, this means traditional torture is out of the question I'm afraid.'

'Oh, I'm broken-hearted,' Malik said, sarcasm being one of his natural abilities and his way of dealing with a stressful situation. 'And I was so looking forward to a bit of fingernail pulling. How about a little electric shock? Go on, just a little one, pl-e-e-ease,' he teased.

'Electric shock?'

'Forget it,' Malik said, secretly thanking heaven such devices had not yet been invented and were not available to Drabek and his strange looking sidekick. *They would make a perfect Doctor Frankenstein and his assistant Igor. I liked that movie.*

Malik had seen enough movies where electricity had been used for evil purposes, and where prisoners were tortured with electric shocks. He knew how lucky he was that they had none at their disposal.

'Where was I?' said Drabek. 'Oh yes, no torture. But we cannot allow a little obstacle like Parlay to get in the way of some questioning now can we, Cork? And as we cannot torture the answers out him, we will have to be content with a little digging...a bit of cranial exploration on the large, stupid green ape.'

'Who are you calling large?' quipped Malik.

Drabek ignored the comment. 'The use of a Mindbender comes somewhere on the thin red line between torture and interrogation, so we are not totally without the means to apply pressure,' Drabek said with a dry smile. 'In fact, you may be ready to spill the beans completely by the time we are finished, begging me to torture you instead.' Drabek laughed and rubbed his hands together, and Malik thought he looked like an excited child about to partake in his favourite game. 'I have questions, and I need answers. Questions like who are you really, and what is your mission? As if we didn't already know,' he added. 'Who are your accomplices and where are the Greens from the ship? These are all important questions. Some you may be able to answer, others not, but the fun of interrogation is in the way we ask, the way we find the truth, even if we already know the answers. Don't you agree, Claustrophobic?'

Malik's cocky confidence evaporated as Drabek explained his plans.

'The art of mind-bending had almost been lost until I discovered Cork at the end of a bottle. That was my little joke if you hadn't noticed,' he added with a humourless sneer. 'Anyway, the poor drunk had been unable to work his magic for so long, he'd almost gone out of his mind. But I'm glad to report with just a little practice and a lot of love from me, Cork has rediscovered his abilities along with his senses. Isn't that right, Cork?'

The ugly man grunted, avoiding eye contact with Drabek while he busied himself setting up the apparatus that looked disturbingly like the torture tools Drabek said he couldn't use. The equipment involved an ominous looking hockey type mask with cables.

Malik wondered if they'd perhaps already discovered electricity as he watched the cables being unravelled.

Malik grew ever more nervous as two guards strapped him into a chair and Cork fitted his head with the strange looking contraption. To Malik's surprise, Drabek received an identical piece of headgear, and they were linked together by more cables. Cork set about preparing a mechanism housed in a wooden box. Full of cogs and gears and other strange parts, it was hardly hi-tech. Cork linked the box with still more cables and fitted a crank handle to a socket on the side.

'Don't worry,' said Drabek, noting Malik's concerned expression. 'My end of this contraption is perfectly safe. Yours on the other hand, well, let's just say you may end up a vegetable, which is quite appropriate really, given your appearance.' Drabek chuckled at his black sense of humour.

Malik felt a tingling in his head. *That's not so bad. If that's the worst he can do, I can take it.*

'Can you tune in to radio city please? All I'm getting is static,' Malik said.

Cork cranked the handle but not much more seemed to happen until Malik began to see double. 'Eh, excuse me. I think we should stop now before someone gets hurt...namely me.' Cork ignored Malik's smart comments. The tingling soon became a vibrating buzz as Cork turned the crank faster. Now Malik was really worried. His sight had begun to fail, and a dark haze clouded his mind. The buzz became a continuous drone as Cork cranked faster still.

'Hello, Mr Cork, I think we should...We should...'

Disoriented and confused, Malik held on to his consciousness, desperate to focus his thoughts as his head became a vibrating mass of confusion. In his mind's eye, he tumbled and turned, tossed by the forces now controlling his brain. A million stars surrounded his fall through virtual space, and a million faces followed his path as unfamiliar voices called his name above the roar of thunder. Explosions crashed around him, he heard the tumbling of rubble, and smelt the acrid smoke of burning flesh. More voices. Babbling voices. Wailing sounds. Women and men are crying in despair, children are screaming.

Plunging once more, Malik sensed the wind go rushing by him, running over his face and catching his breath, making him gasp for air. He wanted to call for help, but he could not speak. He tried to run, but his legs would not move. New voices appealed to him. Angry voices. Pleading voices. *What do you want?*

'*Malik, you know we love you. We always will. But this is something we must do.*'

Mum, Dad?

'*It's time to forgive, Malik.*'

He wanted to cry and say he was sorry, but they had vanished, gone far away into the depths below.

'*Malik, can you hear me? Focus! This is Nim. You must focus and resist.*'

'Nim?'

'*Only you can hear me, Malik. Stay strong. Do not let Drabek take over your mind.*'

'I'm scared, Nim. Where am I?'

'*Where you have always been. This is an illusion, and you are safe if you believe you are safe. Drabek wants your mind, but you are strong, you can resist him and turn the tables. Focus, Malik, do not let him into your head.'*

Nim's voice grew fainter until it was no more than a whisper. And now Drabek spoke, but not to him; he was addressing someone else. Drabek in a dark place lit by candles. Two people stood with him, cowering in a huddle. Drabek passed out blue coloured bottles in the shadows. Their faces unclear, women's faces. *Turn, who are you?* They turned, but their faces blurred and faded away. Malik started to tumble once more, losing sight of Drabek and the two females. He travelled against his will, with no control over his destination. Stars passed him at a million miles an hour, and when he looked below, he saw the world, Earth in all its glory. Music! *Beyoncé... what's she doing here?*

Waterfalls rumbled and thundered all around him. Cadaverines snapped at his flesh. Carried now in a flooded river, he saw Leanne and called out her name, but she disappeared beneath the surface and was gone.

The drone of Cork's cranks returned to assault his ears. Blackness replaced light as the Megaverse stretched out before him into the void. Drabek's voice grew louder, but Malik couldn't hear what he was saying. War! Armies were marching. Battles fought in the mud. Drabek's voice again.

'Stop, stop, stop I tell you!' screamed Drabek.

The visions disappeared in a flash. Instant calm. Silence. Malik opened his eyes with a jolt, and gradually, his swimming head slowed to a stop. He regained his senses and saw he was still in the room with his tormentors who were scrambling to sort out the apparatus. Drabek talked, but his words were mumbled and desperate.

Drabek seethed and threw off the headgear, snarling in anger as he became tangled in the mass of cables around his legs. 'You bungling idiot,' he screamed. Cork tried frantically to help his master out of the equipment. 'Leave it. Get out of my sight! Go!'

Malik breathed deeply. Quick to recover from his ordeal, his heart slowed to a more normal rhythm. He noticed Drabek had turned pale and ill; things had clearly not gone to plan. Cork had failed with his contraption. Though he felt sick after the experience, Malik took the opportunity to antagonise Drabek, after all, it was the kind of opportunity he rarely missed.

'That wasn't so bad, was it,' he lied with a smile. 'I feel quite refreshed, Lord Drabek, don't you?'

Infuriated, Drabek bellowed at the guards. 'Take him back to his cell!'

CHAPTER 21

The green thumb

Knowing that you are going to die, really knowing for sure and then surviving against all the odds, changes a person forever. Leanne had survived and had beaten certain death by a miracle. And now she was changed for all time, aged by her ordeal, and scarred by the experience beyond the physical wounds to her body. Just shy of her sixteenth birthday, she no longer felt like the girl she once was. Within Elandra Mezza, she had found a new self. It was as though her youth had come to an abrupt end, her innocence lost in the process. She had purged all her frailties along with her tears, and now she felt determined, truly at one with Elandra Mezza.

Elandra gave her the hard edge of steel and the determination she needed to succeed. It was as though she had become a new person, a hybrid mix of both identities. *I feel you within me, Elandra.*

Servants had arrived with food, drink, and fresh clothes. A tray of fruit and cheese looked tempting; she had not eaten in days, but she didn't dare to eat in case they had poisoned the food. After bathing, she had dressed in an elegant silk robe of orange and gold and now felt physically refreshed and mentally ready for what might come. But most of all, she just felt different. *What's happened to me?*

Though she was said to have been a guest of the queen under Parlay rules, when she had tried her room door, she had found it locked from the outside. She was very much a prisoner and could do little else but sit in the window seat and wait. The afternoon sun had already set, and a fresh breeze blew from the ocean, causing her to shiver at the coming night. Lights had begun to glow in windows, and she wondered if one of them could be shining on Malik. She worried about him, like a mother over her missing child. He had saved her life, and now she must find a way to save him in return. Her stomach rolled at the thought of him in some dark dungeon, alone and frightened.

She had never been close to anyone before, other than her parents and her grandparents. Other kids had friends their age and in her search to find herself, she had wanted them too, wanted to be like other kids who had all the friends in the world. She knew girls who had collected six or seven hundred friends on Facebook. Kathy Henderson had over a thousand. Her own page had a paltry six, and they were all friends she had requested. No one had ever asked her to be their friend. She always knew how ridiculous it was, and the idea that friends could be collected like comic books and Pokémon cards was laughable, but it didn't stop her wanting them.

Despite herself, she now had someone special, a true friend for all his annoying, no, infuriating remarks and mannerisms. He was the most irritating...Leanne smiled when she thought of his silly jokes. Her mind drifted back to the labyrinth, to the desperate fight for survival, and she wondered how many of Kathy Henderson's friends would have saved her life against all the odds. Leanne vowed to find a way to free Malik.

Lord Krug arrived at Leanne's room to escort her to the Great Hall, where the queen had assembled members of court to join them. She liked Krug instantly, taking his arm as he guided her through the palace and gave her a running commentary about its history as they went. A charming man, he reminded her of that guy from Game of Thrones. *What was his name?* She couldn't remember.

With small talk at an end, he asked her how it was an ambassador, one of Caprine's highest-ranking officials, could arrive on a peace mission in such a secretive way.

'Surely the whole point of Parlay is to meet the queen under controlled conditions?' Lord Krug said.

Leanne told him of her fears for her safety. 'There are forces out to stop us before we can talk about peace. I would never have reached the city if they'd had their way.'

'It is truly a miracle you were able to reach the palace at all, notwithstanding your brush with the cadaverines. Sadly, there are even more vile and deadly creatures who will stop at nothing to keep you from achieving success. This afternoon, the queen has already addressed the counsel about your arrival, and I have to tell you, she does not believe your story. There are few friends ready to stand up and speak on your behalf. Lord Drabek seeks to have you tried as a witch. Those who fear him agree. They say only a witch could have survived the cadaverines.'

Leanne's hands began to shake and sweat as she recalled once more the miracle of her survival. She wondered if she would ever get over the experience. 'Witches and broomsticks,' she said. 'Surely the people of Mariana are beyond such superstitions.'

'I'm afraid not, far from it. People fear anything that cannot easily be explained.'

Leanne could not explain it either. She had been so near death and had given herself over to whatever lay beyond life. But something had happened; she'd cheated the Grim Reaper when it should all have been over. She tried to chase it from her mind.

'I would argue the peace process is more important to explain. I survived a cadaverine bite, so what? The people of Mariana should be more worried about the sickness ravaging the city, not black magic.'

'But that's just it, they blame you for the sickness...they blame you for dispersing the Carchi virus. It would be easy for them to believe you achieved this by witchcraft. Your presence in the tunnels beneath the city is proof of such deeds. Drabek says you were caught spreading the disease into the water supply.'

'Where is this evidence Drabek claims to have?'

'Evidence is in short supply I'm afraid. No one is prepared to force Drabek to produce such proof. His word is all we have, and since you yourself have confirmed to the queen your virus is missing, we have no evidence to the contrary.'

'How is the princess?'

'Nearing the end, I'm sad to say. When the princess dies, Drabek will have all the proof he needs, and the queen will seek vengeance, starting with you, Parlay or not. I am afraid you have stepped from the frying pan into the fire, my dear.'

On her arrival at the great hall, silence descended on the grand room. Guests watched with hateful stares as Lord Krug escorted her to the high table. Seeing the level of hostility amongst members of the royal court, Leanne felt certain the odds were stacked against her. Achieving a peaceful outcome seemed an impossible task while Drabek held influence over everyone.

After her recent ordeals, there were few things left could shock Leanne. She imagined whatever came her way, she was no longer capable of being surprised. Nevertheless, the appearance of Lord Drabek generated the same astonished reaction as it had done in both Alex and Malik. *Phys Ed! Oh my gosh, what next?*

Leanne concealed her shock admirably when Lord Krug introduced them. Stunned at first by his appearance, she had almost called him Mr Evans but stopped herself just in time. Shocked by Phys Ed she may have been, but it was the sight of Alex that truly made her heart leap.

There was no doubt in her mind that the man she saw entering the room was Alexander Bottom. He appeared twenty years older and wore a silly moustache, but this man had to be Alex. At least he's not green, she thought as she studied his handsome features. Age had been kind to him, and he looked mature, impressive, and confident in his new identity. But was he the real Alex? Or, like Queen Cleoron and Lord Drabek, was he just a lookalike, a copy of the original? A discreet wink from Alex when no one was looking confirmed his true identity, much to Leanne's relief. She wanted to rush to him and tell him her stories, but this was neither the time nor the place to reveal their connection.

Stone-faced, the queen arrived at the hall without much fanfare. Everyone bowed low until she had taken her seat at the head of the table. With no hint of genuine hospitality, she curtly invited Leanne to sit at her left side. Next, Lord Krug was instructed to join Leanne as her chaperone, and Alex was ordered to take the seat on the queen's right, much to Drabek's annoyance it only helped in further fuelling his foul mood.

Drabek sat next to Alex with a snarl of distaste. How could the queen consign him to third place at the table while that upstart, Boatman, sat at her right hand? And the witch from Caprine at her left, why wasn't she in chains?

The remaining members of court completed the dining arrangements at random. Leanne's only thought was to get Alex alone so they could talk freely. The queen said very little as dining commenced. Apparently distracted by her daughter's grave condition, she maintained an aloof presence while guests spoke in low whispers amid a sombre mood of pending doom. Lord Krug did his best to indulge Leanne in polite conversation, but it was difficult to be sincere under the circumstances. With the eyes of the room upon him, he felt self-conscious for even trying.

Drabek brooded over his soup course. Thinking the dinner was a farce and muttering of his discontent, he snarled at a group of senators who appeared to be having too much fun. When they realised they were the focus of his attention, they stopped smiling and avoided his gaze by staring down at the table. Eventually, and with enough of the niceties, Drabek threw his soup spoon down in disgust.

'Rules of Parlay they may be, but I for one cannot stomach the pretence.' Drabek rose and bowed to the queen. 'If Your Majesty will permit me, I have matters of state to attend to.'

Queen Cleoron hesitated. Drabek's disrespect would normally attract her strong disapproval, but she agreed with Drabek's sentiments. She felt compelled, however, to follow court protocol, and traditional courtesies must be offered to high ranking officials such as the ambassador. Those travelling under the protection of Parlay were entitled to receive the same hospitality. In the end, she was too weary to challenge Drabek and make a scene, so she nodded her approval and Drabek left the room with a dramatic flourish, leaving the remaining guests to sit in silent embarrassment. The tension in the hall appeared to be at breaking point with several court members seemingly ready to follow Drabek's lead and ask for permission to leave the table.

'Your Majesty,' Leanne said, hoping to ease the volatile situation, 'may I enquire about the princess' condition?'

Stunned silence filled the great hall. Leanne knew she had made a mistake before the last word had left her lips, and if looks could kill, she would've been dead a hundred times over. To her great credit, Queen Cleoron exercised complete control as she answered the enquiry, but nothing could hide the fury and despair in her expression, or the icy threat in her words.

'My daughter lies close to death. My doctors tell me she will not last the night. I am the queen, and yet I cannot see her, cannot hold her hand or comfort her for fear I will be contaminated. I am forbidden from her side in the interests of the realm. Forbidden from being with my own daughter WHEN SHE DIES!' Leanne swallowed hard, feeling sick to her stomach. 'To add to my pain,' the queen continued, lowing her voice back to a normal volume, 'while my daughter lies alone and dying, protocol dictates I must sit with my enemy, an enemy with a probable hand in her murder. Please, do not ask about my daughter's condition out of any desire for polite conversation when you yourself are no doubt complicit in her killing. This night I will lose a daughter, and when I do, there will be others who will lose their heads. Justice will be swift, Ambassador.'

My head first. Leanne could not think of anything to say in response. She wanted to argue in her defence, but she couldn't, she didn't dare.

'Lord Krug,' said the queen. 'Escort the ambassador back to her room. She is done here.'

'We need the air,' Lord Krug said, taking Leanne to her room the long way round via a stroll through the gardens. 'It might be winter, but the gardens catch the warm afternoon sun and hold its heat in the walls and pathways. The pyramid affects the immediate climate. I love to walk through at night when I can be alone with my thoughts, especially when the weight of the world is upon my shoulders.'

'It was stupid of me to ask of the princess. I don't know what I was thinking,' Leanne said, annoyed at herself for her insensitive blunder. *How could I have been so stupid?*

Krug stopped, inclined his head and studied her. 'I believe your concern was genuine, though your timing was awful. The queen is grieving over her child, and tonight was not the night to remind her of who might be responsible.'

They walked on in silence for a while, Leanne stewing over her careless comments, Krug giving her time with her thoughts. The night had a calming effect, enough for Leanne to start taking in her surroundings. Mariana was indeed a beautiful city.

Stopping to allow Leanne time to admire the gardens and the city skyline beyond, Lord Krug pointed to the pyramid and gave her some background on the structure.

'Magnificent, isn't it? No one knows who built it. The Great Pyramid has stood in this place long before modern history. The product of an ancient civilization with advanced skills and knowledge we have somehow lost over time.'

Like an ultramodern skyscraper, the structure glowed with golden light. Against the night sky, Leanne thought it was the most beautiful thing she had ever seen. What great vision those ancient people must have had to build such a monument. She wondered if it might be a tomb for a once great ruler, like the pyramids in Egypt back on Earth.

'It appears to float above the water,' she said.

A square, man-made lake surrounded the base of the pyramid and reflected its glow in a shimmering display of dazzling jewels of light.

'Oh, it more than *appears* to float, Ambassador. It does, in fact, float about a foot above the surface. Mystery surrounds its construction and how such a large edifice can defy the laws of nature. Our scholars have pondered over these questions for a very long time. As far as anyone knows, it has hovered in that place since time began. No wonder the Gods have made it their home. There have been attempts over time to open it up and see what is inside, but nothing can penetrate the surface. And laws were passed long ago to prevent such attempts.'

They continued to walk in the peaceful surroundings, taking Leanne's mind off the queen's harsh words and stopping every few yards to admire the flowers. Leanne stretched to smell what looked like frangipani, and she sighed at the delicate scent.

'That reminds me of my grandmother and her garden. She has a green thumb, and frangipani is her favourite flower.'

'Your grandmother is a Green?' Krug asked in surprise.

Leanne laughed. 'No, she has a green thumb.' Krug looked confused. 'It's just a saying people use where I come from.' Leanne almost said *back on Earth*. 'We say if someone has a natural gift for gardening, they have a green thumb. They say they can grow anything when others might struggle to keep plants alive. Like my grandmother, a green thumb can take the sickest of plants and get them to thrive. My mother often takes her houseplants to my gran for their revival. A green thumb has an almost magical touch tha—' Leanne stopped mid-sentence. Her mind raced. *That's it!* 'Malik!' She turned to Krug and said urgently, 'We have to return to the hall, I must speak to the queen at once. It's a matter of life and death.'

CHAPTER 22

The miracle

When the guards came for Malik, he expected the worst. Another round of Drabek's mind-bending exercises might not have the same favourable outcome. He didn't know if he could hold out a second time around having almost broken down the first time. Of course, it could have been worse; other prisoners had talked of Drabek's ultimate punishment, that of being thrown into the fiery pit known as the Hellefyr. Their descriptions of the legendary natural phenomenon terrified Malik.

Two armed guards escorted Malik and he shuffled along between them, chained at the ankles and wrists. As they navigated the corridors, he felt like a condemned man. He couldn't help comparing it to the times the principal had called him to his office, except this time he was in chains of course. *Somehow I don't think they would get away with manacles in school.*

After a long and awkward walk, where he tripped his way forward in tiny steps ahead of his escort, they arrived at the great hall. Two elaborately dressed sentries stood before a set of ornate doors, high and wide enough to allow passage for even an elephant. *Maybe they knew I was coming.* On Malik's approach, the doors opened to reveal the vast interior of a grand hall and a host of waiting dignitaries.

Malik entered nervously. *What new horrors wait within?*

Curious lords, senators, and various members of court parted to allow him a wide path to the queen. She sat at the far end of the hall on an elegant silver throne. Everyone wanted to catch a glimpse of the proceedings, and even servants jostled for a spot where they could observe the unfolding events from the fringes. Murmurs of amazement rippled through court as Malik passed, for no one had ever seen such a monster. He was the demon who had come with the Caprinese woman to kill them in their beds as they slept.

'A freak of nature,' someone shouted from the rear.

'A wild animal,' someone else called out.

'Burn him,' said another.

Malik recognised the queen as an older version of Jani Nasri, sat imperiously on her throne as he approached. The cold look in her eye made him cautious. It told him this was not the Jani he knew from school. *Dangerous. Be careful, Malik.*

Malik took in the scene and tried to make sense of his thoughts. Bad thoughts. Had he been summoned for execution? A round of public torture or a trial perhaps? Fear of the unknown caused palpitations. He attempted a smile, but it developed into a grimace. The queen responded with a cold, blank disapproving expression. *Definitely dangerous.*

Prodding him forward like the keepers of a savage beast, palace guards brought Malik to their ruler and made him kneel before her. Queen Cleoron ordered him to be unchained. The guards released the bonds and retreated to the rear of the hall, leaving Malik to ponder his predicament and the queen's next move. All eyes focused on Malik.

'Malik,' said a familiar voice.

At first he thought he was hallucinating.

'Malik, it's me,' the voice repeated.

Malik turned to see Leanne, the sight even more beautiful than the sound. He found himself instantly and unexpectedly overcome with emotion, and before anyone could stop him, he rushed to Leanne, picked her up in an enveloping bear hug, and swung her off her feet. Malik spun her around and around until she felt quite dizzy. Disgusted groans of shock rippled around the hall like a wave. It was against all laws to make any kind of intimate contact with a Green. And here was the ugliest giant of all Greens not only making contact, but also looking like he might kiss the woman at any moment, such was his delight.

Alex couldn't believe his eyes for different reasons. Seeing Leanne and Malik embrace like long-lost best friends had taken him by surprise. It made him wonder just what they had been through to bring them together with such obvious affection. The last time he had seen them, they were at each other's throats.

'I thought you were dead,' Malik said, allowing the grinning Leanne to gain her feet and adjust her composure under the gaze of a hundred disapproving eyes.

'You're not crying are you, Malik?' she said.

'Don't be daft...you must have caught me in my eye with your finger. Wow!' he said, wiping his eyes with his sleeve. 'I really thought you were done for! I can't believe you're alive and well. And by the look of it, dressed for a party.'

'Enough!' the queen bellowed. 'Your touching reunion is over.' She focused on Leanne. 'I warn you, Ambassador Mezza, if this is a ploy, you will watch each other die a slow and painful death. This course of action goes against all my instincts.'

Malik and Leanne turned their attention back to the queen. Drabek arrived through the doors, puffing and panting after racing to the scene. He had been summoned as soon as the news broke.

'What is the meaning of this?' Drabek asked in a furious tone. He received a brief update from one of the senators as he came to the queen's side. 'I came as soon as I heard, Your Majesty. You cannot be seriously contemplating this madness. They are surely a team of assassins. Why else would they enter the city in such a way, if not to cause you harm? Mark my words, if you allow this animal access to the princess, he will kill her with his own bare hands.'

Members of court gasped.

Malik noted Alex standing close to the throne. He showed no sign of recognition.

'Your Majesty,' Leanne said above the rumbling voices. 'May I speak?'

Queen Cleoron held up a hand to silence the crowd. 'Speak,' she said.

'I have seen Malik heal before, Your Majesty. A young child with the pestilence lay at death's door, only to be saved by the touch of his hand.'

Heal? What are you talking about? Malik raised his eyebrows in an expression of disbelief. What was Leanne saying? What was she planning?

Leanne continued. 'You have witnessed his miracles yourself, Queen Cleoron. You saw my wounds, and you told me yourself I was as good as dead as no one had ever survived a cadaverine bite. Malik saved me and he saved the child, just as he can save the princess.'

'Witchcraft! Your Majesty, she survived the bite by witchcraft. We should dispense with the formalities and condemn them both immediately to the Hellefyr.'

'Your Majesty, if I may speak?' Alex stepped forward for the first time. 'I have heard of such healers amongst the Greens. Legend tells of miracles in ages past. Temples on Ikadies depict these healers laying hands on the sick and dying to cure them. Surely we must try if it means there's a chance we can save the princess.'

'Nonsense,' said Drabek. 'These are the myths of ignorant savages, stories of the bogeyman.'

Malik shot back with a quick response. 'Well, you're the living proof that the bogeyman exists, why not—'

'Silence everyone!' Queen Cleoron held up a hand and commanded her complete attention. She looked directly at Malik. 'Is this true? Can you save my daughter?'

Malik didn't know what to think or say. He looked around at the expectant faces, all focused on him in silent anticipation. Queen Cleoron, desperate and praying. Drabek, snarling and angry. Alex, the faintest hint of hope in his eyes. Finally, he turned to Leanne, looking for answers and silently pleading for her guidance.

'You were the one who told me to have faith when all seemed lost in the labyrinth, Malik. Now it's time for you to trust me.'

Malik closed his eyes, heaved a sigh of resignation and said, 'Let me see the princess.'

Drabek drew his sword and moved to stop Malik in his tracks. Alex stepped between them with his hand on Drabek's sword as the queen intervened.

'Sheath your weapon, Lord Drabek,' the queen ordered. 'Guards, escort the Green to the princess' chamber. At the first sign of trickery, kill him.'

The guards looked horrified at having to go near the princess.

'I will accompany him, Your Majesty,' Alex said.

Queen Cleoron hesitated. 'And what of the pestilence, are you willing to risk your own life on the word of the ambassador and her Green? If you enter the princess' chamber, you have little hope of avoiding contamination. Are you really so sure of this Green's gift?'

'I am, Your Majesty. I believe he can help the princess.'

'Very well.' The queen nodded her approval. As Malik and Alex passed, Queen Cleoron grasped Malik's arm and leaned in close to his ear. 'Please,' she whispered, 'save my little girl.'

Leaving the guards, who were more than willing and somewhat relieved to be staying outside, Alex led Malik into the princess' chamber. A young woman greeted them, a handmaiden to the princess who had volunteered to care for the dying child. Malik had seen her face before, but he wasn't sure where. Alex instructed her to leave the room, which she did reluctantly. When she had gone and closed the door behind her, he turned to Malik, held out a hand and said with a smile, 'It's good to see you, Malik.'

Malik gave a huge sigh of relief. 'Thank heavens! I wasn't sure it was really you, Alex.'

They shook hands a little too formally until Malik pulled Alex towards him, hugged him, and slapped his back. They stood apart and looked each other up and down to take in the changes, happy to be reunited at last.

'Hey, Malik, you're looking...'

'A little green, I know. How come I got the bum end of the deal?'

'Hey, no Bottom jokes, okay? I'll have you know I'm now Captain Alexander Boatman, forty-four-year-old explorer of the seven seas and close confidant to the Queen of Mariana. Who is *not* Jani Nasri by the way. I thought at first she had made it through after all and almost blew it when I asked her what held her up. Apparently I'm her confidant.'

'Typical! The handsome Alex gets to be a fighting hero with royal privileges to go along with the part, while I get to be Shrek's double and get a trip to prison for good measure. Where's the fairness in that?'

They both laughed, but their excitement at seeing each other was short-lived. Both knew the seriousness of the situation.

'What was Leanne thinking? Was she just trying to buy us time?' asked Malik.

'I don't know, Malik, but whatever she's up to, I hope she knows what she's doing.'

Turning their attention to the princess, they couldn't help thinking they had embarked on a plan doomed to failure. The child was gravely ill. She lay on a large white pillow, while everything else in the room was morbidly black. Black fabric had been draped to adorn the walls and shroud the heavily carved four-poster bed. Like the inside of a vampire's lair, the room had an ominous mood of evil. Dried herbs and plant roots hung from strings, and the bedroom smelled of the garlic that was scattered in large quantities on the floor.

'At least we won't go short of cooking ingredients if we decide to make soup,' Malik said.

'It's like a bedroom scene from a horror movie. I'm half expecting Count Dracula to step out of the shadows at any moment. Not the sort of environment to cheer a sick patient,' said Alex.

'Not the place to cheer anyone,' agreed Malik.

'Can you really help her?' Alex asked seriously.

Malik looked down at the young princess. Fragile and small, she was as pale as fresh snow, her cheeks and eyes were sunken and dark, and her breathing was visibly shallow. He bent close and listened to her breath.

'She's barely alive.' Malik frowned. 'This girl needs a doctor. What are we doing here, Alex?'

Alex shrugged. 'Maybe this is it. Perhaps by saving the princess, we avoid a war between these races. It's all been very confusing so far. It feels like I'm constantly trying to catch up.'

Alex paused. 'Truth is I don't know what we're doing. It looks like it's all down to you.'

'But I'm no doctor, Alex. I can't just heal her.'

'That's not what Leanne says.'

'Yeah, well Leanne needs her head seeing to.'

They stood a while in silence before Alex placed a supportive hand on Malik's shoulder and said, 'Why don't you give it a try? You're all we've got.'

Irritated by the impossible pressure and expectations placed on him, Malik shook off Alex and said a little too aggressively, '*You* give it a try.' The idea of him healing the princess was insane. 'What do you expect me to do, Alex, wave my hands in the air and dance around her bed while chanting?'

'You must be able to do something.'

'Okay, what?'

Alex shrugged.

Malik started dancing stupidly around the bed, waving his arms in the air and chanting. 'Boogie, boogie. Opus pocus boogedy, boogedy.'

'Stop it, Malik. What are you doing?'

'What, am I not doing it right? Maybe if I summon the Gods, they'll help us. Oh, wiggery, wiggery, oh great big eye in the sky, oh big banana, save this princess from whatever plague is killing her. Let my green fingers do the walking, my green lips will do the talking. Woo, woo, woo.'

'Malik, stop. You're not helping by freaking out.'

'No kidding! In case you haven't realised, Alex, we're about to die if I can't save her. This little adventure of ours will all be over just as soon as the princess checks out of this life, which looks as though it could be any minute now. Then we'll really be up to our eyes in it. Oh, I forgot,' he said, smirking with sarcasm, 'you're the queen's right-hand man. You get to watch in safety while Leanne and I face the chop.'

'That's unfair.'

They stood in silence, contemplating their options. It seemed hopeless.

'You do realise we are both likely to catch whatever disease she has?' said Alex eventually. 'If you're not going to cure her, our mission ends here and they may as well kill us because the two of us will die of the plague anyway, and Leanne will get thrown into the pit of hell for her witchcraft.'

'Hellefyr,' Malik corrected. 'She'll get thrown into the Hellefyr.'

The princess stirred. Malik moved to her side and looked down sympathetically. She looked so helpless and weak. He placed a hand on her head.

'She's burning up, and yet her sweat is as cold as ice.' Malik held her tiny hand; it seemed so delicate cradled in his huge palm. 'I wish I could help you, little one, I just don't know how,' he said sadly.

With Malik now calm, they settled on chairs at the bedside and watched the princess sleep. Time passed as they told each other of their adventures, each amazed at the stories of survival. Alex's tales of oceans and warships, volcanoes, and giant ants, only equalled by the floodwaters, prison escapes, and cadaverines encountered by Malik and Leanne.

'Not your average school trip,' joked Alex.

Malik's tone turned serious. 'I never gave it a thought before.'

'Gave what a thought?'

'How it must be for people who don't have the freedom we take for granted. When this is over, if Nim gets us out of here, we will go back to our comfortable lives, safe in our homes and know we will have food on the table, a warm bed to climb into, and people who care for us. We'll sleep without fear of someone knocking on the door to take us away. The Greens have nothing, Alex. They have no rights, no dignity, and no home to call their own. I've never seen cruelty like this, and I never knew people could be mistreated this way. It makes you think about the way you lived your own life.'

'What do you mean?'

'I mean,' said Malik, 'I feel ashamed. I've acted like a real troll, an insensitive idiot. You don't realise what it's like to be treated badly until you've walked in someone else's shoes.'

'I'm as shocked as you by the treatment of Greens, Malik. What's harder to take is Alexander Boatman has been part of the problem. He captured slaves for the queen and brought them to the city. It was his job, *my* job, to round up the last survivors out on the islands. What I keep asking myself is, is this part of who I am? Has there been a little bit of Alexander Boatman hidden away inside me all this time?'

'Perhaps we all have a measure of good and bad inside us,' said Malik.

'Maybe what we are doing here will make up for the bad things.'

A long silence passed between them, each thinking of what they might change if and when they got home.

'Can I have some water please?'

If the words had come from God Himself, they could not have been more surprised. Alex and Malik watched open mouthed as the princess heaved herself up on her pillow and smiled.

'It's a miracle,' Malik said, laughing.

'No,' said Alex. '*You're* a miracle, Malik. You *are* a great blooming miracle.'

CHAPTER 23

Devil or Holy man?

Queen Cleoron watched as Princess Li played happily in the garden with a friend. They chased each other in and out of stone columns, played hide and seek amongst the trees and bushes, and laughed as they tried to catch an elusive butterfly with their hands. If she had not seen the result with her own eyes, she would never have believed the miracle before her. Celebrations had gone on late into the night, and the queen could not have been happier, but now she was troubled.

'You sent for me, Your Majesty,' Alex said.

The queen did not answer; she seemed far away, deep in thought.

'Majesty?'

She spoke without turning to look. 'Alexander, thank you for coming. Please sit.'

Alex sat on the stone bench opposite the queen and watched the children playing.

'You would think she had never been ill,' Alex said.

The queen seemed unable to take her eyes off the princess. 'I can't believe she is here,' she said. 'I'm afraid if I lose sight of her for more than a second, she will disappear, I will wake to find this has all been a dream, and she will be dead.'

Alex smiled as the princess squealed and giggled with her playmate, running around and around in circles until they felt dizzy and fell to the ground. 'I can only imagine what you must have gone through. But this is not a dream. She's safe, thanks to Malik.'

The queen finally turned to look at Alex as she spoke. 'You were there, Alexander, you saw him work his magic. How did he do such a thing? Is this the work of a saint or a devil? The questions trouble me greatly.'

Alex knew he must be careful in the way he answered. He did not want to sound too supportive of Malik and Leanne, but he needed to press home the point. The queen must open her mind to their good intentions.

'Would it matter whether it was the devil or a holy man?' Alex asked. 'Princess Li is alive and well as a result of Malik's powers. For that, we are all grateful, no matter how he achieved her recovery. But to ease your mind and to answer your questions, Your Majesty, I believe there is only good in Malik. I saw no witchcraft or devils at work.'

'The city is abuzz with talk of miracles and magic,' Queen Cleoron said as a deep frown furrowed her brow. 'They are calling Malik a holy man, a spiritual healer sent by the Gods to bring about change. The Greens believe he is their saviour. Unrest is spreading fast.'

Alex hesitated and said, 'Perhaps he brings a change for the good for all of us. If Her Majesty can use these events to bring the people together, maybe you can avoid further unrest.'

'Drabek calls him a demon. He has accused the envoy and her Green of witchcraft. He believes they poisoned the princess and then saved her by using their readymade antidote. The plan being to gain my trust and then infiltrate our inner sanctum.'

Alex wanted the queen to come to her own conclusions, but to still guide her in the right direction. 'Would they go to such bother? If they intended to use the Carchi virus and had already started its spread, why not wait until it had done its work and the whole of Mariana was at Caprine's mercy?'

'It does not make sense, does it?' said the queen. 'But devils are known to work in mysterious ways. I will admit I prayed for the Green to heal my daughter, no matter what the cost.'

The queen knew she would have sold her own soul if it meant saving Princess Li. But had she made a pact with the devil? The thought struck fear into her heart, and so she dismissed the idea. 'Is it possible he has truly been sent by the Gods?' she said.

'He simply laid his hands on her and prayed for her recovery,' Alex said, sensing the queen's concern. 'I saw no witch's chants, no demonic rituals.' *Only Malik's stupid dance.* 'I don't believe he had any evil intentions. I think it is possible that the Gods have sent him to us.'

The queen stood. 'Come, walk with me, Alexander.' They walked in silence for a while as the queen reflected on the miracle. Eventually, she said, 'There is the other possibility to consider.'

'Other possibility?'

'What if he has not only come to us directly from the Gods, but he is himself a God?'

This was getting into crazy ground for Alex. Talk of Gods and devils was insanely bizarre, but *Malik a God*, nothing could be that strange. Alex recalled the moment Malik came into contact with the princess. He had touched her forehead and held her hand. It all seemed unremarkable at the time. There was no moment of revelation, no celestial light, and no angels trumpeting. All he knew was he had witnessed a miracle and Malik was somehow responsible.

'Your Majesty, if I may be so bold?' *Now I'm starting to sound like William Shakespeare.* 'If Malik has truly been sent to us by the Gods, we must acknowledge the gifts he brings. Would we not risk offending those same Gods if we did not make changes and embrace the opportunity for peace? Perhaps we can thank them for Princess Li's life by making peace with the Greens and the Caprinese. Her Majesty could lead a new era of cooperation, building a better future for the whole of Trinity.' Alex was on a roll now, and the queen was listening seriously. He could tell she was coming around to his way of thinking. 'I'm sure Her Majesty will agree, we can no longer keep his people locked up like animals after what has happened. They must be freed before the Gods are angered.' *I don't want to push too hard, too soon, but this might be our best chance of peace while the queen is open to all possibilities.* 'In my opinion, Princess Li's recovery,' Alex went on, 'can only be explained by divine intervention.' *There, he had said it.* 'Majesty, we must waste no time in thanking the Gods by doing what we know to be right.'

'You are right,' she said. 'I have been confused, Alexander, unable to think clearly. Distracted, I have allowed my grief to cloud my judgement, and I have given up my control. I've allowed hatred to dominate my thoughts. War is almost upon us, and Lord Drabek is a persuasive man, blaming the Caprinese for everything that has befallen us. If the Gods want peace, I have made a great error of judgment.'

'Who could blame you under the circumstances,' Alex replied.

'But,' she said, 'I will no longer be swayed by my emotions. I must take time to consider. Perhaps the Caprinese are innocent, perhaps not. Only time will tell. It might be the Caprinese alone are to blame and the Greens are innocent.'

Not quite what I was saying.

'If Lord Drabek is right,' the queen went on, 'our people remain in grave danger. Hundreds, perhaps thousands of our people are sick and dying. If the Caprinese are truly responsible, we must retaliate, we must defend ourselves. Surely the Gods would not deny us our self-defence? Thank you for your advice, Alexander, you have always been honest when offering your opinions. The counsel will convene this afternoon, and we will hear Ambassador Mezza's proposals for peace. By that time, I will have a clear head. But I have to tell you, without evidence of her innocence, it will be hard to convince the counsel of her true intentions.'

As a show of gratitude and good faith from the queen, Malik had been given a room in the palace next door to Leanne. In doing so, the monarch was also hedging her bets in case Malik had indeed been sent by the Gods. Under the watchful eye of a palace guard, Leanne and Malik had been given a certain amount of freedom to roam the palace complex until the grand counsel convened. Queen Cleoron had nominated Alexander to entertain the ambassador and her Green aide, giving the friends the opportunity to talk in private for the first time with all three together.

'Drabek is outraged,' Alex said. 'And when he's angry, he's dangerous.'

'I thought he was going to have a heart attack when the princess walked through the door. I wanted to go up to him and laugh in his face,' said Malik.

'It's not funny, Malik,' Leanne said seriously. 'Don't think for one minute he will step back and let us have our way without a fight. Lord Krug warned me Drabek holds the real power, not the queen. Drabek thinks she has been brainwashed too easily by her daughter's miraculous recovery, and he is determined to get her refocused on war.'

'Leanne is right. We mustn't underestimate him,' said Alex.

Malik agreed. 'I know he's dangerous, but every time I see Phys Ed's face on him, I have to remind myself to be careful. It's Drabek I'm seeing, not Phys. I'm just excited to be out of his blooming cells at last. You have no idea what it was like in there.'

'I can only imagine. But you're out now, thanks to your newly found talent,' said Alex.

'How did you know, Leanne, how did you know the princess would recover?' asked Malik.

'I didn't, at least not for sure. I started to get the feeling something odd was going on after you came in contact with the kid at the pilgrim camp. Within minutes of your comforting him, he was recovering. His sudden turn for the better disturbed me at the time, and I had a strange feeling you had something to do with it but couldn't put my finger on what it was bothered me about the incident. I decided my concern was because you'd risked yourself carelessly, and I thought nothing more about it until later.'

'So you put me on the spot because you had a funny feeling about a boy in a tent?'

'No, Malik. It became much more than a funny feeling. When I was bitten, I knew I was going to die, at least the Elandra Mezza in me knew. Cadaverine bites are lethal, and I knew without doubt my time was up. I won't try to lie, I was terrified of dying. I saw no way out, and it frightened the heck out of me. As we moved through the passage, the pain was unbearable. Soon I couldn't go on. I had given up. Nothing left...no fight.

'I could hear you talking, Malik, you were trying to coax me on. But other voices were calling me, telling me to let go, telling me to accept my fate. And I did,' Leanne said, looking squarely at Malik as moisture welled in her eyes. 'I said goodbye.' Leanne took a moment to wipe her tears. 'I'm sorry, this is hard to talk about.'

Alex and Malik gave her time without comment.

Leanne heaved a big sigh and went on. 'You put your hand on my leg. I felt it like a sharp sting. I suddenly became aware of you, and even though I could not respond, something had stirred in me. You put your hand on my head and the touch was electric, shocking me to my soul's core. I was instantly stronger, but still I could not respond. My limbs would not move, my eyes would not open, my lips would not part, but my mind was racing. I began to see, but not through my eyes. I saw things from somewhere outside my body. I saw you, and I saw me lying propped against your chest...you, your face buried in my hair, your arms enveloping me and willing me to cling to life. That's when it happened. I was startled by what I saw, unable to comprehend it. I saw your life force transferred to me in a visible electric-blue glow, and at that moment I knew I had to make a choice. I screamed, YES! I WANT TO LIVE!' Leanne paused for a long moment to compose herself again. 'My mind raced and I became confused. I didn't know where I was. There were stars, lights, and people's voices. I was desperate to find you again.' Leanne paused again and took a deep breath. 'I must have returned to my body and blacked out. The next thing I remember is waking up in the palace.'

Malik and Alex were stunned.

'It wasn't until I was recovering in my room I started to remember more clearly. I started to understand I had been part of something special, something miraculous. You didn't just save my life, Malik, you *gave* me life.'

Malik shook his head in disbelief. 'You're creeping me out,' he said, trying to get to grips with her story. 'What you're saying just isn't possible.'

'Like travelling across the Megaverse?' Alex asked. 'That wasn't possible either.'

'It's true, Malik, I'm sorry if it freaks you out. I can't explain it any more than you can, but the fact remains, you have a special power and you saved me. When I was in the garden with Lord Krug, we were talking about green thumbs and how some people have a gift, like a special touch that could bring plants back to life. And suddenly everything made sense...you had saved my life, Malik, and if you could save me, maybe you had the power to save the princess. And you did.'

Alex shook his head. 'If we were not sitting here, light years from home and living in bodies that don't belong to us, I would say you were nuts, Leanne. If I hadn't seen Princess Li sit up and smile when she ought to have died, I would say it was impossible. Nothing about this adventure seems possible, yet here we are, living proof miracles do exist.'

They sat for hours, recounting the details of every step they had taken since arriving on Trinity. Leanne and Alex talked about the lives of Elandra Mezza and Alexander Boatman as though they had personal knowledge of their stories. Alex described in detail Alexander's childhood and days of playing around the harbour while watching the ships come and go, dreaming one day he would join them. Leanne had never set foot in Caprine, and yet she now found herself describing her life of privilege, her childhood in a wealthy family, and her rise to political power.

'Elandra Mezza is a powerful woman in her own right,' Leanne told them excitedly. 'She is one of the most trusted members of the Caprinese Assembly and the most popular figure in Caprine after the king. Opposition to the peace mission came from all sides of politics, not because they did not want peace, but because they feared for my safety.' Leanne was now speaking in the first person. 'They felt I should remain in Caprine in case the king died while I was away. I...' Leanne hesitated as she realised what she was about to say. 'Oh my gosh, it's just come to me. Elandra will be the new leader. I...I will be the first president of Caprine.'

Later that afternoon, the grand counsel called Ambassador Mezza to address the counsel and plead her innocence and the case for a peaceful resolution to the crisis between the two nations. Queen Cleoron oversaw the debate while Lord Drabek spoke for the State of Mariana.

The counsel chamber had seats rising to the outer walls in a series of steep marble steps like a Roman amphitheatre. Not a single place stood empty as the noisy and sometimes hostile debate raged on. Queen Cleoron sat on a throne at the head of the chamber, flanked by senior lords and senators. On a small platform located in the middle of the floor, Leanne gave her deposition, struggling at times to be heard above the competing voices.

'And what of the armada of warships standing off our coast?' asked Drabek. 'If not for war, then maybe to take away our dead bodies to be dumped at sea once the deadly disease has completed its lethal work.'

A great rumble of voices filled the counsel chamber as they considered Drabek's words. The queen called for order.

Leanne felt the weight of numbers stacked against her, but not entirely. She had noticed a shift in the overall mood. Some senators viewed the princess' recovery as a sign they should open their minds to the debate. Some voices even supported her cause, swayed by Malik's miracle. She heard calls to reassess the Green threat, and some proposed the return of slaves to their owners. Leanne was in no doubt some counsel members had selfish reasons for wanting their slaves back. But others, growing with confidence in the crowded counsel chambers, had even proposed the freeing of Greens altogether so they would fall in line with Caprine's example.

'If Malik has been sent to us by the Gods, how can we even think of destroying the Green race?' asked a member of counsel. 'It would be to sign our own death warrant. The Gods would not forgive us.'

The bold declaration by a lower order senator caused Drabek to snarl and curse. 'They mass warships at our door while we sit here and debate. Don't you see these devils have been sent to distract us while Caprine prepares to annihilate us?' he said.

'Our warships have been placed on alert only as a defensive measure,' Leanne argued. 'The fleet has assembled in response to events here in Mariana. We have no wish to go to war.'

'You won't have to go to war if you keep spreading the virus,' Drabek responded.

'Your Majesty, senators of the high counsel,' Leanne said above the cackle of battling voices.

'Silence!' the queen ordered. 'Speak, Ambassador.'

'Thank you, Your Majesty. We, the people of Caprine, have a new constitution built on our love for peace. A non-aggression clause is enshrined in law, and in recent years the Caprinese people have embraced the passive ways of the Greens. For a long time now, slavery has been abolished. We live in a free society where everyone is considered equal. Our National Assembly has passed laws intent on making amends for the past, compensating the Greens and investing in the rebuilding of Ikadies and other Green lands. We realised long ago we could learn much from Green culture. Caprinese people enjoy a feeling of wellbeing that comes from the teachings of Green holy leaders. Our culture has been transformed by those we once held prisoner, and we are learning to live as the Gods intended. We practice tolerance and embrace our differences. Why would we risk our peaceful society and go to war? We live in a new era of harmony, and we invite Mariana to join us.' Debate rumbled through the counsel, and Leanne waited for the hall to go quiet enough to continue. 'Your Majesty, we share the same Gods. The Caprinese have been making pilgrimage to Mariana for centuries to pray at the Lux Temple and place a hand of respect on the Great Pyramid. We can also share the future under the protection of those same Gods, the Gods that brought you Malik. We stand with the Greens for peace.'

Drabek sprang to his feet, waving his arms in the air as he drummed up support from the counsel. 'You have it from the witch's own mouth. The Caprinese and the Greens are as one. They will slit our throats while we sleep.'

'We would hardly need to slit your throats if we had done what you say and had already released the virus amongst you!' A loud gasp circulated the counsel in response to Leanne's aggressive defence. 'Your Majesty,' she continued. 'Lord Drabek's pretext for war is based on our supposed use of the Carchi strain. He claims a plague of our making is currently raging through Mariana and its provinces, and we intend to kill every last one of you. I propose an immediate solution that will hold the fragile peace and prove to you once and for all that our intentions are not only peaceful, but we offer our support and an opportunity for the planet to unite as one.'

'Burn them!' cried one of Drabek's cronies.

'Silence,' said the queen. 'Go on, Ambassador.'

'Malik will attend to Mariana's sick. There are many in immediate danger of dying, too many perhaps. He may not be able to save them all, but he is ready and willing to try for as long as it takes. Let him prove to you we come in peace. Give him this chance, and you will see we are here at the will of the Gods.'

CHAPTER 24

The missing proof

M iracle followed miracle as the sick rose from their beds, healthier and fitter than they had ever been. Malik could not believe his powers of healing, for their speedy recovery was nothing short of incredible. Word spread quickly, causing a rush to the palace from all corners of the realm. Long lines formed as desperate citizens looked for a chance to come before the Green Holy Man of Caprine and be cured by his hand. The chronically ill came dragged on stretchers, and those needing help arrived by the wagon load. Many more came out of curiosity, just to see the miracle worker for themselves. Some just wanted to touch him and be blessed. The city of Mariana was in a state of euphoria, joyous in their knowledge Malik had been sent by the Gods.

'It's scary. Don't you think it's scary?' asked Alex.

'I don't know what to think,' said Leanne. 'This goes far beyond anything we could have imagined. Far beyond our understanding. People are starting to talk about Malik as a God himself, and that *is* scary. I wish Nim would appear and help us understand what's going on.'

They sat for a while in silence, watching the gathering as Malik accepted the people like the pope greeting pilgrims at the Vatican.

'I have a confession to make,' Alex said, hesitating, unsure if this was the right time to say more. 'I...'

'Alex, what is it?'

'I should have said something earlier when Malik was with us.'

'Tell me.'

'When I told you of my exploits on the Island of Parisos, I told you everything except for one important detail.'

'Alex?'

'I told you we were following Nim's instructions and searching for an ancient relic. I said the volcano exploded and we had to abandon our search and run for our lives. That was all true, except...I found it. I found it at the last minute.'

'The relic?'

'Yes.'

'Why would you keep it a secret?' asked Leanne. 'What exactly did you find?'

'Nim didn't tell me a lot as usual, only that I should go to the city of Kerano on the slopes of Tiran and search for an icon. She didn't tell me what it was.'

'But you know now?'

'Yes.'

Leanne sensed the anxiety in Alex's voice, and his reluctance to say what was on his mind. 'What did you find, Alex?'

'I found the lost Carchi Pot,' he said at last. 'I have the missing virus in my possession.'

Exhausted, Malik observed the long lines of hopeful, desperate people and wondered when it would end. Since dawn, he had greeted countless numbers of sick and dying as they came to him with every kind of ailment from simple colds to crippled limbs. Now, as the day grew old, it seemed they came to him in good health. Young, old, rich, and poor, they all wanted his blessing.

Eventually, Lord Krug came to call a halt for the day, and it took a platoon of guards to quell the disappointed masses. Krug had been watching from the sidelines and had seen Malik's exhaustion. He came to escort Malik back to his quarters, but he also wanted time to talk alone.

'I'm not happy with this,' Malik said. 'This is more than just healing the sick. They want me to bless them like I'm some holy man. They're starting to look at me like I'm from a different planet.' *You are from a different planet, stupid!*

'I'm afraid things have gotten a little out of hand,' Krug said. 'Tomorrow we will try and organise better so only the sick can gain access. But I agree, it is a disturbing turn of events.'

'Tomorrow!' Malik gasped. 'How many more are there?'

Krug smiled at Malik's shock. 'Not as many as you fear, Malik. Perhaps another five hundred. We estimate you have received over two thousand already.'

'Five hundred? I don't think I have enough skin left on my fingers to shake another hand or pat another head. I'm shattered. Couldn't you put on a green mask and do a few for me?'

'Oh, but if I could,' Krug said, laughing. 'But seriously, we are witnessing more than a cure for disease here. Your gift is remarkable, but your power over the people is even more astounding. Ambassador Mezza tells me you had no prior knowledge of your special ability, is this true?'

'I'm gobsmacked.'

'Gobsmacked?'

'Sorry, it's just an expression where I come from,' said Malik. 'It means I'm stunned by what has happened. I have a reputation for hurting people not healing them. Have you seen the way they act around me? It's not normal, it gives me the creeps.'

They stood in silence and watched the crowd as soldiers tried to disperse them.

'Walk with me back to your chambers,' said Lord Krug.

'When I'm done, when the sick people are all well again, what happens then? Do you think the queen will be convinced of our peaceful intentions and call a halt to this coming war?'

Krug took a moment to answer. 'The queen, yes, I believe she is already convinced by your actions.'

'So that's a good thing, right?' Malik sensed a conflict in the lord, and for a brief moment, he saw an irritated expression pass over his face.

'There are many who, and I believe the queen is one of them, think you are more than just a faith healer, Malik. They believe you are truly a celestial being. Some are afraid of you because they don't understand you. Some already talk of worshipping you.'

Malik laughed aloud. If things weren't weird enough, this was just too much. A joke of immense proportions. 'You can't be serious...worship me?'

'I'm very serious,' Krug said as he waved his hand to indicate the huge crowd now preparing to camp at the palace doors and wait for Malik to appear again in the morning. 'Take a look, Malik, these are your followers. You have become—'

'An overnight rock star,' Malik said. 'I understand people's interest in what looks like a miracle cure for all, but the fuss will blow over. They'll see I'm just an ordinary person.' *Just gigantic and green with powers over life and death. Ordinary!*

Krug smiled. 'You still don't get it, do you? You will never be ordinary again. These people will look to you for their lead. They will follow you to the ends of the planet, and they will follow you into war. Greens will never be allowed to remain imprisoned now you are their leader. Though you may not realise it, the future is in your hands, Malik. The people consider you a Deity.'

'Deity?'

'A God, dear boy!'

Malik waved his hands to dismiss the idea. 'No, no, no. I am not in the least bit a God. I'm not a leader either, not of the Greens, not of the Caprinese, and certainly not of these poor, sick people of Mariana. I'm just the big kid from Morton Bay High,' Malik blurted.

Krug frowned, but let the reference to Morton Bay High go without question.

'You might not like the idea, but that is how these people see you, and Queen Cleoron agrees. This makes you the most powerful enemy of Drabek and the most dangerous man on the planet. Drabek will not allow you to take away his influence and control, or his war, without a fight. Perhaps it is time for you to leave Mariana before things go too far.'

Krug became distracted by a disturbance in the crowd near the prison entrance. He saw the unmistakable shape of Drabek's top hat and watched as the dark lord pushed his way through the mob towards the prison door.

'Speak of the devil, and he is sure to appear,' Krug said, pointing out Drabek's appearance to Malik. 'That man will seek to destroy you, Malik. One way or another, you and he will decide our fate.'

'Who is that girl at his side?'

'That is Dora Dale, the butcher's daughter.'

Drabek appeared to be in a heated conversation with the young woman. She was shouting and waving her arms in protest. Drabek threw her aside, and she fell to the floor. Before she could get back to her feet, he had entered the prison and slammed the door behind him.

'I've seen her before, at the palace.'

'Ah, you mean Katherine Dale, her twin sister. Katherine is Princess Li's handmaid. You would have seen her at the princess' chambers. They are identical twins.'

Malik felt troubled. 'I guess that's it. She doesn't look too happy.'

Dora Dale stormed off towards the city. Whatever had exchanged between them, Drabek had left her in a foul mood.

'I can't believe you kept it to yourself all this time.'

Leanne's reaction was understandable. Alex had allowed her to go to the counsel meeting knowing full well she would be interrogated about the virus, and all the time he had possession of the missing pot.

'Is it still sealed?'

'Yes,' he answered emphatically. Alex had recovered the container of germs from the petrified hands of the King of Caprine. Only Callum knew of the artefact's existence and had promised to keep its whereabouts a closely guarded secret. After hiding the pot on his return to Mariana, Alex had decided to wait before telling the others. 'It's safely hidden until we know what to do next,' he said.

'Wait! We can't wait. It's proof of our innocence, Alex, proof my people have not released the virus against Mariana. Why didn't you say something? We must tell the queen at once.'

'We can't, not yet.'

'What do you mean, we can't?'

Alex took Leanne by the shoulders and urged her to sit. 'Leanne, please understand. I never wanted to make things difficult for you. It was for your protection I decided to keep the pot hidden.'

'My protection! The queen nearly had me thrown in the Hellefyr, some protection that would have been.'

'I would not have let it get that far, Leanne. But ask yourself this, what if Drabek got his hands on the virus, what then? With both strains in his possession, the Caprinese would have no defence whatsoever.' Alex could tell Leanne was unconvinced. She was angry and with good reason. *I should have told her.*

'Without Mutually Assured Destruction, Drabek would hold all the power,' Alex continued. 'The Caprinese would be at his mercy. He would have the power to enslave the Caprinese as he has done the Greens, throwing them in chains, or worse, exterminating them, leaving him free to take over from the queen and rule Trinity in its entirety. Is that what you want?'

'Of course not.' Leanne thought for a moment, agonising over the right course of action. But now there was a more significant problem troubling her mind. Alex had kept the discovery a secret. Why? *Can I trust him?* She suddenly realised they stood on different sides of the conflict. And though she knew it was Alex doing the talking, how could she be sure it wasn't Captain Boatman pulling the strings?

'So what do we do next?' asked Alex.

'You must return the pot to me. It belongs to my people.'

'*Your people?* Don't take me the wrong way, Leanne, but these are not your people. Are you forgetting who you really are?'

'I'm not forgetting anything,' Leanne said with more than a hint of aggression. 'Perhaps it's you who's forgotten. After all, it's you who does Drabek's dirty work. It's you who rounds up Greens and has them thrown into his dungeons. How do we know you won't betray us, give us up along with the Carchi virus to Drabek? How do we know where your loyalties truly lie, Alex?'

Alex could hardly believe his ears. How quickly she had turned on him. It was his own stupid fault for not confiding in her sooner. But now was not the time to hand over the virus, not while she was angry and unable to think clearly.

'I can't let you have it, Leanne. It's too dangerous.'

'Dangerous! Dangerous for whom?' Leanne was about to say things she might regret when she heard Malik's voice.

'Guess who I found?' said Malik.

Alex was relieved to see Malik and Nim. Their timely arrival had stopped Leanne going too far with her accusations. He hoped they would be more rational about the news.

'You look tired, Malik,' said Alex.

'I'm shattered completely. If I have to pat one more head or kiss one more baby, I will scream. And what's wrong with you two? You look like a pair of angry birds.' Malik sensed the tension immediately.

Nim knew what had caused the glum faces.

The Figment flitted about in her usual fashion, before settling down to sit beside Leanne. She held Leanne's hand, and it had an instantly calming effect. Leanne thought Nim's fingers felt like feathers on her skin. She studied Alex's disillusioned face and felt guilty over her outburst.

Alex repeated his story for Malik, who listened without comment. Leanne was surprised to hear Nim side with Alex.

'I think Alex did the right thing by being cautious. Drabek is very cunning, and it would not take long for him to sense a shared secret. If it suited his purpose, he would not hesitate to put Parlay rules aside and use torture to discover the pot's whereabouts. Now you must decide together what to do.'

'Can't you just tell us?' asked Malik, exhausted by the constant lack of direction.

'I am confident you will make the right decisions, Malik,' Nim said. 'But above all, Drabek must not be allowed to take complete control of the virus strains.' Nim turned to Leanne and squeezed her hand. 'My dear, do not be swayed by suspicion and mistrust. These are the weapons Drabek will use against you. Remember, you are all on the same side, and the dark forces of Angra are on the other.'

Leanne looked ashamed. 'I'm sorry, Alex.'

'Don't be. There's nothing to be sorry about,' said Alex. 'I should have told you both sooner.'

On the way to join Alex and Leanne, Malik was relieved to hear his newfound abilities were in no way godlike. Healers of one kind or another lived throughout the Megaverse, Nim had told him.

'Nim says I'm just an ordinary, everyday Green,' Malik said.

'Not quite what I said,' Nim responded. 'But in some worlds, touch healers are as common as modern doctors on Earth. Greens have a long tradition of healing through touch, and it has only been in the last few centuries such skills have disappeared from general use on Trinity. Greens have been endowed with many amazing abilities.'

'So you're not a God after all, Malik... you just think you are,' Leanne said, laughing.

'Malik has some important news,' Nim said after everyone stopped chuckling.

'I think I may know what's making everyone sick,' Malik said as everyone huddled in closer to listen. 'I told you about Drabek's attempt to get inside my head using Cork the Mind-bender. If you remember, it backfired on him and he unwittingly revealed some of his own thoughts to me. The reverse of his intentions. I didn't realise at the time, and their faces were blurred, but I think I saw a memory of Drabek instructing his agents to poison their victims, including Princess Li. I saw him handing over bottles of liquid to someone I now believe to be the Dale twins. Katherine Dale is the handmaid to the princess. We saw her on the night we went to the princess' chamber. Didn't you ever wonder, Alex, why she did not show any signs of the disease herself?'

'I never gave it a thought in all the excitement,' said Alex.

'She had plenty of opportunities to slip the poison to the princess,' Malik continued. 'And she pretended to care for Princess Li knowing she was safe from catching any disease.'

Alex nodded in agreement. 'If she had poisoned the princess, there was never a risk of catching anything.'

'Exactly. Dora, the other sister, had access to food supplies,' said Malik. 'I believe she chose random victims, people who bought meat from her father, the butcher, and laced their purchases with the same poison. Drabek's concoction created all the same symptoms as the pestilence or a lethal virus so no one would suspect their food had been spiked. With Drabek feeding the queen lies and accusations about the release of the virus, and her daughter one of the victims, he was assured of her sympathetic ear.'

Alex saw the pieces of the puzzle falling into place. It all made sense now. 'How can we prove it?' he asked. 'We can't very well accuse him with only Malik's word to go by.'

'We could try...after all, the people do think he's a God, and unless we can get back inside Drabek's head, Malik is all we've got,' said Leanne.

'No, we need hard evidence,' said Alex.

'Katherine Dale has a servant's quarters next door to Princess Li,' Nim said. 'If she had this poison, she may not yet have had a chance to dispose of the evidence. Alex has free access throughout the palace, so perhaps he can search her room without anyone knowing.'

'Search Drabek's room too,' Malik added. 'My guess is he has more supplies at hand.'

'That might be a little harder to arrange,' Alex said, knowing the risks of being caught in the dark lord's chamber. But Malik was right, if Drabek had issued poison, it must have come from his own supplies, and these could only be found in his private rooms.

'Well, Alex, what do you think?' said Leanne.

'I'll do it,' he said.

They agreed on a plan in which Leanne would create a distraction by requesting a meeting with Lord Drabek in the counsel chambers. Meanwhile, as a trusted member of the queen's court, Alex would be able to slip past the guards and into Drabek's rooms without drawing attention. What could go wrong?

'Nim, will you be sticking around this time?'

Nim flitted from one spot to the next to the next. 'I'm always around, Alex, it is just materialising when you need me I'm having trouble with. It seems the pyramid is exerting a powerful force and interfering with my abilities. I'm afraid there is little I can do to overcome it at times.'

CHAPTER 25

Dirty deeds

Avoiding the main entrance meant Alex could make his way through the rear of the palace undetected. Long hallways stretched the entire length of the building, intersected by shorter ones leading to various wings of the complex. As a regular visitor to the palace, Alexander's presence there was unremarkable, allowing him to wander through corridors while being ignored by servants, soldiers, and kitchen staff alike. A few off-duty guards gave him a casual nod of recognition when he passed, but no one appeared curious.

Despite Leanne's earlier outburst, Alex felt the three friends were once again working together in a coordinated fashion. Troubling though the flare-up was, he understood the strain Leanne was under and why she had become so distrustful and defensive. None of them could have been prepared for what they had encountered on Trinity; the pressure was enough to make anyone buckle. He wondered if they would ever have agreed to such an adventure had they known what to expect in advance.

If everything has gone to plan, Leanne should be meeting Drabek right about now. He hoped she would not underestimate him.

The east wing's ground floor accommodated guards, servants, and kitchen and administration staff. Alex passed through without problems. The upper dormitory housed several high-ranking senators and advisors in residence, including Lord Drabek. Alex climbed the stairs to the top level, and from there it was a short walk to Drabek's door. Alex paused outside the room, disturbed by a sign on the door opposite that read: Intelligence & Security Authority. This was the barracks of ISA, Drabek's newly formed secret police. Drabek obviously wanted them close at hand for his protection. Alex was about to turn the handle to Drabek's door when two officers emerged from the barracks.

Sitting up close was disturbing for all the wrong reasons. Leanne felt she was back at school. She pushed the image of Phys Ed teaching classes from her mind and tried to remind herself the man standing before her was not the bungling teacher, but a dangerous and deadly lookalike. Any resemblance, other than his physical appearance, was non-existent.

She couldn't help thinking she saw a hint of recognition in his eyes, as though he were trying hard to place her, to remember where they had met before. Drabek took a seat and invited Leanne to join him. She heard the familiar nasal wheeze as he spoke and had to remind herself once again. *Concentrate, this is Drabek, not Mr Evans.*

Two ISA police officers stood near the door in silence. To Leanne, they looked like thugs. Before they could begin, the door opened and a palace guard entered. He bowed briefly and shuffled inside. Avoiding eye contact with Drabek, he gave one of the ISA officers a message and left quickly. The policeman passed on the contents of the note with a secretive whisper in Drabek's ear. Drabek acknowledged the message with a nod and waved him back to his position by the door.

Drabek smiled. 'Just the little matter of an intruder in the palace grounds,' he said, watching Leanne for a reaction.

Outwardly, she remained stone-faced and impassive, but inwardly, Leanne's heart sank. *Could Alex have been discovered so soon?*

'Before we begin,' Drabek said. 'I have more important news. I'm sure the contents of which will be of great interest to you, Ambassador. The King of Caprine is dead,' he said abruptly. 'Word has just arrived from Caprine.'

Drabek could not contain his delight at being the one to break the news. He almost laughed as the blood drained from Leanne's face, leaving a ghostly mask to tell of her shock.

'And if my information is correct,' Drabek continued, 'that makes you the new leader of the Caprinese Kingdom. The king is dead, long live the president!' he proclaimed in a mocking tone.

Leanne could barely focus a thought. 'Dead?' she said.

'So I am told.' Drabek allowed the news to sink in before continuing. 'I'm also informed that with the royal line at an end, the Grand Assembly of Caprine has decided on a change of rule. The monarchy will no longer preside over the people. They want a president. They want you, Elandra Mezza, to be the very first.'

Leanne was in a state of shock. 'A change of rule, yes,' she said, 'but who will lead the people is yet to be decided. That is a matter for the grand assembly.'

'Oh, I think you're too modest, Ambassador, my sources have you down as a certainty. But I do hope nobody bets their house on the length of your reign.'

'There are few certainties in this life, Lord Drabek.'

'Or any other,' he conceded with a smile.

Leanne's mission had taken on new urgency. Without a peace treaty, there would be no need for a king *or* a president.

'This news changes the complexion of our peace talks, Lord Drabek. I must address Queen Cleoron and her counsel at first light so that I might return to Caprine as soon as possible.' Leanne stood, making herself ready to leave. She appeared anxious.

'Please don't go on my account, Ambassador, or is that Madam President? Either way, we have not had a chance to speak. Tell me what was so urgent we had to meet here so late in the evening.'

Leanne gasped. In her state of shock, she had totally forgotten Alex.

'Lord Drabek is not in his chambers,' one of the ISA officers said. 'Is he expecting you, Captain?'

Drabek's secret police wore uniforms specially designed for the new force. And though their organisation's directives suggested an undercover role, there was nothing secretive about their appearance or their operations. Elaborately decorated with gold embroidery, their red and black tunics might have been elegant had it not been for the skulls, snakes, and monsters depicted by the gilt thread. Tattooed faces of the ISA officers featured fierce images, not unlike the Maori of New Zealand and certain tribes of South America. Alex thought the tats were meant to intimidate. As a sign of their authority, they wore armbands emblazoned with Drabek's coat of arms, a black eagle on a white background with a human skull for a head.

The two men waited for Alex to reply with an expressionless and threatening air of arrogance that made Alex shiver. He was aware that with Drabek's authority, they could detain who they wanted, even a captain of the queen's fleet.

'No,' Alex said at last, 'Lord Drabek is not expecting me. But I can wait.'

Unmoved, the ISA officers stood and waited with him, cold eyes meeting his with suspicion and scorn. Alex maintained eye contact, unwavering and steady.

'You don't have to keep me company,' he said after a long silence. 'I'm sure you have a baby shower to attend.'

Neither policemen reacted to his sarcasm, not that they would have known what a baby shower was. They stared with blank expressions, waiting for Alex to make the next move. Unable to search the room, Alex decided to leave before he had more questions to answer. He was about to tell the men he would return to see Drabek in the morning when a third police officer joined them at a trot.

'Sir,' said the breathless man. 'There has been a breach of the palace grounds. Lord Drabek has been notified and we are searching the area.'

With a final disdainful sneer, the three policemen turned on their heels and hurried from sight, leaving Alex to slip inside Drabek's chambers undetected.

Drabek's room was unusually sparse; it had a hard, uncomfortable feel. There were few signs of warmth or luxury, and no personal touches to identify the occupant. Alex noted the way in which items were arranged in perfect order and made a mental note to leave everything exactly as he found it.

He moved through the chamber, checking drawers and cupboards as he went. When he came to the bedroom, he saw the first personal signs of Drabek in the form of his clothing. Everything else in the room was standard palace issue. Even Drabek's precisely laid out clothes seemed impersonal and bland. Identical in style, they were simply-tailored black pants, plain black tunic tops with long sleeves, black woollen leggings, black boots, and Drabek's signature black top hat. The dark lord had never been seen in any other colour or fashion.

Three top hats sat on a high shelf, precisely aligned. Alex wondered why a man would need three identical pieces of headwear. Curiously, he reached up and lifted one down. As he did so, he noticed a wooden box pushed to the back of the shelf out of sight. Alex took the box and opened it. Inside, just as Malik had described them, he counted five blue glass bottles full of liquid. Alex put one in his pocket as the door to Drabek's room opened, and someone stepped inside.

'I came to plead with you, Lord Drabek,' Leanne said.

She tried hard to focus. It was her role to distract Drabek and keep him busy while Alex searched for evidence. News of the king's sudden passing had left her rattled, and she found it difficult to think of anything else.

'The queen is obviously reliant on your advice, My Lord. Your influence over the counsel is beyond question,' she continued. 'With such power, I can only imagine you will be the ultimate decision maker when it comes to the question of war. On behalf of the people of Caprine, I beg you to rethink your position. One with such power must also have the wisdom to know when to use it.'

'You flatter me, Ambassador. But I see no reason to rethink my position. My position is clear.'

'You might want to consider what you would jeopardise by leading the queen into a war she cannot win. You have an enviable position at her side, and a very comfortable life as her key advisor. Would you risk it all?'

Drabek stood, pressed his hands together, and considered Leanne's statement as though he were looking for humour in her words. 'Comfortable you say? Do you honestly believe I crave comfort, that my purpose in life is to have an easy time as the queen's snivelling lackey?'

'I can't guess what it is you crave, Lord Drabek, or what your motives are for driving recklessly toward war, but I do know to embark any further on this madness would be to condemn all sides to extinction.'

'You seem very sure of yourself, Ambassador. Your confidence seems quite perplexing seeing as you claim to no longer have possession of the Carchi virus. By your own admission, you have nothing to threaten us with as it turns out.'

Leanne decided to double bluff Drabek. 'I lied about that. We still have the virus safe in our hands.'

'Come now, Ambassador Mezza, surely you can do better than that.'

'Will you risk your own survival on the truth or untruth of my words?'

'You don't have the virus. I saw it in your eyes when you addressed the counsel,' Drabek said, but now he looked doubtful.

'Look again,' Leanne said, unflinching. 'Look into my eyes and see the truth.'

The smile disappeared from Drabek's face.

Lord Krug stepped into Drabek's room and closed the door, and Alex slid himself in behind a heavy velvet curtain for cover. Krug went to Drabek's desk and opened a drawer but hesitated, sensing he was not alone. He turned and scanned the room with suspicion, searching for the source of his unease. At last, his gaze came to rest on the curtain.

'You can come out now. I know you are there.'

Alex slowly stepped out from his hiding place and watched as an alarmed and bewildered expression crossed Krug's face like a dark shadow.

'I suppose you're wondering why I'm here?' said Alex.

Krug looked at the box in Alex's hands. 'On the contrary, Alexander, I think it's quite clear why you are here, and it seems you and I have the same thing in mind.'

'You suspect Drabek too?'

'Of course, dear boy, has he not already shown his capacity for treachery? But without evidence my hands are tied, the queen would never take my word over Drabek's. I need proof of his dirty deeds.'

Trusting his old mentor with the story, Alex explained how Malik had seen into Drabek's mind during his mind-bending exercise, how he had come to realise Drabek had been responsible for poisoning the princess among others, and how he had framed the Caprinese for their deaths. Alex outlined the part played by the Dale twins and how he had concluded that evidence would be found in both the Dales' and Drabek's possession.

'And here you have it, Lord Krug, there's no disputing this is the poison used,' said Alex.

'This is terrible news,' said Krug. 'But what if Lord Drabek has found the missing Carchi virus, and the bottles you hold do not contain poison but the virus itself?'

'Drabek could not have found the virus,' Alex said confidently.

'But how can you be so certain?'

'Because I have the Carchi Pot and the seal is unbroken. The pot is safely hidden in my mother's kitchen.'

Alex went on to describe his adventure on Parisos and his eventual discovery of the missing pot in the petrified hands of the old king. He told of Frog's attempt to steal the disease and their narrow escape from the volcano.

Krug listened in silence until Alex had finished. 'You must go to the queen at once, Alexander. Take her the evidence.'

Alex hesitated. 'I will. But we can't tell her of the pots whereabouts, at least not yet. It would be too dangerous before Drabek is safely in chains. Even then, Lord Krug, the virus must be returned to Caprine to maintain the balance of power and preserve the peace.'

Krug thought about the implications before agreeing. 'Very well, Alexander, you must take the evidence to Queen Cleoron, and I will take some guards and find Drabek.'

Queen Cleoron listened in astonishment as Alex told his story. The box of blue bottles was all the proof they needed. Alex promised that the palace pharmacist would undoubtedly confirm the presence of a poison that could imitate the effects of the virus.

'Lord Krug is on his way to arrest Drabek at this very moment. Earlier, I despatched a search party to Katherine Dale's room to look for more evidence. Dora Dale is—'

Before he could finish, the search party returned with Katherine Dale and a matching blue bottle of poison that they found in her personal belongings. Katherine looked terrified by her arrest. She cried and pleaded for mercy.

'Lord Drabek made me do it, Ma'am,' said Dale. 'He threatened to kill me and my whole family if I didn't go through with it. I didn't want no harm to the princess, Ma'am. I loved her, you know that.'

Queen Cleoron silenced everyone while she digested the story. It was beyond imagination; the one man she had come to trust had been responsible for the attempted murder of her daughter. She cursed aloud as the doors opened and Lord Krug arrived with a large detachment of soldiers and secret police. With him, he had Leanne and Lord Drabek. Drabek stepped forward to face the queen.

'Why is this man not in chains?' the queen bellowed.

'Quite right,' said Drabek. 'Guards, arrest Captain Boatman and throw him in chains.'

'But...'

Two burly soldiers stepped forward and grasped Alex by the arms, one on either side, forcing his hands behind his back.

'Take him and Ambassador Mezza to the dungeons,' Drabek continued with a snarl. 'And find the Green giant. I will deal with them all later. Oh, and by the way, Captain, my men are about to make their way to your mother's kitchen. The Carchi virus will be mine if Lord Krug's information is correct. Perhaps you can share the precise location to spare your mother any harm or inconvenience.'

Krug shrugged his shoulders and said, 'I'm sorry, Alexander.'

'Lord Krug, what have you done?' said Alex.

'One has to know which side is best for one's own survival, Alexander. Lord Drabek and I have been allies for a very long time. We have a mutual understanding of the future.'

Queen Cleoron, confused by the drama unfolding before her, now came to the realisation she was witnessing a rebellion. Drabek and Krug were taking power right under her nose and she had to stop them.

'Soldiers, arrest these men.' No one moved. 'Soldiers, I demand you arrest Lords Drabek and Krug.' Still no one moved.

'Guards,' said Drabek with a confident sneer. 'Confine the queen to her quarters until further notice.'

CHAPTER 26

Despair

'I thought I could trust Lord Krug, but I was a fool,' Alex said.

He sat near the corner of his prison cell on the stone floor with his back propped against the cold, mould-ridden wall. A hole the size of an orange had been chiselled out of the wall adjoining two cells, which was at the eye level of a sitting man. The opening had probably been made by a previous prisoner long since departed, and no doubt one of the many names and initials carved into the walls. With a tilt of his head, Alex was able to see Leanne sitting in the dark on the other side. He wondered how many prisoners had sat in these same uncomfortable positions and consoled each other in their shared despair.

'I'm sorry,' he said. The sound of his voice echoed around the barren cell walls and ended in silence. He waited for a response, but there was none. 'Leanne, did you hear me?' She did not answer. In the dim light, Alex saw she had her hands on her face. 'Are you crying?'

Leanne dropped her hands and sighed. 'No, I am not crying. I'm angry.'

'I said I was sorry.'

'Not at you, Alex. I'm not angry at you. I might have made the same mistake if our positions had been reversed. Krug had me fooled too. No, I'm angry at myself for not seeing this coming. How could I have been so stupid as to think Drabek would be willing to negotiate peace when he is the one who engineered this whole crisis as an excuse for war. I should have known he was behind the sickness from the start.'

'Why should you have known, how could you?'

'Why? Because it was my job to know! As the leader of my people, I should have been aware of Drabek's influence over the queen and the likelihood he would try something like this.'

'There you go again, Leanne, taking on a burden that's not yours. You're not the leader of Caprine, and you're not Elandra Mezza. You are Leanne Chambers, fifteen years old, a schoolgirl from class 4C. You can't be expected to take on the responsibility for all that's happened, and you can't blame yourself for what Drabek has done.'

Silence followed while Leanne brooded. She knew Alex was right; she couldn't have known what to expect, but with each passing night's sleep, she felt Elandra's presence growing inside her, and with it, the personal responsibility of her role. There were times she didn't know who she was anymore because so much of Elandra was revealing itself and influencing her thoughts.

'Sixteen,' Leanne said eventually.

'What?'

'You said fifteen years old. It's sixteen...I had my birthday yesterday.'

Alex closed his eyes and felt for Leanne. 'Sorry I missed it. Did you have a party?'

'Yeah,' she chuckled. 'And a big cake with sixteen candles. Mum threw a surprise party and everyone was there. All my Facebook and Instagram friends were there. Well, maybe not all of them, we only have a small house.' She said this with jest, but her voice trailed off into a sad murmur.

'I'll bet Simon Harper was there,' Alex said, continuing the line of humour.

'Sod Simon Harper. I never really liked him. He's so full of himself.'

They did not speak again for several minutes as Leanne's thoughts drifted to her life back home. She wondered what she would make of it all if she ever got back. Her world, her life, it all seemed so different now. She had changed, and with that change, the people and things that mattered to her had become even more important. She missed her parents.

'Did you miss your mum all those years?' she asked Alex. 'I mean if you were so young when she went away, do you remember her and miss her not being around?'

Out of the blue, the question threw Alex for a few moments; he was still thinking of Simon Harper and how popular he was at school.

He had never shared his feelings about his mother, who had disappeared when he was just three years old. 'At first, I did,' he said, thinking back. 'I was too young to know everything that was going on, and no one took the time to explain. Maybe they thought I was just too young to understand. I remember I cried a lot at first. I wanted no one but my mum, and anyone who tried to console me got the tantrum treatment.' A sense of emptiness filled his heart as the memory unwound. Perhaps he remembered more than he cared to admit.

'Slowly it became clear she wasn't coming home. I overheard conversations between my dad and others close to the family. They said she had walked out on us, but my dad never believed it. Time passed, she never returned, I stopped crying eventually, and life took over. My dad did a good job of raising me on his own, with a little help from his sister and my grandparents. We were soon happy again, and I never asked about my mum again. We never looked back. Sometimes I dream about her, but I can never see her face. She's always turning away or just out of sight. She's always wearing a string of white pearls around her neck, and I think how pretty she must look.' Alex reflected on the vision, lost in his thoughts for a while before he snapped back to reality. 'To answer your question,' he said, 'you don't miss what you never had, and for most of my life I've never had a mum.'

'Did you ever wonder why she went away?'

'I just assumed she didn't like us anymore. That whatever she wanted from life, we couldn't give it to her. Sometimes, very rarely, I wondered where she ended up and if she had found happiness with another family, a family she could love. Other times I fantasised she would come knocking on the door and say she had made a mistake, and she'd realised she loved us all along. I knew what I was going to say if she did, and it wouldn't have been nice. But most of the time I didn't care what happened to her. I wasn't angry, wasn't sad, I just didn't care because she was gone and we, me and my dad, were happy without her. That's how it seemed anyway.'

There were times when Leanne thought having parents was a luxury she could do without. Not that they were cruel or uncaring, quite the opposite in fact. An only child and her daddy's little princess, she had been only too happy to delight him with the speed of her advancement. As a young child, she found life easy and fun. Most of all she found pleasure in learning and overcoming new hurdles. When her parents, mostly her father, saw her various talents, they pushed just enough to test her. Nothing gave her more pleasure than seeing her father's face when she did something astonishingly brilliant. She remembered his surprise and delight when she started speaking Spanish within months of her first English words.

As she grew older, the relationship with her father started to change. She only had herself to blame because she saw every push he gave her as a challenge to meet. With every challenge taken on and won, it slowly became a battle between them, and her father sought ever more difficult demands to place on her. She, on the other hand, would fight tooth and nail to take up the gauntlet and succeed where he thought she might falter. Their battles became serious after a while. Winning was everything. These challenges applied to everything in life, but most of all her music. She played the piano as though it were the piano itself she was fighting. She had wanted so badly to be a concert pianist and make her father proud, but the enjoyment of music started to fade as he demanded more and more effort. It seemed nothing would please him, and she saw the love for her father slipping away in the process. That's when she finished playing, and that's when she stopped taking up her father's challenges.

Alex's cell door rattled and opened to reveal Drabek, accompanied by members of ISA. In their custody, they had Malik.

'I thought you might like some company, Captain, seeing as how you two have become so chummy.'

Cautious as ever of the big Green man, the guards forced Malik into Alex's cell using the point of a spear to keep him at arm's length.

Malik turned back to Drabek and said, 'Oh, waiter, when dinner time comes around, can I get a burger and chips? And an ice-cream sundae, or a large cola float with chocolate ice cream to wash it all down. And bring some for my friends too, they must be starving by now.'

'Burger and chips? That must be some of the Green filth you people eat on that island of yours. Anyway, mock all you like, slave, soon you won't be worrying about eating, you will only be worrying about getting eaten.'

Drabek doubled over with a hearty laugh, joined in the fun by his men until Drabek's face changed to a sneer, and his men followed suit again.

'But I'm not one to deny a last wish. I'll have someone bring you some real food in the morning. Mariana food,' Drabek said.

Leanne shouted from the next cell. 'You can't do this, Drabek, we are here under Parlay. I demand our release.'

'Oh, the new president demands, does she? Well Parlay, shmarlay, I don't give a damn for your rules,' Drabek said. 'Anyway, you forfeited your protection under Parlay when you tried to overthrow my government.'

'Your government?' Alex stepped forward aggressively. The guard raised a spear and warned him to stand back. 'Queen

Cleoron is head of state,' Alex continued. 'It's her government ruling over Mariana, not yours, you treasonous dog!'

'*Treasonous dog?*' Malik said, mocking Alex's attempt at an insult.

'Well, it sounded like something Alexander would say,' Alex responded.

Drabek laughed off the personal attack. 'Treasonous? That's not what the people will believe I'm afraid. The only treason will be seen as yours, Captain, for conspiring with the enemy and assisting the ambassador and her Green to commit murder. I will inform them of your attempt to assassinate the queen, a successful attempt, unfortunately.'

'The queen is dead?' Alex asked, shocked by the news.

Drabek smiled. 'Actually, no...not yet at least. But the people won't know that. The queen and her little princess will be disposed of discreetly after I have dealt with you three.'

'You're a monster,' said Leanne.

'Why thank you,' said Drabek. 'So now we come to what to do with the three of you. Normally I would have you all thrown straight into the Hellefyr, but Malik here has become something of an icon to the common masses, and I don't want to risk an uprising. Therefore, I have decided to grant Malik and you, Captain, a reprieve. Your death penalty has been reduced to life imprisonment on the roof of the lighthouse tower. Not a very long life I would imagine, given the exposed location.

But my leniency should keep the people happy, for a while at least.'

'Well, that doesn't sound so bad,' said Malik. 'At least I'll be able to wave at the ships as they depart for far-off lands. And we'll be able to watch the sunset, Alex. We could take up painting.'

'Laugh all you want, Green man. You'll be able to watch more than sunsets from your lofty perch. You'll have the best seats in the house for my grand show,' said Drabek.

'What show?' asked Malik.

'He has something evil in mind,' said Alex. 'I can sense it by the sneer on his face.' Alex suddenly realised where this was going. 'You said the two of us had been sentenced to life in prison, so what about Ambassador Mezza?'

'Oh, you must call her by her new title, *Madam President*. A short-lived president I'm afraid. I'm sorry to say that using the protection of Parlay to murder the queen is punishable by death, and while there are mitigating circumstances allowing your sentence to be commuted, no one would forgive me if I did not make the Caprinese assassin pay the ultimate price. The day after tomorrow is Extinction Day, a fitting anniversary to celebrate with a sacrifice. She will face the Hellefyr and burn while you both enjoy the spectacle from your high vantage point, assuming you last that long. Once she has been dealt with, the people of Mariana will want me to take control. I will send our armies to exact revenge on her people. Having killed our queen with the Carchi virus, the Caprinese will be held accountable, and as such I will declare viral war on those responsible. Mutually Assured Destruction was Carchi's plan, wasn't it? Except, as we all now know, the Caprinese do not have the means to retaliate because, thanks to Captain Boatman, I now have both strains. The only thing mutual about the Caprinese destruction will be that you and I can be mutually assured they will be annihilated.' Drabek fell into uncontrollable hysterics, laughing so hard that tears ran down his cheeks.

'You're mad,' Alex said.

'Mad? I suppose I am in a way. Well, that is what M.A.D. stands for, Mutually Assured Destruction,' Drabek chuckled some more and wiped the tears from his eyes.

'He's the Mad Hatter,' Malik said. 'Lewis Carroll's Mad Hatter. Except he's not a hatter, he's a hater.'

'Enjoy your last night together with the president. In the morning you will be consigned to the tower.'

The cell doors slammed, the lamps extinguished, and silence descended on the inmates. There were no angry shouts from Leanne, no tears or pleas for mercy, no funny gags from Malik or reassuring words from Alex.

Silence.

CHAPTER 27

Resolve

Nim wept. They could not see her, but they could hear her sobs, first in Leanne's cell, next in a corner close to Malik and Alex, then back with Leanne. Her tears reflected her heavy heart. It was she who had brought them to this, and it was she they had trusted with their lives.

'I have no words to describe how I feel,' said Nim between sobs. 'It wasn't supposed to happen like this. I never imagined you would face such dangers. It's my fault, and I must find a way to help you.' No one spoke in response. 'My father has tried everything he knows to get you out of here, but a great force within the pyramid is blocking every effort. Unless you can escape beyond the city walls, you will be unable to cross over to safety.'

Still, no one answered.

'Please say something,' said Nim. 'Shout at me, scream...I deserve it.'

No one did. They knew there was no blame to lay, for they would all have answered Nim's call even if they had known the risks and the severity of the dangers. They also knew it wasn't only their fate hanging in the balance, but the fate of the whole planet, the entire Megaverse. Events on Trinity were being played out on thousands, perhaps millions of worlds across multiple dimensions. Reflections of their failed attempts for peace would have consequences for the existence of life itself, the battle between good and evil. With the extinction of Caprine and the Greens repeated ad infinitum, the balance would shift in favour of Angra. Worlds would become unstable and would collide and collapse. The Big Bang would follow.

'We can't give up,' Alex said eventually.

'Ever,' said Malik.

'Never,' Leanne agreed.

With renewed determination, they discussed their options and the seeds of an idea began to form in Alex's head. 'Nim, can you communicate with John Boatman directly?'

'Maybe. I can try.' Then after a pause, 'I'll find a way.'

Alex explained his plan.

Daylight arrived after a long and sleepless night. The three friends had said little since Nim's departure, reflecting instead on the importance of their lives and their plan for survival.

When the cell door opened, Alex was relieved to see Little Jim, as secretly arranged, carrying a tray of food for a breakfast Drabek had promised as their last.

The guard searched Jim for weapons and found nothing of interest. With his eyes on the food, he failed to notice Little Jim had developed a fatter than usual backside due to the soft, pillow-like packs hidden in his trousers, hardly a threat even if the guard had found them. Jim slipped out the packages and passed them to Alex while the guard checked the food tray, tasting the freshly baked bread in the process and slipping half the loaf along with some honey into his pocket for later.

'Mr Boatman sends his regards, Captain, and those of Nim,' said Little Jim. 'Their meeting was very successful last night. He said to tell you that thankfully, he is already well underway with the prototypes. He's used the finest Red Widow Spider silk in your design. He said it's stronger than Black Spider, stronger than steel, yet lighter than a hummingbird's feather. Strong enough for even three men, he said.'

'What you talking about?' the guard asked, grasping Little Jim roughly by the arm. 'Leave the tray and get your ugly little face out of my sight before I kick you where it hurts.'

The mean looking guard hurried Little Jim to the door. Jim looked back as he went and shouted a message. 'Mr Boatman said to watch out for the changes he made to the airfoil...it's been designed for the fastest rate of descent.'

'Get out of here!'

'Oh, and most important!'

'Go,' said the guard.

'Whatever you do, don't—' The heavy oak door slammed on Little Jim before he could finish his sentence.

The crowds had already gathered in the square before daylight, despite the chilly morning. News of the queen's assassination along with her daughter, Princess Li, had spread quickly, and there were mixed feelings among the population. Some were outraged, some felt betrayed, and some were in denial. How could it be the Green giant known as Malik, could perform his miracles and heal the sick, only to consort with the Caprinese ambassador to assassinate the queen? It didn't make sense.

Now, as soldiers led Malik and Alex to the tower, there was barely a free inch in which to stand. Heated debate amongst those assembled had quickly deteriorated, and fights had broken out between those of opposing views. Uneasy at the fragile mood of the crowd, extra soldiers had been assigned to clear a path and to watch for anyone with thoughts of taking the law into their own hands.

Standing head and shoulders above everyone else, Malik became the immediate focus for the crowds in the square. Some shouted insults, others, words of support.

'Murderers!' a wealthy looking man called out as they passed, but an angry mob shouted him down; clearly, they supported Malik.

'We don't believe in your guilt, Malik. We'll demand a re-trial.'

'Lies and fabrication!' said another. 'We'll call for your release.'

Some even began to insult Drabek. They questioned his hold on power, and safe amid the mass of anonymous faces, they called him a criminal and a liar. Nevertheless, with Drabek's soldiers and secret police evident in large numbers, no one tried to intervene before the condemned duo reached the entrance to the tower.

The lighthouse tower stood eight hundred feet high. A perfect cylinder of polished marble, the sheer walls offered no opportunity for a climber to take a grip. A single entrance at the base proudly displayed a door made of six-inch-thick steel. It opened to a spiralling stone staircase, curling its way up with over one thousand five hundred steps to the summit.

'You've got to be joking,' said Malik, eyeing the long climb. 'Why don't you just kill me now and get it over with? The tallest thing I ever climbed was my bed.'

'Don't tempt me,' said the leading guard as he urged the pair upwards one step at a time.

'I'll never make it,' Malik continued to complain. 'You need to install an elevator.'

'Look on the bright side,' said the guard. 'You won't ever have to walk back down.'

'Ha, ha, very funny,' said Malik.

Almost one hour later and exhausted by the effort, Alex and Malik emerged from a heavy steel trapdoor and out onto an open platform, which turned out to be the roof of the lighthouse tower. It reminded Alex of a helicopter landing pad, like those seen on some city skyscrapers and oil platforms. Bare and exposed to the elements, the shiny marble floor felt slippery underfoot, making them feel unsafe even when standing still. A stiff, cold breeze blew in from the sea, and Alex saw the Caprinese fleet anchored many miles offshore, waiting for orders in the event Elandra Mezza should fail in her mission of peace. The ships appeared as nothing more than black dots on the horizon, too far away to help the ambassador even if they came to know of her predicament.

The Great Pyramid seemed even more colossal from their high vantage point. Its pinnacle glistened like a star on a Christmas tree, some hundreds of feet above the top level of the lighthouse tower. Alex saw them reflected in its shiny glaze.

Four armed guards stood ready in case of resistance, while a fifth took a bucket of sticky goo and slopped the mixture on Malik and Alex with a long-handled paintbrush.

'What is that stinking stuff?' asked Alex as he tried in vain to fend off the slapping brush strokes.

'Goat urine and honey,' the man answered.

'You idiot!' said Malik. 'I asked for a peanut and honey breakfast, not pee and honey. And where's my toast?'

'Go ahead, funny man, make jokes. But you won't be laughing in the morning when you're just a pile of stinking green guts. The vamps will make short work of you, even with all that fat. They can't resist this concoction...they can smell it from ten miles away.'

'Vamps?'

'You don't want to know, Malik,' Alex assured him.

The guards left via the trapdoor, which slammed shut behind them, leaving Alex and Malik to survey their new prison. Not that there was anything much to discover. There were no walls to contain them, no steel bars or chains. In fact, the platform was devoid of anything at all, including any barriers to protect them from falling over the edge. Malik moved tentatively to take a peek over the side. His stomach turned at the sight, and his legs buckled like jelly beneath him as his head swam in a dizzy haze.

'Oh no, I'm afraid of heights.'

'It's a normal reaction,' said Alex. 'You'll get used to it.'

'Get used to it? I don't want to get used to it. Anyway, it's not the height bothers me, it's the thought of falling to the bottom.'

Alex stood without fear right on the edge of the tower and looked down on the city. Below, thousands of people packed the public square and scurried around as tiny dots, looking for all the world like insects. At one end of the square, he saw the dreaded Hellefyr. Glowing red with bubbling, molten lava, the Hellefyr was, in fact, an open volcanic pit. Over centuries, it had been used for sacrifice and as a place of execution for crimes against the Realm. When viewed from this great height, Alex thought it resembled the red eye of a fiery dragon, blinking as clouds of gas erupted from its belching centre. A stage had been built on the edge of the Hellefyr, and a platform stretched out like a diving board over the blazing-hot middle. Alex felt a shiver, and the hairs on his neck bristled; he knew the purpose of the platform.

'What if we want to go to the toilet?' asked Malik.

'Use the poop chute,' Alex said, pointing to a hole the size of a dinner plate near the platform rim.

Malik looked down the chute and smiled. 'There's going to be an awful mess for someone to clean up by the time it hits the ground.'

Alex didn't laugh.

'What kind of lighthouse is this anyway,' asked Malik. 'Where's the light?'

'They once lit bonfires on the platform to warn ships to avoid the rocky coast and to signal the alarm when enemy ships were spotted out at sea. They also believed the light would guide the Gods to Mariana. After the harbour wall was built, they had smaller light towers constructed further out on the rocks.' Alex pointed them out. 'And since then there hasn't been a war in living memory, and the old lighthouse has served only as a prison death sentence for people like us. Prisoners are left to rot up here without food or shelter. If the exposure or the starvation doesn't kill you then...'

'Then what?'

'There's a storm coming,' Alex said, pointing to the horizon. 'Let's hope it gets here before nightfall.'

'Are you crazy? Eh, hello, Earth to Alex...storms come with lightning. If you hadn't noticed, we have nowhere to hide up here.'

'Yeah, but vamps don't like hunting during storms.'

'What happens to us after?' Leanne asked Nim.

They were alone in her cell. The guard had disappeared somewhere to take a nap, confident his prisoner could go nowhere beyond her four walls. Nim was invisible to him.

'After?'

'After they kill us here, what happens to us on Earth?'

Nim hesitated. She knew the answer but did not want to say. In the end, she felt she had no choice. 'You would cease to exist. You'd disappear without trace.'

'That's awful! What about our families, our parents?'

Nim answered sadly. 'They would never know what happened to you, forever wondering where you went.' Nim started to cry again. 'I am sorry,' she said.

'But you could tell them, right? You could appear to them as you did to us, tell them we didn't just disappear and that we didn't just run away and leave them without a word.'

Nim sobbed.

'Nim, you could, couldn't you?'

'It would not be permitted.'

'Permitted by whom?'

'Leanne, there are rules, and rules of the Megaverse are not easily broken. Bringing you here has broken many rules and laws of the Megaverse. We should not even be talking now, and I am afraid if they knew, I would be...'

Leanne's mind started to race. She imagined her grieving parents, heartbroken. The loss alone would be bad enough, but never knowing the truth, that would surely kill her father. And she had so many things she wanted to tell him. She thought of Malik and Alex and their parents; they would suffer the same fate, left to wonder and question for an eternity. And Alex's father, she couldn't imagine how devastated he would be to lose another family member without knowing why.

'Alex's father would go through the whole ordeal again,' said Leanne. 'It just doesn't seem right.'

'Life is not always fair. It wasn't fair the first time.'

'The first time?'

Nim did not answer.

'Nim?' Leanne studied Nim and knew the Figment was hiding something, but she could not hide the guilt on her face.

The realisation sent a quiver through Leanne's body. 'Alex's mother didn't leave him, did she? You said as much that day at the school. You said so because you knew for sure! She didn't run away...she crossed over, didn't she?'

Silence.

'Nim, answer me. She crossed over and never returned. What happened to her?'

Spots of ice-cold rain stung their faces as a prelude to the coming storm. The breeze had increased to a brisk and steady wind, but the eye of the storm had stalled and settled offshore. Billowing cumulonimbus clouds climbed into the stratosphere, providing a light show out to sea that in other circumstances would have been spectacular to watch. As it was, the constant lightning strikes and thunder crashes only served to remind them of what was to come. The alternatives, however, were even more frightening to Malik, especially since Alex had explained what vamps were and how he had already seen them on the hunt.

'When are you going to take those paragliders out of your pants?' asked Malik. 'I think they've had enough of your wind tests by now.'

'Very funny,' said Alex. 'But not until morning. We don't want to lose them. Plus, they make a good pillow for me to sit on.'

Alex did not want to unpack the paragliders just yet. The danger of wind carrying them off the platform before they were ready was a real one. He could not believe John Boatman had managed to create such a compact design from his drawings, but faith in his skills as a sailmaker made Alex confident the sails would work as they should. His only worry was that Little Jim had been unable to communicate his final warning before being thrown out of the cells that morning. Actually, it was far from his only worry. He had serious concerns Malik would be unable to control his glider, having never flown before. The flight was going to be a severe test for an experienced paraglider, let alone a first timer. On the plus side, Malik was an avid gamer so he knew how to handle these types of challenge, in theory at least. And he was smarter, much smarter than he allowed anyone to know, especially when it came to technical things and how stuff worked.

Alex went over and over the instructions with Malik. He wished he had a pencil and paper so he could better explain, but Malik appeared to grasp the concept and gave the impression he could confidently manage the flight without difficulty. Malik was more worried about Leanne and how Alex would complete her rescue alone.

'I should follow you as backup,' Malik said. 'If something happens to you, she'll be done for.'

Alex wished he could say yes, but he knew Malik would have his hands full just getting himself over the city wall. 'It's going to be a difficult enough manoeuvre for me without worrying about you, Malik. What if we collide in mid-air, tangle our canopies and crash, what would happen to Leanne then? No, all you have to do is take off from the tower, glide over the wall and wait for us on the other side. That will allow me to concentrate on Leanne without worrying about you.'

Malik agreed reluctantly, but Alex knew he was unhappy about having to leave Leanne behind, even if only for a minute. 'What's the story between you two anyway?' Alex asked.

'What do you mean?'

'You and Leanne. It's obvious there's some chemistry happening.'

'Chemistry?'

'You know what I'm talking about. I've seen the way you look at each other. And then there was the big hug in the great hall. The one where you almost—'

'You're out of your mind,' Malik interrupted. 'Leanne hates me.'

'Didn't look that way to me, Malik. I definitely saw some reciprocation coming your way.'

'Reciprocation, is that your fancy way of saying she was disgusted?'

'You know what I'm talking about,' Alex persisted.

'Shut up, Alex.'

They sat in silence for a while, watching the storm clouds billow and glow like the dancing embers of a fire. Malik couldn't help thinking about what Alex had said. It was ridiculous to even consider he and Leanne had anything in common beyond them being thrown together on this bizarre adventure. Even if she didn't still hate him, he would always be the big buffoon to her, no matter what he said or did.

The remainder of the day passed slowly, and as night drew nearer, the pyramid began to radiate with orange and gold light, as it had done every night since the dawn of time. The sight had a mesmerising effect on the two captives.

'Who do you suppose built the pyramid, and what makes it glow like that?'

'No one knows, Malik. They say an ancient civilization created the structure before mysteriously dying out, long before recorded history. If that's true, they had an amazing level of technical knowledge. Look at the precision of the polished glass and how it's perfectly engineered. It's resisted all attempts to get inside. The surface is made of something harder than anything known to man. And what about the modern design? It wouldn't look out of place in Dubai, Shanghai, or New York. I'm sure there's something similar in London. And then there's the floating thing, how is that even possible? It defies physics.'

'I know. I can't figure it out. Maybe it's an illusion,' said Malik.

'Oh, it's not an illusion. I've seen it up close. It levitates.'

'It must be magnetism, like magnetic suspension using opposing gravitational fields. It probably uses a dynamic stabiliser like tuned mass dampers to keep it from moving.'

'Wow, you know all that stuff and yet you call Leanne a nerd?'

'Yeah well, don't tell her I'm smart or it will ruin my reputation. I've built gyroscopes and model drones, all controlled by a computer. Stabilisers are an important part of the design process. It's a hobby.'

The storm appeared to be on the move at last, creeping ever closer to the shoreline. Malik and Alex silently cringed when a lightning bolt found its mark on an outlying lighthouse, and thunder crashed almost simultaneously, causing them to worry about where the next one would hit.

'That was close,' said Malik.

They turned their attention back to the pyramid and tried to ignore the approaching danger.

'There are no markings anywhere on the pyramid other than the single symbol of a hand located on the east side where the platform extends across the lake,' Alex said, his knowledge coming from the captain's experience of the monolith. 'The platform allows pilgrims access to the outer edge of the pyramid and the hand, which has come to be known as the Hand of Gods. They come from all over Trinity to touch the symbol and pray to the Gods. Some people believe the pyramid is home to the Gods, others say it was built as a tribute to them by a race of people no longer in existence. Some stories tell of their destruction at the hands of the very Gods they worshipped.'

Malik stared at the perfect, symmetrical structure. *It's beautiful.* He sensed an irresistible connection to the pyramid and an overwhelming attraction he did not understand. 'Every time I look at it, I think it's trying to tell me something,' he said.

'Probably saying, 'Get some sleep Malik, you're going to need it in the morning.''

Malik laughed. 'Yeah, probably.' Malik studied Alex and wondered how he could be so calm. 'I don't get it,' he said eventually.

'Get what?' said Alex.

'You. I don't get you.'

'What's there to get?'

'How is it someone named Bottom is so confident and sure of himself? When I first saw you in class and heard what your name was, I thought you would have to be a geek.'

'And so you thought I'd be an easy target, right? You thought I would crumble and cry every time you made fun of me.' Malik did not reply. 'I've had to deal with my name all my life, Malik. Even before I started school, before I was even five years old, people, kids, adults, anyone with a funny comment to share would make a beeline for me. My dad prepared me for what was to come from people like you. He did his best to warn me. I never figured it would be so relentless and last all my life. But my dad and my grandad were strong characters, and they helped me see it as an advantage.'

'An advantage how?'

'A name like mine makes you independent and strong because you develop a thick skin, and after a while, it takes a lot to bother you. Once you accept yourself for who you are, you become happier with everything else in life. It's also like you're equipped with this personality detector, where you can instantly judge a person's character by the way they react when they hear your name. Like you...I knew straight away you would want to bully me.'

'I didn't bully you.'

'No? So all those names were just friendly fun, right?'

Malik thought in silence for a while as another crash of thunder split the air.

'Sometimes it's hard to see yourself as others do,' Malik said at last. 'I'm not good at making friends, never have been. I stick my foot in it even before I get to first base. In some ways, I'm like you. People take one look at me and make up their minds about who I am and what kind of person I am. I get an instant reaction and react just as they would expect, so it becomes a self-fulfilling circle.'

'Prophecy,' Alex said. 'A self-fulfilling prophecy.'

'Whatever.' Malik paused. 'Anyway, you're wrong.'

'About what?'

'About me seeing you as a target.'

'No?'

'It might surprise you to know you drew my attention because I was curious. I watched you in school and thought you were different from other kids. You seemed to cope with life as though nothing could faze you. You didn't care what others said or did.' Malik hesitated. 'I admired you,' he said, then flushed at the admission.

'What!' Alex said, laughing. 'You're taking the pee, right?'

'I'm not. I picked you out because I thought we could get along together like we had something in common.'

'You went a funny way about it, Malik.'

'I know, that's what I'm saying. I'm my own worst enemy. I want to say one thing, and something completely different comes out of my mouth. And then I get angry because nobody takes me seriously. They see me as an overgrown chump with no brains. They expect the worst of me, so that's what they get.' Alex did not reply. 'Anyway, I didn't mean to act like a bully. So I'm saying sorry, that wasn't my intention. Geez! Why is it so hard to apologise? I feel like an idiot.'

'You're not an idiot, Malik. It takes guts to say stuff like that.'

They said nothing else, allowing the conversation to come to an end naturally but with each feeling they had a better understanding of the other.

'Martha Halligan was a troubled child,' Nim began. 'From a very young age, she had difficulty sleeping. Oh, she slept well enough, but she dreamed more than any child should. She also remembered every dream down to the minutest detail, even days and weeks after. Martha kept Dreamweavers like my father extremely busy trying their best to weave a basic level of normality for the child. She was happy in many ways and enjoyed telling those who would listen of her adventures in dreamland. Martha's parents, teachers, and friends put her stories down to a vivid imagination, but as she grew older, others found her tales to be quite odd, disturbing even.

'Eventually, Martha stopped telling her stories. She had seen how people reacted when she did. She knew people thought she was not only strange, but she was becoming quite mad. Despite her isolation, Martha met Ted Bottom. They married soon after and were thrilled to be blessed with a son. They named him Alexander.'

'Did Martha stop remembering her dreams once Alexander was born?' Leanne asked, watching Nim closely as the beautiful Figment told her tale.

'No, on the contrary, after Alexander was born her dreams became even more real. One day, she started to dream the same dream over and over. Martha dreamed of a woman and child, not unlike herself in appearance, but a poor, desperate woman with an infant child she could ill afford to feed and care for properly. Each night, Martha would witness the woman's suffering and despair as she struggled to survive. The child was a sickly child, malnourished and prone to every illness. She did her best to care for his needs, but with each passing day, the child grew weaker and the woman's hope for his future grew fainter.

'Martha's health suffered. She could not shake off thoughts of the woman and child. Even though she had her own son, Alexander, to raise, she could not find happiness in her life while the woman suffered in her dreams. One night as she slept, Martha watched helplessly as the woman gave up hope entirely, lost the will to live, and plotted her own end. Martha feared for the child.

'Martha knew her own child, Alexander, was a healthy, strong boy who would go on to thrive and live a happy life. He had a loving father and grandparents who would care for him. She took the heart-breaking decision to stay within her dream so she could rescue the woman's child. She crossed over and took on the mother's role before the woman could take her own life and that of the child. Martha knew by making this commitment, she could never return to her own life.'

Leanne thought she could feel Martha's heart breaking, and tears ran from her eyes at her brave sacrifice. 'How was that possible?'

'No one knows. Martha was special, and her will was so strong. Even my father could not unravel the mystery of how

Martha was able to cross over without any help from a Dream-weaver and guide.'

'And what happened to the boy?'

Nim continued the tale, her voice echoing the sadness of Martha's story as it reached its conclusion. 'Martha raised the boy alone. Constantly sick, it was a struggle even for someone with Martha's strength of character. Martha worked when she could, begged when she couldn't, but somehow managed to feed and clothe them both, often going without herself so that the child could grow stronger. But as the boy grew, his true character started to emerge. He was a nasty child, full of resentment and anger. He belittled and bullied Martha, even stole the food from her mouth. She witnessed his cruelty to others and knew she had failed him when she saw what he had become. He had grown up quite evil despite her best efforts. Martha Bottom died of a double broken heart. It broke daily for the child she had given up and left behind, and it broke daily after that for the child she had chosen to save.'

'And what happened to the boy, the man, the evil man?'

Nim sighed. 'Drabek? Why, he went on to continue his evil ways I'm afraid.'

CHAPTER 28

Every storm has a silver lining

With the onset of the night came nature's full fury as wild winds whipped rain into stinging squalls of hail and ice. Alex and Malik endured their lofty perch, clinging to life by frozen fingertips, hoping they could ride out the storm until daybreak. They lay flat on the floor to withstand the hurricane-force gusts. To add to their terror, above the roar of the gale they could hear the shrieks of vamps flying high in the sky. Frustrated cries of hunger pierced through the air as their sensitive noses picked up the scent of prey, but they were too afraid of the storm to descend any closer. It was the one bright spot in an otherwise desperate situation for the two exposed prisoners.

Lightning strikes peppered the darkness with constant flashes of searing light, followed by deafening cracks of thunder. They watched the sizzling forks of untamed power converge on the pyramid. Strike after strike, the electrical discharges were taking the same path to ground, seemingly on a collision course with the tower, only to leap to the pyramid before impact. The storm lasted hours, though it seemed like weeks, and all the while, the pyramid provided protection. Shielding them from the worst of the weather and taking the brunt of lightning strikes like a protective mother, her vulnerable children hid behind her great shining skirt for shelter.

Battered and bruised as daylight dawned, Alex and Malik could only marvel at their miraculous survival. With the storm long gone, the sun had risen against a perfect blue sky. Heat from its rays caused steam to rise from the wet surface of the tower, like the lazy raising of a curtain before the start of a spectacular show. Distant shrieks and the sight of vamps circling high in the cloudless sky drew their attention.

'I thought you said they only hunt at night.'

'They do,' said Alex. 'Normally. They must be able to smell that stinking stuff they put on us. I thought the rain would have washed it all off by now. We're probably safe while the sun's high.'

'Probably?'

Alex went to the edge of the platform and studied the scene below. Crowds had returned and had already filled out the public square. He observed what he thought was a lighter mood amongst those gathered, an almost carnival-like atmosphere as they prepared to celebrate Extinction Day. It was on this date the last Leemon had passed away on the island they in their millions had once called home. Today, the people of Mariana planned to mark the anniversary with a special event, and for once, Drabek had the people firmly on his side. As the killer of their queen, the people of Mariana wanted Elandra Mezza to suffer an agonising death in the flames of Hellefyr. Alex could hear distant laughing and plenty of happy voices in the crowd as they waited for Drabek to begin the festivities. His stomach turned when he thought of the terrifying ordeal Leanne now faced.

The wind had dropped to the slightest of breezes, a little too calm for flying, Alex thought. He studied the direction in which the clouds were moving and worked out his plan of attack. 'We should go over the instructions one more time,' he said to Malik.

'Alex, we have been over them a hundred times. I know what to do.'

They unpacked the paragliders, laid them out on the floor, and meticulously checked the lines. Marvelling at the lightweight gossamer materials, it was impossible for them to understand how such delicate silk could be so strong and stow

345

into such tiny packages. Alex checked every detail for functionality and design. John Boatman had executed his job with precision but had made several small changes meant to enhance performance. Until he was in the air, it was impossible for Alex to understand the impact these changes would have. He could only trust in John Boatman and pray the improvements would work.

Thumping drums and blowing horns signalled the start of festivities below. From their vantage point, Alex and Malik watched a procession of dignitaries arrive at the stage and take their seats for the ceremony. Unmistakable amongst the colourful gathering, the black-clad figure of Drabek stood out at a podium whereupon he began his opening speech. It wouldn't be long now before Leanne would appear before them.

'Time to get ready,' Alex said.

Alex first assisted Malik with his harness. The lightweight webbing used for straps made the fitting comfortable and secure. The breeze whistled across the lighthouse roof with a sudden gust, causing Malik's canopy to fill with air before settling down once more on the floor. Malik took a deep breath and gave Alex an anxious thumbs up. With Malik secured and ready to go, Alex fitted his glider harness and checked out the cords he would use to steer. His heart thumped against his chest, and his mouth felt like blotting paper.

'Okay, ready if you are, Malik.'

Malik rolled his eyes and took another deep breath. His nerves were now in full flight or fight mode. Except this time, the heightened emotions were all about the flight part.

The crowd jeered and cheered to signal the time had finally come as Leanne entered the square to a rowdy reception, escorted to the stage by a troop of heavily armed guards. The almighty roar was deafening.

Alex and Malik stood on the rim of the tower and waited. Adrenaline pumped through their veins as they watched for the right moment to go. Malik's hands trembled.

'Almost time,' Alex said. 'Don't forget, just take off gently, don't jump, and let the canopy lift and carry you in a straight line to the south until you are over the city wall. Don't start pulling cords and trying to force it or you'll end up in a spin.'

'I know! Give it a rest,' said Malik, taking a lungful of air as he tried to focus and settle himself.

They watched with sickening anticipation as Leanne was forced onto the overhanging platform where she began her slow, steady walk over the Hellefyr.

'Okay, let's do this,' said Alex as he inhaled one last breath to steady his nerves.

'Hey, Bubble Butt, good luck,' said Malik.

Malik's canopy billowed and filled with air, tugging at him as he readied to take to the sky.

'Same to you, my friend,' Alex said.

The emphasis on the word friend was not lost on Malik. He smiled and gave another thumbs up.

'You know,' said Alex, 'you look like a superhero ready to take flight.'

'Really? Which one?' said Malik.

Alex allowed his sail to fill and lift, taking him an inch or two off the ground like a fledgling eagle testing its wings for the first flight. 'The Green Willy,' he said with a grin as he stepped over the edge of the tower. 'See you on the other side!'

Malik watched Alex begin his flight in a slow arc, circling the tower as he adjusted to the conditions. Malik said a prayer and let the breeze take him off his feet, and before he even had the chance to think about changing his mind, he too was soaring above the ground far below. 'Green Willy, very funny.'

To say Leanne saw her life flash by before her eyes would be incorrect, it was the life she had yet to live she imagined. She thought of her grand piano, the Steinway she had hardly played and its shining gloss casework that smelled of beeswax, spruce, and maple every time she opened the lid to play. Her family was by no means wealthy, and the magnificent grand piano had been a stretch for her father who had virtually mortgaged the house to afford it. He thought the instrument would rekindle the passion within her. It arrived on her fifteenth birthday. The piano had been a dream come true, but it had come at a time in her life when she struggled to see her future as a musician. Now she could look back with such clarity, she realised how ungrateful she much have appeared. Her parents had given up so much for her future.

She did play the grand occasionally, and only in secret when her parents were out of the house and she was alone. She would get distracted halfway through practice and start playing pop songs instead while singing along to the tunes. Not that she would ever sing in public, but she had a soft, melodic voice that could capture the very soul of the music she played so skilfully. Now, as she stood on the edge of the abyss, it was the keys of that beautiful grand piano she longed to feel beneath her fingers. *Will I ever get the chance again?*

As she neared the end of the platform, Leanne stopped, turned her back to the bubbling cauldron of molten rock, and faced the baying crowd of hostile citizens.

My gosh, they hate me.

Drabek waved his arms in the air to encourage their calls for revenge. Lord Krug stood beside him looking ashamed, unable to look her in the eyes. Drabek called for silence, and the gathering came to be quiet so he could speak.

'Good citizens of Mariana,' he bellowed. 'We have come together today to remember our beloved Queen Cleoron and the Princess Li, taken from us by the treachery of an enemy bent on our annihilation.' The crowd roared in anger as they raised their fists and called for blood. Drabek waited for calm before continuing. 'Our only comfort at this time is in taking a life for a life. This crime will not go unpunished.' Drabek let the masses vent their feelings for a few more minutes before going on. 'Behold, citizens of Mariana, I give you the first and last President of Caprine, and the killer of your queen, Elandra Mezzaaaa!'

Drabek let the name hang in the air as though he were introducing a circus act to an appreciative audience. Booming voices, thousands in number, shook the ground beneath their feet in response. Leanne cringed at the outpouring of hate and thought they would drive her into the Hellefyr by their sheer force of ill will. She steadied herself as Drabek silenced the voices for the last time.

'Has the witch anything to say before we carry out the sentence?'

A bubble of lava erupted from the roiling pool and sent a shower of hot pumice into the air. Leanne felt the searing heat on her back, and the crowd cheered as she cowered forwards away from the sudden hot spew.

'People of Mariana,' Leanne began, but no one could hear her above the aggressive howls for justice. Drabek did not attempt to quiet them.

In her peripheral vision, high in the sky and as yet unnoticed by the angry mob, Leanne saw two paragliders leaving the rim of the lighthouse.

It felt good to be in the air at last. Alex adjusted his line of flight and came around the tower in a wide circle, just in time to see Malik catch the breeze. He nervously watched as Malik struggled to become familiar with the controls. Malik needed to bring the glider around to his left and set a course for the wall, but instead, Malik's handling had sent him in the opposite direction. With nothing he could do to help, Alex had to concentrate on Leanne and hope Malik would gain command of the canopy.

Alex did not catch the loud howls from below because the wind now rushed past his ears, making it impossible to hear anything at all. To gain a rapid rate of descent, he would have to perform a series of dangerous manoeuvres, more hazardous than he had ever attempted. Timing was everything. He closed the cells on the leading edge of the canopy, pulled the brakes on the left side of the trailing edge and shifted his weight, causing the glider to turn sharply while forcing him into a corkscrew-like flight path.

The design changes made by John Boatman had a dramatic effect on his rate of descent, and Alex struggled to maintain control as he became disorientated by the increasing velocity of the spiralling turns. G-forces, never before experienced, threatened to cause him to blackout under the immense pressure, so he shifted his weight again and increased the angle of attack. But Alex knew if he kept his current rate of speed, his descent would conclude with a devastating, probably fatal crash into the ground and his rescue would be over with before it had even started.

Malik overcompensated and made a sudden right turn. Seeing the Great Pyramid was now directly in his path, he groaned helplessly and pulled on the brakes, but it turned out to be too much, too late as his manoeuvre caused him to stall in mid-flight and come to rest with a heavy thud against the mirror-like wall. Malik spread his arms wide as his fingers desperately searched for a handhold. He began to slide like a frog down a window pane as he clambered to find a grip, clinging for dear life as his canopy floated limply below him.

Someone in the crowd called out and pointed skyward as they spotted Alex's paraglider looping wildly above them. A collective gasp followed as others in the mob focused on the phenomenon, a sight they had never seen before, and whispers began circulating that perhaps the spectre had been sent by the devil to rescue the witch. Some fled in panic, others stood like stone and watched as the strange object swept back and forth through the air, seemingly from the heavens. Leanne's heart thumped. Drabek looked horrified.

'Into the Hellefyr with her, now!' he screamed.

Alex regained control, bringing the airfoil back on the trajectory. He saw Leanne balanced near the end of the overhanging platform, and two ISA policemen were approaching her with swords drawn, trying to force her off into the fiery pit. Alex shifted his weight once more, bringing him around in an arcing approach and aligning him with Leanne and the Hellefyr beyond. But now Drabek's men were littered across his flight path, directly between him and Leanne. He trimmed the lines and brought the tips of his canopy underneath to increase airspeed. Extending his legs out before him, he braced himself for the collision. With a mighty blow from his feet to each of the men's backs, one by one he sent them tumbling sideways and into the Hellefyr with a blood-curdling scream. The impact slowed Alex's rate of travel; he hoped he would still have enough speed to complete Leanne's rescue.

Malik pressed his face flat against the glass wall with his hands still spread against the surface as he desperately felt around for a hold. Gradually slipping on the steep slope, he did everything he could to stop himself from sliding down the side of the pyramid. But his attention had been drawn to something quite startling embedded in the glass. The glare of strong sunlight had illuminated a texture within the glass, an unmistakable pattern right before his eyes.

'Photovoltaic cells,' Malik said to no one. Fascinated by his discovery, Malik gasped in shock as his canopy filled with air and momentarily hoisted him away from the surface. Despite his best and most determined efforts, he started to lose his grip on the pyramid.

Alex hit Leanne like a train, almost knocking her into the bubbling vortex as he scooped her up off her feet. He gripped her with his legs and she grasped his harness as planned, wrapping her hands tight around the webbing while clinging to him desperately. Alex cleared the platform, but the sudden additional weight had caused an unexpected shift in trajectory. They were now headed down and into the Hellefyr from which he was trying to save her.

An idea flickered in Alex's mind, inspired by the immense heat rising from the inferno below. He opened the airfoil fully to scoop up the super-heated air. The delicate canopy flapped in the turbulence, and for a moment, all seemed lost as the paraglider deflated. Alex pulled hard on the lines; the unbearable heat seared his legs, but the canopy responded almost instantly, filling like a balloon and sending them skywards as though it were a feather dropped over a campfire. They rose with such speed that Leanne could barely hold on. Alex gained control and rode the incredibly hot thermals high into the sky as the crowd looked on in astonishment. Alex continued to soar, rising in a circular path like an eagle as they climbed higher and higher with every revolution in the upsurge of heated currents.

We'll soon have enough altitude to clear the city wall.

Alex heard it before he saw it. First a shriek, then a grumble, then a roar. The vamp appeared like a bat out of hell, talons raised and ready to strike. Alex shifted his weight, taking the glider into a dive as the giant animal glanced his body and grazed his arm, drawing blood in the process.

Leanne gasped in horror as the ferocious head had come so close she could see her reflection in its black diamond eyes. The vamp turned hard and prepared for another attack. Leanne strengthened her grip on the harness, but G-forces pulled at her arms with such power they threatened to dislodge her completely. Alex banked again, the vamp on his tail as he entered a spiral at speed and headed once more for the ground at an unstoppable rate of descent. The animal followed with a squeal and a snarl, proudly displaying a gleaming set of deadly, razor-sharp teeth.

Malik's canopy had now fully inflated. He pulled on the lines to turn himself to the east and for the first time, he saw the battle for survival unfolding beneath him.

Alex noticed a line he had not seen before, one of John Boatman's additions to the design. The vamp had circled and was coming around for the kill, so Alex decided to test the line and gave it a firm, sharp pull. The mistake soon became apparent, and Little Jim's unfinished last words came back to haunt him. Hearing the snapping and whirring of material above him, Alex realised the canopy had separated from the harness and both he and his passenger were now plummeting towards the ground, leaving the canopy flapping uselessly like a plastic bag in the breeze.

The vamp honed in on its prey. Alex and Leanne tumbled helplessly, and Drabek simply stood open mouthed and stunned by the spectacle. Outstretched talons cut through the air as the vamp committed to a power dive, intending to take them mid-air before they reached the ground. Alex closed his eyes and braced for the impact. But when it came, it was from an unexpected source and direction.

Malik crashed into his friends in an uncontrolled tangle of lines, green flesh, and Red Spider silk sail. Only feet from the ground, he hit them with such speed he caused them to plough into the square like a grounded comet, sending dust and debris into the air behind them as they came to a halt at the foot of the stage. Shell-shocked, the three friends lay in the dirt and watched in terror as the vamp closed in for the kill. Like a supersonic missile, the animal was an unstoppable force. With a deafening screech, the vamp called out in triumph.

'I think this is goodbye,' said Malik, closing his eyes in anticipation of the strike.

It would have been comical had it not saved their lives. It might even have gained a spot on the funniest home videos had someone had a camera and invented a television, but just as the angry vamp reached its elusive prey, the jettisoned canopy of Alex's paraglider floated down and covered the animal's head, blinding it in the process. Unable to see during the closing seconds of its attack, the vamp veered off course, missed its target, and careered instead into the gathered dignitaries on stage, taking out Drabek, Krug, and several others, only coming to rest when it skidded to a halt at the edge of the Hellefyr.

Drabek cursed in disbelief at first, then cursed again in horror as the dazed animal towered its head above him and snarled. The shift in weight caused the platform to creak and groan, instantly causing silence to fall upon the square as everyone held their breath. Another creak echoed around the square, followed by the sound of cracking timber. For a brief, quiet moment, nothing else happened. No one moved, no one spoke, even the vamp seemed to sense the imminent danger and remained perfectly still. With a slight gust of hot air from the volcano, Drabek's top hat tilted to the side. Silence followed. The topper again slipped on his head and now balanced only on the tip of his ear. Everyone gasped as hands shot up to cover open mouths. And then, as if it were the last straw to break the camel's back, the hat fell over Drabek's ear. With one final crash, the platform gave way and plunged them headlong into the fiery depths below. The last two things to be seen entering the Hellefyr were a panicked and stunned vamp, followed by the disbelieving and horrified face of Lord Drabek.

'Curse you, Bottom, we are not done you and I!' were his final words

CHAPTER 29

Revelation

Confusion followed the dramatic rescue of Leanne and the demise of Lord Drabek. In the aftermath, only Malik's presence stopped the volatile crowd from finishing the job Drabek started. He stood before the angry mob while protecting Alex and Leanne, called for calm, brought order to the square, and asked for a chance to explain the truth. Lord Krug had survived the vamp collision but had been left clinging precariously to the rim of the Hellefyr; that was until Malik had pulled him to safety on the condition that Krug admitted his guilt. Forced to confess his treason and while pleading for mercy, Lord Krug reluctantly told the gathered citizens how Drabek had deceived them. The crowd gasped when they heard of Drabek's plans to kill the queen. They also learned of his plot to poison the princess, among others, in order to provoke a war with Caprine. In order to prove Drabek's deception, loyal palace guards were sent at once to free the queen from her confinement, and she emerged with the princess as the final irrefutable evidence of their deceased lord's treachery. Queen Cleoron's trusted officers soon set about restoring order, arresting those who had plotted against her, and releasing those held under Drabek's orders. Mariana was once again in its rightful loyal hands.

By late afternoon, the palace was secure and the crowd had dispersed from the square and all palace grounds. It had taken all day, but Alex, Leanne, and Malik finally found themselves alone and able to talk in private. Leanne couldn't help noticing Malik's excitement. She saw him slink away somewhere earlier when he thought she wouldn't notice. He showed up hours later looking tickled pink with himself. At first she had put his lively condition down to adrenalin, the effects of the traumas still running through his system. But as the day had progressed, she knew there had to be more behind his apparent agitated state.

'Did you hear what Drabek said as he disappeared into the Hellefyr?' said Alex. 'He called me Bottom.'

'I'm not so sure,' said Leanne. 'Maybe it just sounded like that in the confusion.'

'No, it was definitely Bottom,' said Alex. "Curse you, Bottom,' he said, 'we're not done you and I."

'Why would he say Bottom, and what did he mean, not done— he's dead!' said Leanne.

'I don't know, but it gave me the shivers. Maybe he'd known who I was all along. Maybe he'd known all of us.'

'Maybe,' said Leanne.

'What now?' asked Alex. 'Our job is done here. All we have to do now is to walk through the city gates and we could be home before we know it.'

'Ravens have been sent with word to Caprine,' Leanne said. 'I sent my official ring as a sign that we have achieved peace, even if it's so far only temporary. Our navy can stand down. But as for going home, our work is not done here while the Carchi virus exists in any of its forms. Queen Cleoron has agreed to meet later to discuss the issue, but there can be no long-term security until the virus is destroyed. The queen still worries me,' said Leanne. 'She's a strong woman and will do whatever it takes to protect her interests. Life would have been a lot easier if Jani had been able to replace her. It worries me that she now holds both virus strains, as did Drabek. What guarantee do we have she won't use them against Caprine and the Greens at another time of her choosing?'

'I think you underestimate her desire for peace,' said Alex. 'I'm confident she'll do the right thing.'

'Every Green has been released from prison,' said Malik.

'I know, that's great, Malik. I know how much it means to you. It's a good sign of her intentions anyway. At least you can go home feeling we've achieved something special.'

'Thanks, but I won't be returning home,' said Malik. 'That's what I've been wanting to tell you all day. I could hardly contain myself waiting until we were alone.'

Alex looked surprised, thinking Malik was the least likely to want to stay any longer than necessary. 'What are you talking about?'

'You may think you've seen everything by now, and nothing could surprise you, right? Well, I have something to show you that might just take the cake,' said Malik. 'I know exactly why I'm here now and what I have to do. Everything has been revealed to me. It was like someone just turned a key to a vault where all my knowledge had been stored.'

'Malik, you're not making any sense,' said Leanne.

'Come with me,' said Malik.

Malik led the others to the Great Pyramid. The area was deserted as they walked out on the boardwalk across the lake and stood before the Hand of Gods. The sacred symbol had started to pulse.

'I've been struggling to understand my part ever since we arrived on Trinity,' Malik said. 'While you two seemed to know instinctively what your role was, I stuffed around looking daft and thinking I was the butt of a big joke. I felt useless.'

'You weren't useless, Malik, you saved many lives, including ours.'

'I know, Leanne, but I still didn't get it...something was missing from the puzzle but I didn't know what. Then I collided with the pyramid during my *expert* flying performance, and everything became clear.' Alex and Leanne looked puzzled. Malik continued, 'I ended up flat against the pyramid. My face was so close to the glass, and the sun was catching it in such a way that I realised the walls of the pyramid are made up of solar panels.'

'Wow,' said Alex.

'Yeah, wow! But that was nothing compared to what happened next. I had my hands pressed against the surface, trying desperately to find some traction or some way to hang on, when something extraordinary happened. My palms tingled as though they were receiving a mild electric shock. But it wasn't a shock, it was a download of data, everything I had to know to complete my mission.'

'You're still not making any sense, Malik,' Alex said.

'Then I'll show you,' said Malik.

Without further explanation, Malik placed his hand on the sacred Hand of Gods symbol. It was a perfect fit for Malik's massive hand. They heard a series of electronic beeps and the release of locks. With a swoosh and a blast of compressed air, a sliding door opened in the pyramid. Leanne and Alex stood open mouthed before the entrance.

Malik held out a hand of introduction. 'Welcome to the Starship Enterprise!'

Vast. That was the only way Alex could describe the interior. Like the atrium lobby of an ultra-modern city building, glass walls rose up in brilliant sheets of sunshine, creating a cathedral-like experience for the three tiny figures standing on the ground floor looking up. Glass elevator shafts rose from floor to pinnacle, and multiple levels with transparent balconies overlooked the lobby.

'It's not called Starship Enterprise. I just made that up. I always wanted to say that though.'

'This is a spaceship?' Leanne asked in awe.

'It sure is,' said Malik.

'And who do you think you are, Spock, Kirk, or Picard?' asked Leanne.

'It would have to be Worf, I reckon,' said Alex, laughing.

Malik smiled. 'None of them,' he said. 'My name is Malikai Tan, son of Kalikai Tan, Star Warrior of the planet Ikadies.'

Neither Alex nor Leanne spoke. They wanted to laugh but stopped themselves when they saw Malik's serious expression. They took a few moments to digest the declaration.

'I know it sounds like I've gone completely round the bend,' Malik said. 'But I haven't, and I'm not making it up. In that instant of contact with the pyramid, I knew who I was supposed to be, just as you knew you were Elandra Mezza, and you, Alex, you knew you were Alexander Boatman. I'm Malikai Tan, and I'm on a mission from Ikadies. Think about it for a while, you'll get used to the idea. In the meantime, let me show you around.'

'Wait a minute. How did you get in here when thousands, no, millions of pilgrims have done the very same thing over the centuries and placed their hand on that very same sacred symbol? How come it didn't open for them?'

'DNA. The sensor reads my DNA. Come on, follow me.'

With facilities you would expect to find inside any modern city complex, the spacecraft did not look in the least bit capable of flight. It was, in fact, a self-sustained living environment. The three friends made their way through the pyramid using elevators, escalators, and moving walkways. Something they had never seen before were the hover platforms, that appeared to have no means of propulsion yet carried them between floors following Malik's voice command. The contrast to the outside world of Trinity was mind-blowing. Floor after floor of ultra-modern living mirrored the type of advanced office slash apartment developments seen in the most advanced cities on Earth. There were shops and eateries, theatres and gymnasiums, a concert hall on the twenty-third floor, and an art gallery on the twenty-fourth. Indoor gardens accompanied fully-furnished apartments looking out over the atrium, and computer workstations were evident in every room. The only thing missing was the people. Alex and Leanne were stunned, but it wasn't until they reached the fortieth floor that the real excitement came.

Malik made his way through the structure as though he had known it all his life. He could not hide the pride he felt when he showed off each new revelation. When he opened the elevator doors on the fortieth floor, Malik jumped out first, and said in a moment of pure delight, 'I would like to invite my guests to join me on the pilot's flight deck. Da, da!'

Alex could not believe his eyes. Upon their entry, the flight deck automatically flickered and buzzed to life. Hundreds of LED monitors, computer screens, indicators, and various equipment panels immediately appeared active.

'It's all powered by the pyramid's outer skin, which is made up of advanced photovoltaic panels set into a heat-resistant ceramic glass, a thousand times more efficient than any we have previously seen on Earth and virtually indestructible. They also act as a heat shield. The energy created sends power to the advanced nano battery system, and backup is provided by a cold fusion reactor at the heart of the ship. But the entire ship can run off just one quarter of the solar cells, which generate the magnetic fields necessary for transportation. Travel is achieved using the natural gravitational forces of the Megaverse.'

'Holy cow! What happened to you when you fell on your head, Malik?' asked Alex.

'I know, it's like I swallowed Leanne's encyclopaedia of physics,' Malik said, laughing.

Malik explained the Great Pyramid, a colonisation Starship, had arrived on Trinity almost two thousand years ago. The crew and passengers, numbering approximately thirty-five hundred, were a green-skinned race of advanced space travellers from the planet Ikadies. It was that planet the island had been named after.

'What happened to the colony once it arrived is a mystery,' Malik continued. 'All communications with the home planet were lost. For unknown reasons the crew failed to set the ship to an arrival protocol, and it has remained on standby ever since.'

'It's incredible to think Greens went from an advanced technological race, with technology that makes even Earth seem backward, to being enslaved by the primitive cultures we see here on Trinity,' Alex said, shaking his head in disbelief. 'I wonder what happened to turn the tables. Didn't anyone from Ikadies try to rescue them?'

'If they did, they would still be travelling,' said Malik. 'It's not a small hop from Ikadies to Trinity. The original voyage took hundreds of years, and even with periodic suspended animation, the people who landed on Trinity were generations removed from those who'd set off. They lived a kind of normal life during the voyage. They had families, worked, and had leisure time like regular people. The ship is self-sustaining, but there's lots of work needed to support a whole colony. When contact was lost, it was just too difficult for anyone to follow them. At least that was the situation until now, and that is where things get a bit tricky,' Malik said.

'What do you mean, tricky?' said Leanne.

'It seems we are not the only ones crossing over dimensions within the Megaverse. The Ikadiens have found a way, *without* the help of Figments, to use the Dreamscape as a transportation gateway and now travel between worlds just as we did. The only problem being, in their case, it's a one-way ticket. They can travel here okay, but they haven't figured out how to return using the same method. Three Starship Warriors volunteered for a no return mission to cross over via the Dreamscape from Ikadies in a bid to discover the fate of the passengers and crew. After so many years, it was an archaeological voyage, not a rescue, like an expedition searching for the lost Titanic. If the ship was found intact, it was to be reprogrammed and set on a course back to Ikadies. Malikai Tan was one of those volunteers who crossed over to complete the mission.'

'Hold on, you're saying *you're* Malikai Tan, as in, the *original* one?'

'No, Leanne, it's still lovable me here. But by an uncanny coincidence, or by divine intervention, we arrived on Trinity soon after Malikai and his friends crossed over on their own mission, and unfortunately for Malikai, I replaced him. Bad timing. What are the chances, eh?'

'So Malakai crosses over from Ikadies and before he can even meet up with his friends and go looking for the Starship, you show up out of the Dreamscape and take *his* place,' said Alex. 'Why do I get the feeling it was no coincidence, maybe you were always meant to replace Malikai. But accident or design, this whole story is insane, I can't believe this ship has stood here on standby for as long as anyone can remember just waiting for someone to take it home. Would you even know how to reprogram the controls?'

'It's not a problem. The process is almost entirely automated once communication has been re-established with the computers. It could fly home without anyone at the controls if it had to. But ideally, it takes the three of us to prepare it for flight and set it on its way.'

'The three of us?' said Alex.

'Sorry, I mean myself and the other two Greens, Callumikai and Oloikai.'

Leanne laughed. 'Does everyone's name end in kai?'

'Actually, yes,' said Malik.

'Hang on,' said Alex, 'do you mean Callum and Olo?'

Alex went on to remind the others of the two Greens who had accompanied him on his voyage to Parisos and how they had returned with him to Mariana, only to disappear from his cabin on the ship shortly after arrival.

'The very same,' said Malik. 'We met earlier and slipped into the Starship during all the chaos. You can talk to them shortly, but right now they are busy doing some technical checks on the reactor.'

'So this is where you've been all afternoon,' said Leanne.

'What did you mean before when you said you wouldn't be going home?' said Alex.

'I'm going to join them on the voyage to Ikadies,' Malik said.

'Join them?' said Leanne.

'Callumikai, Oloikai, and the rest of the Greens,' said Malik. 'When he saw the plight of his descendants here on Trinity, Callumikai, our leader, decided that he would evacuate as many as could be rescued and set them on a voyage to Ikadies. I've decided to be part of it.'

'You would all die on this ship, Malik. It's just ridiculous to even think about going,' Leanne said, unable to hide the panic in her voice. 'Talk sense into him, Alex. He can't really be thinking of joining them.'

'Why not?' said Malik.

'You said it yourself, the journey would take hundreds of years, and those who left would not live long enough to ever arrive. What would be the point?'

CHAPTER 30

Preparations

Days passed, and everything changed. The planet faced a new turmoil when faced with the rewriting of history, and it seemed Trinity would never be the same again. News of the spacecraft and the arrival of Greens from another planet to claim it soon spread, and people flocked from far and wide to see and confirm the revelation for themselves. Having been the custodians of the Great Pyramid for centuries, it was not easy for the queen and the people of Mariana to accept its real purpose, or its upcoming departure from the city.

As Alex had anticipated, Callum and Callumikai Rah turned out to be one and the same person; as did Oloikai and Olo. Like Malikai Tan, they had been trained to operate the spacecraft and boasted a wide variety of skills, Olo being the chief engineer. It came as no surprise to discover that Malikai's primary role was that of a touch healer, the Ikadien equivalent of the ship's doctor.

Greens had answered the call to leave in their thousands and placed their fate in the hands of Callumikai and his crew, influenced by the already popular figure of Malik as part of the Starship team. Though they would not live to see their home planet, the prospect of a better life for their children and those of future generations made the decision to leave an easy one for most. They agreed almost unanimously that this was a sacrifice worth making.

After much debate over the handover, and with the blessing of Queen Cleoron and her counsel, preparations for the Greens' departure had begun in earnest. Vast hanger doors had opened up on the Great Pyramid, which had come to be known as the Enterprise, mainly thanks to Malik's repetitive use of the name. Ikadien Starships had numbers, not names, but Malik was a Trekkie, and the tribute to Star Trek gave him great amusement and pleasure.

By the tenth day, most of those leaving had already moved into accommodation aboard the ship and were being trained by the three Greens, including Malik who had taken to his new role with enthusiasm. Considered to be crew as well as passengers, each embarking traveller was assigned a specific role for the long journey ahead. Willingly, Greens were pressed into service and excitement grew as they came to grips with a technology they never dreamt possible. Similar to the art of touch healing, many Greens had a unique ability to pass on skills and knowledge through touch alone, an ability almost lost by those on Trinity. But it did not take long for Callum and Olo to teach the others how to tap into their incredible potential. Along with Greens wanting to join the exodus, a delegation of senior officials had arrived from the Caprinese capital. With them, they brought some unexpected news of their own.

Leanne should have felt relieved by the news. After all, a huge burden had been lifted, but instead, she felt grumpy and disappointed. Caprine's newly arrived delegation had come with a surprising twist on recent events. After the king's death, the Caprinese counsel had convened and had indeed elected a new president. But against everyone's expectations, and by a narrow margin, the vote had gone to Senator Zed Irak, a man of considerable influence amongst his peers. The news had stunned Leanne. Perhaps if Elandra Mezza had remained in Caprine and had been present during deliberations, she might have been able to sway the vote in her favour. Instead, while she battled to avoid war and fight for her own life here on Mariana, Senator Irak had been able to comfortably gain the necessary support for the presidency in her absence.

Irak was a good man, she conceded. He had been responsible for much of the work done on Green reforms. In earlier years, it was he who had negotiated new laws and championed equal rights for all. Yes, he would make an excellent president. So why did she feel so down and disheartened? Was it Elandra for whom she felt sorry? Being the first president would be a big enough deal, but being the first female president, now that would have been something to shout about. Leanne decided it might all have been for the best in the end. When she finally returned home, and Elandra took her rightful place once more, she was sure Elandra would need time to adjust to the changes in her world, even after Nim's father had weaved her back to reality.

'Why so glum?' asked Nim.

Leanne raised her head. 'Still popping up out of nowhere I see.'

'Oh, you are not happy to see me?'

'I'm always happy to see you, Nim. I'm just feeling sorry for myself.'

Nim appeared on the bench next to Leanne. 'Ah!' she said, suddenly understanding Leanne's unhappiness. 'You are disappointed by the appointment of the president.'

'A little I suppose, for Elandra at least. But I'm sure she'll be happy with the choice of president. Zed Irak deserves the recognition. I'll soon be headed home, and she will have enough to do just picking up the pieces of her life, so she'll probably be glad it's not her.'

'Home, yes.' Nim watched Leanne and saw a conflict in her eyes. 'You don't seem happy about the idea.'

'Going home? Yes, of course I'm happy. It's just...'

'Malik?' said Nim.

'He's dead set on going to Ikadies aboard the Starship. How can he be so insensitive to his parents?' A shadow of anger passed over Leanne's face like a cloud over the sun as her brow furrowed deeply. 'I mean, why can't he leave it to Callum and Olo? And what about the real Malikai Tan, doesn't he get a say in this? If we left now with Malik, the real Malikai would take his proper place and everyone would be happy. It's just like Malik, he thinks it's all about *him*. What about other people's feelings?'

'By other people, you mean *your* feelings.'

Leanne reacted defensively. 'What? No! I mean...No. My feelings don't come into it.' Nim smiled, looking like the cat who just swallowed the canary. 'No need to be so smug,' Leanne said, breaking into a half smile. 'My feelings too, I suppose. I mean, we all came together so we should go home together. I'm sure Alex would say the same thing.'

'But Alex doesn't feel like you, does he? There's no shame in admitting your feelings, Leanne. Malik is an exceptional person.'

Leanne knew what Nim was getting at. Her and Malik? What a laugh. She didn't have to justify her feeling to anyone, least of all Nim. *Malik is a friend, that's all.*

So why was she feeling sick to her stomach at the thought of him leaving? He had become more than just a friend; she had already acknowledged that. He had saved her life, *again*. It made him special, but it didn't explain the heavy knots she felt inside or the feeling of gloom that had settled over her when he'd announced his plans to join the voyage.

'My gosh, I can't be? It's too ridiculous.'

CHAPTER 31

Finding the way

The sight of peaceful Caprinese ships in the Mariana harbour gave everyone a lift. President Zed Irak had arrived the previous day to sign the peace treaty, and the capital prepared for the biggest party Trinity had ever seen. Celebrations began with a ceremony paying tribute to the heroic efforts of Elandra Mezza, Malik, now known as Malikai Tan, and Mariana's very own Captain Alexander Boatman for their role in Drabek's downfall.

'First of all,' said the queen, 'I want to announce an Admiralty for Captain Boatman for his outstanding contribution in the name of the Realm.' The crowd cheered. 'I also want to thank President Irak and Callumikai Rah for their part in a historic decision to mark the signing of the peace treaty with a declaration of unity,' said the queen, followed by another cheer. 'Together we have recognised a unique opportunity to bond our nations for all time.' The queen took a moment to let the crowd settle. 'At the invitation of Callumakai Rah, President Irak and myself have each selected a group of volunteers to join the voyage to Ikadies.'

Then came the news that knocked Leanne almost off her feet.

'In addition to his award for bravery and as recognition for his daring endeavours,' the queen continued, 'Admiral Alexander Boatman will lead Mariana's participation on the voyage to planet Ikadies.'

The crowd went wild with applause. Leanne slumped as tears filled her eyes, and the all-too-familiar knots twisted in her stomach. This was not how things were supposed to turn out, she thought.

With speeches over, Queen Cleoron and Zed Irak approached the Hellefyr where they were each handed a pot containing the virus, and drums rolled as they stepped to the rim. A bubble of lava burst from the Hellefyr and sent a shower of hot liquid into the air, causing Zed Irak to flinch and stumble, almost dropping the pot as he did so. The crowd gasped as one, but the president recovered his balance with an embarrassed smile. Horns blared, and at the signal of the queen, they completed the ceremony by simultaneously tossing the deadly germs into the Hellefyr to a raucous chorus of deafening cheers.

'Let the festivities begin!' cried the queen.

Devastated by the latest news, Leanne tried her best to hide her feelings as she congratulated Alex and played along with the celebrations. After all, she tried to assure herself, the queen had referred to Alexander Boatman when she declared her new envoy to Ikadies, not Alex. Alex would surely have crossed over by that time, and the captain, or admiral as he was now known, would have taken his proper place. The problem was, she didn't believe it for one second.

Great feasts soon got underway, and food and drink flowed in massive quantities, shared by all races in a show of unity that had never been seen before. Celebrations stretched from the harbour to the Great Pyramid and every corner of the city beyond. Street parties were staged at every venue with the rich and the poor invited, and leaders and dignitaries of the three nations had gathered in the Great Pyramid where they joined thousands of newly commissioned space travellers.

Amid the excitement, Alex, Malik, and Leanne found time to talk. There was much to be said, but Leanne sensed an uneasy atmosphere. Alex looked guilty and Malik much the same.

'Has anyone seen Nim today?' asked Alex, hoping to avoid the debate.

'No, she's gone missing again,' said Leanne. 'I wanted to ask her how all this is going to play out, like how we're going to get home before you two go hopping all over the Megaverse?

Surely now is the time for us to skip out before it all gets too complicated.'

'Come on the voyage with us,' Malik said.

Leanne gave out a short, almost hysterical laugh. 'Malik! We're not going on any voyage. We need to go home.'

'Why?' asked Malik.

'Why! Because we just do. We've done what we had to, now it's time to leave.'

'Just because your character isn't needed anymore, doesn't mean it's over for all of us.'

'My character?'

'You know what I mean,' said Malik.

'This isn't a film set, Malik. It's not Star Trek. My character, as you call it, is a real person, and her name is Elandra Mezza. And right at this moment, she's probably stuck in limbo somewhere in the Dreamscape waiting to wake and get back to her reality. It's time for her, Alexander Boatman, and Malikai Tan to return to their lives, and for Leanne, Alex, and Malik to go home. We've already done more than could have been expected.'

'That's not the point. This trip is the chance of a lifetime! Don't you want to learn what's out there?' argued Malik.

'What's out there is danger and death, and what I want to do is to go home to my mum and dad. I want to go home to *my* life. Nim said if we get beyond the city wall and away from the interference of the pyramid, we can be on our way before another day passes. It's time for us to go. Alex, say something please.'

Alex looked uncomfortable. 'I kind of agree with Malik,' he said. 'Something doesn't feel right about going home just yet. There are answers here to questions I haven't even asked. We've all changed since arriving, and it's no secret we each have more to us than before. There's a piece of Alexander Boatman in me, Elandra Mezza in you, and Malik feels it too... Malikai Tan is woven right in alongside his own thoughts. It's not as simple as just dropping everything, going home and forgetting about it. Anyway, you were the one who said she wanted to stay only a couple of days ago. You said yourself there was more to be done here.'

'I said we weren't finished until the virus was destroyed. Now it's destroyed, we are done. What I didn't say was that we should spend the rest of our lives sailing through space only to die of old age before reaching our destination.'

'Don't you feel even a little bit curious? Don't you want to find out what the future might be like for space travellers, find out more about new civilisations, learn from Greens about things we thought impossible? Callumikai told us there would be many stops along the way and new worlds to explore. Who knows what great adventures are waiting for us. Don't you want to be part of it?'

'No, Malik! I want my life back. I want normal! I want to go home.'

Silence hung in the air between them. Malik looked disappointed. Eventually, he said, 'What's stopping you?'

Leanne could not believe he said that. How could he be so insensitive? Her lip trembled and she stormed off before she started to cry, leaving the boys to make their plans without her. She was determined not to break down again. And Malik was right, she thought, there was nothing stopping her so why should she worry about what they chose to do? Now Zed Irak had arrived and taken over, she could leave without feeling guilty and be proud of what she had accomplished. The virus no longer existed; she had done her job. She should be happy.

Instead, Leanne felt empty, confused, and lost, and not for the first time, she felt alone. Struggling to understand her feelings, she was rapidly becoming a mess of mixed and confused emotions. No blooming wonder, she thought. She had survived death, escaped prison, almost been eaten, and come within a whisker of being burned alive in the Hellefyr. She had done all this while adjusting to the body of a twenty-three-year-old woman with all the mature hormones that came along with the role. And to top it all off, she had these stupid heart palpitations; the result of stress, she told herself. It was just coincidence that it happened every time Malik appeared on the scene.

Help me, Nim! Where are you?

The celebrations went on well into the evening, and Leanne had tried her best to lighten up and enjoy the party. She had watched Malik enjoying a mug full of Honey Bee Ale, and now he was after another. He was sure to make a fool of himself. Alex had surprised her with his enthusiasm for the trip. Maybe it was a boy thing, the two of them all gung-ho about going where no man had gone before, Star Trek all over again.

Malik startled her. 'Hey,' he said. He had a glow about him she was sure came from the ale. 'I wanted to say sorry for what I said. I didn't intend for it to come out like that.'

'Like what?' said Leanne.

'Like I didn't care if you went home or not,' Malik said.

'It's okay, I'm the one who should be sorry. I can see how excited you both are about going. And if you've made up your minds, I'm happy for you.'

'Thanks.' An awkward silence lingered between them. 'Anyway,' he said eventually, 'you're wanted on the twenty-third floor. All the leaders are up there, and we've been summoned.'

'What now, more speeches?'

Alex joined Malik and Leanne on a hover transport, and they made their way to the concert hall on the twenty-third floor. Malik led them in through the stage door, and they emerged on stage behind a dense screen of curtains. As big a shock as anything she had encountered since arriving on Trinity, the grand piano on centre stage astonished Leanne and almost took her breath away. Much larger than any she had ever seen before, the case was nearly three times as broad as her Steinway at home. She studied the instrument carefully and saw, despite its huge proportions, it had the familiar eighty-eight keys, fifty-two of which were white and thirty-six black.

It really is a Grand Piano.

'I thought it might cheer you up,' said Malik.

'What's it doing here?'

'Oh, it's just hanging around because it likes to imitate a musical instrument. What do you think it's doing here?'

'Don't be sarcastic, Malik. I mean, where did it come from?' said Leanne.

'Well, it seems Greens not only have an innovative hi-tech culture, but they also have a musical one. They, we, have our own brand of classical music. I sampled some of it today from the control room. We have a variety of instruments, and many are almost identical to those we have on Earth. Some are a bit strange, I'll admit, and the music's not really my thing. It's kind of like experimental music, like the improvised music you get back home...totally boring and far too way out for my taste.'

'Yeah, well that wouldn't be hard for a Beyoncé groupie,' said Leanne.

'Now who's being sarcastic?' said Malik.

'I listened to a troupe of Mariana musicians playing in the square, all very primitive, flutes, drums, and lutes. I never imagined I would see a refined instrument like this here,' said Leanne.

'It's been right here on the ship all along. There's a whole orchestra of instruments. Take a closer look,' Alex said.

Leanne approached the piano cautiously, as though it were something strange, otherworldly, like the pyramid itself, an alien craft to transport her back to reality. She peeked inside the case and saw all the familiar parts, and apart from the enormous soundboard, it was perfect in every way. She let a single finger tap on the keys gently, allowing the sound to tinkle with barely audible notes that sounded like heaven to her ears. She felt an urge so strong it made her ache inside. Powerless to resist and before she could stop herself, she sat at the keyboard, feet on pedals, and felt breathless.

Malik signalled a helper and the towering curtains parted, opening fully to the sides of the stage. Footlights came on with a clunk, causing Leanne to scrunch up her eyes in response to their sudden brilliance. She adjusted, looked beyond the glow, and saw a packed auditorium up to at least three levels high. The audience waited in silence.

'Malik!'

'No pressure, just enjoy yourself,' Malik said as he stepped back to join Alex in the wings.

All eyes focused on Leanne in utter silence, but she didn't care; the piano had her under its spell. She appeared entranced, pondering the keyboard before her as though she were waiting for it to speak to her and tell her what to play.

Leanne was not a religious person, far from it, and she had never been to church or followed a faith. But even before Nim arrived to turn life upside down, she had believed in spirituality, and that there was more to life than her Earthly existence. She knew it now with certainty. But before Nim, this spiritual awareness manifested itself in her music. Music had always been able to transport her spirit beyond the physical world. The piano was her way to understand the world, to express her feelings, hopes, and dreams.

Leanne let her fingers float over the keys. Surprised by the clarity and depth of tone, she marvelled at the ease of action. Shoeless feet slipped onto the pedals, and so sensitive was the touch, she felt she only had to twitch a toe to get a response. She paused, aware of the faces now focused on her. She was ready to tell them her story. As a seasoned performer, an audience had little effect on Leanne. Once she started playing, she was oblivious to anything beyond her own imagination.

She closed her eyelids and imagined the ocean; she could almost smell its salty spray. In her mind's eye, she saw the waves crashing as restless tides where the ocean met the shore. Beyond the rocks, she followed a path and left the sea for the mountains and the cool, moist mountain air. She saw the sky, felt the warmth of the sun, and she started to play.

With a touch like dancing butterflies, her fingers caressed the keys with delicate precision. No sheet music was necessary; she played with spontaneity, allowing herself to succumb to the feelings within as she gave herself over to the music. Her fingers followed her heart. Leanne had no particular piece in mind; her music came from her deepest emotions.

At first, through a series of scales, she expressed the textures of the instrument and allowed the music to communicate through the unison of notes. She was showing off and acknowledging the skill of the craftsmen who had created the marvellous instrument. But soon, as it always did, her emotions began to drive her performance beyond skill and technique. The music played to her mood.

The resulting sounds soon became an unsettling expression of conflict as the tempo increased and Leanne allowed her feelings to come to the fore. Her fingers picked out the notes, fluid and precise. She felt the music building, threatening, bullying. And now she was moving, swaying back and forth, living every note, every expression of passion and of pain and hurt. She brought in the robust bass, a tone dark and rich, echoing her soul into the depths of despair. She saw death calling in the catacombs, the cadaverines, Drabek, the vamps, and the terrible red eye of the Hellefyr; she played through it as she relived her ordeal.

She hammered the keys till her fingers felt numb. Furiously expressing every angry thought and every frantic effort of survival; desperate and terrifying, the music represented her darkest moments. She felt naked, gutted, brought to her knees in the blackness and despair.

Silence, a pause, a breath of hope, a glimmer of light. One finger, tapping. Two fingers, tapping. Three fingers, four fingers, tiptoeing delicately over notes of optimism. Salted jewels of teardrops seeped from her closed eyes as she searched for the way. She held the last note, allowing it to resonate. She breathed deeply, slowly, felt the rhythm of her chest, felt the warmth of home again, the sureness of love creeping into her soul like the thawing of spring. Her fingers began to pick out a melody, a lighter, cheerful melody that spoke of the future. Very soon, the music had taken control once again, buoyant and bubbling, bright and sublime. Entranced, she poured her heart into a building whirlwind of joy and divine expression, to a crescendo of staggering power as the last keys crashed and the final E chord thundered to a sustained conclusion.

Silence. Leanne's cheeks ran wet with tears; her eyelids remained closed, her heart beating like the heart of a captive animal. Slowly she opened her eyes as if she were waking from a dream, blinded by the footlights. Still silence. The concert hall lights came alive. She had never seen so many stunned faces. People sat like stone statues, unable to move after what they had witnessed during the fifteen minutes of utter raw emotion.

Queen Cleoron was first to blink, suddenly bursting into tears and crying uncontrollably. Others followed, laughing and crying, overcome with feelings of intense passion. No one had ever heard such a performance; the music was as foreign and marvellous as anything they had ever experienced. Leanne searched for Malik. When she saw him, he had his face in his massive hands and was weeping like a baby. Alex stood next to him, eyes moist, but with a smile that could have brightened the darkest night. He was ecstatic. He started to clap, slowly and alone at first. Another joined in, and another, and another until the audience erupted in a deafening show of heartfelt appreciation. This was a moment they would remember forever; the moment music came to Trinity and made the world weep.

The clamour to congratulate Leanne went on for well over an hour. Even Queen Cleoron and President Irak had to wait their turn to get close enough to speak, such was the enthusiastic outpouring of adoration and awe. When he finally reached her, the president had a bewildered expression.

'I'm overwhelmed, Ambassador Mezza. We have known each other for many years. I have never heard such music and can't imagine how you came to be so familiar with this instrument. Tell me, how did you come to play with such passion and obvious experience?'

Leanne had no ready answer. All she could say was she must have been inspired by a greater force, or perhaps it was the influence of the Great Pyramid.

'I'm afraid I am as mystified as you, Mister President.'

Zed Irak appeared unconvinced by her answer, but let the subject drop. Queen Cleoron asked if it would be possible to know more about this form of music, but Leanne pleaded ignorance and changed the subject, referring her instead to Callumakai for more information. She had something more important on her mind. During her performance, as was often the case, Leanne had been able to find answers to her problems. She now had a way forward; she was about to follow her heart.

'I have a request, President Irak,' she said.

'Please, Elandra, call me Zed, we have been friends for a long time.'

'I wish to represent Caprine on the voyage to Ikadies,' said Leanne.

CHAPTER 32

Last goodbyes

L aunch Day. Alex woke early. The sun had yet to rise, and during the night a thick fall of late-season snow had blanketed the city. Eager to take one last look at Mariana before leaving the strange world forever, Alex dressed and headed for the door of his new apartment. As he came outside, he found Leanne about to knock. She had the same plan in mind and had thought Alex might appreciate the morning air. They exited the pyramid and walked in the fresh snow, sinking their boots into the undisturbed and pristine powder.

'Great ski conditions,' said Alex. 'That's what I'd be wanting to do if we were back home right now.'

'Me too,' said Leanne with a hint of longing.

They walked in silence for a while, taking in the crisp, fresh air and listening only to the crunch of snow underfoot. Like the top of a Christmas cake, the city appeared magical. A new fall of snow brought with it a unique brand of silence, a serenity found in no other way. There were few people about and active. Most lay huddled in their warm beds away from the cold no doubt. They walked as far as the Hellefyr where they stood for a while, enjoying the warmth of its glow but remembering its evil past. Leanne shuddered at the thought.

'This was almost as far as we got,' she said.

'Almost,' Alex replied. They turned and looked back to the Great Pyramid, the only structure not covered in white. The golden glow had taken on a pulsing appearance over the last few days as it readied for launch. It had always had a life of its own, but now life seemed even more powerful and real, as though the Gods once thought to reside within had woken and were restless to return to the heavens.

'That's the biggest Christmas tree you'll ever see,' said Leanne.

'It's quite something isn't it,' said Alex.

'I can't believe we're really going,' she said. 'I still feel uneasy about it.'

'What made you change your mind?' asked Alex.

Leanne considered the question for some time before replying. 'Nim told me destiny is not ours to choose,' she said at last. 'I mean, have we ever really had a choice about anything since we agreed to leave home?' Alex did not answer. 'We are all in this together, like it or not, Alex. You, me, Malik...we are bound together in this adventure, and we must see it out together. When I played in the concert hall, I found my answers. I found the way to proceed, and that way was with the two of you. You were right when you said we are not who we once were. I sometimes wonder if when Nim's father weaved his magic, he got us all mixed up. Not only have we become part of Elandra, Malikai, and Alexander, but we have also somehow gained a little bit of each other. We're like three planets caught in each other's gravitational pull, revolving around and around in a wobbly, ungainly orbit.'

'You're right. I feel closer to you both than I've ever been to anyone else, other than my father.' Alex thought back to the concert hall. 'I'm glad you found the way forward.'

'Music does that to me,' said Leanne.

'Your performance may have had an impact on your decision, but I have never heard anything like it in my life. It blew me away. I've never been a great fan of music, it's always been just background stuff for me. I had no idea it could be so powerful, that it could literally bring a person to tears, let alone hundreds. It touched everyone. You were amazing, Leanne.'

Leanne smiled bashfully. She had never reached such heights while playing, and to have caused such a reaction was as surprising to her as to anyone.

'Are you ready for today?' Alex asked, changing the subject.

'I'm frightened. Perhaps more frightened than I've ever been since this thing started, but I'm ready. I don't know if

Malik is though.' Leanne giggled. 'He's still trying to get over the Honey Bee Ale. I knew he would drink too much and make a fool of himself. And you didn't do so bad either. I never had you down as an Elvis impersonator.'

As the party had progressed two nights previously, Malik had sat down at the piano and performed chopsticks with Leanne. He had then asked if she knew any Elvis Presley songs, and she had obliged. Influenced by the alcoholic drinks and with his inhibitions gone, Malik had stood in front of the audience and performed a rattling rendition of Blue Suede Shoes. His off-key singing only matched by his wobbly-kneed dance routine had produced a hilarious result. After that, there was no stopping him. Alex joined him on the floor for a duet performance of Hound Dog, and before they knew it, the pair had encouraged a line dance numbering in the hundreds as partygoers took to the strange sounds of rock and roll like they had known Elvis all their lives.

'We had some fun, and we deserved it. I don't think Drabek would have been impressed,' Alex said.

Leanne's thoughts turned to Martha Bottom and Nim's sad story. It was as though Drabek had stolen her away from Alex. She had given up everything only to be betrayed by his evil soul.

'Alex,' she said, desperately looking for the right words.

'What is it? You look like you're about to cry.'

The words stuck in Leanne's throat. At last, she said, 'We should get back. We have a big day ahead.'

Throughout the morning, a steady stream of dignitaries, friends, family, and well-wishers bid their farewells. Queen Cleoron repeated her gratitude, saying she would never forget their courage and determination, even in the face of her own blind stupidity. She praised them once again for saving Princess Li and bringing peace to Trinity. The queen wept as they said their goodbyes.

Malik picked out Shari and her daughter, Loti, in the crowd. Reunited with her husband and Loti with her father, the family had decided to stay and make a new life as free folk in Mariana. Malik stooped and told Loti to be good for her parents. They rubbed noses and parted with tears in their eyes.

It had come as no surprise that John and Ida Boatman had decided to join the Starship voyage. John could barely contain his enthusiasm for new worlds, and poor Olo had not had a minutes' peace from John and his endless questions.

Little Jim stepped forward, trying hard to remain manly in the face of his sadness. Alex hugged him and asked him to keep an eye on the newly promoted Captain Stark. 'I'll never forget you,' said Little Jim with a trembling lip.

When the fuss had died down and the crowd dispersed to a safe distance, Nim appeared beside the three friends. If a face could launch a thousand ships, then Nim's could launch a million. Yet even her beauty could not mask her sadness and utter misery, marking the end of their time together. They found no words to express their sorrow. When each came to speak, the words caught in their throats and tears rolled down their faces. They contented with silent hugs and kisses, each knowing what would have been said had they found their sad voices. Finally, Nim embraced Leanne and whispered so that only she could hear, 'Have faith child, your journey is already decided and your destiny is beyond the will of mortals.' And in the blink of an eye, Nim was gone.

With the doors closed and the tears now dry, the Great Pyramid prepared for launch. Malik was excited. He could not hide his enthusiasm for the journey, fidgeting and taking off to the bathroom every few minutes to steady his nerves. The three friends were now seated in pride of place on the flight deck of the Starship, waiting for pre-flight checks to be carried out and for the thousands on board to confirm their take-off positions. Sitting side by side with Leanne flanked by the boys, the three chatted nervously as an automated sequence ran through the control system, marking off functions in readiness for the countdown.

'You may feel nauseous during takeoff,' Malik said knowingly. 'The whole structure will feel like it's about to disintegrate, but that's normal, and it will calm down as we leave Trinity atmosphere.'

No sooner had Malik said it than an announcement came over the PA system telling everyone of the last phase of preparation. Everyone should be in their launch positions now without exceptions. Countdown would begin in thirty seconds. Malik reached down and wrapped his massive hand around Leanne's. She felt a lump in her throat.

'Malik, there's something I want to tell you,' said Leanne, suddenly aware how vital it was to say what she was feeling before liftoff.

The countdown began. 'Ten, nine, eight...'

'Hang on,' Malik said. 'Tell me later. Here we go.' He squeezed Leanne's hand.

'Seven, six, five...'

'Malik,' Leanne felt panicked. Not because of the upcoming voyage, but because she had to tell him something and it would not wait until later.

'This is it,' said Alex as he reached out and took Leanne's other hand, distracting her for a second.

'Four, three, two...'

'But...'

'One. We have liftoff.'

A tremor shook the pyramid. Alex gripped Leanne's hand hard as Malik did likewise on the other side. Strangely numb, their minds were now fighting forces unknown while sensing deep vibrations that shook their bodies. The titanic Starship began a slow ascent, rumbling like an earthquake as it made its way skyward. For centuries, this monolith had hovered in place, awaiting this moment. There was no stopping it now; the planet could no longer hold its sacred prize.

Unable to think clearly, the sensations they felt came from alternative laws of physics. They were not simply lifting off; they were somehow being transported beyond the pyramid. They lost sight of the flight deck and watched as the pyramid receded into space, but they were not in control. A steady stream of images began to play in each mind. Strange images, familiar images, people, worlds, random images, horrifying images, peaceful images. Stars arrayed before them, colourful and bright. More worlds, more stars; they were travelling. They encountered people, familiar faces, long-lost souls, the faces they were yet to meet. And now they were spinning, turning head over heels, tumbling beyond worlds. They had experienced this before, this very sensation.

With a blinding flash, every thought ceased. Silence. Blackness. Isolation. Time passed. Distant voices, faint, barely discernible. Louder now, growing stronger.

'I knew it,' Malik said. 'I knew we shouldn't have fallen for this.'

Leanne opened her eyes and focused on the light fitting in the centre of the ceiling; it had a Batman shade and looked particularly childish in design. 'I think I must have dropped off,' she said, dazed. 'I dreamt I was in a tunnel with water and...um...No, it's gone, I can't remember. Ooh,' she said, 'my head hurts.'

Leanne felt Malik's hand gripping hers, and she pulled away quickly as though she had been shocked. She stared at Malik who stared back confused by the exchange.

'What?' he said.

'Nothing,' Leanne answered, looking away.

'What time is it?' Malik asked.

Alex stretched. 'I think I must have slept too.'

Leanne reached for her phone and checked the time. 'My goodness, we've been here almost an hour!'

'Nim's gone,' said Alex.

Malik had risen to his feet. 'Idiots. We're all idiots. I told you we were being made to look like fools. She's disappeared and left us lying on the floor, holding hands and looking ridiculous. Any bets we'll find photos of us on Instagram in the morning. What were we thinking?'

Malik went to his computer and clicked on the mouse, bringing up a saved game in which he boasted a high score of two million four thousand points. 'Anyone fancy a game of Star Trek?'

Alex looked at the characters on screen. 'Who are you,' he asked, 'Spock, Kirk, Picard, or Worf?'

'None of them,' Malik replied. 'I'm Mal...' Malik did not finish his sentence. He exchanged a spooky look with Alex. Both boys shrugged, and the feeling of déjà vu disappeared.

Jani Nasri appeared at the bedroom door. 'Sorry I'm late,' she said. 'My sister is in the hospital, and I was the only one able to visit her today. I felt terrible about leaving her. Where is Nim?'

'Nim's gone,' said Alex. 'I think we've all been taken in by her joke.'

'I'm sorry about your sister,' said Malik. 'Which hospital is she in?'

'Saint Lucia,' said Jani.

'Well, don't worry, she's in good hands,' Malik said. A frown appeared on his face, and he raised his own hands in front of him and looked at them puzzled.

'Malik?' said Leanne. 'Are you alright?'

Malik shook off the strange feeling. 'I'm fine. I was just going to say she's in good hands because my mum works there, and all the doctors and nurses are great.'

'Thank you, Malik,' said Jani. 'That makes me feel better. Seeing as Nim is not here, I won't stay, if no one has any objections.'

'Do you want anything to eat before you go?' asked Malik.

'No, it's okay,' said Jani. 'I ate a snack at the hospital.'

'Well, maybe we could all meet up for burgers some other night,' Malik said, smiling.

'I'd like that,' said Jani.

'That would be cool,' said Alex. 'Let's make it soon.' Alex rubbed his eyes. 'I must have been tired,' he said, yawning. 'I don't remember nodding off, but I do remember dreaming, I just can't recall what I dreamed. I think Phys Ed was in it. Must be all the odd goings on in school this morning. Isn't it funny how dreams just melt away the moment you open your eyes?'

'Maybe Nim tried to hypnotise us,' said Malik.

'Maybe. Anyway, I'm heading off too,' said Leanne. 'I have an awful urge to play my piano. I don't even remember the last time I played.'

A simultaneous shiver ran down Alex and Malik's spines.

'I didn't know you played,' said Malik.

'Yeah, well, you don't know much about me at all, Malik,' said Leanne.

'Nor you about me,' countered Malik.

'I guess not,' she said, and found herself studying his face. She hadn't noticed before that he was actually good looking in a rustic sort of way. She stopped herself staring before he caught her.

'I do know we all fell for Nim's big joke. If I ever see her again, I'll get my own back, you can count on it,' said Malik.

'She did have us fooled,' Alex agreed. 'I'm going too, Malik.'

'Are you sure you don't want to play the game?'

'No, maybe another time. After what Nim said, I've decided I'm going to ask my dad about my mum. It's time I knew what happened when she went away.'

'Sounds like a good idea, Alex,' said Leanne. 'Sometimes things are not always as they seem.' Leanne had a sudden image of a mother and an infant child. The mother was crying. Leanne shook her head, and the picture was gone.

Malik saw them all to the door.

'Nice home, Malik,' Leanne said sincerely. 'And that was nice what you said to Jani.'

'It was dumb what I said earlier about her and her family. I was trying to be smart, I didn't mean it. Jani seems nice and you never know what other people are going through, do you? Sometimes we need to put ourselves in other's shoes.'

'Maybe you're not such a hard arse after all,' said Leanne.

'Hey! Don't say arse around Bottom.' They all laughed.

As they walked down the path, Malik called out after them. 'Hey, Leanne, maybe you and I could get together, go to the movies or something.'

Leanne turned, walking backwards. 'You and me?' she said smiling. 'In your dreams, Malik...In your dreams.'

The End

ACKNOWLEGEMENTS

My grateful thanks Oliver and Jay for your reading skills and valuable perspective.

Thanks Anthony for your encouragement and for kick-starting this novel into action.

Thanks to Desiree Lewis, Mary Hughes, Eamonn Murphy, and Kristin Houlihan for your comments and wonderful feedback.

Special thanks to Catherine Chester, my fantastic UK Editor.

And finally, thank you to all my family and friends for your undying encouragement, love, and support—Lee Richie.

ABOUT THE AUTHOR

Lee Richie is an emerging Australian author and the creator of Alexander Bottom & The Dreamweaver's Daughter.

Lee was born and grew up in Liverpool England. After leaving school at just fourteen, a teacher made the following prediction: 'You'll never amount to anything, Lee; you're a waste of life.' Those cruel words followed Lee through life, making a successful international business career all the sweeter.

Life was not always easy. Lee says there are many stories to tell, of hard lessons learned. Of reaching heights once thought impossible, of being poor yet feeling rich, of being down but never beaten.

'I want to tell my stories in a way that might inspire others who face daily challenges of their own. I'm so grateful for my life and my family, for the people I've met and the places I've seen along the way. A waste of life? Not mine; not a minute of it.'

Alexander Bottom & the Dreamweaver's Daughter, is Lee's first novel.

Lee now lives in the Southern Highlands of NSW, Australia.

www.leerichie.com

www.ingramcontent.com/pod-product-compliance
Lightning Source LLC
Chambersburg PA
CBHW030335120726
47901CB00007B/1801